Shadows of Good Friday
By
A P Bateman

Text © Anthony Paul Bateman
2017
All rights reserved
No part of this book may be reproduced, or stored in a retrieval system, or transmitted in any form or by any means, electronic, mechanical, photocopying, printing or otherwise, without written permission of the author.

Author contact: authorapbateman@gmail.com
Facebook: @authorapbateman

Website: www.apbateman.com

Also by A P Bateman

The Alex King Series
The Contract Man
Lies and Retribution

The Rob Stone Series
The Ares Virus
The Town
The Island

For my wife Clair.

Without your support and understanding this novel would never have been written.

For Summer and Lewis, my two gorgeous children.

Without you, this novel would have been finished so much sooner…

1

**Autumn 1992,
London**

The night is cold and dark. Despite the usual ambience of the city it is dull and the buildings close in on him in, consolidating the darkness to near total effect. The mist is dense too, surrounding him and dampening his clothes, as well as his spirits.

He watches as the blue light bounces across the damp walls, a strobe-like phosphorescence niggling and teasing at the corners and recesses of the buildings and around the edges of the rubbish bin he is hiding behind. It is an American-style dumpster, and has not been emptied recently. He tucks his legs up closer to his body and pushes himself back against the wall. A gutter has dislodged above and is showering him under a cascade of drips; cold and probing at his collar. The stench is hateful, he has pressed his hand onto something gelatinous, rubbery and wet. He knows what it is, before he glances at it in the gloom. The alley is littered with them, a popular place for quick transactions and ill-conceived urges, and the inevitable walk of shame.

A sweep of a torch lights up the alley. He can hear the crackle of voices, the static of radios. He cannot hear what is said, but he picks up on the tone and urgency of the short message. The net is closing in. The torch beam sweeps back and forth, probing the extremities, casting shadows upon the damp walls. His shadow is not one of them, the dumpster and collection of smaller bins are temporarily projected on the wall behind. The beam retracts and the alley is dark once more. He is about to move when the beam sweeps back. The light refreshed, slashing through the dismal shadow with renewed vigour. He realises it is another officer's torch. The net is not only closing, but strengthening as the police numbers swell. He needs to get out of here, needs to put distance between himself and the search party. The beam sweeps across the walls and the boarded-up doorways. He pulls his legs closer, moves his hand and places it back down on broken glass. There is a distinct 'crack' in the air along with his sharp intake of breath. The alley goes dark and the burst of static suddenly sounds distant.

His hand is badly cut and the blood is running down his wrist as he pulls his hand close to his face to inspect it through the gloom. It is a bad wound and he makes the mistake of pulling the shard of glass clear. It hurts, but he isn't ready for the amount of blood. The wound is open and running like a tap with a worn washer. He pulls his jacket off and removes his T-shirt and uses it to wrap his hand tightly. He is shivering from both cold and adrenalin, and puts the jacket back on.

There are no more signs of movement, light or noise from the street and he gets to his feet unsteadily. The bag is next to him. Both a beacon and an anchor. He picks it up, hefts its weight over his shoulder, holding it by the straps. He feels tentative walking to the entrance of the alleyway; his limbs feel like they are functioning in slow-motion. His heart is thudding against his chest, taking its erratic beat to his ears and affecting his senses. He cannot hear clearly, the pulsating like a bout of irritating tinnitus. He *needs* to hear, *needs* to be alert. His own body is confounding him.

Back in the half-light of the deserted street he walks quickly and purposefully. His hand is still bleeding and has soaked the T-shirt through. He feels lightheaded, his legs are heavy and unsteady. The adrenalin is subsiding and he is suffering because of it.

The heavily laden sports bag is a thorn in his side. It seems heavier somehow. He needs to keep it, but it is an insurmountable piece of evidence that will damn him. And not just to a life behind bars, but one that will threaten the life he has worked hard to attain. The promise to his wife to change, to become an honest man and work an honest day. But he has been weak, and with the weakness has come the risk. Again, he knows the penalty well. He must lose the bag. If he rids himself of the millstone, he will have a better chance of escaping.

He stopped. Snapped out of his thoughts. He had a feeling. The same feeling that had told him to run when the driver hadn't shown. The same feeling, a gut instinct that had told him to take to his heels and get out of the square. Barely a minute later, the square had been full of police and the night air full of blue strobe lights and wailing sirens.

He trusted his instincts and broke into a jog, all the while searching for another hiding place, if not for himself then for the bag. Ahead of him he could hear tyres squealing. Not braking sharply, but cornering at speed, the rubber parting company with traction. He looked to his right. Shop fronts. Shallow shop doorways with no alleyways or cover. To his left are the two single lanes of road. Across the road is a churchyard. The church is derelict, the trees overgrown and unkempt. It is perfect and he crosses the road quickly and climbs through the broken and rusted iron railings.

As he re-enters the street at the north end of the churchyard he is relieved to be without the incriminating evidence. He tucks up the collar of his sodden jacket and walks briefly across the road and back onto the side with the shops. There is no obvious place to hide, the shops are terraced. There is most likely an alleyway behind them, a ginnel of some sort, but unless he can access it from the street then it is pointless to speculate.

He is in familiar territory and knows that there is a myriad of roadways and walkways at a large housing estate half-a-mile further on. He has friends there, people who will give him a place to crash for the night. In the morning rush-hour he will fade away. The police will not search house to house without a good reason, and logistically they would not be prepared for thousands of tower block flats and outlying ground level terraced bungalows. There was now only four hours until the city would be gridlocked and people were up and out and he would disappear.

The street wound around to the right sharply. He only has another two minutes of being out in the open, another two minutes exposed to danger. Sanctuary lies ahead. But before sanctuary stands two armed police officers and a group of uniformed police officers huddled together who appeared to be studying or comparing notes. The armed police worry him. They have been a fixture on the streets since the mortar bombing in Downing Street the previous year, and with the Baltic Exchange bombing in April, the city has been a different place to walk the streets. The police were putting large numbers of paramilitary-looking officers on the streets and they were armed to the teeth.

He eases between two parked cars and takes a breath, curses inwardly. He had only agreed to take the job because of his set of skills. The share would set him up. His recruitment had been persuasive. It was agreed this would be his last job, and then he would be left alone. There was never meant to be weapons, no violence of any sort. Now a security guard lay dead or dying and the idiot with the gun was out on the streets. The driver must have got wind of it, because he hadn't shown. The police had been on the scene within minutes and now armed police were blocking his escape. But how did they know he would head for the housing estate? Did they already know his identity?

He can usually think quickly, but tonight he is floundering. Stunned at seeing the guard shot, nauseous from the wound to his hand. Exhausted from the chase through the streets. He checks the wound quickly, the T-shirt is now completely blood-soaked and dripping like a filled sponge. He needs medical attention, but that will create a trail. He *needs* the sanctuary of that estate, the place where he grew up. The place he once called home. He cannot go onwards, but he will have to backtrack carefully. He moves slowly, not wanting his movements to catch their eye. He nears the bend in the street, but is illuminated in the bright headlights of an approaching vehicle. There are shouts behind him but he doesn't hear what was said. He is running blindly across the road. The vehicle is reversing after him, blue strobes flashing and now the siren is wailing. It sounds so loud in the confines of the street. More shouts and now the sound of heavy footsteps.

There is a Victorian garden ahead of him. The wrought iron railings are five-feet high and rusted. He scrambles over them, catches his clothes on top, his jacket rips and he falls heavily to the sodden earth. There is broken glass and empty beer cans in the undergrowth. The council has given up on the mini oasis of garden in the city, and much of it is like a jungle as he pushes through thick rhododendron bushes and untended roses that snag and tear at his flesh. He pushes through and out into an overgrown lawn. He can hear the footsteps behind him, faster than his own, and then the inevitable happens and he is barrelled to the floor. The landing winds him. Rough hands roll him over. The police officer is big and red faced. He is heaving for breath as he straddles him, a rugby player pinning him to the ground. He raises his fist, grips his prisoner tightly by the scruff of his jacket and smashes the large bunched fist down into his face. He raises the fist again, the prisoner offers no resistance but the officer grits his teeth cursing him, then smashes down, a great hammer blow and the man is out cold.

The lights have faded, as have his hopes of freedom.

2

April 2nd, 1998
HM Prison Wormwood Scrubs, London

His pace fell into rhythm with the guard's purposefully unhurried stride. The guard had nowhere to go, nothing to rush for. For Simon Grant, there was a whole life to live, six stolen years to make up for.

The footsteps were hollow, echoing off the damp limestone walls. The corridor was cold and smelled of mildew. Everything smelled of mildew. His clothes, his hair, even his breath.

"Any plans?"

"The usual."

The guard smiled. "A shag and a steak then."

"I doubt in that order," he said quietly.

"I thought you had someone waiting?"

"No."

The guard looked at the ring on his finger. He had just watched him put it on when he had been handed his envelope of processions. It had slipped on easily. He had lost weight. "What's with the ring then?"

"Habit."

"She's moved on then?"

"We'll see."

The guard nodded. He saw it every day. He watched prisoner visits wane, stop altogether. He saw the change in the men stuck behind bars, their minds running away in the dark hours, the vivid pictures of their loved ones in another's arms.

They stopped at a pair of metal doors. The guard unlocked them with a key and when they walked through he slammed it shut and it locked automatically. They walked on through an open courtyard and into a second corridor, as equally cold and damp as the previous.

"Have you got a lift?"

"No."

The guard nodded. "Money?"

"Subs."

The guard nodded. "Don't spend it all at once."

"Wouldn't take long."

Another guard stood ahead of them. He was a tough, often cruel Scotsman named McGivney. He had ginger hair and a hard demeanour, although he was as white as copy paper.

"I know, he's an asshole," the guard said quietly as they neared. "He'll try and wind you up. See if he can get a rise out of you. Ignore it, or you'll be back in here tonight."

Grant knew the guard, hadn't had many dealings with him in the three years since he had been transferred to The Scrubs. He looked straight ahead, took the guard in, then cast his eyes to the ground.

"Who have we got here then?"

"Grant, Simon."

"Wasn't asking you, Pat."

Grant avoided the Scotsman's eyes. "Grant, Simon, FA7214, Sir."

"And is Grant pleased to be getting out of here?"

"Yes, Sir."

"I'll take it from here, Pat."

The guard hesitated, but McGivney was senior in rank. He nodded to Grant and turned sharply. Grant looked at the Scotsman. The man held the keys and there was only one door between The Scrubs and the street.

"A friend of a friend was shot in your heist. The security guard working the diamond exchange. Remember him?"

Grant nodded. He had tried to forget, but the man's screams and pleading as he lay bleeding on the ground haunted him most nights.

"Well, he lives on sick benefit and shits in a bag." McGivney said. "How does that sound to you?"

"I didn't shoot him."

Grant didn't see the punch coming. It came upwards and into his diaphragm. The air spilled out of him and he dropped to his knees. "No. But you know who did! You played an ignorant little shit in court. You never disclosed where the money went, and got a longer sentence because of it. Now you're free to collect your share. I have friends and they'll be watching you and waiting. That guard needs compensation and you'll fucking well give it to him or you'll fucking well learn to swim in the Thames chained to a couple of concrete blocks. Got it?"

Grant nodded. He was spluttering, gasping for air. "Look, I'm sorry, but I didn't know anybody would have a shooter."

McGivney helped him to his feet. "Of course you didn't, sunshine." The Scotsman brought his knee up into Grant's groin and he folded in two. He looked casually around him and patted him on the back. There was newly installed CCTV throughout much of the prison, but this alleyway and courtyard was a blind spot. It was how some of the guards got the contraband into the prison to sell to the inmates. "Let me tell you, sunshine, watch your back. And don't spend the money. They will be in touch." He pulled Grant back up straight and unbolted the final metal door. "Mind how you go."

Grant felt himself propelled into the outside world. The great metal door shut behind him with a deep echo that resonated off the limestone walls of the courtyard, and the stillness and quietness that followed hit him all at once. His ears felt as if they had popped, such was the magnitude of the silence. Still within the city, and surrounded by residential streets, Grant had never experienced such silence. The world slowly came back, as if somebody was slowly turning up the volume - a car horn sounding in the distance, birds singing in the trees, a door closing, the gentle hum of distant traffic. It was suddenly back. The sounds of the outside world.

He rubbed his stomach, cupped his balls and looked down the street. It was empty one way, but there was a large black Mercedes heading down from the other. It slowed as it neared, then stopped in front of him. Grant felt a chill. The tinted window lowered. And the man it revealed filled more than half the front.

"Get in Simon."

3

Port of Holyhead, Anglesey

The fog was dense and had stopped all other shipping traffic, the harbour master confining them to port until it lifted. With the exception of the Dublin ferry, that was late, due an hour ago and holding a circular pattern out in the Irish Sea, there was no further shipping movements. Which was good. Because it had given the two MI5 officers waiting outside the ferry-port time to check the passenger manifests via ship-to-shore radio.

The man put down the binoculars and turned to his colleague in the passenger seat. "Nothing."

"There won't be for a few more minutes," he replied. "The pilot is bringing it in, escorted by a tug."

"It's like pea soup out there."

"It's going to be difficult to follow them, let's just hope it doesn't extend inland too much."

"It's Wales. It's either foggy or raining. And we've got to get across Anglesey first."

The man with the binoculars was called Randal. He was forty, ex-Army and from a working-class background. He had worked hard to become a watcher, the term MI5 used for its surveillance officers. The man next to him, who seldom drove by choice, was called Charles Forester. He was a graduate with a first-class degree from Oxford. He had seriously ruined his career in MI5 after a hunch had not played out, and had been demoted from what had been a promising eight-years climbing the ladder at a startling rate. He was thirty-four and knew he was destined for better things. He was determined to reach the top and the sooner he could get off watcher detail and back behind a desk on the higher floors of Thames House, the better.

"The routes are going to be covered after we clear the island," Forester said. "Once we can confirm the vehicle I have enough units on standby to get an eyes-on and follow. We can all chop and change, get back on route."

"You've thought of everything," Randal said. "Clever boy."

Forester smiled. "Careful. I was your boss once; I will be again."

Randal laughed. "Ok, sonny." He smiled, then seemed to take in what the younger man said. "I mean, boss."

"That's the ticket," he said quietly, almost to himself. He watched the man with the binoculars. "They were observed boarding at Dublin and the manifest checks out. The vehicle is a five-year-old Ford Sierra 2.9L on Eire plates…" He read out the licence plate number and shrugged. "I guess they're trying to be inconspicuous with the car choice. It's old, but not a banger. I guess the engine will be good. Is it more powerful than this?"

They were in a Ford Mondeo, the Sierra's successor. Randal shook his head. "No, although we have a smaller engine, we've got more horsepower and the motor-pool have breathed some magic on the engine."

"And the other cars?"

"The Rover will struggle a bit, but the motor-pool usually do a good job. The others should be alright," Randal said convincingly.

"Good."

The prow of the ferry broke through the fog. It was sudden and quite an impressive sight. Gradually, more and more of the vessel revealed itself. The foghorn sounded as the ferry started to dock. Men in yellow high-visibility vests performed various duties, some with ropes and machinery to engage chains, and others just looking busy.

Randal put down the binoculars and picked up a Motorola hand-held radio. "Do you want to make the call?"

Forester shook his head. He had learned when to put his name to something and when to sit back. It was how he had fallen from grace, and how he would climb back.

"Alpha Lima Two, this is Alpha Bravo One. Sit-rep, over."

"Alpha Bravo One, we are in position at the bottom of the ramp. Will report when we get a visual, over."

"Alpha Lima Two, have that, out." Randal put the handset down. "I can't believe PIRA would try anything with just six days until the peace agreement is signed."

"The Det said that the group was a splinter cell. They want to derail the Good Friday Agreement. They are not happy with the terms Sinn Fein have negotiated."

"What? Getting all of their prisoners pardoned and released?" He ground his teeth. "It's alright for you, but I patrolled Ulster in the green army. I lost comrades across the water and now all those fuckers are being released next month! The agreement isn't bringing our dead soldiers back. Shame the Det couldn't put bullets in them on the way. Say they attacked them, the murdering bastards."

The Det was the undercover wing of 14 Intelligence Company, the British Army's intelligence corps. It was formally called *The Detachment* and worked closely with both MI5 and MI6 in Northern Ireland. The team had illegally followed the terrorists through the Republic of Ireland and confirmed them boarding the ferry at Dublin. Now it was being handed over to the Security Service, often referred to as MI5. Operating on UK soil was the department's remit, with the Secret Intelligence Service, or MI6, gathering intelligence overseas.

"Just murder four Irishmen because of a loose tip-off or because they are acting suspiciously?" Forester smiled. "A little callous, I'd say."

"No more than they deserve, I'm sure," Randal seethed.

"Well, leave the semantics to me. I'll figure out what the signs mean. I'll see what these *boyos* are up to."

Randal took the Browning 9mm pistol out from his jacket pocket and tucked it under his thigh. "That's better, nice and close. Maybe they'll give me an excuse."

Forester eyed the weapon closely. He never carried a weapon himself. MI5 did not officially have a remit to use weapons, however, when detailing the movements of known terrorists on UK soil, certain operatives could arm themselves to provide security for both their team and members of the public. These officers were assigned under the umbrella of Special Branch liaison and detachment. "You'd kill someone rather than let the courts deal with them?"

Randal stared at the younger man. He felt a little cornered by the question. He was suddenly wary. Finally, he said, "No, I suppose not."

"Alpha Bravo One, this is Alpha Lima Two, status report, over."

Randal grabbed the Motorola, thankful for the distraction. "Alpha Bravo One, go ahead, over."

"Tangos have disembarked. We are three vehicles behind, over."

"Alpha Lima Two, have that, out."

"Tell them that's too close, drop them back a couple of vehicles," Forester said.

Randal looked at the younger man and smiled. "And if they lose them, that came from me? I suggest, sunshine..." he said, handing him the handset. "You tell them that yourself."

4

North London

"What kind of proposition?" Simon Grant watched the road ahead. But he couldn't help glancing into the mirror to study Holman's impressive collection of chins.

Holman turned the wheel sharply left, then right, negotiating the mini-roundabout. He let the wheel settle against his ample stomach. "The kind that makes you rich, son. The kind that makes you rich."

Grant studied him. He had put on more weight, if that was possible. His hair had greyed at the sides, perhaps he'd even thinned a little on top. His eyes were the same though, almost black and weasel-like. There was an intensity behind them, a ruthlessness.

"I've heard it before."

"No doubt."

"From you."

Holman tapped the steering wheel. "Haven't done so badly myself lately."

"Nice," said Grant. "I do six years inside and you get a hundred-grand motor."

Holman smiled. "I *am* grateful; you know?"

"Do I?" Grant asked. "You never showed up with a cake with a file in it."

"I couldn't go near *you*!"

"Or they would have had you."

"Exactly," Holman agreed. "Now, like I said, I *am* grateful. Your share is waiting, along with a handsome bonus for keeping your trap shut."

"I should hope so."

"So we'll go and get it, then you can hear my proposition."

"No. I'll take the cash, but I'm not interested in anything else. I'm going to find Lisa."

Holman laughed callously. "Don't waste your time! She's moved on mate. She's got herself a nice businessman, nice house, a dad for her kid…"

"My kid!" Grant snapped.

"Yeah, *your* kid. Jesus wept, what kind of father have you been for six years?"

"Because of your fucking gunman! Because you went out to bring the car round and never came back! Where did you go?"

"The filth turned up with sirens and flashing blue lights!" Holman snapped. "Someone must have heard the gunshot and called the police."

"So you left me."

"I couldn't get back to the square."

Grant shook his head. "What the hell was the bloody shooting about? We could have knocked the security guard out, tied him up. Shit, you could have *sat* on him!"

"I see prison hasn't trimmed your lip any."

Grant looked at Holman's straining gut. "No, just my stomach."

"Bitch." Holman smiled. "I hear little David is calling the bloke Daddy. Of course, he would after six years. How old is he, ten, eleven? Fuck, he won't remember you then, will he?"

"You're a bastard, Frank."

"Aye, son. A bastard's bastard, and no mistake." Holman slowed the car. They had entered a well-healed, tree-lined street with large houses and expensive vehicles parked along both sides. There were large four by four vehicles taking up two spaces. "Look at this lot," Holman said. "All the posh mums are driving these fucking farm vehicles now. That one's a Mercedes with a bloody great five-litre engine like this. BMW are making one next year. BMW making farm equipment! Times are changing. There's big money about now. You need to hear my proposition, or you'll just be some shithead with a few grand in his back pocket. A man who can't get a job because of his criminal record. A man who can't get a mortgage because the bank won't lend money to ex-cons."

Holman slowed for a school crossing and let a group of women across. They were well turned out with neutral tones and expensive hair. He carried on through the crossing when they were clear and stopped on the yellow zig-zags the other side. He kept the engine running.

"What are we doing here?"

"Just watch."

Grant did. He saw children in smart school uniforms. Red ties, white shirts and grey blazers. The sign to the school read *Avingdon Preparatory School, boys & girls, 4 – 11 years.*

A sporty BMW two seater convertible pulled into a drop-off space. The black roof was up and a boy of about ten stepped out. His mother got out and walked around the bonnet. She hugged him close and handed him his mini-rucksack. The boy turned and walked up the steps.

"Handsome lad, eh?" Holman grinned. "Don't know where an ugly shit like you figured. Are you sure he's yours?"

Grant stared at the boy as he reached the top of the steps, turned around and waved at his mother. Grant turned his eyes to the woman. She was mid-thirties, slim and attractive. Her auburn hair was cut short in a bob. It revealed her slender neck, bare shoulders glimpsing out from a thin woollen sweater. She was beautiful. But then, she always had been. Her hair had been long and brunette when Grant had last seen her. Brunette was her natural colour, but the red tone suited her. Grant's stomach seemed to drop through the seat. He reached for the door handle.

Holman flicked the central locking before he could open the door. "Don't be a tosser, sunshine."

Grant glared at him, pulled the door handle but it would not release. "For Christ's sake Frank!" he snapped. "Open the fucking door!"

"Don't be a twat. Take a look at her. She's like a bloody model, isn't she? A bit of money has ironed out the rough edges. No silver Argos jewellery and catalogue clothes for her now. See that car? That's a BMW Z3. James Bond drove one in the last film, but I doubt you would have seen it in the nick. Private school for your boy, a nice sports car, everything your missus could desire... Could you provide all of that? You should see the house!"

"So what have you brought me here for?" Grant asked as he watched the tiny sports car drive away. "To rub my nose in it?"

Holman laughed. He put the gearbox into drive and pulled out. "I wanted to show you what you've lost. And I wanted to show you what you could get back."

"What?"

"You have to listen to my proposition first."

5

Wales

"Keep back! You're getting too close; they'll suss us any minute!" Forester snapped. He picked up the handset. "Hello Alpha Lima Two, this is Alpha Bravo One, message, over."

"Send, over."

"Alpha Lima Two, advance and take point, over."

"Alpha Bravo One, wilco, out."

Forester turned to Randal. "Right, they're on point now, anchor up and we'll leap-frog later."

Randal glared in the mirror as he watched the green Rover 600 overtake and take the lead. He slowed the Mondeo down enough for a delivery van to overtake them and pull closer to the Rover.

They were using the buddy system and along with another vehicle, a blue Peugeot which was driving the anticipated route a mile ahead of the target vehicle, they had enough resources to shadow the target vehicle without becoming suspicious.

***

Ahead of them two more MI5 officers travelling in the Rover were settling into the pace, just on the cusp of the fog. They could see the Sierra's fog lights and braking lights, but little more.

"So who are they then?"

"Top players. An IRA active service unit. Two of them wormed their way out of the Enniskillen bombing. The RUC messed up some evidence and they walked. Another one is a known hitter, a gunman. Wanted for the death of two RUC officers and a solider in the Parachute Regiment. Not sure who else is in the vehicle. The Det haven't filed a completed report yet."

"I can't believe they were so blatant," the man said. "Just hopping on the ferry like that."

"They couldn't lose," Mary Vaughan said, running a hand through her jet black mane. She studied her vanity mirror, but not for her stunning looks, she needed to keep tabs on the vehicle behind. The white delivery van was so close to their bumper, but at least it shielded Forester and Randal in the Ford. "They knew we wouldn't be able to resist. They must have known that someone would pick them up. Perhaps they have a plan to get rid of us along the way."

"That's worrying," Davis said quietly.

"We've got weapons," she said calmly. "Perhaps they just think they can lose us. Or maybe with just six days to go until the peace agreement is signed, they feel empowered. If we act too fast and have no evidence or proof, then we could de-rail the Good Friday Agreement. They are all on the list anyway. Every man in that car is free, in a manner of speaking, after Friday. What are we going to do, arrest them now? No. They're up to something and we need to know what."

"And they know it too," Davis said. "The bastards."

6

North London

Simon Grant stared at the house in genuine admiration. "You've come a long way, Frank," he said, then glanced across at Holman, who was smiling a little smugly at the compliment.

The house was clearly of late Georgian architecture. Big, square and of uncompromisingly bold design, it suited the large man perfectly. It stood four storeys high, with a thick belt of ivy taking over the whole left side. "Got a home in south-west France as well now. I go down a few times a year. That way I can bring a shed-load of wine back. I might even be buying into a vineyard down there. Near Bordeaux."

"Funny, last time I saw you, you didn't know the difference between a fine wine or a bottle of Blue Nun."

"A lot of things have changed."

The Mercedes swept into the entrance over the loose gravel driveway and glided to a halt next to a new Porsche sports car. It was a little two-seater with a canvas roof and looked similar at both ends. Grant studied it, but did not recognise the model. Another reminder of how great swathes of life moved on when you were inside for more than half a decade.

"Eileen's." Holman stated flatly. "I can't get rid of the bitch, so I might just as well keep her quiet."

Eileen and Frank Holman had a marriage of pure convenience, but the convenience was entirely Eileen's. The marriage had been a sham from day one. A peroxide blonde, twelve years his junior. She had been thirty-five when they had married, and had become his wife under the pretence of being pregnant. Money had been her only motivation from the start, and as no evidence of a baby ever appeared, Eileen had made it clear that it would be considerably cheaper for Holman to keep her in the manner to which she had now become accustomed than to let her go. She knew all of her husband's business deals and associates, so it would certainly not pay for him to even consider seeking a divorce. She was happy to live a separate, parasitic existence within Frank Holman's life, and he made only two stipulations: she would have to accompany him to public gatherings to maintain the charade, and neither would bring a partner back to the house. Above all, Frank Holman could never afford to lose face in public.

Frank Holman could live with it. And in truth, he had grown accustomed to their estranged life. He preferred to use his bed for sleep, and whenever he felt the urges he could not satiate with Eileen, even with one of their rare consolations where they seemed to forget they hated one another, he would visit one of the three brothels where he held a financial stake, and collect a freebie. That not only offered more variety, but he was aware he would probably never have found a woman who would have attempted to partake in his particular sexual perversions. Not one outside the world of prostitution at least.

Grant opened the Mercedes, swung his feet out onto the thick bed of gravel, and stared up at the impressive-looking building. He could not help being surprised by the extent of Frank Holman's financial progress during the six-years that he had spent in prison. Sure, Holman had always been financially secure and had always had his fair share of investments, though never the sort to be found on the FTSE 100. But this? The house was worth over a million in this postcode, the Mercedes S600 was worth well over one hundred-thousand pounds, which was around half the value of Holman's previous home.

"I can see what you're wondering sonny," Holman paused. "How in God's name did old Franky-boy make good?" He grinned. "Watch this," he said, stepping away from the car. He pushed the door shut, then grinned as the door eased itself closed on soft-closing electric hinges and the wing mirrors slowly folded flush to the door automatically. "Not your everyday motor, is it? Come on, let's go inside and we can talk a little more about my proposition."

Grant shook his head. "No thanks, Frank. Just get my money and I'll be on my way. I don't mean to be rude or ungrateful, but I need to go straight."

Holman waddled around the rear of the huge car and stared at him coldly. "What for, sunshine? For Lisa? For little David? Do me a favour! They don't want you, that's for damned sure!" Holman stared at him, his face hard, his eyes cold and merciless. Grant opened his mouth to protest, but was cut down by another vicious tongue-lashing. "Wake up shithead! She's with another man! A nice, sensible, successful man. Nice house, nice car, nice possessions. Better than you ever gave her, that's for sure," he paused. "How long did she visit you for? Five, maybe six months? Then she slipped between another man's sheets, while he slipped between her legs.

Wake yourself up and forget about her." Holman's face was hard and cold again, his lightning changes of expression were becoming unnerving. "What were you going to do? Go round there with thirty-grand in your pocket, the rags you're standing in, and try to win her heart back? Get real, thirty- grand barely buys you one of those!" He waved a hand towards the Porsche and laughed. "One of those and a couple of cheap suits!"

Grant cast his eyes to the ground. He had known before the sentencing, known that it had been the last straw, that he would lose her forever. She had reached the end of her tether long before he did what was meant to have been his last job, long before he had been caught. She had given him enough warnings and had told him that if he didn't give up his life of crime and the company he kept, then she would leave him. Grant had never realised that she had really meant those words, not until it was too late.

It was exactly as Frank Holman had said. Six months, ten visits, then the final, dismissing, damning letter. But Grant had known all along. Ever since he had seen her expression in court.

Then had come the endless sleepless nights with only his graphic, subconsciously sadistic imagination as company. How that imagination could run riot during the long, early hours. He would close his eyes and see the two of them. See her laid back, her arms stretched behind her, gripping the headboard in ecstasy, taken to the heights of passion by her new lover. Her eyes closed, that look of concentration on her soft face, which slowly turned to ecstasy as the first violent orgasm shuddered through her and drove her to tears of pleasure, then pain.

He couldn't see her lover's face, of course, but that was even more haunting. He was forever guessing.

"So what are you going to do?" Holman's gravelly voice pulled him away from his painful, innermost thoughts, snapping him back to the harsh reality he now faced.

Grant turned towards his old friend and shrugged haplessly. "I don't know."

"I'll tell you what you're going to do," Holman smiled wryly, knowingly. "You're going to come inside with me. You're going to have yourself a large brandy, and then we are going to talk about how you are going to earn yourself a clear two-million quid," he paused and placed an arm around the younger man's shoulder. "That, my friend, is what you are going to do."

7

"Wait!" Mary Vaughan grabbed her partner's arm, stopping him from opening his door. She glanced back at the entrance to the service station, then looked back at him. "You stay here, keep a watch on the target vehicle," she paused, turning to look back at the building. "If they come back out, get hold of Forester on the net and tell him to take the lead."

Davis nodded. Mary Vaughan was the experienced agent, and technically his superior. He settled back into his seat, his adrenaline subsiding as the woman opened her door and walked purposefully, if not elegantly across the car park towards the main building.

***

Matthew McCormick handed over the money in loose change, then carried his tray to where his three companions were seated, gratefully nursing their cups of tea. As he placed his tray down onto the table, he glanced over towards the entrance and watched the attractive brunette walk into the restaurant.

He had caught her with her guard down. She stared at him for a second, their eyes meeting for far too long. Awkwardly, she looked away, somewhat flustered.

McCormick sat down next to his old friend Patrick Hennessey, a bull of a man with a shock of flame-red hair. He kept his eyes on the woman as she helped herself to an orange juice and walked over to join the queue at the service counter.

As was usually the case in a motorway service station, the queue represented a fair cross section of humanity. Fat man with crew cut, wearing a colourful football strip with loyal pride, stood next to his smaller, but almost identical son. The boy must have been eight and had a matching earing. Like father, like son. Then there was the salesman, outfitted in the obligatory white shirt and floral print tie, trying to hold his personal organiser open whilst dialling on his mobile phone, while also attempting to push his food tray along the counter towards the impatient girl operating the till. Responsible for her ill temper and the queue's near-standstill were a family of clearly limited means, for whom residence in the queue seemed the thing to do, even though only one person was needed to hold the tray of beverages and pay. Grandmother, mother, father, friend and a gaggle of young children who were playing with the clean cutlery in the trays and pulling at the cashier's apron strings.

When Mary Vaughan had finally paid for her drink, she meandered across the dining room, with its criss-cross arrangement of fixed tables and chairs, and sat down two tables away from the four men. McCormick kept his eyes on the attractive woman. Perhaps she had looked at him because she was attracted to him, biding her time until he was on his own, and away from this motley crew of men at his table. But he was a realist. With his well-broken nose, thinning hair and pockmarked complexion, Matthew McCormick was not the most handsome of men. He scanned the rest of the dining room, checking to see if any more MI5 watchers had decided to make an entrance. The woman had that look about her. Not smart enough in appearance for a businesswoman. At an age where she should be coupled-off, perhaps with a couple of children in tow. But on her own, and apparently unhurried. Too obvious by far.

It was late afternoon and the car park was rapidly emptying. Most people were heading for their destinations, with few bothering to stop now and face the extortionate prices that they would undoubtedly be charged.

Dugan, a slightly built, fair-haired man and in his early thirties, turned to McCormick and frowned expectantly. "What do yer think to that, Matt?" he asked in his broad Ulster accent.

McCormick, oblivious to the ongoing conversation and the other men's banter, looked back at his three companions, leant forwards conspiratorially and started to whisper, but turned his eyes back to the woman as he talked.

Mary Vaughan made no attempt to catch what the man had said. Instead, she sipped the remnants of her glass, stood up casually and walked towards the far exit. McCormick suddenly rose to his feet, darted through a quicker path between the tables and chairs and some fake foliage and walked ahead of her. Mary froze, albeit slightly, then continued to walk on. The man's actions were far too abrupt, too sudden. She knew that she had been spotted. She glanced casually over her shoulder, catching a glimpse of the other three men, who were all walking silently behind her. They had all spread themselves out, covering any possible way of escape.

Behind her, and in the path of two of the men were two tables of customers, all eating and drinking. If it came down to a firefight they would undoubtedly be caught in the crossfire.

The man in front of her walked through the doorway and out into the foyer, where he stopped and started to look around suspiciously.

Mary Vaughan reached across her waist and felt the hefty, reassuring butt of her Sig P226 pistol. She made a conscious effort to remain calm; she could not afford to lose control of the situation now. Timing was of the essence; if the men were armed she would be gunned down for sure. Four against one, forget it. She had two options; bluff it out, or draw her weapon and fire first, and blow the entire operation. Ahead of her, the man with the unsightly pockmarked face turned to glare at her.

Shit! She thought. She chose to bluff it out.

She stuck out her shapely breasts, then smoothed her hands over her hips. "I see you've decided to leave your friends behind," she paused, smiling seductively at the man in front of her, then ran a hand through her long, dark hair. "I thought I might have caught your attention back there. Couldn't resist, could you?"

Matthew McCormick smiled. These scenarios really were strictly for the movies. And not great ones. He looked over her head and nodded at Patrick, who by now, was standing directly behind her.

Mary turned around, but it was too late. The big Irishman brought the edge of his hand down across the side of her slim neck, at a point just below and behind her right ear. She fell forwards, and McCormick caught her just in time. He hugged her close, keeping her to her feet, then turned to the rest of the men and scowled. "Get back to the fricking car! Go on, move it!" He glanced to his right and saw the entrance to the men's lavatories, then looked back to the exit where the other three men were now casually leaving the building.

There was nobody in the foyer; the whole scene had passed entirely unobserved. McCormick kept her held close to him and walked towards the men's lavatories, taking a chance that it would be empty. As he entered the brightly-lit, sanitised surroundings he heard the sound of a nearby toilet flushing, and then the sound of a buckle and zip fastening. He rushed her inside the nearest cubicle and slammed the door shut, just as the other occupant opened the door.

McCormick lowered the woman to the toilet seat and listened intently as the man washed his hands, then operated the warm-air dryer. He listened for the departing footsteps, then looked down at the woman, who was slowly starting to regain consciousness. She looked up at him, wincing as pain stabbed through her neck. The Irishman pushed his face almost into hers and grit his teeth together before speaking. "Right, bitch, who the fuck are you? And don't even think about bullshitting me! You're a fucking spook, aren't you?"

She stared up at him tearfully, then brought her knee up into his groin. The blow was savage, and caught him completely off guard. He gasped and fell forward to his knees, cupping his crotch with both hands in a bid to master the pain.

Mary Vaughan saw her chance and took it; she reached across her waist, caught hold of the Sig's thick plastic butt and pulled the pistol free of its leather holster.

McCormick, startled at the sight of the pistol, suddenly forgot the pain to his throbbing groin and made a grab for the weapon. He slipped his index finger behind the trigger, preventing her from firing, then punched a short, fierce jab full in her face. She reeled backwards, cracking the back of her skull against the solid tiled wall. Unfazed by the woman's injury, McCormick followed up the vicious attack with a punch to her sternum, then a back fist to her temple. He looked down at the woman, then calmly slipped the pistol into the waistband of his faded blue jeans.

Mary Vaughan looked up at him pleadingly, a trickle of blood running down over her lips and off the tip of her chin. "Please, please don't…" she sobbed.

"What choice do I have, luv?" McCormick shook his head. "We are at war, us and the likes of you."

"We're not, just give the peace agreement a chance. It will work, you have to start trusting us," she pleaded.

"Trust you! Is that why you were following us? Is that why you were carrying a fucking gun?" McCormick caught hold of her shoulder and steadied her. "You know that I don't have a choice," he paused. "And a right pretty thing you were too." He smiled, then quickly reached down and spun her around. He pressed his knee into the small of her back and pinned her against the toilet cistern, he wrapped his arms around her, pinning her arms to her side and cupped her mouth with his left hand and pinched her nose with his right. She reacted at once, struggling against him, desperately trying to take a breath. His grip was like a vice and she knew she had no time. She started to convulse, but he held firm. Her last moments, dying in a dirty toilet cubicle, were swift and efficiently dealt. Within a minute she passed out and he kept his grip for another two minutes, long after she had died and slumped lifelessly to the floor.

McCormick had not realised just how dramatic suffocating her would be. He turned her around and lifted her body onto the toilet. Her eyes were blank and glossy. Her stare, distant and final. His fingers ached, as did his throbbing forearms, which threatened to spasm into a painful bout of cramp. Sweat poured from his brow as he pulled a length of toilet paper from the wall-mounted dispenser, then dabbed it across his face and neck.

The cadaver looked up at him, the eyes bulging slightly. There was blood seeping from the corner of one, a crimson tear which travelled steadily down the cheek. A thin dribble of saliva ran from its mouth, followed by a thick, pungent-smelling, blood-filled mucus. Once silky-smooth hair was now matted tangled, and the carefully, tastefully applied makeup had been smeared by the final tears of both panic and pain. During the struggle, her blouse had ripped open, exposing a firm breast. McCormick bent down and gently covered her apparent immodesty with the flap of silk.

"Sorry luv, wrong time, wrong place, that's all," he paused, then wrinkled his nose in disgust, as he took in the fetid smell of death. As is usually the case, the cadaver's bladder and bowels had relaxed as the brain died. Death was a nasty business.

He looked down at what had once been a beautiful woman, thoroughly sickened at the sight, and somewhat sickened by what he had been forced to do. He had taken away all she had ever had, and all she would ever have. He had killed before, of course, but this felt different from any of the others. Soldiers were soldiers, they carried guns and they patrolled the country that he loved. The RUC were sell-outs, bastards every one. They strutted with revolvers on their hips and carbines in their hands. War was war, and killing was part of what he had sworn to do until his land was free of British rule. But this woman? It was different to setting up an IED or taking a pot-shot at a soldier from four-hundred metres away. It had felt so different, to watch the life slip helplessly and steadily from her, to witness her last moments on this earth. An assault rifle would clatter away in his hands, filling him with schoolboy excitement, bravado, and an overwhelming rush of adrenaline. A bomb would detonate, but by then he and the rest of his cell would be miles away. This was very different; this had sickened him to the core.

He turned around, eager to leave the body without further contact with those lifeless eyes, and unlocked the door, stepping cautiously out from the cubicle. After a quick, cursory glance, he gently closed the door then re-locked the bolt, using a ten-pence coin to turn the slot.

8

Simon Grant sipped from the balloon brandy glass, watching Frank Holman curiously as the man undertook the ritual of swilling the contents around his oversized glass.

"That's what I said," Holman paused. "Two-million. Impressed?"

Grant watched his old friend. Acting out his self-appointed role as lord of the manor when a few years ago Frank Holman was a lager drinker. He wouldn't have known a vintage brandy from a single malt whiskey. Now he had the look of a man who owned plenty of both, and knew when to serve which.

"Or alternatively, you could just have the thirty-grand I owe you and try to prise Lisa out of that other bloke's bed and back into your own," he paused, then broke into a raucous laugh. "Oh sorry, I forgot, you don't even have a bed of your own for her to go to!" Holman grinned, very pleased with this cruel shaft of irony as he proceeded with the swilling of his glass while the, vapours rose. "It *does* improve the aroma and flavour, you know," he said. "I went on a wine tasting and spirit appreciation tour when I went to see about buying a share in a vineyard."

Grant set his own glass down and stared at him contemptuously. "Why push the subject? I lost everything while I was inside. And still you try and wind me up. We used to be friends," he said sadly. "I have been away from her for six years, I still love her."

Holman smirked. "*Used* to be friends? I invite you into my home, I am willing to cut you into a deal for two-million quid, and you have the front to say, we *used* to be friends!" He struggled out of his deep chair and walked over to a small, Edwardian writing bureau. He opened the drawer and took out a large manila envelope. "Thirty-grand," he announced, throwing the envelope across the room to where Grant was seated. It bounced off his knee and settled at his feet. "Twenty from your share, as agreed, and a further ten on top," he paused breathlessly. "You kept quiet, kept me from doing bird, but you also cost me one hell of a lot of money and influence when you got yourself caught." He glared at him menacingly. "I had trails to cover, bribes to pay. Investors in the enterprise were very edgy after you got caught. They spent six years covering their tracks in case you talked. I think ten-grand is enough compensation."

"You were late, that was the reason that I got caught. And because of that idiot you used as a heavy man. Besides, I stashed the money while I was on the run, avoiding the police dragnet. I didn't have to get word to you to let you know where I hid it," he paused. "As for money and influence..." Grant glanced around the room and noted the luxurious furnishings. "I can see that I must have cost you a great deal of both."

Holman shook his head despondently. "Just take the money and get the hell out of my house, I can't be bothered with you anymore. You know your problem Simon Grant? You're fucking ungrateful! Six years, big deal! I've just given you thirty-grand from a job where I made nothing," he paused, glaring at him harshly. "Now I'm giving you the chance to earn yourself two-million pounds, but you just forget it! Go to your beloved Lisa, show her your handful of notes and whisk her off into the sunset. Just don't hold your breath! She was tired of you before you got yourself nicked - if she wasn't, she wouldn't have sat on another man's dick before you were even sentenced!"

"That's not true!" Grant flung himself out of his chair and rushed forward towards Holman, his fist raised in childish rage. Holman sidestepped quickly, surprisingly so for such an overweight individual, and punched Grant in his solar plexus, dropping him to the floor instantly.

"I thought you'd have toughened up a bit in a *real* prison." Holman looked down at Grant and offered his hand. "Do you know what? If my grandmother was alive today, she could kick your bloody arse!"

Grant refused the offered hand and slowly pulled himself to his feet, pressing a comforting hand to the pain in his chest. The blow had knocked the wind out of his lungs and shaken him. The speed in which the big man moved had unnerved him. "Lisa didn't cheat on me as soon as that. It's not true, and you know it…" he said.

"Whatever," he replied. "It was soon after though. Six months, I reckon." Holman turned his back on him and walked over to the coffee table where he had left his brandy. He picked up the oversized glass, swirled the remnants around for a brief second or two, and casually sank the contents in one mouthful. He savoured the taste for a moment, then turned back towards Grant and smiled. "This is pretty good. One hundred years old, believe it or not. Not your everyday drink, but then again, this is not a day to be taken lightly."

Grant returned unsteadily to his chair and flopped down, still rubbing his chest. He reached for the remnants of brandy and took a sip, before replacing the glass on the table. It was getting late. He hadn't eaten and the brandy was taking effect.

Holman walked towards the door, then looked sombrely back at his old friend. "It's two-million, Simon. More money than you could ever dream of. A few days planning, a few hours' work, and a lifetime spending," he paused. "If you're interested, you can take the bedroom at the top of the stairs and we'll talk some more in the morning. If not, then drink up and get the fuck out of my house." He walked through the open doorway and closed the door silently behind him.

Simon Grant stared at the glass on the table beside him. He took shallow breaths, his chest still aching from the savage, unexpected blow. The man had caught him completely off guard. Frank Holman was certainly not a man to underestimate. In all the years he had known him, this was the first time they had come to blows. He closed his eyes. The warmth of the central heating and the comfort of the soft leather chair, combined with the alcohol, none of which had he been accustomed to for so long, started to influence his senses. Soon he was peacefully asleep, unable to wake from his familiar dream, as Lisa reached back for the headboard, arched her back and accepted her new man, the man whose face Grant could never see.

***

"We could force them off the road, take the bastards out and end it now!" Randle snapped. "We'd be justified!

They've killed one of our colleagues! We could force their hand, take them out!"

"What, murder them? Take retribution for Mary?" Forester shook his head despondently. "Just keep calm, for Christ's sake. Mary was a good friend of mine as well. Keep your distance and wait for control to respond. Until the police get the CCTV footage, we can't be sure they were even involved. There will also be a bigger picture to consider. If they are intending to target something over here, it could kill hundreds of people. We need to retain an eyes-on and learn more."

After the four Irishmen had left the services and Mary Vaughan had not returned to her vehicle, the two men had received a curt message from Davis for them to follow the target vehicle. Four miles down the motorway, almost out of the hand-held Motorola's range, they had heard Davis give Control the news of Mary Vaughan's gruesome death. Both men had been aware that Davis had been greatly distressed, possibly sobbing; yet neither man had commented about it. No doubt they would both shed a tear or two for their team-mate as they tried to sleep in the early hours.

"Hello Alpha Bravo One, this is Control, message, over."

"Alpha Bravo One, send, over."

"Control, stay with target vehicle for now. Replacement vehicle will relieve you at the junction for Reading Over."

"No way, we're staying…"

Forester snatched the handset from the man's clasp, fumbled with the pressel switch and started to speak. "Alpha Bravo One, static interference, all is correct now, understood. Will be relieved at junction eleven, Luton. Wilco, out." He turned towards Randle as he returned the handset to the centre console. "How you made it this far in Five is beyond me. No wonder the police kicked you out."

***

"Is he in?"
"I would think so; he hasn't left just yet."
"Make sure that you get him, Holman. Nothing more can go ahead without him. If he declines, then up the offer as you see fit."
"No, he'll be happy with two. He's out to impress. He'll agree to it in the morning."
"Still wants her then?"
"Absolutely."
"Very well, but I'll sort out an insurance policy, just in case."
"Well, whatever needs to be done. I'll keep you informed from this end, I'm going to check on him now, I'll see you soon…" Holman heard the click of the receiver being replaced, which always infuriated him. The other man always broke the conversation in that manner; one day he would do the same to him. He replaced the receiver and walked back down the staircase, crossed the hall and gently opened the lounge door. As he peered inside he could see Simon Grant sleeping. The man was slumped in the comfortable leather armchair, his head resting on the silk cushion. Quiet, warmth and too many brandies. Holman knew he would be out for a while, and he wouldn't wake and

leave in the middle of the night. He had nowhere to go, and then he'd be thinking about the money. In the cold light of day, the money would speak to him. Quietly, Holman pulled the door to and headed for his study. There was more brandy in there, and there were the plans. The plans needed fine-tuning, but they were sound. Simon Grant would help bring the plan closer to fruition, as long as he agreed. And Holman knew he would. It simply depended on how much leverage was needed.

9

"What the bloody hell was all that about?" Alex King shook his head in bewilderment then replaced the tiny earpiece, and looked down at his scribbled transcript of the telephone conversation. "And who the bloody hell is this Holman guy?"

"No idea."

"O'Shea said to up the offer, then this guy Holman says that he's sure that he'll be happy with *two*," he paused and looked across at his liaison officer. "Two what? Two-thousand, two-million?"

"Beyond me, old chap. It might as well be two lumps of sugar in his bloody tea, for all I know." Ian Forsyth lit another cigarette and expelled a smoky sigh. "It's traced to a St. Albans telephone number, no name, but I can soon sort that out."

"I don't like it. Especially the bit about an *insurance policy*, sounds a bit dodgy to me," King paused, stood up and paced over to the window. "Danny Neeson, O'Shea's driver, he's more than he seems isn't he?"

Forsyth smiled wryly. "Oh, Danny-boy is his bloody right-hand man, his bodyguard as well. Had the front to come across the water and train with an established close protection agency. The ironic thing is the agency was run by British ex-special forces." He inhaled another lung-full of smoke, then rested his head against the chair and blew a smoke ring towards the ceiling. "Ex-SAS soldiers actually trained an IRA terrorist in the art and craft of close protection and anti-terrorism." He chuckled and looked back at him.

"Danny's not just our chap's right-hand man, he's a top player in his own right. He killed three of your lot at Crossmaglen security base. Used an old Soviet-stock mortar."

King frowned. "My lot?"

"Yes, you know, soldier johnnies," he paused, a little ponderously. "Marines I think."

King stared at the MI6 officer in bewilderment. Forsyth was outfitted like the archetypal sixties British spy. Double-breasted, pinstriped suit, trench coat and trilby hat. He also spoke with not one, but a whole bag of plums in his mouth. "I'm not a soldier. I work for MI6, but was seconded to the SAS for field experience."

"Private soldier then."

"I'm not for hire."

"Not yet, old boy, not yet. You're a blunt instrument for the service. We refer to you lot as soldiers. And that's the same, as the marines or green army," he paused, exhaling a thin plume of cigarette smoke. "You all get a little muddy and bloody, from time to time."

10

It was a powerful kick. Not a tap, nor a half-hearted shunt, but a kick of sheer, unimaginable, pent-up aggression. The quick run had helped. Three paces, a quick shuffle and then, side of the foot and in for the kill.

Then came the sudden realisation of what he had done.

The boy watched the ball, studying its trajectory, the gradual curve, and then the sudden deviation, which could only spell inevitable disaster. There was no way that it would make the makeshift goal, not even the post, not even close. The guttering gave way upon impact, crashing to the ground as the ball continued on its path of destruction and bounced to the conservatory roof, cracking the glass into a spider's web, then turning at an acute angle and rattling against the two metal dustbins.

"David!"

The boy looked up, startled, and then horrified that the shout had come so quickly after the event. He turned his attention back to the ball, which now rolled across the neatly kept lawn, and halted, somewhat incriminatingly, at his feet.

"Are you deaf, boy?"

The boy looked at the fearsome expression on the man's face, as he strode across the neatly cut lawn towards him. He started to tremble at the thought of what might be coming. "No, sir."

"Then come here." The voice was calm and patient, yet the eyes seemed to scream at him, agonisingly loud, threatening to shatter his eardrums.

The boy walked forward hesitantly. He knew the tone - frighteningly calm, but devastatingly deceiving. He stood before him, head bowed, eyes staring hopelessly at the ground. The man reached out and gently touched his face, stroking the boy's cheek as lightly as a caress with a pinch of down. He stared up at the smiling man, then cringed as he noticed the expression change. Slowly at first, then abruptly, glaring hatefully at him, as if he wanted the boy dead. He gripped hard, fastening his hold on the boy's soft, puppyish skin, then twisting, spitefully so, until tears started to well in the young eyes.

"What have I told you about playing in the garden with that bloody ball?" He stared at the boy then clenched his teeth as he squeezed with all his might. "Play! Play! Play! That's all you ever do! Have you done your homework? No, of course you haven't!"

The boy sobbed, the tone threatening to burst into a tearful wail at any moment. He looked up at the man pleadingly. "I don't have any home..."

"Don't bloody interrupt me!" He released his grip on the boy's soft cheek, only to catch and twist his earlobe. Earlobes were better. They turned red, but they didn't leave a bruise. The man knew which parts of the body bruised and which parts concealed the evidence of violence. He twisted, and the sob instantly became a wail, as a searing stab of pain ripped through the soft skin of the lobe, and all his imagination focused on whether the ear was about to rip clean from his head.

"God, you're so soft, so bloody weak!" The man shook his head disdainfully, then released his grip and swiped his hand across the boy's cheek, catching him with the back of his knuckles, sending him to his knees. "If somebody doesn't sort you out now, then you'll grow up to be a loser! Do you want that?"

The boy held his flaming cheek and blinked through the salty intrusion of tears. "No, Sir," he replied meekly. He knew what would come next, and it would hurt, it always did. He wished it wouldn't, yet something inside told him that it was worse than any physical pain that the man could ever inflict. More than his cheek, more than the stretched ear, more than the spiteful dig in the ribs he received every single morning before breakfast.

The man looked at him in disgusted pity and shook his head. "A loser," he paused. "A loser, just like your pathetic father."

***

Grant opened his eyes, slowly at first, feeling a little groggy. He was not used to the dry heat from the radiators, or the brandy, which now reminded him of its presence by fuelling the headache that was threatening to beat his brain into a gelatinous pulp. He eased himself out of the deep leather chair then felt the sudden rush of blood surge through his body and leap into his brain. He wobbled slightly but regained his balance as his head gradually began to acknowledge the feeling and compensate. He blinked several times, and gently rubbed his tired eyes.

His first hangover in six years, and already he was promising that it would be his last. He sniffed the air, the unmistakable aroma only noticeable now that he had started his slow progress to recovery. He turned towards the door, sniffing the air and following his nose.

Frank Holman stood at the stove, looking almost comical in a plastic apron with the strings fastened loosely across his back. Last night the man had swilled his brandy as if to the manor born, now he wore a plastic apron with *Kiss the Cook* emblazoned across the front. Frank Holman had never presented a balanced persona.

Simon Grant declined the written instruction and made his way unsteadily across the kitchen, perching himself against the side of the large mahogany worktop.

Holman turned and grinned. "I see you're still here," he said, a little patronisingly. "Good night's sleep? Must be nice with nobody trying to bugger you in the middle of the night."

Grant forced a grin. "That never happened. Maybe I'm not that good looking."

"You're right there."

"Fuck off."

"Two eggs or three?"

Grant blinked. "Three?" He shook his head. "No, one will be just fine. Who the hell eats three eggs?"

"No appetite, eh?" He walked nimbly across the kitchen and set two plates on the large, matching oval mahogany table. "Enjoy."

Grant drew up to the considerably smaller of the portions and started to pick his way through some of the bacon and sausage.

"Never could stand the way you ate," Holman commented. He speared a sausage and forced the whole thing into his mouth, long end first, then switching to broadside with a well-practised twist. He chewed twice, perhaps three times, then swallowed. He smacked his lips in satisfaction, then smiled. "Gorgeous!" He tore a slice of greasy, over-cooked fried bread with his hands then dipped it into the yolk of the first of his three fried eggs. "Food is there to be eaten, not bloody looked at." He bit a large mouthful of fried bread, then sucked in huge mouthfuls of air to quell the sizzling fat on his tongue.

Grant watched the trickle of egg-yolk down his host's chin, then turned back to his breakfast. "I just like to take my time, that's all."

Holman patted his chest to speed the passage of a loud belch. He smiled, obviously pleased with the result, then looked back at his old friend. "That's the thing about time, isn't it?" He stabbed a whole tomato, jabbed a round of black pudding and forced the stack into his mouth. "You let time pass you by without seizing the opportunities," he paused, thinking it better to swallow the obstruction first. "And what are you left with?" Grant shrugged haplessly. He knew the answer, knew that it had nothing to do with eating fast or slow. It was purely rhetorical, an excuse for Frank Holman to pontificate. "I'll tell you what you're left with." Holman sneered. "Nothing!" He took another deep breath between mouthfuls, allowing at least some of his food to start its journey towards his ample stomach, before stabbing a whole rasher of bacon with his fork and expertly twisting it into a mouth-sized piece, like a skilled native Italian, about to eat a forkful of spaghetti. "You come into this world with nothing. You can't take anything when you go, that's for damn sure, but you can sure as hell try to get yourself as much as you can in between."

Grant nodded. "I tried that six years ago, so did you. Only, I was the one who ended up in prison. I was the one who lost everything."

Holman shovelled the last remaining fried tomato into his mouth, chewed once, then swallowed. He pursed his thick lips together in satisfaction, then smiled. "Mmm, superb!" He sipped from his mug of sweet tea, then replaced on the table and grinned. "Can't beat that little lot to start the day."

"You eat like that every morning?" Grant asked, somewhat surprised that the man was still on this earth, let alone walking it.

Holman grinned. "Each and every day, sometimes I end the day on that too. Some famous guy, I don't know who, said that if you want to eat well in England, then eat breakfast three times a day," he paused, adopting a heavier tone. "Seriously though, I am offering you the chance of a dead cert, big money job. You got yourself caught last time, this time will be different."

"Why should you care?"

"You didn't grass on me," Holman smiled. "You could have, and you could have got your sentence cut as a result. However, you stayed loyal to your friend. I admire that."

Grant chuckled. "Loyal? Do you think that my kneecaps would still be functioning if I grassed you up?

One of your contacts would have paid me an early morning visit, sooner or later."

Holman gave him a look of mock surprise. "Simon, I am deeply offended."

Grant pushed his unfinished meal aside and took a sip of lukewarm tea.

"Like my old grandmother used to say; waste not, want not." Holman reached forward and pulled the plate towards him, exchanged Grant's cutlery for his own and started to eat.

"Was that the grandmother who could have kicked my arse?"

Holman smiled through a mouthful of sausage. "Kicked it, skinned it and hung it on the fucking shed door."

Grant smiled at the thought then looked at his host seriously. "So what is it?" he asked. "I mean, two-million is an awful lot of money, just for one man's share."

Holman smiled wryly. Occasionally, on the hottest of summer days, he would go fishing. Rod, tackle, bait, a few beers, the sun on his face and a pleasurable drive down to the coast. His uncle had taught him to fish at an early age, amongst other things. The secret, above all else, was to tease. Move the bait gently and never strike the rod upon the first bite. If you did, you would be guaranteed to arouse suspicion, lose the fish and scare it off for good. Always wait until the bait and hook was firmly in its mouth, preferably swallowed, only then would you make the strike. "Two-million *is* a hell of an amount of dosh for a few days' work," Holman agreed. He wiped a piece of fried bread around the newly acquired plate, mopping up the egg yolk and grease, then popped the morsel into his avid mouth. "Excellent! Fry-up, food of the Gods! Tried that caviar stuff once. Fish eggs?" He laughed raucously. "More like fish shit!"

11

The yellow works-van pulled into the quiet street, crawled along the line of parked cars, then parked in a nearby space opposite a row of terraced houses. The larger of the two men, muscular and bulky, but by no means fat, got out of the driver's door and walked to the rear of the vehicle. He rubbed his fingers through his bushy beard, relieving himself of an irritating itch, then reached out and opened the double doors. The smaller man opened the passenger door and stepped onto the pavement, a huge smile upon his face, which was rapidly turning into a laugh. "...So then he says…"

"I know; I've already heard it."

The smaller man stopped in his tracks and frowned. "What do you mean?"

"I mean, I've heard it," the larger man paused. "The grave digger says, I know but I had to have somewhere to park my bike…"

"Sod off Dave!" The smaller man snapped, his expression turning from anger to a childish sulk. "I went through the whole of that joke for nothing."

"Yeah well, you missed a bit out."

"Bollocks!"

The large man started lifting the wrought iron manhole cover to expose the drain. He stood back in disgust, then glanced at his companion and swept a welcoming hand towards the open hole.

"No way!" The smaller man shook his head defiantly, still sulking. "I went down the bastard hole yesterday!"

"Tough," he replied, then tensed his arm to reveal a bulging set of biceps. "Looks like you're going down today as well."

McCormick smiled as he watched the smaller of the two men protest. He glanced at his watch, then replaced the net curtain and walked over to the television set.

"Ah, shut that shit off Matt! What the hell do yer want it on so early for anyway?" Patrick padded across the lounge on his way back from the bathroom, wearing only a faded pair of cotton boxer shorts. He picked some of the material out of his arse crack and let out a belch. "Who wants a brew?"

McCormick nodded. "Breakfast news. I want to see if they got a good picture of me at the service station," he paused, switching to another channel with the remote control. "There was bound to be a camera somewhere."

The big Irishman let out another belch and scratched his bare stomach. "Aye, well they won't mention her. The bloody bitch was intelligence; they'll not say a bloody thing. If you're not mentioned, then we'll know MI5 were on to us for sure." He walked around the side of the breakfast bar and opened the refrigerator door. "Bloody sodding cheek! I thought Neeson was going to stock this place up? Lazy, fucking bastard!"

"Aye, I can really see yer telling him so." McCormick laughed. "As big as yer are, and as fucking butt-ugly as yer are, you're scared shitless of the bastard."

"Too bloody right I am! And you're not I suppose?"

Matthew McCormick didn't answer. He picked up the remote control and switched to another channel. Patrick was probably right. The intelligence services would undoubtedly cover up the incident. Bad press was never needed, especially as the British government continued with the peace agreement charade. They needed a calm sea, plain sailing until the agreement was signed.

McCormick stood up and threw the remote control on the sofa, and walked back to the window.

"Will you calm down? Jesus, Mary and Joseph, you're making me nervous! We're well in the clear. We lost our tail at the service station, just relax." Patrick walked back towards the bedroom, letting out a prize-winning belch as he closed the door behind him.

McCormick pulled back the net curtain and stared outside again. The street was residential, therefore reasonably quiet, as most of the inhabitants had already left for work. The two workmen had covered up the open drain with a red and white striped weather cover, looking much like a large tent. He watched the larger of the two men carry what appeared to be a battered metal tool box into the weather cover, then fasten the opening behind him. McCormick replaced the net curtain and walked back to the television set. He flicked over to *The Jerry Springer Show*. A woman was about to ruin her husband's life with her confession to an affair with his brother. He watched animatedly. *You never really knew what people were up to behind your back,* he reflected.

"Hello, Control, this is X-ray Delta One, message, over."

"Control, send, over."

"X-ray Delta One, in position, out."

"All right Dave." The smaller of the two men kept his eyes on the monitor in front of him. The image showed McCormick replacing the net curtain opposite them. There would be a two second delay at this distance, the camera was using VHF radio frequency to the hub unit connected to the monitor. The man patiently waited for his colleague to replace the handset, check the fastening to the opening of the work tent, then he grinned. "I've got another one - this time, tell me if you've heard it before I go round the houses. A camel without a hump goes into a vasectomy clinic…"

"Heard it."

"Bastard!"

12

He depressed the clutch and shifted down into third gear, emitting a mighty, bellowing roar from the two cavernous exhaust pipes. He entered the tight corner, slowing on engine braking alone, then dabbed his left foot on the brake, as he kept the revs on the accelerator with his right foot. The car's rear end twitched. Then, just as he was through the bend, he dropped into second and floored the accelerator. The rear wheels screeched loudly, letting out a bluish smoke and for a brief instant, the whole vehicle started to float as if it were on slushy ice. The car gently played towards the right, and then suddenly slewed sideways.

"Keep the throttle on, don't take your foot off..." The man in the passenger seat said calmly, his hand hovering near the steering wheel. "Opposite lock, and more throttle. Now!"

Neeson responded accordingly, compensated the tail-slide and changed up into third. "That felt much better!" He caught sight of the look of excitement on his face in the rear-view mirror and tried to suppress the broad smile. Never in his wildest dreams would he have expected to drive such a car.

"You're getting the hang of it now. Goes well, doesn't she?" the salesman paused. "Best of both worlds, performance and reliability, which is exactly what you have to think about when buying a performance car. After all, you might be driving it every day, and can soon become tired of a specialist sports car. Sure, TVR's are good to drive. Astonishing performance, but I guarantee that this will only ever see the inside of a garage for servicing. That is why this costs just over seventy-grand, and the TVR Cerbera which you said you liked costs only fifty. That and the fact in ten years' time the TVR will be a tatty mess inside and this will still look like new."

"Doesn't feel as quick though," he commented.

"Nought to sixty in just under five seconds, one hundred and seventy miles per hour! How fast do you want to go?" the salesman laughed. "All right, maybe so. Let's face it, nothing is going to keep up with the four and a half-litre TVR Cerbera. Not even the lottery winner's super-cars. Christ, even a Ferrari F40 doesn't catch a Cerbera on acceleration, and it would cost you six or seven times as much. But most cars are compared to each other on paper. Let's just say, if you put the Cerbera through that last bend, just like you did with this, then you would have been road kill. Did I mention our track days? We are giving all Porsche 911 buyers a day learning to drive fast down at Thruxton race track. It's something we're doing for the 996 new engine models."

Neeson wasn't listening. He was having too much fun. He downshifted again, taking the vehicle confidently into the approaching corner. He positioned the nose of the car through the bend, dropped to second, and then kicked the accelerator hard to the floor.

"No, watch it!" The salesman made a grab for the steering wheel, but it was far too late. The tail of the Porsche 911 went wide, too wide to be corrected, and under the influence of inertia and the weight of the rear-mounted engine creating a pendulum effect, slewed round one hundred and eighty degrees. The vehicle shuddered to an abrupt halt, the wheels smoking. A stench of burnt rubber in the air. "I told you to watch it! You're a bloody madman!" The young salesman caught hold of the door handle. "Move over, I'm driving us back to the showroom," he ordered, in a voice too scared and plaintive for any ring of authority.

Neeson grabbed the man's arm and gripped firmly, forcing him to remain where he was. He looked down at him, and the man was instantly intimidated by the cold stare. At five-foot-ten Danny Neeson was not overly tall, yet he was thick set, two-days' dark-stubble covered his face, framing his cold blue eyes and well-broken nose. A thick scar ran from the corner of his left eye to the tip of his chin. Scars told stories, and you just knew the man who gave him that scar came off worse. The young salesman decided to hear him out.

"If you want to sell this baby, then you're going to have to allow me to try it out thoroughly," he said quietly, relaxing his grip. "After all, you wouldn't take a woman to the altar without finding out what she's like in the sack first, would you?" He smiled wryly. "I'm happy now, I know exactly how far I can push it, so just sit yourself back in your seat and enjoy the ride home." The tone was calm yet firm, even though his soft Irish accent had an easy rhythm to it.

The salesman settled back into his seat and smiled, certainly seeming a little more relaxed. He was starting to see his commission. "Certainly, Mr Bircher, I was just a little shaken up, that's all. This is a seventy-grand vehicle after all."

Neeson nodded and smiled amiably. "Understandable. Now, if you don't mind, I'd like to return by a more scenic route," he paused. "I want to get used to my new car."

The salesman beamed. "Feel free. I'm only too glad that you chose German reliability and technology over rustic British performance."

Neeson slipped the gearbox into first and pulled back into the road, heading back in the opposite direction to which they had been travelling.

After travelling about a mile, Neeson signalled left and took a sharp forked turning, away from what had passed as a main road.

The Hampshire countryside was certainly beautiful in early spring. The buds on the trees were shooting, and some had even burst open to release delicate early leaves. The grass was wet, still beaded with morning dew, which gave it a fresh look, contrasting strongly with the occasional field of yellow rape seed. With the neatly trimmed hedges and the uniform fields, it was very different from Neeson's native Armagh.

He took another left fork, followed almost immediately by a narrow right-hand turning, which was shrouded by trees from either side.

"A bit out in the sticks, aren't we?" The salesman looked at his watch and frowned. "We'd better be getting back, if we have to sort out the finance."

"I won't be needing any finance."

"Oh, I see." The salesman nodded. Cash sales were good, but finance sales gave him another commission. Times were changing in the motor industry. *Facilitators for debt*, was what the showroom's managing director called his sales team.

Neeson slowed the vehicle and turned off to the left at a minor junction, then swung the car across the road and into a narrow lane on the right. The lane was pitted and muddy, and the front spoiler caught briefly on a piece of raised ground, scraping noisily underneath.

The salesman frowned. "What's going on?"

"Nothing to be concerned about, the car's as good as mine. Just relax, I have to check on something while we're here."

The Porsche was awkward at low revs, a feature of many high-performance sports cars, the torque effecting a shudder at not receiving enough throttle, forcing Neeson to ride the clutch to keep from stalling. After approximately half a mile, the lane widened. Ahead of them, on the left-hand side of the track, was a large flatbed removal lorry. The rear doors were open and two heavy-duty metal skids protruded down onto the muddy ground. The salesman stared at the metal skids, his mind suddenly working overtime. He made a move towards the door but stopped when he felt the cold metal on the side of his neck.

"No, son, sorry." Neeson cocked the hammer of the pistol then removed it from the man's neck and rammed it into his stomach. There was no escaping, no taking the weapon from him. It dug in deeply, a squeeze of the trigger and it would blow out the man's liver.

"Oh for god's sake!" The man stared in horror at the menacing weapon then looked up into Neeson's cold eyes and started to shake. "Please, don't kill me! It's just a fucking car... Take it!"

Neeson remained silent but kept the pistol pressed firmly into the man's gut. He looked back towards the lorry and watched the two thickset men, dressed in identical work overalls, walk purposefully towards them. The tough-looking Irishman looked back at his prisoner and smiled. "That will sort of depend on you," he commented. He slipped the gearbox into neutral and engaged the handbrake. "All right son, out you get."

The young salesman opened his door nervously and stepped out into the muddy lane. He shut the door, looked across the roof of the vehicle and fixed his eyes on the pistol, which was pointing directly into his face. One of the thickset men slipped effortlessly into the driver's seat, while the other stood directly in front of the Porsche's bonnet and started to walk backwards towards the lorry and up into the container, directing the driver with hand signals to keep the front wheels straight. He quickly stepped to one side, checked that the rear wheels lined up appropriately, then waved the other man forwards. The revs climbed, the rear wheels spun briefly on the stony ground before gaining traction, then in one graceful motion, the Porsche was aboard.

Neeson smiled. The frightened young man was still staring at the pistol. "Come with me," he ordered, and walked casually across the lane to where a light blue Saab was parked, almost out of view in an offset gateway.

The young salesman stood beside the vehicle, his legs shaking uncontrollably. As he kept his eyes on the pistol, he lost control of his breathing as well. "Please, take the car, just don't kill me!" he pleaded raggedly.

Neeson grinned and without warning slapped him hard across the cheek. The young man fell backwards into the muddy gateway. The Irishman stepped back a few paces, putting a safe distance between them. He turned around as he heard the lorry's noisy diesel engine fire and watched the driver execute an admirable three-point turn in the narrow lane. The passenger held up a thumb and Neeson nodded an acknowledgement as he watched the vehicle move away. He looked back at the salesman, who was sitting miserably in a waterlogged tractor track. He smiled to himself, aware that the man had no survival instinct. He had simply given up, too scared to attempt to escape with his life.

"Please..." the salesman started to sob. "...Please don't kill me!"

"How old are you?" Neeson asked, taking a thick bulbous suppressor, or what the inexperienced called a silencer, from his jacket pocket.

The man's eyes were transfixed. "Twenty-nine," he replied solemnly. His limbs were shaking violently and for a moment it looked as if he were about to convulse.

"Stop it! For fuck's sake! Can't you make this easy on me? I don't want to kill you, but I have very little choice in the matter," he paused, screwing the suppressor into the specially fitted adapter on the end of the tiny pistol's barrel. "Standing or sitting?" he asked, then aimed the weapon steadily at the centre of the man's forehead.

"What?"

"Standing or sitting? I'm giving you a choice. You only die once. I want to make it good for you, too."

"Oh god, you're sick!" The salesman scrabbled in the mud in an attempt to get up but his smooth leather soles slipped, and he was suddenly sitting once more. He looked up in hatred and despair and shook his head. "You're out of your mind!"

"Or running?" Neeson shrugged. "It's just another option. Come on, you can't say that I'm not being fair, can you?"

The young salesman had tears in his eyes. "Just get it over with, you sick bastard!"

Neeson squeezed the trigger twice. The two 9mm bullets impacted just short of the salesman's groin, spraying his astonished face with a spume of muddy water. The man screamed. "I was only trying to help!" Neeson shouted. "You could be more grateful. People don't spend enough time thinking about their own death. We plan our lives, right down to the last detail, but not death. Isn't that strange?" The salesman sobbed loudly, cupping his head between his hands. Neeson leant back against the bonnet of the Saab and lowered the pistol. "I'd bet that before today you've never even given your death a second thought. Sure, you probably told all of your mates that you'd like to be balls-deep in a Playboy model when the time came, but I bet you never even considered the possibility of it ending like this. On your arse in a muddy ditch with a bullet through your face." He smirked as he savoured the young man's situation. "I gave you the choice, standing, sitting or running. Clean through the head, or peppered with random fire. The choice is still yours." He raised the gun and aimed it carefully at the man's forehead. "Personally, I'd prefer it clean through the head, but then again, if you were running, you might not feel the fatal shot if you were high on adrenaline. Plus, you would have at least a tiny chance of surviving."

The young salesman looked up at him pleadingly and shook his head in desperation. "Please..."

"For Christ's sake, have some fucking dignity! Think of yourself as already dead. That way, it's merely a matter of how it happens, not when." He stepped forwards, the pistol less than a foot from the man's face. "Come on Jason, it won't be that bad."

The sobbing ceased and there was a look of bewilderment on the man's face. It was a blast from his past. He hadn't gone by that name for five years. "How do you know my name?"

Neeson smiled wryly. "I know many things, Jason. Jason Porter. Actually thirty-one years old, live-in girlfriend called Samantha Jenkins, with a baby on the way. Or could it be twins, like your uncle and your father? These things tend to run in the family." He stepped backwards then reached inside the open driver's window and retrieved a large envelope. "The thing is Jason, you have a wee bit of a past, don't you?"

Jason Porter shook his head in disbelief as the man walked towards him and threw the envelope into his muddy lap.

"Open it," he ordered. "Look, listen and learn time." Porter struggled to keep his hands from shaking, as he fumbled with the adhesive seal. He tore straight across the edge of the envelope, then upended it and tipped the contents into his lap. "Happy snaps Jason."

Neeson informed him. "You could almost put them in your family album."

Jason Porter stared in disbelief at the assorted of photographs, then looked up coldly at the Irishman. "You bastard!"

"Aye, more than likely," he grinned. "They're all in there, Jason. Mum, Dad, brother, uncle Robert, Sister Emma, grandpa Jones, your whole family. Even your girlfriend Samantha, and your unborn baby. Or is it babies? I'm not sure, I fell short of obtaining her hospital records."

Porter shook his head, tears flowing steadily down his cheeks. "Why? What have I ever done to you?"

"Nothing. It doesn't always have to work like that." Neeson rested himself against the bonnet of the vehicle and smiled. "You have three convictions for joyriding against you, which were dealt with by the young offenders' court, but you soon grew out of it when you were old enough to drive legally. At nineteen, you decided to try the big time and filled in as a getaway driver in an armed robbery. So, you weren't caught driving. In fact, you outran three separate police forces, in an eighty-mile chase, and evaded capture by driving into a multi-storey car park, where the camera in the pursuing helicopter couldn't see you abandon the vehicle. Pretty smart that was," Neeson paused. "Just a pity that you didn't exercise the same degree of caution when you started to spend the money. You blew it too soon and on too much, and got yourself caught as a result. Still, the six years you served in prison must have given you a chance to think? I mean, a good job, and in a prestige car showroom. I wonder what they'd have said if they knew?" Neeson laughed. "You'd think they might have checked your history more closely before letting you loose in Porsches and all those lovely marques you take in part-exchange, wouldn't you?" Porter remained silent, his eyes on the photographs of his family in his lap. "Maybe your brother had something to do with that? Maybe *Prestige Showrooms* are happy with their employee, and top salesperson? But then again, they think that your name is Mike. Michael Porter, your younger brother, to be precise." He smiled cynically. "That was really nice of your brother to lend his name, especially as he doesn't have a criminal record. Does your girlfriend know about your little charade?"

Jason Porter threw the photographs down into the mud and tried to get to his feet. Neeson fired two shots near the man's right foot and he screamed and held his hands over his cowering face. He fell back down into the mud then looked up at the man with the gun. "What is all this about?" he asked sombrely, the last of his energy exhausted.

"A driving job. Plain and simple. If you accept, then there's a clear quarter-million in it for you."

"And if I refuse?"

"Then everybody in those photographs dies, starting with the oldest. From old grandpa Jones, right down the list to your unborn child. Tell me, what would grandpa Jones look like with his tongue hanging out through a slit in his neck?" Jason Porter stared at the ground. He held a hand over his mouth but couldn't suppress the urge, turning his head aside to vomit in the mud. Neeson laughed. "If that makes you feel sick, just wait until I tell you what's in store for young Samantha, unborn child and all!"

Porter shook his head frantically. "Stop it, you sick bastard!" He glared up at the Irishman, then frowned. "You're offering two-hundred and fifty thousand pounds? Why not just ask me, why threaten me with my entire family?"

"I like my team to be fully committed," Neeson smiled. "So tell me, what is it to be?"

13

"Your break." Holman smiled. He had already won the first two frames, and his opening break of fifty-four had sealed the second game virtually from the start.

Grant methodically chalked his cue, then walked over to the opposite end of the table. He positioned the white ball next to the green, then rested his fingers gently on the soft baize. Taking the cue and resting it delicately on his left hand, he raised his fingers to form a bridge and sighted along the shaft.

"When you're good and ready," Holman commented tiresomely.

Grant ignored his host as he sighted down the wooden cue. He drew back his right hand, then pushed it forwards smoothly and remained in position as he watched the white ball travel gently down the table, rebound off the bottom cushion and kiss one of the red balls, ever so slightly.

"No balls, Simon!" Holman struggled out of the deep leather armchair and walked over to the bottom end of the table. "I wouldn't have bothered sitting down if I'd known that was the best you could do." He leaned forwards, easing his straining gut onto the edge of the table, then bent his left knee. "Ever wanted to know the secret of playing a successful game of snooker?" he asked, laughing out loud. "Play it like pool!"

Grant watched, astonished as the man belted the white into the pack of red balls, scattering them in all directions. A lone red impacted against the blue ball, cannoned off a cushion, then found its way into the bottom-left pocket. He was sure that there was something about a rule that all balls had to be played for, and not *smacked* indiscriminately, but this was Holman's house. Holman's game. Holman's rules.

"Blue, I think." Holman leaned his weight across the table and smiled at Grant before sinking the ball with notable force. "You like my little playroom then?"

Grant dutifully retrieved the blue ball from the pocket and replaced it on the centre spot. He glanced at the somewhat ostentatious mini-bar, with its neon sign - *Frank's Place* - then looked back at Holman. "It's very you."

Holman smiled triumphantly. "That's what I think. I spend a great deal of time in here. Doing business with my associates, mainly."

"Eileen must lose you for hours," Grant he chided.

Frank Holman bent across the table and sighted for his next shot. "She never tries to find me, doesn't even know if I'm in the bloody house half the time." He potted the red into the middle pocket then walked around the table to take a shot at the black. "Didn't come cheap, this," he said.

"I can imagine."

Holman smiled and hit the black ball, with such force that it rattled in the pocket before dropping down into the net. "But hey, it's only money!" He nodded to Grant, indicating that he should retrieve the black from the pocket for him.

Grant dutifully replaced the black ball on its spot, then looked seriously at his host. "So what does it involve?"

"Well, to get the highest score, you have to try and pot the black as many times as you can," he paused. "It's worth seven points." Holman grinned, then leaned forwards and took a shot at a nearby red, which was hovering precariously over the bottom right-hand pocket.

"You know what I mean Frank, don't play any more games."

"Oh, the *job*, you mean." Holman raised an eyebrow as he chalked his cue. "Well, I would have to know if you were in or not first. It's very hush-hush, need to know only."

Grant nodded knowingly. "But two-million would be my share?" He stepped forwards, blocking Holman from his shot. "That's an awful lot of money for just a few days' work, Frank."

"An obscene amount of money, wouldn't you say?" Holman agreed. "More than you deserve, that's for sure!" He prodded Grant in the stomach with the tip of his cue and glared. "Better not stop me, I'm on a roll. I would hate for you to make me miss my next shot."

Grant stepped aside reluctantly. He knew Holman well, knew his ways. If Holman was not in control, then the man was never happy.

Holman leaned forwards and sighted on the pink ball. He pulled back the cue, then rushed it forward, sending the ball into the middle pocket. The white ball gave chase, wobbled dramatically over the pocket, then followed the pink home.

"Bastard!" he shouted. He threw the cue across the table, scattering the remainder of the balls in every direction. He turned back to Grant and scowled. "You want to know, do you? Well I can tell you! Just tell me, are you in or out?"

"I'm not sure."

"Well make up your bloody mind, there's not much time and I need a bloody cracksman!"

"I can't, I don't know what it involves yet!"

Holman clenched his fist tightly and banged it down onto the table, venting his frustration. "Two-million quid! Two-million, just sitting and waiting for you!" He clenched his teeth together and stared at him, his eyes blazing. "Now are you fucking in, or are you going to fuck off out of my house and try and win back your wife and kid with the pittance you've got to your name?"

Grant took a deep breath, then smiled. "In."

14

Alex King took another sip of tea, then dropped the thick file on the table. He turned towards Forsyth, who was leaning back in his chair, calmly blowing smoke rings up to the ceiling.

"What's the likes of him doing with someone like O'Shea?"

"Couldn't possibly tell you, old boy," Forsyth paused, then looked at him tiresomely. "That is for you to find out, I suppose."

King stared at his MI6 liaison officer with amusement. Ian Forsyth's casual daywear was even more bazaar than that of his classic British spy attire. Brown brogues, tweed jacket, mustard-coloured corduroys, tattersall check shirt and a cream cravat. He almost smiled at the sight. Forsyth was still a young man, maybe a decade older than himself, late-thirties, certainly no more. He glanced down at his own attire; blue jeans, trainers, grey sweatshirt and the leather bomber jacket hung over the back of the chair. The attire of the average field operative. The two men were worlds apart.

"He is just a petty criminal with fingers in a lot of pies. No radical political persuasions, he's not even on the electoral roll." King paused. "What the hell is an old-school London criminal doing with the IRA?"

"I trust you are merely thinking out loud?" Forsyth blew another smoke ring then smiled gleefully, obviously impressed with the result. "An Executive Termination Order will arrive shortly. That was the extent of your mission with your detachment to The

Increment - *to gather enough background intelligence to terminate effectively.*"

King shook his head in protest. "I think we may be jumping the gun a bit. O'Shea is up to something with this bloke, Frank Holman."

"Not for us old boy." Forsyth stubbed out his cigarette out in the ashtray which balanced precariously on the arm of the tatty wooden chair. "I just brought over the file so that you could get some background information on whoever O'Shea was talking to. Never thought for a minute that you might want to turn detective on me," he paused. "The Northern Ireland peace agreement is in tatters. Factions of the IRA are ruining the whole sweet deal for everyone. Mark O'Shea is one of the main culprits. If he continues to run his own little private vendetta, then the government will end up with a great deal of egg on their pretty little faces. Our job is to remove O'Shea as soon as possible, take him out of the equation, and get the peace deal back on track. It is due to be signed on Good Friday. Teams from The Increment, like our happy little twosome are operating all over the British Isles removing unpleasant little shits like O'Shea. With any luck, the path will be clear for peace."

King wasn't taken in by this. He knew that the agreement meant that the British government had to release all IRA prisoners as part of the deal. These "rogue" cells were just being taken out of the equation. A silent show of force. "I just think it should be looked at in a little more depth," he said. "This guy Holman sounded to be in deep with O'Shea. He has no political or fanatical history, but he does have a wealth of assets, and not one shred of evidence as to how he accumulated it. The police know that he's a crook, the Inland Revenue suspect the same, yet he's still walking free."

Forsyth leaned forward in his seat, suddenly appearing intrigued for the first time. "What exactly are you getting at, old boy?"

"Perhaps it's fund-raising? Maybe O'Shea and this guy Holman are planning something that we should know about, something that could have an effect on the peace agreement. It could be weapons, money, drugs, who knows? There seems to be little that PIRA won't touch lately," King paused. "I have been assigned the mission to kill O'Shea, and I'll do it. There's no question about that. But if I take him out now, we may never know what the two of them are planning. Besides, who is to say that Frank Holman won't deal with another IRA quartermaster?"

Forsyth remained thoughtfully silent. He opened his silver cigarette case, extracted a handmade cigarette and tapped the tip against the lid, removing loose strands of tobacco. He flicked the wheel of the lighter, brought the flame to the tip, then pulled the cigarette towards his overly full lips.

King tried not to smile. He had never seen such ceremony, such a gratuitously complex approach to such a simple task. He no longer smoked, but he remembered simply sticking a cigarette in his mouth and lighting it.

"What do you want to do?" Forsyth asked, amid a cloud of pungent, mildly scented cigarette smoke.

King relaxed, knowing that now he had his liaison officer's cooperation - or at least his attention. As operation controller, Ian Forsyth had the final authority in the field, at least while the task was building up. He would not report events until he saw fit, which would probably mean until he had the result he wanted.

"I want a communications tap on Frank Holman's telephone line, and a scanner in place, in case he uses a mobile. A list of the people that he's telephoned during the past two weeks, and taps on their own phone lines."

Forsyth chuckled and shook his head, dismissing King's request with a disconcerting smile. "This is a closed shop, old boy, SIS only. Box would have to be involved for an operation on that scale, and with their methods, that means a force of approximately twenty operatives. There is no way I can get a sanction on that, it will only attract unwanted attention. The mandarins will give their two-pence worth, and the whole deal will be called off." He inhaled deeply on the Turkish-blend cigarette, then blew out a thin plume of smoke as he pondered. "I could get you a tap on the man's line, and provide you with a file on the person or persons most called from his number during... say... the past week. And I can buy you twenty-four hours, after I receive the Executive Termination Order," he paused. "It will be easy to delay the hit on the grounds of a lack of, or insufficient intelligence. After that, O'Shea takes a bullet and we go home."

15

The vehicle swept over the bumpy surface spraying muddy water over the windscreen. Neeson quickly applied the wipers, but soon wished he hadn't, as the mud smeared a thin film over the entire screen. He cursed as he swung the Saab into the farmyard and skidded to a halt. As he switched off the engine he studied the house before him.

The farm had been purchased from a major high-street bank's quarterly repossession sale. Its previous owner had been unable to work off the debts which he had incurred during the mad cow disease beef crisis, where he had to slaughter his entire herd. With a minimum age of two-and-a-half years before beef cattle were ready for the food chain, the farmer was left with no income and was not equipped with either the equipment or legislative know how to diversify in time. His fields were grass for the sole purpose of grazing, and crops took time to sow and establish. Markets were in place for existing growers and not easily negotiated. The property had received no attention in almost three years, and had been bought for a relatively small sum, considering its vast potential to an affluent owner. The farmhouse was habitable, albeit after some vigorous housework, but the outside had a feel and appearance of long-standing dereliction.

Jason Porter sat in the passenger seat, somewhat subdued. His ordeal in the ditch far from forgotten, he was still at a low ebb and covered in mud, which had yet started to dry on the fabric of his Hugo Boss suit. He stared at the dilapidated building and frowned. "What's this place?"

Neeson smiled. "This? This, my new found friend, is home for the next few days." He opened the door, swung his leg over a particularly large puddle and stepped out onto the muddy ground. "Come on, move yourself, there's work to be done. You'll not earn your quarter million by sitting on your arse!"

Porter stepped out, failed to notice the puddle, and waded almost ankle-deep. "Shit!" he said. He looked at Neeson, who had started to walk away. "Why me? What have I got to do?"

"Questions, bloody questions! Do you want to earn your money or not?" Neeson frowned. "I told you, it's a driving job." He held up his hand. "Now that's all you fucking need to know for now! A week's work, a little risk and you'll be a rich man," he paused. "What's more, you'll have the added bonus of allowing your entire family to carry on with their lives." He turned and walked across the farmyard to the derelict-looking barn, leaving the threat to hang in the air.

Porter followed. He was uneasy. In his experience, it was either stick or carrot. One or the other, but never both. When they reached the barn, Neeson opened a narrow door next to the enormous double doors, which were obviously intended for the passage of heavy farm machinery. He stood aside, allowing Porter to enter first.

Inside, the two thickset men had started work on the Porsche. They had fastened a series of large square polythene sheets to the ceiling of the barn, creating an almost sterile environment in which to work on the vehicle. They had already removed the front and rear quarter panels and registration plates, and were now going about the time-consuming business of taping sheets of newspaper and patches of masking tape over the windows, logos and headlights. The two men glanced up from their work, nodded a silent acknowledgement to their fellow Irishman, then continued to prepare for the vehicle's new colour scheme.

Neeson led the way through the barn to a small room at the end of the vast building. It had been constructed quickly and haphazardly, consisting merely of a space divided off by plywood partitions, with three single beds and a small portable colour television set on top of a rickety-looking table which also had a kettle and a pile of dirty cups and empty biscuit packets.

"There are some clothes and toiletries on your bed," he paused, pointing at the bed in the furthest corner. "You do not attempt to contact anyone. From this day forward, you are simply missing. You will stick to both Ross and Sean like shit to a wee baby's blanket. They are hard at work, so I will expect you to give them a hand. Meals will be served in the farmhouse, but you are not to go there without either Ross or Sean accompanying you. Those are the rules; do you understand them?" Jason Porter nodded, starting to feel somewhat overwhelmed. Neeson patted him on the back and grinned. "Just a week, that's all. After that, I will arrange for you to leave the country, go down to Spain for a bit. You can buy a nice place down there, fly your missus out." He reached into his jacket pocket and took out another envelope then noticed the man's expression and smiled. "No, nothing like that..." He reassured him "We are partners now and partners look out for one another," he paused, and handed over the envelope. "Call it a little bonus. Non-deductible from our agreed sum."

Porter ripped open the envelope and let the bundle of fifty-pound notes drop into the palm of his hand. He grinned gleefully, too enthralled by his new wealth to notice that the Irishman had left the room.

16

"It's no bloody good, I'm damned near starving!" Patrick stood up abruptly and walked to the door. "I'm going to go and get us some food. That idle bastard Neeson must be trying to wind us up or something. Anyone coming with me?"

"Aye, right enough," Liam said, then slowly rose to his feet. "I could do with a bit of a walk." He looked across at McCormick and raised an eyebrow expectantly.

"That's all right, isn't it Matt?"

McCormick glanced at his watch, then shrugged. "Not exactly given much choice, are we?" he paused. "Just find a shop, then get yourselves straight back here. No trouble, no quick pints in a pub, and no fucking about. All right?"

"Aye, mother, as if we would." Patrick smiled and picked up his leather jacket, which was draped over the arm of the chair. He looked back towards McCormick, his expression suddenly serious. "You don't think that anything has gone wrong, do you Matt?" He looked at his watch and frowned. "I mean, Danny was meant to have this place stocked up for our stay, and he was going to meet us first thing. It's past lunchtime now."

"Will yer ever think about anything but yer gut, big man?" McCormick said, his Belfast accent so much stronger than the others. He grinned. "No, I'm sure everything's fine. Danny's just fucking us around, yer know what he's like. Go get us some food and don't eat it all on yer bloody way back, all right? Me and Dugan are hungry as well."

"Yes, mother." Liam ginned. "If we promise to be good, can we buy some sweets for the way home?"

"*Feck* off!" McCormick laughed, then picked up a nearby cushion and threw it across the room at him. "Someone has to keep you lads in line!"

***

"Hello Control, this is X-ray Delta One, message, over."

"Control, send, over."

"X-ray Delta One, two of the targets are mobile, over."

"Control, state which targets, over."

"X-ray Delta One, appears to be Red Two and Red Four, over."

"Control, Roger that, Red Two and Red Four, stay advised, wait-out."

***

Patrick reached the bottom of the concrete steps, then looked each way down the quiet street. He jovially slapped his companion on the shoulder, then nodded for him to follow. The two men walked casually, doing their best to look as if they knew the way. Neither man had no idea that a team of a dozen MI5 watchers were observing them from both static locations and passing vehicles. They were well past the two men posing as council workers outside their safe-house. Between the four Irishmen arriving and the first observation post being set up, a series or vehicles had been parked at various points under various guises. A post office van, a courier vehicle, two plain-looking cars and a motorcyclist checking his tyres. The watchers from MI5 were among the best in the world. When the two men came back, number plates would be swapped, positions changed – even the clothes and appearance of the surveillance officers would change drastically.

Patrick looked up as he walked then pulled a disdainful face before looking back at Liam. "Ah, shit!" he cursed loudly, then pointed. "Bloody charity worker. Cross over the road. Quickly!"

"You don't have to give anything, you big lug! Just ignore the bitch," Liam said with amusement. "Besides, what's wrong with charity workers anyway?"

"Bloody charity! Don't get me started about bloody charity..." the big Irishman paused. "Get off your arses and work for it, that's what I say about fucking charity!"

"Ah, so you do," Liam paused, his mouth cracking into a wry smirk. "Have you never tossed your loose change into a bucket for the *cause* then?"

"That's bloody different!" Patrick brushed past the old woman, ignoring the collection tin, then glared at his companion. "You're trying to wind me up right enough!"

"Calm down big man, just having myself a laugh."

***

"Hello Control, this is Papa Whiskey Three, sit-rep, over."

"Control, send, over."

"Papa Whiskey Three, targets are heading towards Green Two, over."

"Control. Roger that, Green Two, wait-out."

"Papa Whiskey Three, Wilco, out." The old woman with the charity tin covered the tiny button transmitter with her head scarf, then crossed over the road and continued on her way, swinging the charity tin as she went. For today, and this operation, her task was complete.

***

Patrick stopped walking outside a corner shop, just a few paces short of a pedestrian crossing. He tapped Liam on the shoulder and nodded towards the shop door. "This'll do, we only need a bit of snack food and some coffee. Wait here while I stock up." He opened the door, which activated a loud bell as he walked into the cramped shop.

The shop was three times too small for the stock that it held, and was cluttered from floor to ceiling with a haphazard array of shelves and racks. Patrick nodded an acknowledgement to the Indian shopkeeper and picked up a wire convenience basket. The shopkeeper ignored the silent greeting and continued to cover the Irishman with a beady-eyed stare, blatantly studying him as he walked through the narrow aisles.

Patrick paused at the upright refrigerator unit, conscious that he was the sole subject of much attentive scrutiny. He opened the glass door, selected half a dozen packets of processed sandwiches and dropped them into the wire basket. He looked back at the shopkeeper and glared. "You got a problem, pal?" The shopkeeper said nothing, but maintained his blank stare. Patrick threw a few more random items into the basket and walked towards the counter. He placed the basket on top, then walked back to the refrigerator and picked up a carton of milk. He looked back at the silent shopkeeper, who had been joined by a middle-aged Indian woman, and pointed to the shelf behind them. "Give us two packets of Marlborough and a box of matches," he said as the shopkeeper totalled up the items and put them in a thin carrier bag. He waited for the man to reach his total then picked up a handful of Mars Bars, and smirked at him. "And those, if it's not too much trouble?" He turned his back on the man, then reached up to the top shelf of the magazine rack and caught hold of a copy of *Men Only*.

The shopkeeper watched as his customer turned the magazine to its centre pages and started to ogle at the contents. He raised his hand and coughed politely, then pointed to the magazine. "Will you be buying that as well?"

Patrick kept his eyes on the two naked women spread-eagled across the centre-fold. "No, I've seen the best bits now," he paused, turning the pages slowly and admiring the sights. "Not a bad pair of jugs on that one. What do you think?" He turned the page towards the startled woman and grinned. "Not many of those to the pound, hey?"

"Kindly put the magazine down if you do not intend to buy it!" The man raged. "How dare you show such filth to my wife?"

The Irishman snapped. "It's okay for you to sell it though!" He dropped the magazine on a pile of children's comics and stepped back to the counter, where the shopkeeper was holding out his hand for the money. "How much then?" he asked. "I'm not bloody psychic!"

The shopkeeper simply glanced down at the digital display on top of the till and remained silent, as he continued to hold out his hand for the money.

The big Irishman pulled a large handful of change out of his trouser pocket and slapped it down onto the counter where most of it rolled onto the floor at the shopkeeper's feet. "Here, pick the fucking pieces out of that!" He picked up his purchases, turned and marched towards the door, sounding a bell as he opened it, then slammed it violently behind him.

Liam, who was leaning casually against the shop window as he smoked a cigarette, looked up in surprise as he felt the window shake. "All right, big man?"

"No I'm bloody not!" He thrust the bag into his companion's hand then fumbled with one of the packets of cigarettes. "Surly bastard watched me like I was going to rip him off," he paused as he slipped a cigarette into his mouth. "Then he gets in a mood when I have a quick look at a fanny mag. Probably had his wife entered in the reader's wives section, and didn't want her to see!"

"*Did* you rip him off?" Liam asked, all too knowingly.

"Of course, teach the bastard a lesson!" He reached into his pocket and pulled out a small packet of mints somewhat triumphantly. "Serves the bugger right."

Liam laughed out loud. "Was that the best you could do, you daft sod?"

"It's the principle," Patrick paused, shaking his head dejectedly. "Never did trust them."

"Who?"

"The bloody Indians," he paused thoughtfully. "Not after what they did to General Custer at Little Bighorn…"

17

"That bloody boy is out there playing football again! I already told him about it this morning," he paused and looked over at her. "He is not going to get anywhere in life, until he learns some much-needed discipline."

She tensed as she placed the clean dish onto the draining board. It was all she could do to force the smile. The same smile she forced every single day. She looked at him, hoping that just this once, the conversation would not go the way of all the others.

"Please Keith, he is only ten years old."

He stared back at her, his eyes blazing. "What the hell do you think his father was doing at ten years of age? No discipline instilled there!" he paused and smiled wryly. "That's why *he* ended up in prison, a low-level criminal, and *I* became a successful businessman. Discipline, plain and simple."

Lisa dried her hands on the hand towel and stared meekly at the floor. "Please Keith, I was just saying, David is only ten-years old. There's plenty of time for discipline, he should be allowed to play football in his free time."

"Oh yes plenty of time," he replied sardonically. "My father instilled discipline into me at an early age, and I turned out all right, didn't I?"

She should have agreed instantly. Just as a woman should always reply with an instant *yes*, when a man asks if he is big enough for her, or better in bed than her last lover. Or just as a man should instantly reply with an emphatic *no*, when asked by a woman if she looks fat in a new dress. She should have simply bit her lip and nodded at the very least, but something inside stopped her. It was the same something which had made her stop loving him, if she ever truly had, and was now making her life so unbearable. She turned back to the sink and plunged her hands into the soapy water, thankful for the distraction.

"Didn't I?" The man fumed, his tone so frighteningly familiar. "Damn you, woman, answer me!"

She flinched at his sudden rage but continued to work in the sink, keeping her back to him to hide the tears. "Yes. You turned out just fine." She couldn't help her tone, although she regretted it more than he would ever know.

He stood up quickly, tipping his chair to the floor. "Mocking me now, are you?" He walked towards her and reached out, gripping her ponytail. He pulled savagely, wrenching her head around until their eyes met. "Because if you are..." The threat hung in the air, teasing her resolve.

"No! No I wasn't! I promise I wasn't mocking you! Please Keith, you're hurting me!" She closed her eyes, then opened them tearfully. "Please Keith, just forget it."

"I'm sorry," he said quietly, his tone suddenly softer. He spun her around gently, then reached out and smoothed his hand down the side of her soft cheek. She shivered involuntarily, yet all too visibly. Nowadays his mere touch repulsed her to the very pit of her stomach, filling her throat with bile.

He glared at her reaction, gripped her firmly by the shoulders and started to shake her violently. "Bitch! You fucking, ungrateful bitch!" He stopped shaking her and moved his hands towards her throat, where they rested, as if at the ready to wring her delicate neck. "I take you on, take on another man's child, and you can't so much as tolerate me touching you! What's wrong? You used to like me touching you! I've apologised for what I did that night. You said that you weren't in the mood, and I should have respected that, but I was drunk, I just couldn't stop myself. I *had* to have you. You can't keep punishing me for it, I said I was sorry!" He pulled her close and moved his hands gently up her neck, where he rested them delicately upon her flushed cheeks. "This has got to stop, Lisa. Why don't we go upstairs and make a fresh start? Come on, you want me to make love to you, don't you?"

Make love *to* me, she thought, not *with* me. He would dominate her, make her feel vulnerable, worthless. No mutual tenderness, or togetherness. Simply force himself inside her and take pleasure in watching the pain rise on her face. She stared tearfully over his shoulder, her blank stare fixed on the wall. Simply staring into blankness, wishing that she were far away, anywhere but here.

He pushed her away from him and looked at her with an almost kindly expression, which instantly turned to rage when he noticed the tears in her eyes. "Crying! Why in God's name are you crying?" He shook his head in bewilderment then stared coldly into her frightened eyes. "If you want to cry, I'll give you something worth crying about!" He lashed out suddenly, catching her in the right eye with loosely held fingertips. They whipped her eyeball and she reeled backwards and fell against the sink. She brought her hand tentatively to her eye, cupped the socket. She was screaming a mixture of pain and surprise at the vicious attack. She looked up at her attacker, choking back her tears as she readied herself for more to come. "Please, Keith…"

Her plea had no effect, he was feeding on the adrenalin, he was enjoying himself. He walked purposefully towards her, looked down at her and laughed. "You are pathetic!" He raged. "You always make it come to this. I give you everything, what more do you want from me?"

She pushed herself off the kitchen counter where she had slumped. "Love," she replied indignantly. "All I ever wanted, was for you to show me love," she paused. "Not material things, just love." She regretted her words. He had a habit of twisting things.

Keith had not always been like this. He was her first love. They had dated for a year before she had left him for Simon Grant. Keith had been her first love, but Simon and been her true love. At her lowest point, when bills could not be paid and life with her husband in prison had taken her to her lowest ebb, Keith had come back into her life. A drink, a meal… it had been innocent enough at first on her part, but loneliness and alcohol had done their parts and all too soon she had crossed the line. Enraged that Simon had gone back to crime, left her alone with a child to raise, she had taken another path. Sex with Keith was something she had done before, before she had even met Simon, so hadn't felt overly wrong on the moral scale. However, for Keith there was an underlying hatred of being second best, of being dumped for Simon Grant, and these feelings had manifested themselves in violence. He saw her years with Simon, her lawfully married years to which she had conceived, birthed and raised their child, as a long-term affair. That every moment with Simon had been insidious. That David was a bastard born from an affair. Keith could not break the thread. That it was his second chance with her, a fresh start. And that he had finally secured what he had always wanted.

Keith laughed at her comment, regarded her with little more than a sneer. "Well, if it's love you want..." He reached down and unfastened his leather belt. "Then, it's love you're going to get!" He stepped forwards, hastily pulling at his trousers.

"No Keith, please!" She stared up at him, as he towered over her. All six-foot-four of him, his trousers now down around his knees.

He caught hold of her by her neck and pushed her down onto the floor. He forced her legs apart and pulled frantically at her short skirt, ripping the seams. He hooked his fingers around her satin pants and yanked hard, snapping the elastic and ripping enough of the material away. Lisa struggled, but he was too strong, too big to fight against. He was close now, fumbling. She could feel his hardness on her thigh. She kept her eyes clenched tightly shut, as she felt his weight on her, and his clumsy fumble to get himself into position. Then came the pain of his savage thrust, and the humiliation of him riding her dry, using her body like a worthless whore. Still she kept her eyes closed; that was her only refuge. Dry and dispassionate, every thrust stabbed deeply into her, searing her most tender parts. His hands smoothed themselves gently over her cheek, and his breath crept into her ear, stale, vulgar.

"That's better, isn't it?" he spoke quietly, almost a soft whisper. "Just relax and let me make love to you."

Her only comfort came from the knowledge that it would not last long. It was brutal and savage, but predictably quick.

***

From his vantage point, high in the boughs of an oak tree, near the conservatory and overlooking the glass vaulted ceiling of the kitchen, little David Grant could not bear to watch any longer. He jumped down onto the grass and ran along the well-kept lawn to his secret hiding place amongst the row of conifer bushes. The ground was often dry here, a bed of fallen fronds and dried twigs. He sat down on the ground, tucked his legs to his chest and rested his head in his hands and started to sob uncontrollably. He rocked a little to and fro. The sob gradually turned into a mournful wail and then a sudden cry of anger. "Daddy, Daddy, please come back!" He wiped the tears from his eyes with the sleeve of his jacket. "Please come home!"

18

He kept the newspaper at arm's length, turning the pages methodically, shaking the crease out as he did so. The newspaper was purely for show, a cover to hide him from suspicion while his eyes remained fixed firmly on the pocket-sized display monitor resting in his lap. There was no need to worry about looking conspicuous now, for his back was to the target, as he sat casually in plain sight on the secluded park bench.

It was only a small park, a village green really. A few oak trees lining the fringe of a small pond, a scattering of willows here and there and in the infrequent clearings the occasional bench-seat.

The target house had been rented from a large property agency based in Reigate under the alias of Peter Harrison. A substantial cash deposit had been put down, and three monthly payments made in advance. The tenancy was for a period of one year and was now entering its second month.

King paid no attention to the long tenancy agreement; anything less than a year in these parts would have seemed suspicious to any reputable property letting agency. As was proving all too true, PIRA, or the Provisional Irish Republican Army, was becoming most adept at counter-surveillance techniques, attracting little attention to their operations on the mainland and elsewhere.

The video camera was safely secured beneath the passenger seat in King's Ford Escort van. It was equipped with a detachable lens and a fibre-optic cable, currently out of view on the vehicle's dashboard. King could now observe the front entrance of the house from a safe distance, picking up the picture on a hand-held monitor, which received the signal on a dedicated microwave frequency. To any casual observer, he was a faceless man taking his lunch break in the tranquillity of a quiet park.

The light blue Saab came into view, drove steadily to the entrance of the Mock-Tudor style house and came to a halt. Danny Neeson stepped out of the vehicle, glanced cautiously around, then climbed the six granite steps to the large oak door. He pressed a small, ornate brass doorbell and stood back, patiently waiting to be greeted. After about thirty seconds, the large, oak door opened, somewhat hesitantly, and Neeson stepped inside.

With the monitor's five-second-relay delay, King wasted no time. He knew that the Irishman was well inside the building. He folded his paper, slipped the monitor inside his jacket pocket and strolled casually back towards the tatty-looking van, which was parked just past Mark O'Shea's house.

King reached into his other pocket and took out a small black box, approximately the size of a cigarette packet. He ambled casually, apparently unhurried, as he walked past the bonnet of the blue Saab. He turned the device over in the palm of his hand, so that the magnetic strip was on top, then took a cursory glance towards the front of the house. Satisfied that he was not being observed, he quickly bent down and slipped the box under the vehicle's rear wheel arch and continued on his way.

The lay-by was situated some three-hundred metres from the quiet park, and the house that was the subject of his attention. In the short time in which he had been parked, no vehicles had driven past him, and he was satisfied it was an inconspicuous location. King reached up under the passenger seat and retrieved the IBM laptop. He uncoiled the lead, then plugged it into the specially adapted cigarette lighter in the dashboard. The computer was now linked to the dedicated frequency of the tracking device, gaining the signal through the vehicle's high-frequency antenna. He switched on the laptop, then typed a command that brought up the menu, from which he selected the relevant file. A detailed road map of Epsom and a three-mile radius appeared on the screen, with a stationary red dot in the centre of the display. King sat back in his seat and relaxed a little as he realised that the Saab was still stationary. At present there was no sound, but if the Saab moved its speed would be indicated by an intermittent 'bleep' which would rise in both tone and volume, according to its distance from the receiver. If the tracking device reached its maximum range of two-thousand metres, the laptop would sound an alarm.

King settled back in his seat and kept his eyes on the display. The only thing left to do now, was wait. He took out a sandwich he had made earlier and unwrapped the foil package. King had two rules when he was inactive: sleep or eat. When he wasn't doing one, he was usually doing the other.

***

Simon Grant walked across Holman's gravelled driveway and stood in the gateway. He turned around and looked back at the house. It was impressive. Holman had grown up on the same council estate as himself. The man had come far, that was for sure. He watched the man as he paced to and fro in front of the house. He was talking animatedly into his mobile phone. It was no bigger than his hand. Grant had never owned one, but he remembered the sheer size of Holman's portable phone before the last job. It had been too large to put in his pocket and had a large pull out metal antenna, and he wore it on a holster on his belt. Now his phone was no bigger than a TV remote. Progress. They would have games or cameras on them next.

"Moved up in the world?"

Grant spun around. The man was as big as an outhouse door. "Sorry?" he said.

"My ex-colleague had a word with you," the man said. "When you left the nick. He told you what he expected you to do. Our friend, the security guard on your last job, he's in dire straits. And I don't mean the fucking band."

"I'm sorry, I..."

The man looked over at Holman, who was still talking on his phone. He stepped closer and punched Grant in the face. Grant reeled backwards and tripped, slamming down onto his backside on the gravel. He looked down at him. "We'll be in touch," he said, then turned around and walked on down the quiet street.

Grant held his hand up to his nose, then stared at the blood. He pinched the bridge of his nose and looked at Holman as he walked over.

"Friend of yours?"

"And yours."

"What do you mean?" he asked, offering him a hand.

Grant took it and got up easily. "A friend of the security guard your bloke shot on that job," he paused. "Now I'm out, they want a payday for him. They want my share."

Holman rubbed his chin thoughtfully. "We can arrange something. I don't want them getting in the way and ruining this thing for us," he said. He caught Grant by the shoulder and guided him across the drive. "How do you get in touch with them?"

"I don't," Grant replied. "I think they plan to shadow me. That bastard prison guard, McGivney. He laid down the law pretty thick yesterday."

Holman nodded. "Leave it to me." He opened the driver's door of the Mercedes and waited for Grant to walk around the other side of the vehicle. "Now, let's take a little drive," he said.

Grant got in and sunk down into the comfortable leather seat and closed his eyes, feeling the warm sun on his face through the tinted windscreen. His nose ached, but it had been the shock which had shaken him more.

The day was bright and mild, his first full day of freedom. He savoured it, wanting it to last. His greed had taken him into the unknown, a destination he had always been wary of, yet so often found himself visiting.

"Thinking of what you can do with two big ones?" Holman asked, as he swung the Mercedes around a parked car, then pulled to a sudden halt at a busy crossroads. "The world's your oyster with that amount of money," he paused. "Ever had oysters, Simon?"

Grant shook his head, his knowledge of seafood ending at paper-wrapped fish and chips, smothered with salt, vinegar and perhaps a dab of curry sauce.

"Most places serve them raw, in their shells," Holman informed him, his face screwed tightly in distaste. "Don't bother, just sniff hard when you've got a cold and swallow, you get the same effect!"

Grant tensed as the car almost collided with a cyclist. Holman swung the Mercedes out into the crown of the road and cursed loudly. "Bloody pansy! Fancy wearing shorts like that?" He shook his head, then broke into a wry smile. "They were so fucking tight, I could damn near see what religion he was!"

"Where are we going?" Grant asked, not wishing to pursue either the topic of raw shellfish, nor male cyclists in tight shorts.

"Time to get things moving," Holman stated, matter-of-factly. "New accommodation for you."

"What do you mean, I thought that I was staying with you? What about my bag?"

"Forget it. I've arranged for some clothes to fit you, as well as everything else that you might need for the next few days," Holman smiled wryly, a sign that sarcasm would soon be flowing. "For the duration of the operation, subject to the occasional reconnaissance, you'll be living in the countryside. Won't that be nice?"

"What about my possessions? I need to see Lisa and pick up my things."

"All gone, her new man dumped the lot. I spoke to her about it before you were released. Seems that all you own, is on your back."

"You *saw* her?" Grant asked. "How was she?"

"No, I said I spoke to her. On the telephone, a few days before you were released. I thought I'd test the water for you at the same time." Holman shrugged. "Like I said; forget the life you had before, just look ahead," he paused. "Two-million quid will help you to do that."

"What if I can't?"

Holman smiled and raised an eyebrow. "Do you know just how much pussy can be bought with that amount of money?" He looked at the road ahead and started to laugh. "There's not a woman alive who wouldn't sell herself for that! Go into any night-club in the country, drop five-grand on the table and ask a single girl for a suck and a fuck, two minutes and you'll be out the door and into something else."

"I don't buy it, never have," Grant paused, staring at him coldly. "You're not a happy man, deep down, are you Frank?"

Holman scoffed. "Don't start that amateur, prison psychology bullshit with me!" He broke into a grin. "Men always buy it! You go out for a drink, meet a woman and start chatting. You buy her drinks all night; she doesn't put her hand in her purse once. You take her for something to eat, and it's the same deal. Then, if you're extremely lucky, you get to fuck her. You've already paid for it; you were paying all bloody night!" He shook his head despairingly. "Say you get married? You work all damn day, you bring home your pay packet at the end of the week, and she takes the bloody lot! You pay for everything; you clothe her, feed her, and buy her everything she needs. Once in a while, she repays you with sex. It's only in her best interest, otherwise you'd go elsewhere for it and she loses her meal ticket. And to top it all, when the courtship is out of the way, when the novelty has worn off, the sex isn't so damned spectacular either! No, men pay for it from puberty onwards, the sooner men wake up and realise that, the better."

"It's not always like that Frank. You can't base everybody's relationship on your own experiences," Grant said. "There is such a thing as love, or haven't you heard of that yet?"

"Like you for instance?" Holman spat at him venomously. "Don't make me laugh! You went to prison; your wife went straight to another man's bed. That's love, is it? Her income went, so it was simply time for another punter. Wives? Live-in whores if you ask me."

"I didn't."

Holman smiled. "Just letting you see it as it is, sonny. There's an awful lot at stake. You keep yourself a clear mind in that head of yours, don't go chasing rainbows. In my experience, there's bugger all at the end of them anyway."

Holman slowed the car suddenly and turned left without indicating. The driver in the vehicle behind them sounded his horn then overtook, leaving them with a familiar hand-gesture.

"Bloody idiot!" Holman raged. "Couldn't he see I was going to turn?" The road ahead narrowed dramatically and the hedges seemed to close in on them from both sides.

Grant looked at the tree-lined hedgerows, then turned back to Holman. "A bit out in the sticks, aren't we?" he commented, hoping to divert the conversation away from Holman's apercus on the virtues of monogamy.

"Best place for us. Eyes and ears everywhere in town," Holman paused, a visible scowl on his face. "You never know who's watching you these days."

***

King kept his distance. He was entirely out of sight, so there was no point in risking a visual. The electronic tracking device was already doing the work for him. He watched the signal slow, and the detailed road map told him that the Saab had turned into a narrow residential street, which eventually led to a network of cul-de-sacs. He accelerated for a few seconds to reduce the Saab's lead on him, then turned into a quiet street, which was signposted as *Holben Drive*.

Neeson parked the Saab in front of the yellow works van, then stepped onto the pavement. He casually surveyed the surroundings, before giving a quick nod to O'Shea, who was sitting patiently in the passenger seat. Satisfied that his personal bodyguard regarded it as safe, O'Shea stepped out and crossed to the row of terraced houses. Neeson followed close behind, his eyes darting everywhere, constantly wary of the security forces. He glanced across at the workmen's weather cover, heard a sudden raucous burst of laughter come from inside, then turned and climbed the flight of steps, just a few paces behind O'Shea.

King swung the van around the corner in time to see the two Irishmen climb the short flight of steps. He hesitated for a second, wondering what action to take then reversed a few metres until he was safely out of sight. Secure in the knowledge that the enemy could not observe his presence, he switched off the vehicle's engine and took the secure link cellular phone out from his jacket pocket.

***

"Hello, Control, this is X-ray Delta One, message, over."

"Control, send, over."

"X-ray Delta One, two subjects, ID unknown, just entered target building, over."

"Control, are you recording? Over."

"X-ray Delta One, Roger that, will send, stay advised, wait-out." The larger of the two men turned to his slightly built companion and pointed to the display monitor. "Get the tape ready, we're sending the footage of those two guys who just entered." He waited patiently, turning the handset over between his fingers. The smaller man held up his thumb, then bent over the satellite transmitter, his finger hovering over the Send button. The larger of the two men pressed the pressel button on his handset, then started to report. "Hello, Control, this is X-ray Delta One, message, over."

"Control, send, over."

"X-ray Delta One, goods ready to be delivered, over."

"Control, send, over."

The smaller of the two men dutifully pressed *send*, then stood back and watched the clock counter begin its rapid countdown. The images of the two Irishmen entering the house were on the way to Control in an instant. The images would be received with virtually no delay, much like a telephone conversation, but travelling via Secure Satellite Linkup (SSLU), using one of the many sophisticated military satellites orbiting the globe and constantly ready for such traffic.

"X-ray Delta One, delivery process complete, over."

"Control, goods received, stay advised, over."

"X-ray Delta One, Roger, out."

The smaller of the two men poured some hot tea from his flask, then sipped a mouthful before looking seriously at his colleague. "All right, here goes: A prostitute, a paedophile and a politician walk into a church..."

"Heard it."

"Bastard!"

***

King had dialled the telephone number from memory and now sat patiently as he waited for the line to be answered.

"Hello?" Forsyth inquired cautiously.

"Forsyth, this is Alex."

"On secure?"

"Of course."

Forsyth hesitated for a moment. *"All right, old boy, go ahead."*

King had a feeling the man was not alone, most probably in one of his many daily meetings. "I followed our two friends to Holben Drive. Does that ring any bells?"

"Holben?" Forsyth asked quietly as if muffling the telephone. *"Are you sure?"*

"Yes, of course."

"In Epsom?"

"Yes," King answered tersely. "What's the problem?"

"Oh for god's sake, get out of there now!" Forsyth spoke quietly, but his agitation was obvious. *"Don't get yourself seen or you'll bugger up things for sure. Go on, man, get moving!"*

King switched off his mobile phone without further question and dropped it carelessly onto the passenger seat. He looked around cautiously as he started the vehicle's engine then, drove away, maintaining a moderate speed to avoid suspicion.

***

Simon Grant stepped out of the car, stretching his legs awkwardly over the large puddle, that Holman had managed to park in the middle of.

"This way," Holman said, then tiptoed among the farmyard's myriad of muddy puddles towards the large barn. There he stopped and turned around impatiently, as he waited for Grant to catch up with him. Grant turned his eyes from the derelict-looking farmhouse towards the barn, noticing the flatbed lorry parked alongside, almost out of view. He looked back towards Holman, who had by now run out of patience and was opening the door to the barn. "Come on Simon, get your bloody arse in gear!" Holman shouted, then stepped into the doorway and waited while Grant picked his way through the ankle-deep mud.

***

King pulled into the quiet forecourt of a petrol station and switched off the engine. He was damned if he was going to run home like a little schoolboy after Forsyth's unexpected reaction. He picked up the Nokia mobile phone from the passenger seat and pressed the re-dial button. The dialling tone rang for a few moments, and then Forsyth came onto the line.

"Hello?" he answered cautiously, not giving away his name.

"Ian, this is Alex. What the hell's going on?"

"My god man, you're not still there, are you?"

"Of course not, half a mile away at a guess," he paused, glancing around cautiously. "Now come on, play it straight. What's happening in Holben Drive?"

Forsyth hesitated for a moment, then sighed somewhat tiresomely. *"A team of watchers from Box have been in place since last night. The Security Service intercepted a PIRA Active Service Unit at Holyhead, earlier yesterday,"* he paused and King had a clear picture of him blowing out another ponderous smoke ring, then smiling at the result. *"A woman from one of the MI5 watcher units got too close in a service station on the motorway. Managed to get herself throttled as a result. At least that is what they think the post mortem will confirm."*

"What about O'Shea? Where does he fit in?"

"Not entirely sure, old boy. Although at a guess, I would say that Danny-boy Neeson and his boss are in with them," he paused. *"Looks like the two services are working on the same case but from opposite ends. I shall attempt to find out more, see who was playing first. Meet me at the safe-house at nine o'clock."*

King switched off the phone and thought for a moment. Forsyth's comment about *who was playing first* seemed to sum up King's experience working with both MI5 and MI6. Both services tended to treat their work as a game, often withholding relevant information from one another, merely to be the one to come up with the result. In his opinion the sooner the two services merged to become the country's complete intelligence service, the better. He was still new to the game, but he was learning fast.

He turned his eyes back to the laptop computer and watched the stationary red dot. Forsyth had told him to get out, but he hadn't mentioned leaving the assignment. Until it was time to meet with Forsyth, he would stay with the Saab.

***

"Nice, isn't she?"

Grant stared at the Porsche 911 and nodded. The bodywork had been prepared for paint spraying, with all glasswork, mirrors and logos taped over. Sean checked the nozzle of the sprayer, then signalled for Ross to start the compressor. Both men wore facemasks to protect themselves from the harmful toxins, and as the paint spraying commenced, Holman stepped back outside, holding the polythene curtain aside for Grant to follow.

"Hot?" Grant asked as he stepped into the cleaner air.

"Of course, straight out of the showroom." Holman turned his attention towards Jason Porter, who was working on something in the corner of the barn. He looked back at Grant and smiled. "Come on, I want to introduce you to someone."

Porter was busy, hard at work sanding down the Porsche's front and rear bumpers. He looked up quizzically at the two men as they approached, and frowned.

"You're the lad that I was told about," Holman stated almost accusingly. "I hear that you're something of a genius behind the wheel. Glad to be aboard?"

"Not given a lot of choice, was I?"

Holman's amiable smile turned to a cruel scowl as he stared at the man in front of him. "Well don't complain, laddie, you'll be rich at the end of it," he paused and turned to Grant. "The two of you should have a lot in common, you're both bloody ungrateful for the opportunity to become richer than you deserve." Jason Porter bowed his head and continued with his sanding work. Frank Holman shook his head despairingly, then walked back to the other two men. He peered inside the polythene curtain, spoke briefly with one of them, then walked back to where Grant was waiting, somewhat uncomfortably, as he watched Porter work silently on the bumpers. "Seems that the man I wanted to introduce you to is out for a while, but he should be back within the hour. How about a cup of coffee?" he asked

***

The little red dot flickered momentarily, then started to race across the screen. King switched on the ignition and started the engine. With any luck, the dot would edge down the road in the direction that he was facing. "Bollocks!" he shouted in irritation. He quickly engaged reverse and accelerated hard out of the forecourt, the van's front tyres screeching in protest against the wet surface of the road. The dot was rapidly moving towards the edge of the screen, and at half a mile the distance was nearing the receiver's cut-off point. If he failed to close the distance, finding the target vehicle might become impossible.

He swung the steering wheel hard to the left, veering the vehicle erratically across both lanes, then crunched the van's notchy gearbox as he struggled to select first gear. He floored the accelerator then slipped the gearbox into second gear almost immediately. The van's engine whined and screamed in protest, at the ill treatment, overtaking a series of slower moving vehicles that had built up behind the Saab.

King glanced at the intermittent flashing red dot, which was cutting a path across the laptop's screen. The note was weaker than mere seconds ago, struggling to make itself heard as it approached the signal cut-off point. He swung the van out across the white line on the crown of the road and floored the accelerator, as he attempted to overtake a row of three cars. He passed the first, then had to take refuge behind a silver Audi while he waited for another suitable gap in the oncoming traffic.

The warning alarm started to wail and he quickly turned his eyes down to the screen of the laptop. The Saab was exactly one-thousand metres from the receiver, and from the roundabout ahead, Neeson could take any number of routes.

King decided to chance it. He pulled out into the crown of the road, dropped to third gear, then kicked the accelerator to the floor as he headed straight for the oncoming bend. The driver of the Audi displayed his surprise, as the tatty Ford Escort van pulled alongside him, and whined past in the other lane. There was now only one vehicle between King and a clear stretch of road. He pulled into the tight gap behind the Vauxhall Vectra, cutting up the Audi to the sound of its horn.

The road swept around to the right in a long drawn-out curve. The road ahead was clear. King pulled out and accelerated hard, nearing maximum revs, then changed up into top. Predictably, the Vectra's pace increased gradually, matching the van's speed, the driver clearly unable to accept the manoeuvre as less than a challenge to his ego. The Vectra, with its considerably more powerful engine, kept King out in the middle of the road as the two vehicles charged side by side towards the blind corner.

King was driving at maximum revs, the Vectra was little above cruising, its engine taking the speed in its stride. Side by side, the two vehicles entered the bend, both braking for the approaching tight corner. King had to lose the driver. If he succeeded in overtaking the Vectra, which was looking ever less likely, the driver might follow in a fit of road rage. That would only draw attention to him, as he caught up with the Saab. He was out of options, as to ram the Vectra was not to be considered; the two vehicles were travelling far too fast and were evenly matched in weight. At this speed both drivers would end up as another accident statistic. The driver of the Vectra was grinning from ear to ear, thoroughly enjoying King's predicament, or at least what he thought it to be. The Vectra had the power advantage; the driver of the out-powered van would have to back off.

King maintained his pace, then with only moments to spare, he reached into his jacket and pulled the Browning 9 mm pistol from his shoulder holster. He aimed it steadily at the driver and glared. The driver of the Vectra braked suddenly, desperate to evade the pistol, the vehicle's ABS brakes bringing it to a dramatic halt.

The Audi was not so lucky.

The driver had been transfixed by the sight of the two vehicles duelling for road supremacy. His brakes had worked, but only in response to his reflexes. They proved wanting. The Audi impacted the rear of the Vectra and shunted it violently into the hedge.

King glanced in his rear view mirror as he slipped back across the crown of the road, barely making it to the bend. He smiled, adrenaline flushing wildly round his veins. "Sorry, pal," he said. "Wrong time, wrong driver."

He quickly turned his attention back to the laptop and the small, intermittently flashing dot. He could not help but to sigh with relief, in the comfortable knowledge that the Saab was now approximately six-hundred metres ahead of him, about to negotiate a series of mini-roundabouts. He settled back in his seat and increased his speed slightly, as the narrow single lane suddenly merged into a dual carriageway. As he closed the gap to around four-hundred metres, he caught his first glimpse of the target vehicle, confirming the much-needed visual. He watched as it slowed and turned off the stretch of dual carriageway and onto a slightly narrower road. The manoeuvre was followed in tandem by a Ford Sierra, which was keeping purposefully close to the blue Saab.

King slowed, then turned off, deciding to keep out of sight and use the tracking device to its full potential. It was always more comforting and reassuring to follow visually but it made no sense to risk being spotted. He noticed a red saloon tailgating him. It wouldn't hurt to put another vehicle between him and the target vehicle, now that he was following on the tracker. He slowed a little and kept close to the grass verge. The Ford Mondeo sped past and King glanced across and saw the man in the passenger seat speaking into the radio handset. He frowned, noting the look of the two men. They were police for sure, maybe Special Branch. Or perhaps MI5. It seemed to be a security forces day out. He just hoped that they would not get too close to the Saab and scare the target off.

***

Danny Neeson glanced into his rear-view mirror and checked that the Sierra was not too close before he slowed and pulled into the narrow entrance on his right. The Sierra copied the manoeuvre, directly behind him, just before the Mondeo flew past the entrance, its brakes squealing as the driver attempted to avoid a collision.

"Christ, Randle!" Forester tensed in his seat, gripping the door's armrest. "Could you get any closer?"

"It wasn't my fault, the bloody turning's on a blind corner!" He shook his head, more out of relief than in protest, before looking back at Charles Forester. "If that damned van hadn't of held us up for so long, it would never have happened."

Forester relaxed a little. It had been close, but he was confident that they had no need to expect anything untoward. "Alright," he paused. "I think we're in the clear. Keep going for a few hundred metres then find somewhere to pull over."

***

King noticed that the flashing red dot was slowing considerably, and adjusted his speed accordingly. He pulled over to the left-hand side of the quiet road and parked the van in an overgrown gateway. The Rover was all too visible, parked further up the road where it looked a little too obvious beside a wooden post and rail fence.

King looked across the fields at the distant farmhouse. The exterior looked derelict, although the inside might have another story to tell. The property was surrounded by a constellation of outbuildings and large barns, but dominated by the large Dutch-style barn to the left. The yard was steadily filling with vehicles, as the two new arrivals parked alongside two other cars. He picked up his powerful field glasses and the compact video camera, then stepped out of the van and closed the door as quietly as possible. He had decided not to take the pistol with him as there seemed to be a lot of people at the farm. Should he be compromised; he would probably fare better with a story of ornithology and confusion of boundaries.

King surveyed the farmyard and the surrounding area, then turned his attention towards the parked Mondeo, approximately three hundred metres further down the road. As it was obvious that the two men were observing the farm, he just hoped that the *players* wouldn't spot them as easily as he had. He tracked the field glasses in a wide arc and smiled to himself, as he watched the infamous IRA man, Danny Neeson step out of the Saab and walk towards the farmhouse.

***

"Ah, here they are!" Holman stood up from the kitchen table, knocked back the last of his whisky from the coffee mug, then walked across the kitchen and placed the mug on the cluttered draining board. He turned back towards Grant and smiled. "Time to introduce you to the team."

Grant stood up and followed Holman, as the man padded across the kitchen and out of the back door.

"Didn't expect to see you, Mr O'Shea, I thought I'd be dealing with Danny-boy here." Holman nodded towards the hard-looking man who was sounding off a series of instructions to the four new arrivals.

Grant watched as the tough-looking Irishman glanced briefly at Holman. He couldn't work out whether the man's look was one of disgust or contempt. He settled on indifference. There was certainly no love lost between Holman and the man he had referred to as Danny-boy.

O'Shea turned around and stared at Grant then looked back at Holman. There was as much indifference in his eyes as his companion's. "Is this the man?"

Holman nodded. "Allow me to introduce you to Simon Grant... The best safecracker ever to grace Her Majesty's Prison!" He turned to Grant and smiled. "Simon, this is Mr O'Shea."

Grant looked warily at the slightly built man with the pale, almost sickly complexion and flame-red hair. He was not a big man, not in the physical sense at least, but Grant had seen the type before, the type of man who has a great deal of power at his fingertips. It was not often that Frank Holman was courteous. But he made a flamboyant exception in favour of the man whom he had greeted as O'Shea. Grant stepped forwards, extending his right hand.

The sickly-looking Irishman smirked, blatantly ignoring the outstretched hand. "The best safecracker ever to grace Her Majesty's Prison," he mused quietly. "We shall soon see." He turned his attention back to Holman. "We have a little test for your man here. Myself, I'm more than a little fucking dubious. If he's the best, then how did he end up doing time?"

19

At six-foot and a well-muscled fourteen stone, King was a big man. A former middle-weight and light-heavyweight boxer, he moved with a catlike grace and stealth. Well-practised in the art of covert advancement, his footsteps were silent and precisely placed. His breathing, calm and unlaboured. He edged his way down the side of the hedge, making sure not to step on any loose twigs, or such debris that could give his position away. At the bottom of the slight hill he slipped under a barbed-wire fence, then stepped over the narrow brook which divided the two fields. The second field was a mass of thistles and nettles, which conspired to slow his progress considerably.

As he neared the top of the incline, he stood close to the hedge and watched for movement in the farmyard. It seemed to have gone quiet, the gathering of men had moved on. He looked at the large barn, where he observed the group walking through the smaller of the two doors. King quickly edged his way along the hedgerow, then paused as he came to a rusted iron gate. He promptly vaulted the obstacle, then jogged the rest of the way down the lane, until he came to the entrance of the farmyard. There, he slowed and walked confidently to the rear of the barn.

Approximately three-quarters of a mile away, the valley below gave way to a small lake where a variety of birds flocked to and fro. It could provide him with an appropriate cover if necessary; using the farm to take a short cut. With the video camera and his powerful field glasses, King would pass as a bird-watcher, although to sustain the image a garment or two from Ian Forsyth's tweed and herringboned wardrobe would have been handy.

Easing his way over the piles of slate and rusted metal which so often seem to accumulate on farms, King made his way towards the middle section of the barn, searching the timber frame until he found what he had hoped for. He carefully eased the loose wooden board, tentatively working it free from the panel, until he had a small slit through which he could observe the scene within.

***

"A little test, sonny," said O'Shea and he beckoned Grant towards him with a grin. "Come on, laddie, don't be shy now!"

Simon Grant stepped forwards hesitantly, glancing briefly at Holman who shrugged helplessly. He looked as worried as Grant did.

Danny Neeson walked to the centre of the floor space and pulled a sheet to reveal an old, yet solid-looking, wall safe. "There you go, wonder boy, open it," he paused. "If you can!"

Grant turned around helplessly and stared at O'Shea. "But I don't have my tools and equipment with me!"

Neeson took the small, but lethal-looking pistol out from his jacket pocket and pointed it at Grant's midriff. "Best be using your initiative then. Oh, and I forgot to say, if you can't open it, I'll waste you, and the boys will bury you out back."

Grant stared at his old friend for assistance, but Holman merely shrugged and stepped over to stand at O'Shea's shoulder. It was clear where Frank Holman's loyalty now lay. Grant had to think fast. He bent down, caught hold of the front corners of the safe and heaved. It was heavy, but he managed to roll the old safe over on the earth. It was constructed entirely of solid wrought iron, with overlapping inserts around the doorframe. The locks were of two types, as was often the case with wall safes. The first to be attempted was the combination dial, usually a four-digit code for a safe of this size. Next would be the lock, a basic tumbler device, which could take anywhere between one and four turns. Without a stethoscope and a selection of picklocks he would be there forever, unless he attempted a less orthodox method of entry. He looked around, trying to overcome his feeling of helplessness, then spotted the bag of chemical fertiliser. He walked over and picked up the nearby feed-dipper and started to open the bag. O'Shea glanced across at Neeson, who merely shrugged and returned his attention to Grant, who by now had half-filled the dipper with the chemical fertiliser. Grant then turned the safe over again and decided that the back offered the best point of entry. He checked that the safe was stable on the slightly uneven ground, then poured the chemical fertiliser into a pile. With the bottom of the dipper, he started to grind the fertiliser to a fine, white powder, which he then returned to the dipper.

Oil was the next ingredient in this basic, yet powerful mixture, and for this he walked over to the tractor, lifted the engine cover and pulled out the oil dipstick, letting the thick black oil run down the stick and into the dipper. He repeated the process a few times, then peered into the container and smiled in satisfaction. Grant mixed the compound into a thick pulp with the aid of the dipstick and continued to stir until it formed a smooth dirty-grey coloured paste. All eyes were on him, the men silently huddled, craning their necks to watch the man work.

Grant then picked up an old shovel and went over the other side of the barn, where a rusted metal gate was propped against the wall. He worked the tip of the shovel blade on the underside of the rails and the rust gathered in the shovel pan. He collected a good sized handful, then walked it back to the pile and scattered the rust on top. He moulded the paste with his hands, then formed it into a ring, approximately ten inches in diameter on the inside and thirteen inches on the outside. He stood up; looking around the barn then walked over to the far wall where several lengths of various sorts of wire were bundled together in hoops and coils. First he selected a length of common household lighting wire, which he frayed against the rusty wheel arch of the old tractor and stripped down until he had a single strand of bright copper, which he then twisted until it snapped. He coiled this into a broken ring, which he embedded into the paste, making sure that it didn't touch the metal surface of the safe. He left two bright ends protruding. Then he selected a thin roll of the type used in electric cattle fences, and walked back to the safe where he started to twist the wire until it broke under friction. He then connected the two separate lengths of wire to the copper protruding from the compound, and walked steadily backwards towards the tractor, making sure not to disturb the ends of the wire from the dangerous mixture, and doubly sure not to allow the two lengths to touch.

All that Simon Grant prayed for now was for the tractor battery to retain some residual charge. He wrapped one of the ends of wire around the negative terminal, then searched for something that would act as a suitable insulator. There was nothing that he could see, so in desperation, he kicked off his left trainer and pulled the rubber insole away from the shoe. He wrapped the rubber insole carefully around the wire then rubbed the tip of the wire against the bonnet of the tractor to make a cleaner connection. Grant was ready, only the battery's uncertain charge could let him down now. He glanced across at the group, who were all waiting with abated breath, then without further word, he touched the tip of the wire against the positive terminal.

The electrically charged copper ignited the oil-soaked chemical fertiliser compound, causing it to flash instantly in a sudden rush of bluish flame. Without hesitation, for this was the most critical part, Grant rushed forwards to the smouldering safe and kicked down hard on the centre of the ring. It gave way with little resistance, creating a cleanly cut hole.

Grant turned back to the group of men and settled his stare on O'Shea. "Crude, but effective," he paused, breaking into a wry grin. "But it *is* easier with the right tools."

After the excitement had subsided, Ross, Sean and Jason went back to working on the Porsche, while the four new arrivals talked quietly amongst themselves leaving Neeson, O'Shea and Grant to listen to Frank Holman's jubilant elation.

"I bloody told you! I told you that he was the best! How many men do you know who could pull off something like that? And with no planning?" He slapped Grant upon the shoulder grinning happily.

O'Shea smiled. "I'm impressed, I like a man who shows initiative and works well under pressure," he paused, then nodded towards the four men, who were standing in the corner admiring the Porsche and its damp, glistening coat of paint. "This will be your team. You start planning tonight in the farmhouse."

"What is it? The job, I mean…" Grant asked.

"It's a safecracking job." Holman grinned excitedly. "Time locks, dead locks and a state-of-the-art security system!"

O'Shea glared at the obese Londoner, as if the man were divulging far too much. He quickly looked back at Grant and smiled. "Of course, you understand that you are *in* this now, in it far too deep to be thinking of backing out." He looked across at Danny Neeson and grinned. "We're used to playing the game a bit on the rough side, are we not Danny-boy?"

"Aye, right enough." The tough-looking Irishman paused and stared coldly at Grant. "Cross us or back out, and you'll not live to regret it. Believe me, you'd just be another name on a very long list."

O'Shea chuckled out loud. "That said, I think we can all go over to the farmhouse and have a wee drink," he smiled. "A toast to the job, and new friends so to speak."

***

King walked cautiously along the hedgerow, as alert now as he had been earlier. He had made it this far, but there was no sense in becoming complacent now. He climbed over the rickety wooden fence, then crossed over the road to where he had parked the van. He removed the field glasses from where they had hung loosely around his neck, and placed them upon the roof of the van, along with the video camera while he unlocked the door.

"Stand still!" The voice was commanding, yet thoroughly calm. The voice of a professional used to giving orders.

King did as he was ordered. He heard the man move tentatively, slightly to his left. Behind him and to the right, he could hear, or rather, sense, the presence of another person, standing still but breathing heavily, almost nervously. King kept the keys of the vehicle in his hand, working them around into position so that the largest key protruded from his knuckle, between his fore and index fingers. A punch with the tip of a key is a formidable weapon, especially to the eyes or the throat. He glanced down at the wing mirror and could see the second man quite clearly. He was fairly well built, but he didn't hold himself with the confidence of a professional. Hired help. King was convinced that he could overpower him if it came to that. Out of the corner of his left eye, using his peripheral vision, he could make out the shape and form of the man who had given the command. He stood approximately eight-feet away and was considerably taller but less well built than his silent companion.

King breathed calmly. Tall thin men were easily overcome. With their higher centre of gravity, tall men always go down quickly; what's more, they tended to stay down.

"Hold your arms out to the sides and drop those keys." The man let out a sarcastic chuckle. "Do you think we're stupid?"

Damn it! King thought. With his crude weapon discovered, he did as he was ordered, dropping the keys where they could be recovered quickly, on the bonnet of the van. He was sure that the two men were security forces, the two from the Mondeo three-hundred metres further up the road, but could hardly confide that he was on the same side. Both Frank Holman and the safecracker were English, speaking with London accents and not the broad Ulster twang the others had so freely demonstrated. It was not out of the question, then, to assume that these two characters could be acting as an outside security team, keeping watch from beyond the boundary of the property.

"Check him." The tall man to his left gave the curt command, and the other man walked dutifully forward. King was left in no doubt to which of the two men was in charge. He felt the man's hands clasp firmly to his sides, then expertly frisk him, searching for any concealed weapon. The man then caught hold of both his shoulders and attempted to spin him.

King tensed his whole body rigid, resisting the man's grip and forcing him to pull harder. Then, as the man attempted to turn him again, this time more forcefully, he spun with the turn using all of his might and the momentum the other man had created, and brought his elbow up to a point striking the man in his ear. The man started to fall but King was already moving. He grabbed the man, one hand gripping his throat, the other grasping the tuft of hair on his forehead. Then using all his strength, he rushed him backwards into the man with the pistol. The tall, thin man dropped, as tall, thin men do, sprawling onto the wet grass and releasing his grip on the weapon, as his companion cannoned into him with great force. King kept hold of the other man and without delay, he thrust his knee up into his groin. The blow was barely given chance to smart before King brought his forehead down onto the bridge of his opponent's nose. There was a sickening sound of cartilage and bone flattening and the man's face turned a crimson-red, as blood surged down over his mouth.

The MI6 operative did not have to wait and see if his opponent had been overcome, nor did he follow the attack up with anything else. His long training and experience told him that the man was out of the equation before he hit the ground. He spun around quickly, just in time to see the tall man reaching for the pistol amongst the twigs and leaves, which made up a belt of scattered debris along the grass verge. King was already lunging forwards. The man brought the pistol up to aim, but was not quick enough. The kick caught him full in the face. He reeled backwards then lay still. King was already upon him, his left hand clasped around the man's throat, his right hand raised for an execution blow to the side of the neck. He'd done it before, a world away and what felt like a lifetime ago. A poorly controlled temper and a lack of thought, that had ultimately set him on a very different path. He was a different man now. He could choose.

His breathing was heavy and his pulse was pounding in his ears. He looked down at his felled opponent, then relaxed a little as he began to regain rational control. During the confrontation, which had lasted merely seconds, his entire being had been completely absorbed from the moment of the initial strike, as if he were operating on automatic pilot. An experience which only the most highly trained of individuals can know, or ever truly understand. His heart hammered against his chest in the ensuing silence as he bent down and retrieved the pistol. The first man, the one with the very broken nose, lay worryingly still. King approached him cautiously, bent down and retrieved the pistol from his shoulder holster, then checked the carotid artery for a pulse. It was beating like a drum and even without checking, he could see that the man was still breathing. Even so, he quickly and expertly placed him into the recovery position then turned round and went over to the taller man, who had begun to stir.

He slipped one of the pistols into his belt, then gently eased back the slide of the other, and checked that the breach was engaged. Live and ready to go.

"Who are you?" the man asked, his voice shaky yet superlatively defiant.

King shook his head. "I'm the one asking the questions now." He aimed the pistol at the man's knee. "I'm telling you straight, piss me about and I will start low and aim higher with every shot. Now, who the hell are you?"

The man squinted up at him, his vision obviously still blurred from the concussion and shock of the blow. "Police," he stated flatly.

"Bullshit!" King paused, waving the pistol in front of him. "This is not police issue, not in this calibre anyway. The police use 9 mm in autos, and .38 or .357 magnum in revolvers. This is a Sig-Sauer P220 .45 ACP. Cops can't pick and choose their weapons to that degree." He shook his head. "No, I'm afraid you'll have to do better than that."

"All right, we're Special Branch."

King raised the pistol and aimed it at the man's head. "Same deal, SB don't use irregular calibres either."

The man stared down the barrel of his own weapon and started to shake. "Please, don't shoot me! I told you, we're Special Branch!"

King shook his head. "I'm asking you for the last time, who are you and what are you doing here?" He tightened his grip on the pistol, his index finger taking up the excess pull on the trigger. "If I have to use this thing on your knee, the players at that farm will hear and your operation will be blown. Not to mention the problems you'll have doing the conga at this year's office party."

"Are *you* security forces as well?"

"I said, I'm the one asking the questions," he paused. "Last chance, I'll blow your kneecap off and walk away, leave you and your friend to face the music.

That is, unless half a dozen known IRA terrorists not far from here don't find you both first."

"Okay!" The man glanced across at his unconscious partner, then shook his head dejectedly. "We're MI5. We have been involved in the surveillance of four men, believed to be an IRA Active Service Unit. They were in the Ford Sierra which drove up to that farm."

King frowned. He had been following the Saab. He already knew that another car had arrived at the farm, but it wasn't proof they were in fact MI5. What he needed to ask was something that only a Security Service operative, or select members of the other security forces would know. King had previously accompanied his MI6 mentor, the man who had recruited him into the service, to a meeting at MI5 headquarters. "Tell me, are you aware of the tasks performed by C5 (c) section?"

The man nodded. "Yes, surveillance of ports and airports."

"Good," King paused. "What's your name?"

"Forester," the man replied. "Charles Forester."

"Box are based on the Thames. But tell me, where are their secondary headquarters? The one where most of the counter-terrorist operations are over-seen from?"

"In Reigate." The man lowered his hands and started to look more relaxed. "You're SAS, aren't you?"

King shrugged. He'd trained with them, from day one in selection to the second from last day. The pass-out. No sand-coloured beret for him. Just a new assignment, and no opportunity to say good-bye.

"I thought so," Forester said. "I'm not a fan of the mandarins using the likes of you. Intelligence work should be done by more qualified individuals."

King tightened his grip on the weapon. This man didn't have to know who he worked for. His mentor, Peter Stewart, the man who took him from a prison cell on Dartmoor, had told him never to offer information, never to divulge it freely. *If they really want it, they'll get it alright, and you'll know when that moment is, you'll be at death's door. Give up what you know, or open the door and step inside, it's up to you...* King smiled. "But I'm not the one on the wrong end of a gun."

"You're with six," he said decisively. "The Increment. You're not meant to be operating on the mainland."

"Lodge a complaint."

"Oh, I intend to," Forester said. "There's no room for assassinations in this society. We have the armed forces to settle things by force, and the police to make arrests, and a justice system to try people and sentence them. That's why you lot don't officially exist, because even MI6 knows it's wrong and doesn't want to be held to account."

"Well, by the looks of it, we handle ourselves better than the operatives from Box," he paused, glancing down at the man on the ground, who was stirring. "I'll be reporting your lack of surveillance drills. Your driver damn near rear-ended the target vehicle."

"You lot are after the four who came in on the ferry?" Forester asked.

"No. I don't know anything about a bloody ferry. I'm following O'Shea," King said. "I'll be keeping the weapons. It will give you something tricky to report when you lodge your complaint. I expect we'll see each other again," he said, as he turned and walked back to the driver's side of the van. "Better luck next time."

20

Frank Holman poured himself a large measure of whisky, then placed the bottle in front of Grant, who declined the offer and slid it across the table towards O'Shea. Judging by the man's grateful expression, he was glad of another refill. "Not have the belly for it?" O'Shea smirked at Grant as he poured himself another generous measure.

"No," Grant paused. "Not got the head." He looked at each of the men in turn, then fixed his stare on Holman. "Reminds me of a couple of men that I met in the nick, a gang of five in all, but two of them ended up in the same prison. They spent weeks going over the events, discussing every detail from the planning, right up to their capture. It took over, plagued their minds, they just couldn't let it go," Grant paused and glanced over to O'Shea who, having emptied his glass again, was reaching for the bottle once more. "Then one day, one of the men actually figured it out. It was so blatantly obvious. They planned the job for months and met every night to revise the procedures, only once they got the whisky out, all they talked about was how they were going to spend the money. The whole affair wound up more like a social gathering than a proper planning session. Too much drinking, not enough planning."

"So how come *you* were caught then?" Neeson asked patronisingly, his hand clenched around his own glass.

Grant stared at Holman, who suddenly seemed uncomfortable with the topic of conversation. "Someone wasn't where they said they would be. Got nervous, left me to fend for myself. We had a few contingency plans, but they seemed to be forgotten," he paused, looking back at the Irishman. "Again, too much drinking, not enough listening to the planning."

O'Shea smiled as he picked up his glass and unhurriedly downed the remnants in one smooth motion. "Fair enough." He placed the empty glass down onto the table and glanced at each of the men in turn. "No more booze then. Let's get down to it, shall we?"

Neeson stood up from his chair and walked to the dresser in the far corner of the kitchen. He opened a drawer and took out two manila envelopes, one large and one small. He hefted the smaller package in his hand, then replaced it and closed the drawer. Upon returning to his seat at the table he opened the larger envelope and tipped out a selection of colour aerial prints, which he spread across the table.

"I commissioned a pilot friend to get these for me," he said, proud of the array of photographs. "An hour after the last race, when the crowds have mostly gone and the big clean-up is underway," Neeson said, gesturing for McCormick to pass the photographs around the table. "We hit the central office safe."

"Race?" Grant asked as he picked up a large, glossy photograph and studied the layout of buildings closely.

"Yes." O'Shea smiled. "Kempton Park race course. No military or armed police. Plenty of roads in and out and a hell of a lot of money on site."

***

King pulled the van into the narrow alleyway and drove steadily along, until it widened into a turning-space with a row of lock-up garages and private storage units. Leaving the engine idling, he got out of the van and walked the short distance to one of the garages. He unlocked the metal up-and-over door and raised it quickly above his head, then glanced around casually to check that no one was tailing him. Satisfied that he was not being followed or observed, he walked back to the van and parked it inside. With the vehicle locked safely away and hidden from sight he walked briskly through the alleyway, out onto the pavement, and then the four hundred metres or so to the large multi-storey car park. He jogged up the stairs to the third floor, where he crossed to the other side of the building and took the stairs to the fifth level, then crossed back over to the opposite corner, where he had earlier parked the well-used BMW 5 Series. He glanced round casually then operated the remote on the key fob.

The art of successful counter-surveillance is to become as paranoid as you possibly can and not relax for a second. If you can be seen and followed, you can just as easily be killed. King was never entirely certain if he had been followed by some other entity, whether security forces or the very terrorists he was hunting, but changing vehicles and carrying out counter-surveillance drills could only help him to stay ahead of the opposition. He had walked to the multi-storey car park, including on his route, a one-way street against the oncoming traffic. He had crossed over the floors of the car park and changed his vehicle, so if anybody had followed him, he was confident that he would either have lost them, or spotted them.

Once he was out of the car park and into the one-way traffic system, he took the A240 to Ewell, and then the A3 to Esher, still confident that he was not being followed. He parked the BMW in the private cobbled courtyard, which was almost completely encircled by apartments, but for the tiny entrance onto the main road. The building was mainly of limestone construction and each apartment was equipped with its own external, wrought iron stairway, with wooden banisters that added at least a little anonymity to the building's many residents.

King quickly made his way around the neatly tended lawn and climbed the stairs to a second floor apartment. As he approached the door he noticed the head of a tiny red drawing pin sticking out of the wooden banister. It was only a small detail, but one which told him that his MI6 liaison officer was inside. Forsyth had insisted that it would be the simplest, and possibly safest option. He knew what special operatives were like in the field, and the last thing he wanted to do was surprise an edgy King with his unannounced presence. Forsyth would have placed the pin discreetly, holding it in the palm of his hand as he climbed the stairs then simply reach for the banister on the last step and insert the pin as he unlocked the door with his other hand.

King unlocked the door but entered cautiously all the same. "Ian?" he called quietly, as he entered the sparse hallway, but he needn't have bothered; there was a fog of cigarette smoke wafting out of the lounge. The sweet, scented blend of Forsyth's bespoke cigarettes.

"Over here, old boy." Forsyth walked breezily from the direction of the bathroom. "Time for a debrief, I should imagine. Been a jolly busy day so far."

The two men walked into the smoke-filled lounge and sat down on the less than comfy chairs that had been quickly provided by the residential wing of the SIS. They chose not to draw the curtains but sat away from the windows all the same. Two men meeting regularly behind closed curtains could only attract unwanted attention from a gossip-hungry neighbour.

Forsyth had made a pot of tea and was now carrying out the ritual of swirling the tea around the china teapot, allowing the leaves and the specially filtered water to infuse. King, who had only ever been a teabag and mug man, smiled at the mannerisms of his companion.

"Sugar?" Forsyth raised an expectant eyebrow, his hand hovering over the pile of cubes.

King nodded somewhat impatiently. "Yes, two." He caught Forsyth's expression then relaxed a little. "Please," he added, knowing that the man could not, and would not be hurried.

Forsyth dropped two cubes of sugar into the cup and stirred it carefully before tapping the spoon against the rim. "I don't know what it is about you soldier types, but you all seem to have the heathenish habit of ruining a jolly good cup of tea with the uncouth addition of sugar." He smiled as he handed the cup and saucer over to King.

"Not given the choice I suppose," he paused, deciding to explain his comment further. "Long runs or route marches are usually broken up by a quick brew of tea. Sugar is tossed in as a matter of course, extra energy. It soon becomes habit." He glanced down at the man's hands noticing how immaculate they were. Neatly manicured fingernails, long but filed smooth, with a shiny appearance that could well have been a colourless varnish. Part of him seriously doubted whether Forsyth had ever done anything more strenuous in life than wield a fountain pen. However, King was not completely taken in by the man's foppish appearance. He was sure that if push came to shove, Ian Forsyth could shove very hard indeed, although probably with a stiletto dagger and most definitely from behind.

King sipped from his cup then replaced it to the saucer. "What have you found out? Today could very nearly have become a total lash-up."

Forsyth nodded and sat back in the chair with a sigh "I know. It would seem that we were very lucky indeed." He reached into his jacket pocket and retrieved his silver cigarette case, then casually opened the lid. "It would appear that both services found themselves stumbling over each other, albeit momentarily." He extracted a rather thick-looking, handmade Turkish cigarette and gently tapped the tip against the lid of the silver case. "Yesterday morning the Security Service's ports and airports division received an emergency telephone call from a senior officer of 14 Intelligence Company operating illegally in Eire. They had tracked known terrorists on a watch list from Ulster," Forsyth paused. "You're familiar with The Det I hear, did some work for them. Before signing on with The Increment."

"A while ago, yes. Another secondment," King replied, not divulging anything.

"My, you get around."

"Where I'm sent."

"Peter Stewart sees potential," Forsyth smirked. "So I suppose we should all respect that. A little unorthodox though. What was it that got you locked up in prison?"

"I'm sure you already know," King replied coldly. "Anyway, back to the telephone call. What did this senior officer have to say?"

Forsyth smiled. "Ah yes, well it would seem that four known players, PIRA boys, were followed down to Dublin and observed boarding a ferry to Holyhead. Bold as bloody brass they were, old boy."

"What about names? Presumably they used aliases."

Forsyth nodded, then carefully lit the cigarette. He inhaled deeply, smiled briefly, as the smoke had the desired effect, then blew out a thin plume of the mildly scented smoke. "Oh they had cover aliases old boy, but the fact remains that the agent from 14 INT positively identified them. Appears he knew two of them very well indeed," Forsyth paused as he inhaled, then let a smoke ring drift lazily across the room, before it disintegrated in front of King's face. "What he didn't get was the registration number of the car. The two players that he followed down from the north did the trip in an old green Ford Fiesta. They then met up with the other two men who were driving the Sierra. The agent had to slip aboard the ship and get the details." Forsyth chuckled sardonically and shook his head. "Would you believe that there were two identical Fords parked on the same deck? The agent contacted Five on his mobile phone, then had to wait until the ferry had docked, and the men got into the car before he could give a positive ID on the vehicle."

King smiled. *Sod's Law*, they called it. If it could go wrong, it usually did.

The fact that operatives from the British Army's Northern Ireland intelligence gathering body, otherwise known as The Det (The Detachment) was operating in Ireland contravened their official brief, as they could only legally operate inside Northern Ireland. When matters went outside of Northern Ireland, they should hand all matters over to MI5, who in turn should liaise with Northern Ireland's Special Branch, part of the Royal Ulster Constabulary (RUC). This procedure naturally resulted in lost time, and is often conveniently forgotten. The South, or Eire remains strictly out of bounds, but only for the British security forces. The terrorists used the south as a safe zone. King knew this only too well and had slipped over the border on surveillance operations in the past. It went on.

Forsyth smiled at the shape of his next smoke ring then turned his concentration back to the debrief. "After the MI5 watchers took over at Holyhead, they followed the players using two vehicle units and a mobile control. The Provos stopped in a motorway service station, again, as bold as bloody brass. One of the watchers got a little too close for her own good. According to Howard, Deputy Director of the Security

Service and Director General of Operations, the woman, Mary Vaughan was killed in the men's lavatories," he paused then added, "Strangled by the looks of it."

"Poor girl. Was she an experienced agent?"

Forsyth nodded. "A copper for six years, then criminal intelligence for two years before being recruited into Five. She was a serving Security Service agent for four years, even spent some time over the water, Belfast apparently." He stubbed out the cigarette in the rapidly filling ashtray then leant back in his chair. "The players were followed by several teams to an address in Epsom, where a static unit was placed on them this morning. Then, our man O'Shea was observed paying them a little visit."

"I know." King took a sip of his tea, which by now had become tepid. He casually wiped a drip of tea from his chin with his sleeve, then turned back to his liaison officer. "I arrived at Holben Drive just in time to see O'Shea and Danny Neeson enter the house. After I spoke to you, and you warned me off, I followed the pair of them to a farm near Send, in Surrey. The Sierra was following them closely, along with an overeager team of watchers from the Security Service in a Mondeo.

"What then?" Forsyth asked, leaning forwards, intrigued by the development.

"I got this." King pulled a Hi-8 video cassette out of his jacket pocket and placed it on the table. "I made my way cross-country to the secluded farmyard and got a look inside the large barn where everybody had congregated," he paused. "That criminal, Frank Holman was there as well, along with someone else he had brought along. They set up a test for him..."

"Who?" Forsyth quickly interrupted.

"The guy that Holman brought with him. Cracking a safe without the use of tools. He did it as well. Used a sort of oil and chemical fertiliser compound. Pack it tight and it's a highly volatile explosive, leave it slack and it's an incendiary. The heat cut through the back of the safe like a thermal lance, and as long as he applied enough force to the area before it cooled then it would naturally give way."

"And he's on the tape?"

"Of course."

Forsyth opened his silver cigarette case and carefully extracted another handmade cigarette. They had three gold bands around the end. King remembered reading an early Fleming or Le Carré novel where the character had them custom made by Moorlands. Maybe Forsyth had read the same book.

"What the hell are they up to?" Forsyth tapped the tip of the cigarette against the lid of the case, then closed the lid with a snap. "PIRA don't collaborate with the English in their operations. It goes against everything they believe in." He slipped the cigarette into the corner of his mouth, then flicked the wheel of the lighter, allowing the flame to hover perilously close to his face. "I know they use the Yanks from time to time, and Middle Eastern countries more often than not. And the Russian Mafia are getting in on the scene of late now the wall's come down, but only supplying resources and training, not in actual operations." Forsyth drifted the flame to the tip of the cigarette then slipped the lighter back into his pocket as he inhaled. "There's less than a week to go before the peace agreement is signed. What the hell are they playing at?"

"It has to be fund-raising," King stated flatly. "They're going to do a money job, using Frank Holman and this safecracker guy. They're hedging their bets, getting money into their accounts for the future."

Forsyth nodded in agreement, then blew out a plume of pungent smelling smoke, subtly different from the smoke of his previous cigarette. "It could well be fund-raising, but we're still left with the same question: why use the English? We know that they've been assisted by the Welsh, even in the bloody Scots in the past, but that's simply a silly Celtic thing," he added quietly. "They're close to ETA in Spain, and the ARB, the Breton nationalists in France. Why use English criminals?"

"Perhaps it is just that this friend of Holman's is the only person available for a specialist job. Holman has contacts in the underworld," King smirked. "Hell, he *is* the underworld. It wouldn't be the first time that the IRA lost sight of politics. We all know that by now Northern Ireland is as much about business as it ever was about ideals. I mean, they're into everything that makes money - drugs, protection rackets, prostitution - the whole political situation has been completely overshadowed by the pursuit of money. It's as much about gangland control as it is about what they consider to be their freedom from Britain."

Forsyth nodded. "What about this team from Five?" he asked, changing the subject suddenly. "Do you think they saw you?"

King nodded, a wry smile cracking. "They got a bit too close to me, I sent them packing. I'm surprised Howard didn't mention it."

"Well, from your schoolboy expression, you got the better of them. They wouldn't exactly advertise that, old boy."

King shrugged, casually dismissing the comment. "What about now, what position are Five taking on this?"

"They have agreed to back off, too many cooks and so forth." Forsyth smiled. "The whole operation is now in your capable hands."

"You mean *ours*, don't you?" King corrected him warily.

Forsyth returned a wry smile. "Of course, old boy, that's exactly what I meant."

***

The blue Saab sped rapidly away, its headlights scything across the courtyard as Danny Neeson turned the vehicle in a tight arc.

Frank Holman walked back into the kitchen, closed the door, and smiled at Grant who sat alone at the table. "I bet you can't believe it, Kempton Park racecourse!" He eased his substantial bulk onto the wooden chair and reached for the whisky bottle. "What do you think to that, son?"

"So now you know," Grant stated flatly, the hint of a smirk on his lips. "They'd kept you in the dark all this time," he paused. "All this time, and Mr Bigshot knew as little as I did. What the fuck have you got us into, Frank?"

The rest of the team had retired to watch television in the lounge, where they were enthusiastically discussing the impending heist, amid generous measures of Irish Whiskey and Scotch single malts. The operation had been outlined but nothing more would unfold until both O'Shea and Neeson were ready. This team was tight.

Holman glared at Grant then sneered contemptuously. "Don't go getting lippy on me, son, I'd hate to have to teach you a lesson."

Grant looked away from the man's cold eyes and found himself reaching for the whiskey bottle. Perhaps it would help. "Forget it, Frank, I don't give a damn what happens." He looked back at him, his eyes hard and narrow. Holman was momentarily stunned; Simon Grant had always been a push-over, he had never seen the man display such calm aggression. He was about to respond in kind when Grant cut him off. "How the hell did you get yourself mixed up with this bunch of thugs, Frank? I know you're into everything, but this? These guys are crazy," he paused. "That mad bastard Neeson would have shot me if I'd failed the test with that safe, he wouldn't even have hesitated. In fact, I got the feeling that he actually wanted me to fail, I could see it in his eyes. If that battery had been flat…"

"Yeah they're tough lads," Holman agreed matter-of-factly.

Grant shook his head despondently. "And why the Irish? They're no good for anything except digging up the bloody roads! That's what you used to say, wasn't it?" He grinned at his old friend who was grinning back at him. Grant suddenly flinched at the realisation. "Oh shit… They're bloody terrorists!"

Holman sipped his drink calmly, then smiled. "Does it matter?"

"Terrorists! Of course it fucking matters!" Grant stared at him in astonishment. "Who the hell are they Frank?"

"Republican Army. The IRA," Holman paused. "And before you say anything else, you should see what they're paying me." He leaned against the hard back of the wooden chair with a look of immense satisfaction upon his face. "More than what you're getting, that's for sure."

Grant shook his head, near dumbfounded. "They kill innocent people, Frank. Easy victims! Off duty soldiers, bombings in shopping centres…" He stood up quickly, a little too quickly with the whiskey inside him. He clutched the table for a moment. "I can't believe it," he said quietly, almost to himself. He let go of the table and walked over to the window, stared at the darkness.

"Believe it. Two-million is a hell of an amount of money. You can live like a king for the rest of your life. Anyway, these guys won't be terrorists next week. They'll all be exonerated as part of the peace agreement. They're looking for new employment, new opportunities for people with their skillset." He took another sip, then shook his head sullenly. "Besides, you're in this now, you can't just walk away from it."

"The hell I can't!" Grant spun round and pointed an accusing finger at him. "You never mentioned a damned thing about the IRA!"

"So sue me!"

"You bastard," Grant said quietly.

"Fine, if you want out, then go! But just be sure to look over your shoulder for the rest of your short life!"

Grant walked back to the table and slumped down onto his hard seat. He sighed deeply and rested his head in his hands. "You are a bloody idiot, Frank. Don't you realise that we're only useful to them until this job is done?" He raised his head and frowned at him. "Haven't you given that any thought?"

Holman scoffed at the suggestion. "You don't know what you're talking about. I've been with them for a few years now, well with Danny Neeson and O'Shea. I'm useful to them all of the time, and they pay me well for it. We have quite a lucrative fund-raising scheme going on over here, they've got their sticky fingers into everything. Not just dodgy schemes and bank-jobs, but legitimate businesses as well. Estate agents, video hire stores. Mobile phones are going to be big, everyone will have one soon, even teenagers. They're looking into that market too," he paused and smiled. "And did you ever wonder why Irish theme pubs have been all the rage for so long?" he asked gleefully. "Take my house - do you think that I could just suddenly afford a place like that in six short years? Of course not! All bought and paid for out of *The Cause*. That stupid car of Eileen's, her toy-boy puller? Paid for by the paddies. I agree with them as well; we should leave Ireland to the Irish."

Grant leaned back in exasperation. "Fuck, Frank! You're a terrorist! What the hell do you know about it all anyway? What about the other Irish organisations? They were born there, and their ancestors for generations before them. They don't want to be separated from Britain. What about them?" He shook his head and stared at the man with a look of contempt. "You know nothing, Frank. You're pig-ignorant and blind to the facts. Ireland is far too complicated for a twat like you to figure out, so just go on taking their money. But if I were you, I'd be looking over my shoulder pretty bloody soon. Or maybe under that fancy car of yours. As for me? Well I'm out of it, right now."

Holman laughed out loud. "I only have to worry if I cross them, son, only if I cross them! Which I don't intend on doing, ever." He stood up from his seat and walked across the kitchen to the large dresser where Neeson had earlier taken out the aerial photographs of Kempton Park. He pulled out the left-hand drawer, then reached inside and retrieved an A4 envelope. "I'm sorry that it had to come down to this, but I thought that for once, just once, you would show some good sense." He walked back to the table and dropped the envelope in front of Grant. "I think that you'll find it's for your own good, I'd hate for you to do anything foolish."

Simon Grant watched Holman leave through the front door, then looked back at the envelope. He was still staring blankly at it when he heard Holman's Mercedes drive out of the farmyard. He reached out and picked up the mysterious package. It was not fastened, so he tipped it up, allowing the contents to slide out onto the table.

For six years she had merely been a distant memory. A somewhat blurred memory both of fondness, and of sadness, but now the image was crystal clear once more. Here she stood with young David. How he had grown! Holding his mother's hand tightly, somewhat insecurely, as the pair waited at a bus stop. Standing in the shelter away from the drizzling rain, little David wore the drab grey colours of a school uniform. He had seen them both with his own eyes yesterday. A glimpse of her hair, her profile. The smile and hug with his son. And then he was gone, and she was driving away from him. A minute to see what his prison sentence had cost him.

Grant flicked through the photographs one by one, all the same but taken with different degrees of magnification. Lisa looked as she always had. Apart from her hair, which was now reddish on the brunette scale. That was new, but she wore it well. She was beautiful. Although there was a visible difference, a distance in her eyes.

A sullen, unmistakable sadness.

The final photograph was upside down and by the look of it, had been placed purposely that way. Grant turned it over and instantly felt a shiver run down his spine. They had been drawn onto the photograph using a fine black pen and much attention to detail. A perfect circle surrounded both Lisa and David's heads, and a thin cross had been drawn in the middle of each circle, centring on their foreheads. Rifle sights.

Superimposed cross-hairs.

Of course, he doubted they would kill them both in such a way if the moment arose, but the elaborate image did everything to enforce their intentions. Grant closed his eyes, a tear rolling gently down his cheek. Now he knew he had no choice in the matter; he was in this as deep as he could get.

He would have to crack that safe.

***

The two men concentrated on the image on the screen and as they did so, Forsyth pressed the pause button on the remote control. The picture in front of them froze, leaving a perfect close up on a man's face. "That ugly-looking bugger is Matthew McCormick." He let the image play on, then froze it again as McCormick walked forwards and stood next to Danny Neeson. "He's the supposed leader of the cell. As you know, they arrived into the country at Holyhead on the ferry yesterday. According to the MI5 agents who followed them, he is the one most likely to have killed Mary Vaughan in the services."

"Why so sure?" King took another sip of steaming hot coffee, his eyes still fixed on McCormick's pock-marked face.

"Last one out, old boy. The other three left in a hurry, but he returned to the vehicle a full ten-minutes later. Security tapes have been collected from the service station, whether he is on them or not, only time will tell. The services management was not keeping a clear security system. You know, recording over the tapes too soon, not filing them. In some cases, the cameras were not recording in certain areas." Forsyth let the tape play for a while, glanced down at the dossier resting in his lap, then pressed the pause button again. "The big bugger is Patrick Hennessey, sometimes goes under Collier. He is a bit of a Machine Gun Kelly type. Four years ago he shot a fish and chip shop all to hell with an

M60, you know, one of those chain-fed guns that Rambo used. Killed the owner, his wife and five customers. Injured sixteen in total, just to attempt to kill two RUC officers eating their chips outside. That was the last anybody saw of him. Combined intelligence sources thought that he holed up in the south for a while, then slipped over to America and hid among the other paddies in Boston." Forsyth inhaled deeply on the remaining stub of cigarette, then blew out a thin plume of mildly scented smoke. "Maybe he didn't after all. Either way, the bastard's a menace. He's back on the scene and extremely dangerous." He released the pause button on the remote control then pressed it again soon after. Simon Grant could be seen bent down over the safe, his face in full view. King smiled. The quality of the film footage was extremely good. Now and again the picture would be lost, only to slip away from the gap and take a close up of the wooden panel through which he had filmed. However, these brief interludes were rare and on the whole the footage was of an excellent standard. "I can take this tape back to the lab and get a photograph of this chap. If he has a past, then I can have a file on him by morning," said Forsyth.

"I expect you'll find he has a past. He's a professional, and most professionals start off small time and learn from their mistakes. He probably has a record for something."

"Well, you'd know all about that."

King ignored him. "Why did Five pull off so quickly?"

Forsyth grinned and slipped the cigarette into the corner of his mouth. "Baying for blood, old boy. Our department usually gets the dirty work, not that they knew The Increment were on to them, but I think they had their suspicions. It's rare for SIS to be so concerned, so focused on a terrorist cell on home soil. Maybe they saw a chance to avenge their female officer."

King frowned. "But the termination order was for Mark O'Shea, with an unofficial by-line for Danny Neeson, should the man get in the way and pose a threat to the operation's objective. It wasn't for the Active Service Unit responsible for the death of their agent."

Forsyth smiled a wry, deceptive smile. "But they don't know that, old boy, they don't know that."

21

Grant woke with a start, prematurely dragged from a fitful sleep by a prolonged crashing and banging. The thunderous clatter seemed to emanate from the general direction of the barn, but for a brief moment he had thought that he was back in prison, with the toughened steel doors slamming shut and the monotony of another tedious day about to commence. Somehow, though, the thought of being back in the security of a cell almost appealed to him. Right now, given the company he was keeping, it would probably be a sight safer.

He squinted through the bright light, which shone somewhat obtrusively through the gap between the curtains, then found himself studying the sparsely furnished room. Only a bed and a hard-backed wooden chair in the far corner next to an old, cracked enamel sink, broke the monotony of the four bare walls. In fact, his last prison cell would have put this room to shame.

A bag of clothes lay strewn on the floor and a toiletries bag hung from an adhesive peg which had been applied somewhat asymmetrically to the back of the wooden door. He swung his legs out over the edge of the bed and rose unsteadily to his feet, feeling the adverse effects of the previous night's whiskey. An unsteady walk to the sink followed by a quick wash with the cold water, there being no hot on offer, made him feel a little more human. Thus refreshed, he put on his old clothes and walked to the door.

The glorious aroma of frying bacon and eggs greeted him at the top of the stairs and he ambled smartly down into the kitchen where Dugan, the smallest of the four men, had obviously been designated chef and was mastering the frying pan on the gas stove. The little Irishman turned and grinned amiably at the new arrival as he cracked another egg into the hot oil. "Mornin' matey, fancy some scoff?"

Grant glanced at the other three men who were tucking into great mounds of fried bacon and sausage, then turned his gaze back to the competent cook. "No thanks, just coffee will be fine." Somehow this selection of table companions had evaporated his earlier appetite.

"Here, fresh pot on the table," McCormick said amiably. "Just help yourself." He patted the table and pulled out a wooden chair. "Have to say, you certainly knew your stuff yesterday with that safe, pretty impressive."

"Thanks," Grant acknowledged the compliment somewhat dismissively. He didn't like the company, though instinct told him that had the four men not been terrorists, he could quite possibly have enjoyed it wholeheartedly. They seemed like nice guys, only his knowledge of what they were and what they had done prejudiced it.

"I've used a similar mix myself, mixed with a residue of boiled-down bleach and petroleum jelly," Patrick paused. "Pack it tightly with nails and screws, or even broken glass, and it serves an entirely different purpose." He smiled at Dugan, who was placing a rack of toast down on the table in front of him.

Grant put down his steaming coffee cup and stared at the big man. "I can imagine," he replied. "And how many innocent people did that kill? How many widows or orphans owe their status to you for that?"

Patrick glared at him coldly and was about to reply when McCormick cut in hastily, "Now lads, I think we had best steer clear of politics and ideals. Money is the only common denominator here. And we're all in this together, as a team." The other three men nodded in unison and resumed devouring their ample breakfasts.

Grant picked up his cup and took a shallow sip, more for a distraction than to slake his thirst. He looked around the table. He was starting to feel very much the outsider, although it was not the first time that he had felt this way. Prison was like a club. Granted, it was a club which nobody ever wanted to join in the first place, but very much a club all the same. Even though its rules were never written down. There were new members arriving all the time, and every new arrival has to tread carefully at first, to establish his place in the pecking order. This was no different. He felt compelled to speak, to establish himself amongst this villainous crew. "So what are we meant to do?" he asked, forcing a smile. "The Indians are here, but where are the chiefs?"

McCormick placed his knife and fork down, having finished his last mouthful. "Mr O'Shea telephoned earlier, he's coming over with Danny Neeson a little later on," he said, then picked up his empty plate and carried it over to the sink. "They will lay out the finer points. Then, I guess we do the job."

Grant picked up his coffee and took a deep gulp of the strong liquid. He felt that he was being swept along by the tide, unable to swim against the current or stop and change direction. For now, all he could do was to go with the flow. There was so much that he wanted to ask, needed to know, but every time he was about to speak, he pictured his wife and child instead. It was better to resign his will to events and hope that he would find a way to resolve things before the actual job took place. He snapped out of this train of thought when he heard the vehicle pull into the farmyard. The driver switched off the engine, and Grant heard the sound of heavy footsteps. He turned his head as the front door opened, then quickly returned his attention to his coffee, suddenly uninterested as he saw Holman's bulk filling the doorway.

"Morning gents, nice night?" Holman stepped into the kitchen and glanced at the frying pan, which was cooling on the stovetop. He looked over at McCormick who was standing beside the sink and smiled. "Any chance of a bite?" His face fell, as McCormick returned to his seat without a word, and the other three went on eating.

Patrick raised his head and pointed towards the empty frying pan. "Aye, help yourself. The food is in the fridge and the pan is on top of the cooker," he said around a mouthful of buttered toast.

All four chuckled, aware that Holman had expected to be waited on. Holman made light of the comment and stepped over behind Grant, placing a hand on his shoulder in a parody of affection. "What about you, son. Not hungry?"

Grant stared stonily ahead. The mere sight of Holman was enough to turn his stomach, forcing him to think of his family and what terrible fate might befall them, should he not go ahead with what was now expected of him. The situation seemed utterly hopeless.

"No appetite," he replied bluntly and took a sip of tepid coffee, rebuffing Holman's attempts at conversation.

Holman removed his hand and smiled lecherously. "Ah, well perhaps you're hungry for something, or *someone* else?" He turned and walked out of the kitchen and into the cramped hallway.

Grant stood up, pushing his chair back violently as he did so. He followed the large man out of the kitchen and slammed the door shut behind him. The rest of the men glanced furtively at one another, and Patrick made to stand up.

"Leave 'em be, Pat," McCormick said quietly. "There's obviously some history there, best be letting them pick at it on their own."

Holman stood with his back to Grant, his head bowed sullenly to the floor. "Not my idea, Simon." He turned around, a look of sorrow in his beady eyes. "I'm as upset as you are."

"Don't bloody patronise me!" Grant spat at him venomously. "You didn't level with me, and you bloody should have, I had no idea what I was getting into!"

Holman smiled wryly. "You didn't need levelling. Two million was all I had to say, your greed did the rest, as usual." He rested his elbow against the wall and leaned, taking the considerable weight off both his stubby legs. "Do what you will afterwards, but play along and the pair of them will be safe and sound. You can go round there and play happy families with two-million quid in your pocket."

Grant shook his head. "How could you do this? How could you allow it? For God's sake, you were at our wedding!" He rubbed his eyes. "What if the bloody job doesn't come off, will they be safe then?"

Holman shrugged haplessly, then avoided Grant's stare. "These are big boys Simon, they play by a completely different set of rules, a very different game to what we're both used to. I don't condone everything they do, but I have to say, they certainly get the job done," he paused. "You understand what I'm saying? There won't be any room for mistakes."

Grant spun around and kicked the wall in fury. A piece of plaster chipped off and settled at his feet. He looked up from the momentary distraction. "How could you do this? I did time for you, I didn't grass you up, and it reflected in my sentence. I stashed the money and got word to you, telling you where to find it. Christ Almighty, I was only caught with the tools from the fucking job! I shouldn't have been sent down for seven years!"

"It was six," Holman corrected him flippantly. "Six, and a few of months."

Grant glared at him. "Good behaviour Frank! I spent most of the time counting down from seven..." He shook his head in bewilderment. "I just can't believe it. I agreed to do the job, now if I don't, it's not only my life at stake, but my family's!"

"Hardly your family any more though, are they?" Holman reminded him flatly. "You're not the man in Lisa's bed, and you're not putting food on the table. Not that you were ever any good at that sort of thing when you were with them. Christ, if Lisa didn't work nights in the social club bar, you'd have barely eaten twice a week..."

"You bastard!"

Holman suddenly looked genuinely sorry for this cruel comment. He hung his head, perplexed, then looked up apologetically. "Look, I'm sorry, mate. Things just got out of hand. Trust me, this job is a piece of piss. You and the boys will make it in and out in no time at all."

"And what about you? What about those arseholes in there? What about Neeson and O'Shea? What about the other three men in the barn, what do you all do?"

Holman smiled wryly. "We're all on something else. In this job, two wrongs definitely make a right." He pushed himself away from the wall, looked around for somewhere to sit, then rested his broad backside on the foot of the stairs.

"What is it? Come on, level with me this time, what aren't you telling me?"

"I'm telling you what you need to know. Just do the job you've been given and everything else will be all right."

Both men turned their heads, as they heard a vehicle pull into the muddy driveway and enter the courtyard. Holman stood up, patted Grant on the shoulder and grinned. "Come on, lad," he said. "Sounds like things are getting underway."

***

King watched attentively from the wooded fringe that ran parallel to the quiet roadside. He pressed the field glasses to his eyes and studied the man that he had been ordered to kill. As he watched Mark O'Shea step out of the passenger-side of the Saab, he felt an overwhelming familiarity with the man. He knew his mannerisms, the way that he held himself, his usual gait, with its short purposeful strides. He knew his characteristic expression: an officious pout, bordering on pomposity.

This was about as close as he had ever been to this man, but he recognized him instantly, from the laborious hours that had been spent studying the surveillance tapes, the file photographs, and reading and rereading the man's dossier. He had been made privy to all the material which had been accumulated by the likes of MI5, MI6, Special Branch and combined military intelligence.

It would surely not be long now. Forsyth had warned him the night before that the executive order would not take much longer to assign. It would soon pass through the final channels and end up on the SIS Home Desk, at the heart of a certain monstrosity on the bank of the River Thames.

King had barely begun to read the file on Simon Alan Grant before he was interrupted by a beep from his laptop computer, indicating that Neeson's Saab was on the move. He dropped the file in the van's foot well and started in pursuit. However, on the basis of even a cursory glance at his file, King was sure about one thing: Simon Grant was without the political ideals to be drawn into terrorism.

He kept the field glasses on Neeson's back. The man was walking towards a dull-brown car that had arrived ahead of them. He had watched the Saab pull into the end of the lane and box the brown car in. A horn had sounded and the brown car had driven ahead of Neeson's Saab and pulled into the farmyard. Neeson's Saab now blocked the exit. King adjusted the focus on the binoculars. He couldn't make out what was being said, but the tough Irishman seemed hostile. A man in his late-fifties or early-sixties got out, his hands in front of him. It was a gesture of de-escalation, of calming the mood. The passenger door opened and the man who got out was big, both wide and tall, but he looked a great deal older than Neeson and as he moved in front of the car, pointed at the Mercedes and the farmhouse, he looked stiff and unfit. He also pointed a finger at Neeson, and unlike his companion, it looked like a gesture to escalate rather than subdue the mood.

He thought of repeating his trip to the barn, getting closer, but King was a great believer in fate. He had been successful once, but it did not necessarily follow that he would be successful a second time. No, for the moment, regardless of the fact that he could not hear what was going on, he would simply have to watch and wait.

***

Holman opened the door and saw Mark O'Shea standing in front of him.

"Get the fucking boys out here now!" O'Shea glared at Holman, watching his indecision. "Move your arse, you fat bastard and go and get them!"

Holman jumped to it and barged his twenty-five stone bulk past Grant. Grant watched the big, grey-haired man pointing aggressively at Neeson and shaking his head. The man looked at Grant in the doorway. Grant recognised him as the man who had hit him in Holman's driveway yesterday morning. The man took a few steps toward him, but Neeson stepped in front of him. Then Grant felt himself barged out of the way into the doorframe as the four Irishmen, led by McCormick, filed out of the door and into the farmyard. Holman held back, standing behind Grant as he straightened himself up.

"What the fuck's going on?" Holman said breathlessly.

"I was hoping you would tell *me*," replied Grant. He stepped out and walked closer. Holman followed.

"Do you know these guys?" Neeson shouted to Holman. Holman shook his head. "Seems they have a deal going with your man here," he added, nodding towards Grant. "You know them?"

Grant shrugged. "That bloke hit me yesterday," he said. "They have a problem with the job I ended up inside for. Their colleague was shot," he paused, then added, "Not by me though."

O'Shea walked over to Holman. "How the fuck did they end up here?" Holman shrugged and O'Shea said, "They must have followed you. They were right on your arse, must have parked up, didn't expect me and Danny to drive in behind them. How long have you been here?"

"Five-minutes, tops," Holman replied.

"Then that works out." O'Shea looked at Grant. "What's this fucking job?"

"I cracked the safe. Holman brought in a psycho trigger-man who went *Reservoir Dogs* on the job. Started shooting at the unarmed guard, then shot the poor bloke in the back as he ran away. Holman was the driver..." Grant looked at his old friend. "He sodded off and left me to face the music. I got caught and went down for it. The guard got shot, now he drinks through a straw and shits in a bag, according to that bloke over there," Grant paused. "They want compensation for him."

"Fair enough," O'Shea said. "But life ain't fucking fair, is it?" He looked coldly at Holman. "So this is down to you?"

Holman stuttered. Grant noted he was scared. He'd never seen him like this before. "I... I guess so."

O'Shea turned and spoke over his shoulder as he walked back into the farmyard. "Then you'll sort this shit out, you fat bastard."

"I think he likes you," Grant said quietly.

"Fuck off."

Grant watched as O'Shea spoke briefly with Neeson and McCormick. The two men nodded and spoke to the other three. The big, grey-haired man was looking on in bemusement, but that soon changed to fear and then aggression as the driver was set upon with fists and feet and fell quickly to the ground. He did not put up a good fight, and as the big man watched he was already rounded up on by Neeson at the rear and McCormick head on. Both men were savage fighters and although blows were exchanged on both sides, the two men were all over him. Neeson bent low and pulled the older man's leg off the ground. The man responded by pounding on his back and neck with his fists, but Neeson kept lifting despite the beating and the man pivoted and fell to the ground. Both men switched to feet and kicked him repeatedly around the head and ribs. Neeson stamped on the man's fingers and as he recoiled and clutched his hand, he was no longer able to defend himself. The fight was over in no more than a minute and the five men were heaving for breath over the two inert forms on the muddy ground.

Grant looked on as the men worked together. Both of the unconscious men were picked up and dragged to the barn. Dugan drove their car over to the barn and through the open doors. He watched Patrick close the doors and walk back into the barn through the smaller door to the side. The door closed and it was as if the incident had never happened.

O'Shea walked over to them and pointed to the door. "Get back inside. We've matters to discuss."

"See, I told you he likes you," Grant said under his breath.

Holman shook his head. His expression had changed. He had been exuberant and self-assured before; now he was looking anxious. O'Shea led the way and pushed the door open. He walked on into the kitchen and paused at the table, staring at both men as they caught up.

"Sit." Holman did as he was told and Grant followed suit. Both remained silent, but Grant drummed his fingers on the table. O'Shea looked at him, but he did not stop. "I don't like what has just transpired. How many more men are going to come looking for you?"

"Less than will be looking for you, or so I hear," Grant said.

O'Shea looked at Holman. "You told him?"

"He worked it out."

165

"So," O'Shea said to Grant. "Is that a problem for you?"

"I just want to do the job, get my fee and walk away."

"Good." He looked at Holman. "Not so simple for you though." Holman didn't reply. "I guess you're in this up to your neck."

Grant ventured, "The job. Can we talk about it now?"

O'Shea shrugged. "I suppose. You will need to make a list of the equipment that you will require and give it to Holman. He will get hold of everything you need. There will be two reinforced glass doors, a seismic alarm system with thermal detection, and a safe with an electronic alarm system and dual time locks."

Grant leaned back in his chair. "What kind of time locks? There are a great many different systems on the market, what are Kempton Park equipped with?"

O'Shea shook his head, then admitted, "We don't know for sure, so I'm afraid you will have to plan for every contingency," he paused and grinned. "You're the professional, so make a list."

Grant shook his head slowly, in exasperation. "What about the alarm system? I always do a thorough reconnaissance of the location. It always helps to know exactly what you're walking into, you must be able to tell me that, at least?"

O'Shea glared at him as he stood up from the table. "You should be able to find that out for yourself," he paused. "You're going there today to have a wee look round. And before you get any wild ideas about taking off, Danny Neeson will be there to hold your hand, so he will. There's an antique fair on there today, outside and in. It should give you the opportunity that you need to familiarise yourself with the surroundings, so if you encounter anything unexpected, make sure to add it to the list when you get back. Neeson will phone it through to Holman for you. It's your only chance for a thorough reconnaissance, so make it good."

"I need more details than that," Grant protested. "I will be able to see their CCTV placement, the alarm facia boxes, but those will be bullshit. Kempton Park will have plenty of built-in details that a quick scout round won't pick up. I thought you lot were connected. A set of blueprints would be helpful, or an insider's account and drawings."

"We know that after the last race, the money is held in a central safe until the tellers count it and make it ready for the security company come for it next morning. There is a window of one hour in which to work. The last tote commission comes in and the tellers start work when the park is closed. There's around an hour before the shift comes on. We know the location, and my boys will get you there. But you will need to work every contingency."

Grant shrugged.

Holman smirked. "What more do you want? The fucking key?"

O'Shea smiled. "No, he'll do okay. I guess it's because of his vested interest. Family will do that for you," he paused. "It's you I have a problem with now, Frank."

"What?" Holman shook his head. Grant had never seen the man so scared. "Mr O'Shea, I've done everything to set this up. I have never let you down in the past."

"No," the Irishman conceded. "But it only takes one mistake to lose the trust. Like a dog that runs away, or a wife who shags somebody else. You never truly regain the trust. You messed things up when you allowed yourself to be followed. And all the way from London no less. You must have been damn near asleep at the wheel…"

"Look, Mark," Holman swallowed. "Mr O'Shea, please, I've given you the contacts, pulled in favours, even got you the cracksman you needed," he said, nodding towards Grant. "I've even brought in an investor…" O'Shea shot Holman a look and he stopped talking, glancing at Grant. "Look, you can trust me. It was one silly mistake…"

"Jesus, Mary and Joseph," O'Shea laughed. "The look on your face!" He stood up and smiled. "It's okay, Frank. I trust you. I forgive you. I need a *favour*, that's all."

"Yes, of course," Holman looked relieved. "Anything."

"Good, good." O'Shea walked to the door. "Come on then, both of you. Let's see how things are working out up at the barn." He walked ahead of them, out into the yard and stood to one side as a lorry drove past them and down the lane towards the road. The three men who had been in the barn when Grant first arrived were seated in the front. "They're off to get the other two cars we need," he said, matter-of-factly. O'Shea pushed the door open and stepped into the bright light.

Powerful lamps had been rigged and Grant could see the Porsche sitting behind a tent of clear plastic sheeting, a red lamp glowing, drying the recent paintwork. The car was squat and wide and compact. Purposeful, fast-looking even at a standstill.

There was another area of plastic sheeting a dozen paces away. This had been hastily erected, draped over hay bales and the side of the barn and the floor. The two men knelt in the middle of the sheet. Their hands bound behind their backs, their heads bowed.

Grant looked at Holman, but the big man looked straight ahead, his eyes transfixed on the scene before him.

O'Shea spoke with Danny Neeson for a moment. He nodded, asked something, then shook his head. It was a hasty conversation. He turned back to Holman and beckoned him forward. Neeson took out his pistol, screwed the bulbous suppressor into the adaptor that had been fitted to the muzzle. He readied the weapon.

"Trust," O'Shea said. "A little test, Frank. A little favour to me to show your commitment. These men are the loose ends from something you orchestrated many years ago. It's time to sever those loose ends, before they ruin what we've planned here."

"No! Please..." one of the men cried out, but was struck on the back of the head by a piece of pipe that Patrick had been holding. The man slumped forwards onto his stomach and the other man grimaced. He started to shake, his foot creasing the plastic sheeting and sending ripples outwards.

"I need to see your commitment, Frank."

"I *am* committed!" Holman shouted.

"Then in that case, I need to see an act of penance." He nodded to Neeson, who put the weapon in Holman's hand and pointed it towards the two men. "Pull the trigger, Frank. Pull the trigger and everything will be right between you and me."

Holman's hand started to shake. Neeson smirked as he released his grip and the weapon seemed to bounce around in the thick, sausage-like fingers at the end of Holman's thick arms. "I... can't," he said quietly.

"Can't or won't?" O'Shea asked.

"Mr O'Shea, please," begged Holman. "I haven't let you down before…"

"And nor will you again," the Irishman said. "Point the gun at his head, pull the trigger. It's simple."

"Please…" the man who remained kneeling begged. He was dealt with as swiftly as his companion. Both men now lay on their stomachs. The first man to go down was sobbing into the sheet.

O'Shea shook his head. "Last chance, Holman. You'll be fucking joining them in a moment." Holman tried to steady his hand. He closed his eyes at the last moment and fired. The bullet thudded into the ground between the two men and they both flinched as a clump of earth blew out of the ground and showered them with dried mud and tiny stones. "That's the stuff!" O'Shea grinned. "Commitment, Frank. Commitment." He walked over to Holman and took the pistol off him. He pointed it down to the men on the sheet and fired twice, so quick it sounded almost as if the weapon coughed just once, the suppressor drowning out the noise to nothing more than a loud cough. Both men kicked out, a spasm of violent movement, then lay quite still. There was a sudden tremor in one of the men's legs on the ground. Holman lurched backwards and all of the men, except for Grant, laughed and jeered.

O'Shea handed the pistol back to Neeson and nodded towards the door. "Right, now the fun and shenanigans are over, let's get a brew."

22

King filmed the unmarked lorry as it drove out from behind the building and parked with its engine running, outside the double doors of the huge barn. The driver sounded the horn, and almost instantly a man jogged out from the barn, around the front of the lorry and got into the passenger side of the cab. King kept filming, panning with the camera as the lorry travelled down the lane, until he had a perfect close shot of both men in the cab. He then gently placed the camera at his feet and crouched low, keeping perfectly still amongst the foliage to avoid detection.

As the lorry eased out onto the road he noticed that the driver was the same man who had brought the van in, but this time he wasn't going back the way he had come. Instead, he took the other direction, travelling towards Guildford. He relaxed as the lorry passed his vantage point. He stood up, yet kept behind the foliage and stretched his aching muscles. His secure cellular telephone vibrated suddenly, pre-set for silent ringing. He reached into his pocket and retrieved it, keeping his eyes on the farm and its entrance. He could not afford to let down his guard for a second.

"Hello?" he answered quietly.

"Mac, it's Forsyth. How's it going?"

"Busy," King commented. He watched as a man walked out of the barn towards the farmhouse. "It's a real hive of activity here. And there's more. Two unknowns turned up, they followed Holman. O'Shea and Neeson arrived shortly afterwards. There was an altercation, and then a proper kick-in. Both of the men were taken to the barn, and someone drove their car in there as well. I don't think they'll be coming back out anytime soon."

"Interesting. However, one can't be responsible for the company others keep. I would say that there is no honour amongst thieves. I'm not sure we should risk derailing our intelligence gathering phase by looking too closely at the minute details."

"Ian, it's not *minute* details. I think two guys have been either executed or imprisoned in the barn…"

"I know!" Forsyth snapped. *"But the Executive Order has been signed off on. We are now officially The Increment, and we have an execution or two to perform of our own. We've got rid of MI5 on this, we don't need plod looking at a gangland killing now that we are so close. The peace agreement will be signed in less than a week and then all bets are off."*

King kept his eyes on the farmyard and spoke quietly into the tiny telephone. "Well, there's also the fact that something else, something major is going on here. We've got this Grant fellow, the safe-cracker, and Frank Holman. There are vehicles coming and going, and that barn is where it's all going on."

"We have our own task."

"But they could be planning a huge event."

"Not our problem," Forsyth replied. *"Maybe you should have gone and worked for MI5?"*

"I'm a serving operative of MI6. I didn't get to pick and choose."

"Shame."

"A major terrorist event would derail the peace process."

"Good. Then we get to play cowboys and Indians again."

"Sorry, I thought that's what we were doing here," King said. "I thought eliminating the likes of Neeson and O'Shea was meant to protect the peace agreement. Or is that just a load of old bollocks?"

"There's always a bigger picture, Alex. You and I may not be a part of it, but that's no reason to find issues our end. Our task was to find a way to take out Mark O'Shea, and Danny Neeson if he poses a threat to life. We had to find a way for it to be done without witnesses, harm to others and it had to be done before the peace agreement was signed. That is all we had to do, and that is all we are going to do."

King may have been relatively new to the Secret Intelligence Service, and particular The Increment, but had been around long enough to know when to hold, and know when to fold. There wasn't much room for negotiation here. "After it's done," King ventured. "Do we hand our findings over to the Security Service and Special Branch?"

"Yes," Forsyth paused. *"Absolutely."*

King knew a lie when he heard it. But he also knew that there would be no mileage in exposing it. He had gathered the intelligence, and knew the details. If he felt that his duty to Queen and country would be better served informing the security forces or the police, then he had no qualms about giving them an anonymous tip-off. But for now, he would play the game and keep his relationship with his liaison officer on workable terms. The trouble with MI6 was that when they used the skills of a specialist, they never truly accepted that the men were intelligent enough to know their own mind. King knew that more important than pulling a trigger was knowing when not to. He lifted the binoculars and looked at the farmhouse and the barn. He needed to know more. He needed to lull the intelligence officer into thinking it was solely for the purpose of killing the two known IRA terrorists. "Well that's good to know Ian," King said. "Now, let's get back to the operation. It's going to pay to know more. I'll carry on here and meet you tonight at the flat."

"Very well, say around nine?"

"Twenty-one-hundred?" King verified.

"Oh have it your way, old boy. Have it your way."

23

"Right, come with me, we're going on a little outing," Neeson said, looking down at Grant, who was seated at the table having just finished making a lengthy list. "If you're quite ready," he added sardonically. He put his empty cup down on the table.

Grant folded the sheet of paper and passed it to Holman, who took it and started to read without a word. Grant had never seen Holman so shaken. Neither of them had ever seen anything like it in the barn. Holman, for all his swagger and talk, had never seen a man killed before.

Neeson turned and led the way out of the house. Grant followed him across the courtyard towards the blue Saab then stood at the passenger door while the Irishman unlocked the driver's door, activating the vehicle's central locking.

Neeson stared at him contemptuously. "You know the deal by now. Don't mess us around, there's more than just *your* life at stake." He opened his door and smiled. "I shouldn't have to threaten you anymore. If you cross us, I'll enjoy seeing to your wife. After all, she is quite a peach."

Grant opened his door, ignoring Neeson's comment. He knew that the man was trying to get under his skin, he had to try to resist the temptation to bite. Instead, he stared straight ahead, avoiding eye-contact with the man. "What are we doing?"

Neeson scowled. He had hoped for some form of reaction from Grant, he always enjoyed baiting people, prided himself on being good at it. "We are going to the race track. They have some sort of antique fair going on today, and Mr O'Shea wants you to spot the security systems." He turned the key in the ignition and the Saab's quiet, refined engine gently fired into life.

"Well, it wouldn't be a bad idea if we had a camera. It's best to take pictures of the systems, that way we can study them further when we get back."

Neeson chuckled. "Aye, already thought of, got one in the boot. I have a facility to develop the film back at the farmhouse. Not bad with a camera myself, but you already know that." He smirked, as he drove out into the lane. "Got some good close ups of your beloved wife, didn't I? She really is a looker, too bad she's shagging someone else, isn't it?"

Grant glared at him. "I heard the same about your mother."

Neeson spun around in his seat, brought his hand up under Grant's chin and seized him savagely by the throat. "You watch that mouth of yours, laddie!" He glared icily at him, as his lips formed a cruel, deceptive smile. "I can't wait for you to mess up, and you will, it's just a matter of time. And when you do, I'll take pleasure in wiping your family out." His grip tightened even more, and Grant felt the blood drain from his head, threatening to make him pass out. "But it won't be before I've given your wife a damn good seeing to. I'll tie her up, spread her out. Have a damn good time with her. I haven't decided quite what I'll do, yet. Either way, she'll be screaming, and I'll be smiling."

Grant smacked the man's hand away and took a deep breath. "Cut the crap! You need me for a job and if you give me anymore shit, I swear to god I'll fuck it all up for you," he paused, expecting the Irishman to try and hit him, but to his surprise, the man simply glared at him. "You know," he added. "You're throwing down your bargaining chips too soon. You've already got me wishing I was back inside, don't push me. There's not much for me out here, maybe I'd be better off in prison again. You know, maybe I won't be able to get into that safe before the law comes crashing the party. Thought about that?"

Neeson looked at him, then started the vehicle. As he drove across the yard and towards the lane, he said without looking at him, "You *will* fuck-up, Grant. It's in your nature. O'Shea has got it into his head that your man Holman is the vital link, and he trusts his opinion on you," he paused as he swung the car onto the road and accelerated harshly. "But I'm here to look after the interests of the cause. Cross me, fail me or betray me and I'll make you wish you'd never been born."

Grant looked out of his window, casually bringing a hand up to rub his throat. He closed his eyes, wanting only to be out of this impossible situation, but he was in too deep. There was no way to go but forward. Forward with the job, which by now he found utterly hateful.

***

King had moved back deeper into the undergrowth. Not wanting to tempt fate, he had thrown himself down onto the ground and lain perfectly still until the Saab had pulled out onto the road. Now that he could hear the vehicle's engine accelerating into the distance, he had to move fast. If it reached the one-thousand metre maximum range of the tracking device, finding it could well prove to be near impossible.

He sprang to his feet and pushed his way through the newly sprouting foliage, until he reached the clearing where he had parked the van out of sight of the road. He quickly unlocked the door and dropped down into the seat. The engine fired instantly and he engaged first gear and floored the accelerator. The front wheels spun briefly on the wet ground, spinning up clumps of mud and gravel, then gained traction and propelled the van erratically towards the road. A cursory check to the right was all that King had time for as he sped out onto the tarmac, changing gear as soon as his speed allowed. As he rounded the first corner onto a straight stretch of road, he opened the laptop on the seat beside him and switched on the tracking receiver. As he negotiated the next bend he precariously glanced down and selected the relevant file with the built-in mouse and waited for the dot to appear on the screen. He breathed a sigh of relief. The Saab was right on the cusp of the one-thousand metre cut off point, but at least he knew that he was on the right track. Further ahead lay a myriad of lanes, turnings and smaller roads, invariably leading to larger roads. At least he was in with a chance.

The dot on the screen was flashing intermittently. He was at a good distance, keeping to a minimum of three-hundred metres, but never allowing more than eight-hundred metres separate the two vehicles.

***

Neeson had travelled cross-country, keeping off the motorway. He had taken the A3 towards Esher then turned off onto the A309 towards Sunbury. The traffic had slowed the Saab down considerably. "We'll not get into the park, it's full of dealers and bargain-hunters. Besides, I don't want to get stuck in any queues in case we're sussed and need to bug out," Neeson paused, looking down each side of the street as he drove. "Keep an eye out for a parking space."

Grant nodded dutifully and glanced down the street. "Over there." He pointed unenthusiastically, then added, "Behind the red sports car."

Neeson nodded and drove up to the car in front. The car in front pulled past the space, its near side indicator flashing, then its reverse lights came on. Neeson drove right up to its bumper and blocked the driver's manoeuvre. The driver held up his hands in despair then pointed towards the space, indicating that he had intended to park.

"I know, pal," Neeson muttered to himself. "But you're shit out of luck."

The driver hurriedly unfastened his seat belt and got out of his car slamming his door shut. He stood in front of the Saab and mouthed an expletive, which he backed it up with a succession of insulting hand gestures.

Grant turned to Neeson in protest. "Give him the space, you bloody idiot! We don't want to draw attention to ourselves."

Neeson scowled. "Shut up! I've got this, I know what I'm bloody well doing!" He glared at the driver and held up his middle finger in mindless retaliation. The driver held up both his arms in exasperation then conceded and went back to his car. "See, I told you I knew what I was doing." Neeson gloated, then pulled further forward when the car moved away. He took several attempts at manoeuvring the Saab, then after much effort slipped into the space between a classic MGB GT and a Volvo estate.

Grant gritted his teeth. They had escaped a violent confrontation with the harassed driver and had finally got into the space. But at what cost? There was more and more CCTV going up these days, and the last thing they needed was to attract attention. He had also noted that Neeson was not a particularly skilful driver. The space had not been excessively small and would not have posed a problem for the majority of motorists. He hoped Neeson wasn't going to be driving on the heist.

The entrance to the park was awash with people coming and going. Grant watched as satisfied bargain and treasure hunters came out with their arms full of what they obviously considered to be great finds.

"They have three inside stalls. The gold ring, the silver ring and the bronze ring, which also houses the tote hall. The inside stalls sell jewellery and fine antiques, while the outside stalls are nothing more than a glorified car boot sale." Neeson smiled as a middle-aged woman struggled through the main gates, carrying a rather dire-looking stuffed moose head, much ravaged by moths. "That's where we're going. Through that gate, then straight across and into the first building."

***

King had to squeeze the van into a nearby gap where it fitted too snugly for comfort, well aware that it might prove a problem when he needed to leave. He got out and walked to the end of the street, peered around and was just in time to see the two men walk towards the entrance of the park. He noted any possible VDM's (visual distinguishing marks), then set about following them towards the main gate.

Simon Grant was wearing a blue and white ski jacket; with a red, fleece-lined hood. It was a poor pairing, he looked like a Union Jack. That became his VDM. Danny Neeson wore a pair of white, high-top running shoes, they were too chunky for his jeans and the bottoms stuck into the trainers. It was fashionable, had Neeson been ten-years younger. And a black American rapper. These became his VDM. Now, at a momentary glance, King would be able to pick the two men out without looking directly at their faces. Both men turned to their right, and walked casually to the entrance. He walked straight past the gate, glancing to his right as he did so. Satisfied that neither man was aware of his presence, he turned back and walked into the grounds. He kept a distance of approximately fifty-metres behind the two men, never looking directly at either of them and never standing out in the open.

King noticed an attractive blonde woman in her early thirties who was browsing the stalls, which were a mixture of genuine antiques and timeworn bric-a-brac. She perused the stalls in the manner of one who knew exactly what she is looking for, disregarding items quickly upon inspection and not hiding her distaste.

Most probably a dealer herself. He moved over towards her, then trailed behind, following her every move. To anyone who might have been watching, he was accompanying her as her somewhat bored, yet loyal partner.

***

The two men stood at the far end of the cavernous building, with hordes of people dodging or pushing past them, as they hurriedly, almost frantically, went about their business. There were bargains to be had, deals to be made. It was a pleasant day out for bargain hunters, but just another day for traders. They snapped up deals, took them back to their stalls and traded them on.

"This way," Neeson ordered. "Let's get a good look at the inside of the building. I want you to check over the layout."

"No." Grant turned and looked at Neeson. "I want to check out the outside first. After all, it's where we'll have to start from."

Neeson scowled, but followed all the same. To a certain degree, Grant's word would have to go, he knew more about this sort of work than he did. He slipped the Pentax camera off his shoulder, held it by the strap then swung it towards Grant. "Here, take what pictures you want, but don't be too bloody obvious."

Grant felt a shiver run down his spine. Just the thought of Neeson hidden away with that very camera, taking pictures of Lisa and David, made him feel sick to his stomach. They had been oblivious to the fact that they were being watched. How easily the camera could have been a rifle sight. He snatched the camera off him then held it down by his side. "I don't understand. Surely if we're going in after the last race has finished, we won't have to bypass the security systems, as they won't be operating. The security staff will be the main problem."

"Not so loud!" Neeson hissed at him, then caught hold of him by his shoulder. "You're going in after the security staff have finished. We weren't quite straight with you. The job will commence much later than we first said. Just take note of the systems, and we'll talk later."

Grant kept walking. Something wasn't right. The whole set-up seemed sketchy, only partly thought-out. Unless they were omitting to divulge all the details for another reason.

***

"Charlotte, darling!" The man called out, waving a patterned silk handkerchief in theatrical manner. "I haven't seen you in an age!"

The woman held out her arms in an equally theatrical manner and waited for the imminent embrace. The man duplicated the reaction and leapt elegantly towards her. He was around six-foot-three and pear-shaped, with womanly hips. His dress was neo-gothic, with great cuffs and his coat was fastened with large, silver buckles. The two air kissed with a foot between them.

King dodged down the side of a car and around into the next thoroughfare of trading stalls. He slipped around the group of traders talking at the edge of the stalls, and backtracked. He'd lost them. He looked all around, and felt the familiar feeling in the pit of his stomach, the one that tells you that you just may have blown it. He scanned the crowds. There were hordes of people, the majority practically stationary, browsing the stalls on both sides. Between these were people moving both from and towards the main building. Mostly, they had filtered to one side or the other, like a road, but there were always a few people who didn't get on board and occasionally the crowds would part. He caught sight of Grant, standing near a stall and aiming a camera at the building. To anyone who might have observed, he looked as if he were just becoming familiar with his new purchase. Instead, King could see that Grant had just taken a picture of the closed circuit camera system that was mounted halfway up the tall streetlamp on the near side of the racing track. Sure enough, Danny Neeson was standing beside him scanning the crowd.

Neeson glanced around, his stare fixing on King's gaze. King moved to his right, keeping tight against the nearby stall. He had to think quickly, direct eye contact usually meant that the game was over. He quickly pretended to browse over the nearby stall. A collection of teddy bears, a tarnished sabre, some medals, pieces of porcelain and cut glass, and furniture.

Furniture, that was it. Nobody following a known terrorist would buy a bulky piece of furniture. King pointed to a pine milking-stool towards the back of the stall. "How much for the stool?"

The woman put down her foam coffee cup and reached backwards. She caught hold of a leg then pulled the stool over a small chest of drawers. "Fifteen quid, luv." King caught hold of it then quickly thrust his hand into his pocket. He pulled out a ten-pound note, then raised an eyebrow. "A tenner any good to you?" He didn't want to wait for change.

The woman looked annoyed. However, realising it was probably one of the better offers that she would get that day, she nodded reluctantly and held out her hand. King handed over the note, took the stool and turned around. The trick now was to avoid the temptation of checking whether Neeson and Grant were both still there. If he did and Neeson saw him, it would all be over. He held the stool by his side and casually went with the flow of the crowd, which now appeared to be going in a counter-clockwise direction with very few people heading his way out of the building. At least with a prop in his hands he would appear to look like a genuine buyer.

***

Neeson stared at the second closed circuit camera system, which was mounted on a large, purpose-built post in the centre of the walkway. "That one will be a problem. The cable runs underground, most probably. Cutting it without detection will be difficult."

"It's only the power which runs underground, the images are sent by receiver, much like a radio, or mobile telephone. The lens is aimed at the public conveniences and the tote stands. It has a forty-five-degree line of sight, so we should make it undetected,"

Grant paused. "Unless, that is, it operates from a control centre, automatically changing its variables."

Neeson shook his head. "I doubt it, security looks pretty shoddy, all in all."

Grant nodded, then said, "That seems to be all we can check outside, we'd better take a look inside the main building."

Neeson swung around, suddenly changing direction. He pushed through the oncoming crowd, dodged past a large rotund woman, then caught his leg on a hard object. "Ah! Watch it will yer!" He rubbed his leg, where the foot of the stool had banged into him. "What's your fucking problem?"

"Pardon, Monsieur…"

Neeson looked perplexed at the unexpected reply, then scowled. He kept walking then as he rubbed his leg he turned around. "Bloody frogs!" he shouted gleefully.

"Sshh, we don't want to draw attention to ourselves." Grant caught hold of Neeson's lapel and pulled him along. "Just keep walking."

Neeson pushed his hand away and grinned. "That told him! Fucking French prick!"

***

King let out a deep breath. He had not seen Neeson until the last minute and by then it was too late. He had circled around the row of stalls and had come up behind the two men, momentarily losing them as he became stuck behind a group of people walking slower than the rest. The crowd had become compact; growing in both volume and density as the day went on. The last thing that King had expected was for the two men to change direction so suddenly.

Only his extensive training, quick thinking and brass neck had enabled him to bluff it out so well. A simple *sorry* would not have been sufficient. He could see from Neeson's retaliation that he was a violent man, ever-eager for a confrontation. However, if neither man spoke the same language, a confrontation would be pointless. King had assumed correctly that Neeson would not be familiar with another language, and was extremely grateful he had been proved correct. After all, he had just used up almost half his entire French vocabulary.

He watched the two men enter the main building, where the smaller, more delicate antiques were on display, as well as silverware and fine jewellery. There was a lot on display, but King felt that he had seen enough. Neeson would recognise him for sure, and there was no point in pushing his luck. He knew what the two men were up to; with his security training, it had been obvious from the first glance that the two men were carrying out a reconnaissance. Kempton Park was definitely the target for something.

King walked past the silver ring and out of the main entrance. He would return to his vehicle, manoeuvre it into a more practical position then wait for the two men to return to the Saab.

***

"Nothing special, is it?" Neeson commented flatly, as he led the way past a row of stalls.

"What, the stalls?" Grant asked, glancing at the vast array of valuables.

"No, the building," he paused at a stall, doing his best to appear interested. He turned to Grant who was watching an Orthodox Jew wearing a prayer shawl, or *Tallit*. The man was examining a diamond and sapphire encrusted necklace. "To think what a wealth of valuables are for sale in this drab building, not to mention the amount of money being carried around."

Grant nodded. "And bugger all in the way of security." He stared at the Orthodox Jew, who handed the necklace back to the woman behind the counter, then reached into his pocket as she smiled and started to wrap the necklace. To Grant's left, an Arab dressed in a white dish-dasha, complete with a business-suited minder carrying a metal briefcase chained to his wrist, studied antique silver at a neighbouring stall. Orthodox Jews and robe-clad Arabs in the same room. For a brief moment all beliefs and old scores looked to be forgotten. The only common interest was money and obtaining the best possible deal.

Grant turned back to Neeson, who was watching the Arab's minder unlock the briefcase. "Seems you might just as well have planned to do this venue. There's little or no security; an armed gang would have a fortune in no time. Besides, I think it would be more your style."

"What do you mean, more my style?"

"I mean, it's less complicated, quicker and there is a fortune in here," he paused, then glanced at the Arab and the Orthodox Jew. "You see that? Those two men couldn't be further apart in beliefs or ideals. Their countries and religion have been at conflict for centuries. And what are they doing? They're ignoring each other, and getting on with their business. I think that there's some sort of lesson in that, especially for you and your comrades."

Neeson sneered. "You have no idea." He looked around the densely populated room then turned towards Grant. "Come on hotshot, do what you were brought here for, and study the security systems." He walked away, radiating hostility through the crowd, elbowing his way through a barrier of people huddling around a particular stall.

Grant followed, quietly pleased with himself. He had succeeded in rattling the man's cage. He might well pay for it later, but for now, he was happy.

Neeson stood next to the double doors which would lead to the stairwell. To his right, a group of Hasidic Jews were examining each other's purchases. They talked in low voices, offering each other a small profit, or a part exchange on another deal. Grant caught up with Neeson, who was leaning against the drab, off-white wall. A huge plaster crack ran from the floor to the ceiling, and in places, huge flakes of dried gloss paint hung from the walls. "This leads to the central office. Just two flights of stairs stand between us and the safe." Neeson took a cursory glance around the room then pushed his way through the double doors.

Grant followed, noticing that the doors were fitted with a basic pressure connector alarm system. That would be no problem, just a simple snip with the wire-cutters and it would be easily defeated. He counted the steps, eleven in all, then a turn to the left. Another thirteen steps and they reached the top.

"Sorry, upstairs is off limits today." A tough-looking man in his mid-thirties stood to the right of the staircase, wearing a yellow vest, marked: SECURITY. He held a compact two-way radio and stared defiantly at the two men. "It isn't open up here until race day."

"Is that a fact?" Neeson asked somewhat mockingly, his Belfast accent, hard and confrontational.

"Sorry, we were just looking for the toilets," Grant explained, apologetically. The security guard stared at them, straight-faced, his arms folded across his chest. "Downstairs and on the right, just follow the smell."

Grant nodded, then turned around and walked down the first flight of stairs. Neeson caught him up before he reached the bottom and grabbed hold of his arm. "Where the hell are you off to?"

Grant pulled his arm back, breaking Neeson's grasp. "It's closed, if we'd stayed and argued, we would only have aroused suspicion. He would have radioed for assistance and we would have been escorted off the site, we may even have got arrested." Grant pushed his way through the double doors at the bottom of the stairwell, then picked his way through the growing crowd.

"Yer daft bastard!" Neeson chuckled. "He's half-ass security. Minimum wage has just come in and it would have been a fucking big raise for that tosser. I could have bought him off. For Christ's sake, I've got more in my pocket than he'll see in three months," he paused. "As a last resort, I could have done him."

Grant stopped just short of the side exit. "Don't judge everyone by your own standards, he liked his job. I could see that from the moment he opened his mouth. He relished telling us that it was off limits, not everyone can be bought," Grant sneered, eager to get one over on Neeson. "As for doing him, well, he looked pretty handy to me. I reckon he would have kicked your arse."

Neeson smiled wryly. He edged himself away from the doorway and lifted his jacket slightly, revealing the small semi-automatic pistol. The same pistol that had killed two men pushing their luck this morning. He let the material go, then patted Grant on the shoulder. "Doesn't matter how handy someone is; nobody wins a confrontation better than the man with the gun." He smiled then added, "As for buying people, they all give in, in the end. You did, we just threw in the extra little sweetener for free. And boy, is she sweet…"

24

"So what you are saying, old boy..." Forsyth paused to inhale and blow yet another perfect smoke ring. "Is that they actually intend to knock-off the race track?"

King nodded and replaced his coffee cup to the small wooden table, which was now covered with paperwork. "Either that or plant an IED…"

"A what?"

"An Improvised Explosive Device," King said. "A bomb."

"Well why on earth don't you just say *bomb*?"

King shrugged. "They were taking pictures of the CCTV system and the alarm systems. But all in all, there isn't a great deal in the way of security. Not cutting edge anyway. It could do with a huge update."

"Maybe if this assassination work doesn't work out you could become a security consultant…" Forsyth took another long drag on the cigarette.

King looked at the man, who seemed even more terse and argumentative than usual. What his colleagues in the special operations unit would say, *in need of a good softener*. A good punch in the face should just about do it. Instead, tempting though it was, King said, "I mean, enough money changes hands on the race days, but the only time that it would be worthwhile to pull something would be at the end of the day."

"Indeed," Forsyth mused.

"But surely that is when security would be at its tightest, until the money is off-loaded elsewhere, by ballistic-proof security vehicle. The money packed in cases with indelible dye canisters."

"One would presume so, yes." Forsyth stubbed the cigarette into ashtray on the table. "I will look into it, find out what the procedures are before, during and after the event. Although, I imagine that between the stewards, officials, security staff and even the cleaners, there must be a great deal of presence long after the public have left the site." He took his time to open the ornate silver cigarette case. "Of course, it could be a bombing. The whole Northern Ireland situation is in a right old pickle. Splinter groups abound, and there is a great divide between the political parties. What the republicans say isn't always what goes."

"So, what about Neeson and O'Shea, what is their official stance on the peace agreement?" King asked. "This team that came over for something, and it certainly looks like *something* is going to happen. What have Five said about them?"

Forsyth smiled wryly. "The details are a bit sketchy. All in all, they're fanatical about a united Ireland, but how they fare after the agreement, has not yet been determined."

"And why the need for Simon Grant? He's a safe-cracker." King stared thoughtfully past the MI6 officer, then shook his head decisively. "No, it has to be a robbery, there is no other explanation."

Forsyth carefully lit his cigarette then blew out a thin plume of sweet, sickly smelling smoke. "Yes there is, old boy, there always is," he smirked. "We just aren't seeing it yet."

***

"You can't be serious!"

"Aye, laddie, just you see if we're not!" O'Shea stared at Grant, he was hostile in both tone and manner. "You can do it. Do you not have initiative?"

Grant shook his head despairingly. "But we didn't even get to have a look upstairs!" He stood up, walked over to the window and looked out into the night. He couldn't see anything, the lights from within made the windows look like dark mirrors. "How the hell can I do the job if I haven't even checked out the security system properly? I have just been released from prison, I'm damned if I am going to go back because you want to rush this job instead of making a proper job!"

Neeson rose steadily to his feet and stared at him. "You have no other choice." He slipped his hand inside his jacket and pulled out the pistol. "Now sit your arse back down."

Grant knew that it was no empty threat, he could see the look in the man's eyes. The barrel of the pistol was fitted with the silencer and remained perfectly still in his unwavering hand. Grant had no idea what type of pistol it was, nor did he care. It was a gun, plain and simple, and the business end was pointing at him. He turned towards Holman, looking for support but could tell that none would come from that quarter.

"Sit down, son, and stop wasting precious time." Holman did not look at him; instead, he slowly shook his head. "You will not get another chance, mate." Grant walked back to the table, reluctantly pulled his chair straight then sat down in silence. Holman seemed a different man since the killing of the two men in the barn. He was monosyllabic and withdrawn. This was the first time he had spoken during the meeting.

Neeson smirked at Grant. "As I was saying, I think that we have a very good chance of success." He spread the newly developed photographs on the table. "I've been upstairs before. I've drawn a diagram of the area, it was only two weeks ago, it will be the same."

McCormick studied the photographs in front of him, then looked at Neeson with concern. "Danny, what are we supposed to do?" He glanced over at Grant, then looked back at his fellow Irishman. "I mean, Grant here will do the alarms, the cameras and the safe, but what's our job? We don't know anything about this sort of work."

"You know your instincts boys." O'Shea interjected. He looked at the four men in turn. "You don't want to get caught, do you? Of course not! So you now know enough about robbery."

"You lads will be guardian angels to golden bollocks here." Neeson nodded vaguely in Grant's direction. "You will get him into the building, you will take out any security personnel and you will carry the equipment in, and the money back out."

Patrick sat up in his seat. "Take out security with what?"

Neeson grinned, leaning back contentedly in his chair. "Some nice, shiny Colt M16-A2 Armalites. A gift from our American friends."

Patrick let out an exaggerated wolf whistle, then beamed a smile at the other three men before looking back at Neeson. "With grenade launchers fitted?"

Neeson laughed. "Leave it out, it's not fucking Christmas!"

Grant bowed his head and caught Holman's expression. They looked as sick as each other.

***

"Why is he so horrible to us mummy?" The boy looked tearfully into his mother's kind, yet somewhat distant eyes, then rested his head back down onto the soft pillow. She flicked a lock of her hair away from her forehead then smiled at her son as she pulled the covers up over his shoulders. "He's not, he's been very good to us."

The boy shook his head in silent protest. "He isn't, he shouts and hits us all the time. I don't like it when he makes you cry, mummy." He looked lovingly at his mother, his eyes glistening from his recent cry. "If I had a big gun, I would shoot him to make him stop hurting you."

Lisa sat up, propped herself onto her elbow and looked at him. "Now, darling, you mustn't say such things. Guns are terrible, evil things, nobody should ever want to shoot another person."

"I don't want to shoot another person; I only want to shoot *him*."

She looked down at her son, saddened by what he had just said. There really wasn't much she could say; the man's actions were taking away the boy's childhood, forcing him to think evil, murderous thoughts. Thoughts that no ten-year-old should ever have.

"I'd get a big gun, a machine gun," the boy smiled innocently. "Then I'd stop him from hurting us."

"He doesn't mean to, it's just his way, he's very sorry now." Lisa looked away, barely able to keep her tears back. She stroked his brow then reached under the covers and held his hand gently.

"I saw him hit you mummy, yesterday, in the kitchen," David paused, as he watched a single tear trickle down his mother's cheek then drip off the point of her chin and onto the clean duvet cover. "Why was he so nasty to you?"

Lisa hung her head. She knew what her son had seen. He had not been himself all day, and now she knew why. He had seen his own mother violated, raped. Now, he would carry that image around with him for the rest of his life. She nudged him over and lay back down beside him, holding him tightly in her comforting arms. They both stared at the ceiling. The arrangement of model airplanes hanging from fishing line. "Hush now, sweetheart, go to sleep." She rubbed the tears from her eyes, then squeezed him reassuringly. "You must never tell a soul what you saw. Please David, do it for mummy."

Her son nodded meekly, then cuddled into her. "Did daddy ever hurt you?"

"No."

"Why not?"

Lisa paused, almost losing herself in her own montage of memories. "Because he was a different person to Keith."

"Why did you leave daddy?"

She bit her lip in a desperate effort not to sob out loud. "I've told you, daddy had to go away. Mummy was so scared that she wouldn't have coped on her own."

"You wouldn't have been alone, mummy. You would have had me. We would have coped together."

She started to cry. "I'm sorry, David. Mummy is so very sorry."

"Keith said that daddy went to prison, he said that daddy will always be in prison. He says that I will end up in prison as well. Is that true, mummy?"

For an instant she had an image of her son, grown up and killing Keith with a machine gun, standing over him and desecrating the corpse with bullet after bullet, cutting the man into viscous lumps of flesh, innards and bone. She snapped the thought from her mind, sickened, scared. "Of course not," she said with conviction, then soothed her hand over her son's face. "Don't listen to him, your daddy will come and see us soon, he loves you dearly."

"Does he love you?"

Lisa closed her eyes. "I don't know."

David remained silent, his mind working overtime, with the simple, innocent logic that only children are blessed with, but inevitably lose with time. "Do you love him, mummy?"

Lisa rolled onto her side and stared, tearfully at the wall. She did not want her son to see her tears. "Yes. Yes, I do." There was a quiver to her voice, as she struggled not to be overcome with emotion. "I always have, and I'm sure that I always will."

***

Frank Holman swung the Mercedes into his gravel driveway and parked next to his wife's sports car. The outside security light came on, its motion sensor triggered by the movement of the vehicle. It would stay lit for another minute, giving him enough time to walk his considerable bulk across the drive and up the granite steps to the front door.

He heard the car before he saw it. It slowed rapidly, using both brakes, and an excessive amount of engine braking. It swung erratically into the driveway, throwing up a cloud of gravel in its wake. Holman realised that he was in its path and leapt out of the way in a less than graceful fashion. He squinted, blinded by the lights then bashfully realised that his leap had been prematurely judged, as the car stopped just short of his original position.

The driver switched off the vehicle's lights, finally allowing Holman to regain some composure and at the same time, recognise the intruder's identity.

The man behind the wheel of the gold BMW 740i made no attempt to leave his car, he merely lowered the electric window as Holman walked hesitantly around the bonnet. "I trust that all is well?" the man paused. "I have more than just money at stake in this, I will not accept failure."

"Everything is going according to plan, Mr Parker." Holman smiled nervously. "All aspects have been looked at and countered accordingly."

The man was tall, slim and gaunt, and had the eyes of a hawk. He nodded thoughtfully then stared coldly, directly into Holman's eyes. "And the Irish contingent are happy with the split?"

"Exceedingly. It seems that both sides will get the result that they want," Holman reassured him. "In a few days, we shall all be extremely wealthy men indeed."

Parker looked at Holman with distaste. "Only you are solely interested in wealth. Both the Irish and myself have an interest in this deal that is not merely financial. Just see that my interest is taken care of Holman, or your life will not be worth living." He raised the window three-quarters of the way without waiting for a reply, then started the engine. "Here," he said and held out an envelope, poking it through the six-inch gap. "That's the details of the safe. And there's more. Read it tonight and pass it on."

Holman took the envelope and stood back as the man accelerated out of the driveway as quickly as he had entered. Some of the gravel showered both of the cars, but Holman didn't care. There were more important things to worry about.

***

Forsyth sipped from his cup then replaced it to the saucer. He slipped another cigarette between his thin lips and fixed his eyes on King. "Tomorrow, I would suggest that you take another look at that barn." He casually flicked the wheel of his lighter, gazed dreamily into the flickering flame, then brought it to the tip of his cigarette. He inhaled deeply then rested his head against the back of his chair and blew a long, thin plume of the pungent smoke to the ceiling. "It would be jolly handy indeed, if we could have the place bugged. You have the equipment, don't you?"

King nodded cautiously. "Yes, but if it's to be done, it had best be done tonight. Preferably, it is a two-man job."

Forsyth nodded. "I am quite aware of that, old boy. However, I have other matters to attend to, so I'm afraid that you will be on your own." He smiled. "They're serving roast rib of beef at the club. I try never to miss it. So the business I have to take care of will be conducted there," he said casually. "Do you have dinner arrangements?"

"Looks like a corned beef sandwich in the van," King said sardonically. He knew Forsyth's problem, the underlying abrasiveness. The man was a graduate with a first class degree, and had let it be known that he had been recruited from Cambridge University in his final year. He most likely had an uncle in politics who had rubbed shoulders with the intelligence community, held the door open for him. Meanwhile, Alex King was born Mark Jeffries. He was the son of a prostitute from a council estate in south London and been expelled from school at fifteen with a list of qualifications that could have been written on a cigarette paper. After his mother had died from an overdose, King had gone into a string of care homes and eventually lost contact with his brothers and sisters. He was sent to prison for a string of offences from theft to assault, then finally for two counts of manslaughter when he was in his early twenties. King was a handy boxer. The two Royal Marines were abusive and drunk. King's fists were fast, the slate floors of the Portsmouth pub were hard and unforgiving. He had a temper which didn't stop when the two men were down. That wasn't the man he was now. He had been shown how to be more, to be a better man, to serve his country and he had vowed to as penance. He didn't have much in common with Forsyth, and Forsyth didn't have much time for the new influx of people being recruited into the service. But with the world getting tougher, MI6 had to get dirtier.

"Why the change of heart?" King asked.

"I'm sorry?"

"Well, earlier you just wanted them dead. Now you want more surveillance done."

"Bigger picture, old boy." Forsyth stared at his cigarette, which burnt lazily between his fingers. The smoke wafted through the air, creating an eerie haze in between them. "Perhaps you were right, old boy. Let's see what these buggers are up to. But I want them both dead before the peace agreement is signed."

"Both? Neeson is only sanctioned if he is a danger to civilians or stands in the way of O'Shea."

"Well, just see that he does," Forsyth said. "You know Alex; you need to learn to read between the lines in this sort of work. Danny Neeson has no right being a part of a peaceful solution to the troubles. He's killed too many people, ruined too many lives. And he'll be scheming and killing whether the peace agreement is signed or not."

King nodded. "And we'll hand our findings over to the police?"

"Of course," Forsyth nodded. "Now, tell me what equipment you have? One would hate for them to pick up their own conversations whilst they listened to breakfast radio."

King smiled at the thought. That sort of mistake had been known to have happened in the past. Many private investigators invest, foolishly so, in cheap, throwaway transmitters and receivers. These not only succeed in throwing television and radio reception out of sync, but all too often, the targets get to hear their own conversations as they listen to the radio. "No, it's the latest equipment, produced by a private firm in Switzerland. As you know, the private sector produces the best quality gear."

"Oh, I know that, old boy. It just costs a bloody fortune though."

King nodded. "Only the best will do. Most transmitters put out a signal at around 375MHZ and most scanners can only reach 485MHZ. But these can put out at over twice that, and are on a dedicated frequency."

"Jolly good, old boy," Forsyth replied, apparently uninterested and equally unimpressed. "See if you can get close enough to plant some visual equipment. Eyes *and* ears. Remember that O'Shea goes down in two days. Don't lose sight of that," he paused, somewhat ponderously. "By the way, what equipment do you want for the take-down?"

Take-down. That was a new one. Now King had heard it all. It sounded more like a lion killing a gazelle on the plains of the Serengeti. He couldn't help wondering where the likes of Forsyth, the men who called the shots within the very fabric of Britain's intelligence services, got their phrases from. Did they go to special classes where they would be taught a hundred different dispassionate ways to refer to a man's execution? Did they take special training to become so dangerously out of touch with the rest of the world? Or were they simply born that way? Sheltered by money and influence, shaped at public boarding schools from the age of three, socially educated in the holidays by a governess, and finely chiselled at either of the two universities. The only two universities that seemed to matter to the supposedly well-bred; so much so that they hold their own exclusive boat race every year, comfortable in the knowledge that the off-spring of the working class cannot beat them by default. The cliques that shadowed the corridors of power are not so far removed from the men raised in such a way, to them, it is perfectly normal.

King studied the man curiously. The SIS officer sat almost regal in his immaculate appearance, pontificating on a man's death, smoking his eastern-scented, hand-rolled cigarettes at around a pound each, and asking for the summary execution equipment as if it were a shopping list for the local supermarket. King suddenly snapped out of his thoughts. He was here for a job, albeit one he had been ordered to do, but a job all the same. It was what he agreed to sign up to. Do it, then get on to the next mission. "I want a machine pistol, or carbine, something with a suppressor."

"What about your pistol, can't you do it with that?"

King shook his head. This was his speciality; he would call the shots. "No, I want something that requires less precision. I'll keep the Browning as a back-up weapon. A Heckler and Koch MP5 SD will do the job, four magazines and one hundred and twenty rounds of nine-millimetre ammunition."

"Somewhat excessive, is it not?" Forsyth looked doubtful as to the choice of weapon.

King did his best to remain composed. Forsyth's opinion on this matter was entirely unwanted. "No, I don't consider that to be excessive at all. In fact, I haven't finished yet. If Danny Neeson is to be killed as well, then I have to consider the odds. These are seasoned pros. And Neeson is hardly ever away from O'Shea's side. I don't want to be caught out when the time comes," he paused, keeping his eyes firmly fixed on Forsyth's own. "And I want a shotgun. A pump action, .12 gauge of course. Remington or Winchester if possible, five shot minimum, with a box of twenty-five 00 buckshot, in three-inch magnum."

"What the hell for?" he asked, shaking his head. "It sounds like you're planning a blood bath!"

"It's always a blood bath, Ian," he said quietly. "For me, it's simply a matter of how many and how often."

25

King switched off the van's headlights and crawled along the road, guided only by the light from the half-moon in the relatively cloud-free sky. He had decided to approach from the other direction. Not wanting to become a creature of habit, he would park further down the road and travel across the fields from the other side of the private lane into the property. Although he was now entering the unknown, it was never good practice to become complacent through familiarity.

He pulled into a side turning then switched off the engine. The lights from the farmhouse were clearly visible from his distance of approximately half a mile. He would wait and watch, not making a move until he felt ready. The lights might well stay on all night, from this distance he had no way of telling what kind of light it was. It could well be that it was an outside light, permanently in operation to deter unwanted visitors. If that were the case, he would not know until he got close enough for a more thorough look.

He glanced at the luminous dials of his watch. It was zero-one-thirty hundred hours. In the dark it could well take him an hour to cover the ground, avoiding obstacles or keeping alert for the opposition, should they have a roving patrol in operation.

Next to him, resting on the passenger seat, was a small backpack containing all the equipment that he would need: a small tool-kit, consisting mainly of screwdrivers in various sizes, a hand-operated drill with a selection of drill-bits, a staple gun, a set of professional pick-locks, four voice-activated transmitters approximately the size of a small box of matches and a pinhole camera fitted with a fibre-optic lens.

On his previous visit, King had gone to the farm unarmed. The heavy manpower present, and the broad daylight, had meant that if he had indeed been sighted he would most probably have been captured, and his weapon would have proven his hostile intentions. But on this occasion, he had the one thing on his side that should help him evade any force the enemy could deploy: The dark.

He knew that if he was compromised at this hour, no amount of excuses would save him, his only option was to go in armed. He reached into the glove box and retrieved his 9 mm Browning HP-35 pistol. The design was over sixty years old, yet it remained a firm favourite with many professional marksmen and military forces around the world. He released the thirteen-round magazine, and checked the pistol's action. Once satisfied that it was free and clear, he inserted the magazine and pulled back the slide, chambering the first round. With the safety applied, the weapon could be brought into use with just the flick of his thumb upon the safety catch. He placed the pistol on the passenger seat then clipped the soft leather holster to his belt, just above and in front of his left hip. King favoured the cross-draw. Next, he checked that his bootlaces were firmly fastened, with the ends tucked inside, before carefully opening the door and stepping onto the soft earth. He swung the backpack over his shoulders, then checked that nothing would rattle or flap with his movements. Finally, he slipped the luminous watch off his wrist and tucked it into his pocket. Only a small detail but they are the ones that let you down if ignored. The luminous dials could disclose his position to the well-trained eye.

Once across the road and over the fence, he kept close to the hedge, taking the precaution to stop and crouch every thirty-metres or so. He would hold his breath, minimising background noise, then he would listen out for the slightest, misplaced sound. In early spring the countryside is alive at night. Rabbits or foxes bolting through the hedgerows, the call of an owl, the rustle of bats emerging to hunt, and probably a hundred other sounds, but to the trained or experienced ear, these sounds are all in their place, just nature doing what nature so noisily does. What he was checking for was any form of patrol. If the players were keeping it tight, it would not be out of character to mount a roving patrol; after all, it did happen in Ireland - both in the north and in the south.

He preferred not to rely on night-vision aids although on some occasions they were necessary. In these conditions, relatively cloud-free, with a half moon, he favoured his instincts every time. At moments like this he felt at his most alive - as alive as anyone could be, thriving on the adrenaline rush. Some people sought the same feeling from such activities as skiing or skydiving, others obtain it directly from drugs, but all King ever needed was the primal source that came with the real chance of combat.

He rose steadily to his feet, keeping his movements slow and purposeful. After a further thirty-metres he reached the brook. The wire fence was just a few steps beyond. He wanted to avoid getting his feet wet, as the sound of sodden boots is highly audible at night when sound is amplified five-fold because of the loss of ambient noise. He took a few steps backwards then ran, taking off at the last minute, clearing the brook but landing heavily on the other side. He crouched low, holding his breath for a moment, then breathed deeply but steadily, listening out for any signs of the opposition. Confident that he was alone, he rose slowly, advancing towards the wire fence.

On this approach the fence was doubled, with a strand of barbed wire near the ground as well as one at waist level. He eased himself between the two lines of wire, careful not to snag his backpack on the top line. He was not worried about the chance of the fence being electrified, but more concerned that it might have been rigged to detect movement. Had he wanted to check for an electric current, he would have dabbed a length of grass on the wire and would only have felt a mild tingle, no matter how high the voltage. However, as he was sure that he could fit between the strands so there seemed little point in being over-cautious. Operating effectively always required a balance between sophisticated training and common sense: when to use the knowledge obtained, and when to choose to ignore it.

He walked the slight gradient, placing his steps around the large tufts of thistles and other weeds that had been allowed to thrive through neglect. As he reached the top of the field, he paused in the gateway and studied the farmhouse and its surroundings. The light that he had originally seen from the road shone from an upstairs room, most probably coming from a bedroom or an upper corridor. In the courtyard two new arrivals accompanied the Sierra: a saloon, possibly a Ford

Mondeo or a Rover 600 series, from this distance King could not be certain. Next to the saloon was a small hatchback, again he could not identify the make or model.

He looked over at the barn, which was completely shrouded in darkness and appeared to be empty. After a brief pause to assess potential danger, he eased himself over the gate, careful to distribute his weight evenly, not wanting to put too much trust in it. Crouching low to keep his movement and silhouette unseen, he studied both the house and the barn. One would be easier than the other. The choice was his.

***

As he lay on the bed unable to sleep, Simon Grant stared thoughtfully at the ceiling. He tried to make sense of it all, but too much failed to add up. The location itself was perfect. The security precautions were second-rate, both in systems and personnel, although Grant was aware of the possibility that extra security staff might be hired for the event. If so, most likely from a first rate company. It was true, the racecourse administration would be holding a great deal of money, but the whole job seemed more tailored to an armed robbery, not forced entry followed by safecracking and security overrides. The Irish would be armed to the teeth: although Grant knew nothing about guns and had no idea what M16 Armalites looked like, the men who did have experience in such matters had obviously been pleased with them.

The most important area to be viewed - the offices that would be holding the money - had been off limits. He only had Neeson's description of what it would be like, and Grant preferred to take that with a pinch of salt. Then there was Holman. A man whom Grant had once been able to call a friend. Frank Holman had even attended his and Lisa's wedding. The two men had gone back years, almost as long as he could remember. Grant and Frank Holman had grown up together on a high-rise council estate in south London. Frank had always been up to something, always in trouble with the police but usually successfully avoiding them. With his flashy suits, the cars that he drove, his jewellery and expensive-looking counterfeit watches, he had become something of a role model for the younger boys on the estate. Frank Holman had taken Grant under his wing, and they had been partners in crime ever since.

Holman was in this up to his eyeballs. If Grant's family had been used to coerce him, then what could they possibly be holding on Holman?

***

King stood with his back to the stone wall of the barn. Its construction was clearly different to what he had first anticipated. The side furthest from the road and the side of the adjoining corner were constructed from solid stone, the other two sides were finished with timber planks. King guessed that the building had decayed over the years, and had been repaired, like so many farms, on a tight budget.

He edged his way along the side of the barn, feeling the wall as he went, testing it for strength. It was sturdy, which was not what he wanted. He needed to be able to drill through the wall with the minimum amount of resistance. He watched his step, placing his feet carefully on the uneven ground and avoiding the clutter that had been discarded between the building and the overgrown hedge. When he reached the timber side of the barn, he stopped and carefully removed the backpack from his shoulders. Inside, everything had been packed securely, each tool in the order in which it would be needed. He reached inside and removed a small, soft leather pouch. He unfastened it and took out a small black box, approximately the size of a cigarette packet. Attached to the box were two wires - one with an earpiece, the other connected to a disk about the size of a ten pence coin. He slipped the earpiece into his ear, and then pressed the button on the side of the box. His ear filled with the sound of distorted atmospherics then fell silent as he gently turned the tuning dial. He pressed the disk against the wall and adjusted the volume control. The device magnified the sound from within the barn one hundred times. It was now imperative that he did not drop or scrape the device, if he did, the magnified sound could well shatter his eardrum.

He heard the unmistakable sound of breathing and estimated that there were at least three people sleeping in the building. He moved the device cautiously, taking care not to knock it against the wall, then placed it gently against a flat piece of stone. He could tell that there was another sleeper, on his own by the sound of it. He took a few more paces, watching where he placed his feet, then, as he reached the join where the stone and timber construction met, he placed the device carefully against the wood. A welcoming silence. He walked the last ten-feet, then placed the device against the door. There was no sound. He adjusted the volume control, and could hear the faint sound of breathing in the distance, which meant that the timber part of the building must be empty, a separate unit in itself.

He removed the earpiece and switched off the device before returning it to the leather pouch and dropping it back inside the backpack. He decided that the side door, next to the large double doors, would be the best point of entry. Given that there were so many people within the building, he seriously doubted that it would be locked. He carefully felt around the door-jam, on the off chance that it would be alarmed or booby-trapped, then, satisfied that it was clear, he tried the door handle. To his relief it clicked open and pushed easily inwards. The moonlight beaming through the two windows at the far end of the barn, illuminated the storage area sufficiently for him to make his way across to where the vehicle was parked, shrouded by a covering of white sheets.

He lifted the fringe of a sheet, and even in the gloom, instantly recognised the vehicle as one of his lottery daydream favourites - a Porsche 911. He replaced the material and walked over to the old tractor, which was parked beside the far wall.

Normally he would have only planted a transmitter in a static position, but he noticed that one of the machine's well-worn tyres was flat. The rim of the wheel was misshapen and the tyres on the other wheel looked to be perforated. From the look of it, the tractor had seen better days. About thirty years ago. Confident that the tractor would not be moved in the near future, King bent down beside the nearside rear wheel and eased the backpack off his shoulders. He reached inside and retrieved a small plastic box then opened it to reveal a selection of dedicated frequency transmitters. He selected one, around an inch square with a twelve-inch strand of wire hanging out of it. This was the antenna and if it touched the rim of the wheel the tractor itself would act as a frequency booster, becoming the aerial.

The transmitter was voice-activated and had been fitted with a new battery, less than two hours ago, which would give it an effective life of five-days continuous use. King reached around the rear of the wheel, placing the transmitter on the brake pad, letting the antenna trail to the rim of the wheel. Next, he walked over to the far timber wall, dropped the backpack onto the ground and took out the hand drill. He placed the bit against the wood, then gently started to turn the handle.

Wood, especially tannin-treated timber of the type used in the barn's construction, tends to splinter when drilled, so when installing surveillance equipment, where the whole point is for it to be fitted quickly and to remain undetected, it is best to drill from the inside and lessen the chance of detection. After a couple, of minutes drilling he had a large enough hole, and replaced the drill in his equipment bag. He would not be able to install the pinhole camera from this side, but once the hole is prepared, installation takes less than a minute.

He reached into the bottom of the backpack and took out the next transmitter, which was ingeniously disguised as a piece of dog's excrement. Placed strategically on the floor, it is the one object that nobody tends to be keen to pick up and examine. Its one drawback was that it could only be placed on the floor, whereas a transmitter's best clarity comes from waist to head level. King smiled as he placed the dog's business on the soil floor next to the wall. It was an extremely clever design, which had fooled the players every time so far. He picked up a handful of straw and carefully scattered it over the device.

King stood up straight and looked all around the barn. It was a good size, and full of farm tools and machinery. He did not know much about agriculture, but he recognised a plough and a chain contraption he had once seen a farmer towing around a field. It was a harrow, or so he thought. Next to it there was a large bundle of polythene, tied with bailer twine. The bundle was around six-feet or so long, maybe a bit more, and four-feet in diameter. King walked over to it and crouched down for a closer look. He prodded it. It was soft but gave a little resistance. He tugged at a fold and opened an edge. He figured what it was before he saw the dead man's face. It was still a shock, but he processed it quickly. From the size of the bundle he figured that it was the bodies of both men he had seen beaten and dragged into the barn. He tucked the fold of plastic back and stood back up. *Poor sods*, he thought. King had no idea who the two men had been, nor of their integrity, but he could imagine how it had gone down. It would have been a terrifying end. It made him think about the task ahead of him, whether he could do it when it finally played out. He had killed before, but fuelled by alcohol and in the days when he was a hot-head. A young man driven only by ego and a need, a desire, to be respected. He hadn't intended it, but it had happened nonetheless. Since his training, it had been talked about, and he was sure he would be fine with it, but seeing the two men, dead and discarded, gave him something to think about. It would be easier to kill if he held all the aces, but easier to live with if it was in the heat of a standoff, with both men having a fighting chance. But it wasn't all about him, it was about the mission. And the mission needed to succeed.

He decided to plant one more transmitter just in case of damage or technical failure. He walked over to the window and felt along the top of the rusty metal frame. Clumps of straw and dust fell, along with a couple of large spiders. It would be perfect; it had obviously not been disturbed for quite some time, if ever. He took a transmitter out of the plastic case and carefully placed it on top of the window frame, then trailed out the length of antenna. This one would probably provide the best reception, with the transmitter at the perfect height for audio quality.

King walked into the centre of the barn and checked his surroundings. Satisfied that he had left everything undisturbed, he walked to the doorway and cautiously stepped out into the night. With the door carefully closed behind him, he eased himself down the side of the building, running his right hand over the wood, at the approximate height that he had drilled the hole. Realising that he had found the spot, when he snagged his finger on a protruding splinter, he dropped his pack to the ground and squatted on his haunches while he retrieved the relevant equipment. A pinhole camera is basically a length of fibre-optic cable with a tiny lens and receiver unit. The lens is pushed through the wall or obstruction and the receiver unit picks up the image and relays it to a base receiver, utilising the same system that is used by mobile telephones.

King gently eased the lens through the hole, which was a tight fit, but far better than too loose as the hole needed to remain unnoticeable. It would also hold the lens in place and not allow it to skew off centre. On the rear of the lens unit, he had applied a small piece of tape with an arrow made in pen, which acted as a marker. He had seen the results of hastily fitted fibre optic lenses, and had seen playbacks of people who appeared to sit on the ceiling and walk up walls. He twisted the lens until his marker was at the top, then let the twelve-inch length of cable hang free. At the bottom of the cable were the receiver and transmitter, which would be capable of sending an image up to four miles on a similar frequency to that of the three audio transmitters. The whole system was movement activated, which in turn eliminated the need for constant viewing on a display monitor.

With the surveillance systems in place King's task at the barn was complete, but deep down, and as risky as it was, he knew that the farmhouse would be the place where most of the sensitive business would be discussed. He stared towards the eastern horizon, then took his watch out of his pocket. It was nearly half-past-three. Dawn would not be breaking for some time yet. If he moved immediately, he might just have enough time.

He peered around the side of the barn and noted that the light that had shone from upstairs was no longer on. He studied the house intently. He had achieved what he had set out to do, this would just be a bonus, but one which he had not planned for. He just hoped that it would not prove to be an unnecessary risk.

Keeping to the relative safety of the shadows, he moved quickly across the courtyard then paused behind the large limestone wall that separated the farmyard from the unkempt garden. He kept his wary eyes on the house, then gave the courtyard behind him a cursory glance. So far, so good.

He placed both hands on top of the stone wall then in one smooth motion, vaulted the obstacle and landed softly on the damp grass. He crept up the concrete pathway, then placed the backpack carefully on the doorstep. The door was rustic in design, a traditional stable type, split into two equal parts. He tried the handle, but as he had expected, it was locked. No harm in trying though. He reached into his bag of tricks and withdrew a small tool kit. Inside the kit was a piece of neatly folded crepe paper. He unfolded it, smoothing out the creases, then slipped it under the door. Next, he took out a length of thick wire and gently inserted it into the lock. He felt what he had hoped for; the key was in place. Like most people, whoever had locked the door had ignored one of the most basic rules of personal security. He pushed the wire gently, gradually easing the key out of the lock. He tensed as the key fell to the floor, but as it bounced on the layer of crepe paper, it made next to no sound. King turned for a quick, cursory glance around, to make sure that he did not become so absorbed in his work that he became complacent. Then he returned to his task, and gently pulled the crepe paper back towards him, revealing the key, which glistened in the moonlight. Relieved, he picked it up and placed it smoothly into the lock. The lock, although rusty in appearance from the outside, opened easily. He pulled down on the handle and pushed the top half of the door inwards, then reached inside, caught hold of the bolt and gently opened the bottom half of the door.

King opened the backpack and took out a roll of cloth. He unwrapped it, then separated the two pieces of material. Each piece had been specially made, and consisted of a foot-shaped piece of cotton with elasticated seams. He bent down and quickly placed the pieces over his feet, the elastic holding the makeshift footwear in place. Now he did not have to worry about tell-tale muddy footprints on the tiled floor. He cautiously stepped inside, observing his surroundings, studying every detail, so as to disturb nothing.

Used cups and glasses cluttered the pine table in the centre of the room, and this first glance told King that this room, like kitchens in most houses, was the focal point. He wasted no time, quickly taking the box of transmitters from his pack. He selected a voice-activated transmitter that would put out its signal on a secondary frequency, then walked over to the dresser.

It was a strain lifting out the large piece of furniture, yet trying to remain silent. He eased one side of it back, tensing suddenly as it squeaked on the quarry tiles. He held his breath, listening out for any sound that would tell him he had been detected, but all he could hear was the sound of his own pulse, pounding savagely in his ears.

King relaxed a little, satisfied that he was in the clear. He peeled off the self-adhesive sticker from the back of the transmitter and carefully pressed it against the rear of the dresser, making sure that the antenna hung down free from any obstructions.

This time, he was ready for the dresser to stick against the quarry tiles, and avoided the sound by lifting from the corner. He had just replaced it back to its original position, when he heard the thud from upstairs. He tensed, his heart pounding voraciously. The sound had been clearly audible through the thin, uneven ceiling. He stood stock-still, waiting for another sound, praying that the first had just been a one-off.

It wasn't.

The thud was accompanied by another, clearly recognisable as footsteps on a hard, wooden floor. King snatched up the backpack, drew the Browning from its holster and bolted for the door. He quietly opened both doors and slipped outside, just as he heard the door open upstairs. He frantically closed the bottom door and re-bolted it, trying to strike a balance between speed and stealth. The footsteps became louder, then ceased altogether. He could hear running water, as he gently slipped the key into the lock, then, as he started to pull the top door towards him, he heard the sound of a toilet flushing. He dropped the pack to the ground and reached inside for the tool kit, which was housed in a soft leather case. He frantically pulled the case apart and caught hold of the required instrument. He raised his head, listening intently. He could hear the sound of approaching footsteps; whoever was up and about was coming down the stairs. The tool that he had selected for the task was a slim pair of pliers, which looked not unlike a pair of exaggerated tweezers. He carefully slipped them into the lock and caught hold of the tip of the key, the magnetised tips almost guiding him, before clamping down tight. His hands were shaking slightly, a response that he had seldom felt before. Maybe it was because someone was getting far too close, or maybe it was because he was operating alone and had no back-up. Either way, he did not spend time analysing it; he merely bit the side of his cheek and concentrated on the task at hand. He eased the key backwards a touch, closed the top half of the stable door, then turned the pliers anti-clockwise, through a three-hundred and sixty-degree rotation. He heard the click of the lock as it rotated a full turn, then he hastily snatched the pliers out from the lock.

The door opened and the light came on instantly, almost blinding King through the glass of the top door. He dropped down out of sight and quickly gathered up the bag of equipment, before hastily retreating across the garden and over the stone wall.

He hesitated behind the wall. From this vantage point and could clearly see a man filling a kettle at the kitchen sink. King wiped his brow and slipped the pistol back into the holster. Although it was cool outside he was perspiring by the bucket load. That had been far too close.

***

Simon Grant placed the kettle on top of the gas ring and turned the igniter. It clicked rapidly for a few seconds, then exploded into life, the blue flame playing off the bottom of the kettle and enveloping the sides. He adjusted the dial, settling the flame, then walked over to the window and stared out into the night.

It would be easy to escape, simply open the door and run. He had many friends in London, and to the south on the coast. Friends who would help him lie low, help him to rebuild his life. Unless Frank Holman had got to them as well and paid them off. Unlikely, but it seemed that money could buy anybody.

They had been clever. They had known that he might want to pull out, so to hedge their bets, they had played one extra chip. There was no way that they could lose, now. Lisa and David Grant were their insurance policy. If he did not co-operate, they would be killed. Simple. Grant closed his eyes, filling his mind with images of his son. His four-year old son, who had cried on his one and only prison visit. David was ten-years old now, yet Grant could not picture him. He had seen him fleetingly at the school steps, but even now, when he closed his eyes he struggled to picture him. The realisation that he did not know his son made him want to weep. He wiped a tear from his eye, and walked over to the table. He pushed an empty cup aside, rested his elbows on the table, and buried his face in his hands.

If he could get to Lisa in time, would she want him? Or would she be settled and in love with this man? There was so much to think about, and so little choice. Deep down, he knew that he had no option but to proceed as planned. He was penned in, a prisoner once more. Grant seriously doubted their chances of success at the racetrack, and it was almost too easy to wish for the relative safety of prison.

Every way he looked, the view was bleak.

***

King placed the heavy box of equipment on the ground at the foot of the large beech tree, and picked up the long rubber aerial. He took two rubber clamp-ties out of the box and carefully strapped the twelve-foot aerial to the tree. The rubber-coated aerial, which had come in three screw-in segments, was connected to the power unit by a length of fibre-optic cable, which in turn, connected with the receiver and the secure transmitter. He screwed the length of fibre-optic cable into the receiver unit, then covered it with the camouflaged plastic weather covering. He bent down and scraped up a handful of twigs and loose leaves, then scattered them over the covering. King seriously doubted that the relay system would be detected. From the look of this area of woodland, although it was only about a hundred-metres from the road, nobody ever came here.

The unit was powered by a car battery, and would give the system six days of unlimited use. The audio and visual recordings would be transmitted from the farm and received by the large rubber aerial and receiver. In turn, these recordings would be transmitted on a secure airwave, of unlimited range, to King's master receiver at the flat which he and Ian Forsyth had made their base for the life of the operation.

26

O'Shea beamed an enthusiastic smile as he walked briskly into the kitchen. "Morning, lads," he called breezily to the four Irishmen, who stared blankly at him, obviously puzzled by his easy mood. "Change of plan, we go tomorrow."

McCormick looked up, apparently concerned. "What's the problem?" he asked.

Neeson walked into the kitchen a few paces behind O'Shea and glared at McCormick disdainfully. "Nothing for you to worry on," he paused. "You're paid to do your job, not ask fucking questions."

"I'm not paid at all," McCormick said, then looked to backtrack when he caught Neeson's eye. "I'm in it for the cause," he said. "Like we all are, or should be."

"You wouldn't be saying that I'm not, would you Matt?" Neeson asked. "I wouldn't recommend bringing my loyalty to the cause up again."

"I wasn't," McCormick countered hesitantly. "I just don't understand all this heist shit. I get planting a bomb for the police to try and find. I get shooting a soldier. I don't really get this."

O'Shea held up a hand to stop Neeson from answering. He looked at McCormick and the other three men in turn. "There are dark days ahead of us. We've decommissioned weapons and have to hand over locations of weapon caches to the British as part of the agreement. Funds have been set by to hand over as well." O'Shea shook his head. "But what about when the Brit bastards go back on their word? What about when they wage a secret war on us? We'll have little funds and a limited arsenal to take the fight back to them. This *heist*, as you call it Matt, is one of many scheduled this week around the mainland to look after our futures. They have been aimed as a shot in the arse for the British. And all in the last few days before the peace agreement has been signed. The British won't connect the dots until it is too late. By then, we'll have our boys out of prison, in line with the terms of the agreement."

"Fucking win-win," Neeson laughed. "A load of new funds, clean and unaccounted for. And our lads back where they belong. English muppets!" He walked around the table, pulled out a chair and sat down. He smiled at Dugan, then reached out and swiped a sausage from the little man's plate. "Where's Grant?"

Dugan stared dejectedly at the half-eaten sausage in Neeson's hand, then nodded towards the ceiling. "Upstairs, not sure if he slept too good," he replied in his soft monotone.

Patrick roared with laughter. "Best not tell him we go tomorrow; he'll not sleep tonight for sure!"

"Mister O'Shea," McCormick said respectfully. "How can the job move forward if it's money from the race that we're after?"

"Ah for fuck's sake…" Neeson looked at him.

Again, O'Shea held up a hand. "We have a man on the inside. He has delivered the information on the safe to us, and he has also informed us that on day one there will not only be the tote money for the first day's betting wins, but forecast betting figures for day two. Essentially, day one will carry more money because the odds favour runners on day one more. Day two should be the bookmakers' day. Also, day two will have more staff in place."

The six men all turned simultaneously as the door opened and Grant appeared in the doorway. His bloodshot eyes sat deeply in dark, skeletal sockets, and his face was a ghastly, ashen grey. It looked as if he had had no sleep for a week.

"Aye, the main man!" O'Shea beamed a yellow-toothed grin, oblivious to the man's sickly appearance, then winked at the others around the table. "Got some news, not sure you'll like it though."

Patrick shook his head despondently, then grinned. "His heart's not in it, you just see if I'm wrong."

Grant glared at the big man. "Piss-off, ginger!" he snapped. "You haven't had your family's lives threatened to get you here!" Grant shook his head and walked over to where the kettle was boiling away on the gas stove. He threw a tea bag into an oversized mug, then lifted the kettle and poured the hot water. He turned around and stared at Patrick defiantly. "If you had, I seriously doubt that you'd find room for a smile on that ugly face of yours."

For a second, Patrick looked as if he was going to respond to the insult with physical violence, but he suddenly relented. Instead, he looked down at his hands, shame appearing on his face. Grant stared at McCormick, Dugan and Liam. He could tell that none of them had known. That piece of information had been the preserve of the few at the top.

"Well..." O'Shea said, breaking the awkward silence that Grant's outburst brought on. "Behave yourself, and tomorrow, you'll be a very wealthy man indeed. And, your wife and wee one will be safe." O'Shea turned to the other men and nodded towards the door. "Go on now, get yourselves over to the barn, you've all got work to do."

***

King sat up in his seat and shouted to Forsyth. "They're going out to the barn. Come and take a look!" He turned back to the monitor and adjusted the volume. Forsyth walked out from the kitchen, a tray of tea and biscuits in his hands.

King glanced over his shoulder at him, then returned to the monitor in anticipation. "I just heard why Grant is mixed up in all of this," he said, helping himself to a biscuit. "He had his family threatened."

Forsyth stared forlornly at the empty space where the lone chocolate-coated crinkle crunch had been, then dejectedly picked up a plain digestive.

The picture flickered, as the sudden movement activated the lens, then both men were able to observe Mark O'Shea walk into the barn, followed by the others. There was a momentary delay between the audio and the visual, but nothing that should prove too tiresome. "Didn't have the time for a more sophisticated system, just one pair of hands, I'm afraid," he said, tongue in cheek.

Forsyth sipped from his cup of tea then shook his head vigorously before saying, "Nonsense old boy, you've done a remarkable job."

"The farmhouse comes up on a different receiver. That way, we can tape conversations in each location." He picked up his cup of tea, then patted the other receiver. "The job is going ahead tomorrow. Grant doesn't seem too impressed."

Forsyth nodded his acknowledgement, then rubbed his chin thoughtfully. "I suppose we could put a close protection team on his family," he mused, then shook his head. "But then again, just for two people, I don't think that it would be worth the risk or resources."

"Resources?"

"Yes."

"Is it worth checking higher up the SIS ladder?"

"I shouldn't have thought so, old boy."

"So Grant's wife and child don't matter?"

"I think they're separated."

"They are," said King. "And last time I checked, the lives of a woman and child still mattered."

"Bigger picture, old boy," replied Forsyth. "Look, it doesn't matter if it gets us O'Shea. That is the operation. Now, if they were going to put a bomb in a shopping centre, then I would risk the operation to keep the public safe. But this woman is someone who has mixed in the criminal fraternity for most of her life. She's happy to do that for the life she's lived."

"And the boy?"

"It probably won't come to it."

"Probably?"

"No," Forsyth said sharply. "Now shush, I want to listen…"

King bit his lip, refraining from further comment. Only a man like Forsyth would disregard an innocent woman and her child as not worth the risk. Personally, King didn't care for the bigger picture. As pictures went, it wasn't the best he'd seen.

They watched Neeson open a trunk. He pulled out a bundle and placed it carefully on the earth floor. He opened it up and stood back.

"There you go lads, America's finest," He paused for dramatic effect as the men stared at the weapons on the ground, each coated in an oily smear of factory gun oil. *"Enjoy."*

King leaned in towards the screen. "M16's," he said. "Or AR-15's. And a whole load of magazines."

"Damn and blast!" Forsyth shifted in his seat and studied the pile of weaponry on the ground.

"Four, I think," King guessed what the other man was thinking. "They could do a lot of damage with those."

"One each lads. Just help yourselves. And four clips a piece." Neeson paused and grinned. *"Don't be afraid to use them, the bastards do call us terrorists after all!"*

"What are clips?" Forsyth asked.

"Magazines. It's not accurate though, the term goes back to world war one. Bullets clipped onto a small rail and were slotted down into either a fixed or detachable magazine. They saved weight and metal." King glanced up at Forsyth, but the man didn't seem interested. "Those are magazines."

"Thanks for the history lesson," Forsyth chided.

"You asked."

There were whoops and cheers as the four men collected their weapons.

"Go and check them over, but don't fire them. The sights are factory-fitted so you'll just have to take your chances with them. They should be bang-on though. Besides, you won't really need sights, it will all be close work." Neeson turned around, as Grant walked into the entrance of the barn, carrying his mug of tea casually in his left hand. *"I've got your kit in the car, you can make yourself useful and give me a hand."* Grant went to place his mug on the ground, but thought better of it when he noticed a pile of dog's excrement. He looked around, then placed the mug on top of a nearby upturned oil drum and followed Neeson outside.

King's heart rate was beginning to subside. He had felt sure that Grant was going to detect the transmitter. He sat back in his seat and looked across at Forsyth, who was beginning the ritual of lighting one of his handmade cigarettes. "This is recording, isn't it, old chap?" Forsyth asked, not taking his eyes from his cigarette. He slipped it between his thin lips then inhaled deeply, with apparently life-giving effect.

"Yes," King replied, as he watched Forsyth sink back in his chair to appreciate the soothing smoke. "The audio is running as well. As soon as anyone speaks, the whole system is activated." The men on the screen were busy loading the weapon's magazines with 5.56 mm full metal-jacketed ammunition. King turned to Forsyth, who was watching the monitor intently. "What about Mark O'Shea? He's meant to go down tomorrow or the day after."

Forsyth blew out a plume of pungent smoke, then furrowed his brow. "I know, but to tell you the truth, I find myself somewhat intrigued. If we can bag this lot, and secure the money, which would no doubt go towards PIRA funds, we will be glory boys, through and through." He inhaled on his cigarette and ponderously released a perfect smoke ring across the room. "Might just help my career prospects out no end. Yours too, old boy. This peace agreement will affect the likes of us. The middle east threat isn't what it's made out to be. Saddam Hussain is finally playing ball now that he's been given a bloody nose. People like us need feathers in our caps, otherwise when things go slack, we'll be swept along in the subsequent layoffs."

King couldn't imagine a time when the middle-east didn't pose a threat, but he was merely a foot soldier. "I think it would be best if the hit went ahead as planned, things could soon spiral out of control," he ventured, watching him, but the man seemed more intent on blowing another smoke ring. "It could cut both ways; we could become *glory boys*, as you say. Or, or we could become the biggest joke within the intelligence and security community. If we fail, we'll both be finished."

Forsyth shook his head, then stubbed the cigarette into the nearby ashtray. "The job that they have planned will go ahead, with or without Mark O'Shea. Another IRA quartermaster, another time. If we can recover the money and take out the main man, it might just put those little men off trying something like this again. We could hold it over Sinn Fein and cash it in for some further bargaining chips in the future."

King nodded. "I see your point, but it's too risky," he paused, watching the screen and seeing the Irishmen stripping down the M16 rifles. He looked back at Forsyth. "Does this mean that you intend to come off the side-lines for O'Shea's assassination?"

Forsyth's expression did not change. He took out his silver cigarette case then smiled wryly. "That is what *you* are trained for, old boy." He opened the lid, extracted a hand-made cigarette and snapped the case shut with a loud click. "That's why I have a first class degree and a masters, and you have an eleven plus. Horses for courses dear chap, horses for courses. You gather the information, and I'll use it. You put a bullet in the man's head, and I'll dine out on the success of the mission. Sorry, old boy, it's just the way of things."

"You really are a proper bastard," King said emphatically.

"Oh, absolutely, old boy. Absolutely."

***

Grant returned to the barn and spread the equipment out on a blanket that Neeson had laid out for him. It was all there, everything that he had requested.

"Impressed?" O'Shea asked with a smile. "Gelignite, nitro-glycerine, a butane blowtorch, even the magnetic picklocks and the diamond-tipped lock-breaker," he paused. "Everything that you requested is there."

Grant picked up the cordless drill and checked the charge. He nodded as he replaced it, then set about checking the selection of hand tools. "What about the hydrochloric acid?"

O'Shea pointed to the unopened bag. "In there, don't spill any. We got you some sulphuric acid as well, it's in the same bag."

Neeson appeared at O'Shea's shoulder, then looked at the other four, who were checking over their weapons. "Right lads, put your toys down and bring the cars inside."

They brought the cars into the barn. Dugan and Patrick driving while McCormick and Liam held the doors open closed them again when the two cars were parked inside. The cars were a green Ford Mondeo a light blue Peugeot 306 hatchback.

"Right lads," Neeson said as the men gathered around him. "It's tomorrow at seven o'clock in the morning." O'Shea glanced across at Danny Neeson, then turned back to the rest of the men. "We have information, from a reliable source, that the safe will contain an unspeakable amount of money, but will be emptied just after seven o'clock and distributed to the cashier booths and concessions."

Grant shook his head. "That makes no sense whatsoever. Surely the safe would be full at the end of the day, after the races! If it contains money, then why not hit it in the early hours, why wait until people have started to arrive? Or do it the next day after the second race meet."

O'Shea smiled. "I understand that you're wary, and to a certain extent, I understand why," he said pointedly, then glanced at the other men. "We want this to succeed, we have invested a great deal of time, money and resources into the venture. We have it on reliable authority that the safe will contain a small fortune. At seven o'clock, the time-lock will be switched off, for no more than ten minutes, during which time you will defeat the secondary devices, and the rest of your team will defeat any security personnel who want to become heroes."

Grant stuck out his chin obstinately and frowned. "Why would it be full of money? Surely it would only hold a few thousand pounds to act as a float?" He glanced at the other four men, but could see that from their expressions that no one shared his doubts.

Neeson stepped forward, his face contorted in anger. "Because we have reliable information!" He shook his head then slipped into an unsettling smile. "That is the way that it will be. We have an insider in the contract security firm that deals with Kempton Park racecourse. They have a secure enough facility to keep the money held at the park. Security vans take the money to three various banks on random days to avoid creating a pattern. That is the way that the track operates. Now, if you want to see how we operate, just carry on the way you are!"

Grant hung his head, his mind briefly filling with images of Lisa and his son. He looked up; there was no point in pressing his luck. This organisation wanted their money. The details may sound strange, but the other men seemed to have taken their information at face value, and they had all worked together in the past, perhaps he should take their word as well. "Alright, I'm just used to working differently, that's all."

O'Shea smiled. "Aye, and you went to prison on your last job as well. Just trust us, and I guarantee that you'll not see the inside of a prison cell again."

Grant nodded humbly, then sat back against a small stack of straw bales.

Neeson took a few steps backwards and perched himself on the bonnet of the Ford Mondeo. "You will go in these two vehicles." He slapped the bonnet of the Ford, then nodded towards the Peugeot. "Ross and Sean will be the drivers. They're the best in the business, so rest assured, you couldn't be in safer hands."

"Where are they?" Grant asked.

Neeson stared at the Englishman despairingly. "Questions, questions, always with the fucking questions!" he paused, grinning at the rest of the men. "Ross and Sean are surveying the area, checking out all the possible escape routes. They want to check now to get the lie of the land. The last thing you all need is to run into road works that have suddenly sprung up since they last checked the area. And, before you ask, Jason Porter is working on something else, safer all round if you don't know what. Let's just call it, a diversion."

O'Shea nodded in agreement then said, "You are effectively two teams; this operation will be run in two parts. And neither part knows the full extent of the operation. It's the basic cell system. Although you do know who else is involved, it is better not to know where they are, or what they will be doing." He glanced across at Neeson, then turned back to the rest of the group. "While you are inside the race track, Neeson and Jason will be causing a wee diversion for the police."

"We will not meet up here again." Neeson shook his head slowly, emphasising the point, then added, as if regarding the emphasis as inadequate. "Under any circumstances."

O'Shea nodded. "Once you have the goods and return to the vehicles, Ross and Sean will be in absolute charge. They will take you to the secondary location, where we will re-group and sort things out."

"It couldn't be simpler. The time locks go off, you pull up in the cars. You leg it to the offices, Grant cracks the safe, while the rest of you keep him covered. You dump the equipment, then fill the bags with the money, leg it back and then get driven away." Neeson smiled. "It's not usual procedure, but all four of you will be given a substantial wedge for your efforts. Enough to start a good life with your loved ones."

The four Irishmen hooted in unison then sat back, grinning excitedly at the news of their unexpected windfall.

O'Shea smiled. "After we meet at the new location, I will have your travel arrangements ready. We're going to Northern Spain and using an ETA safe-house for a couple of weeks and then we'll take a sea crossing via Spanish fishing boat to the west coast of Ireland."

***

"Do you think it will work?" Forsyth sat back in his seat and blew out a thin plume of smoke. The two men had watched and listened to the entire briefing, then sat in silence with their own thoughts, once the team had been dismissed.

King looked up from the empty screen, turned to darkness with lack of movement. He shook his head. "Not a chance. At first, it sounds so simple." He picked up his cup, and sipped his tea, which by now had become tepid. He screwed up his face in distaste, and hastily returned the cup to the table. "I don't believe that there will be such a large amount of money left in the safe. It's a race course, not a bloody bank, after all," he paused. "Sure, there will be plenty of money there after a race, but why leave it there between races?"

"It *isn't* done like that, old boy." Forsyth watched his newly formed smoke ring drift lazily across the room, then turned back towards King. "I checked. Apparently, the security van arrives in the morning with the float. It is certainly a substantial amount and well worth the trouble, but it's nowhere near the figures they're quoting. It's in the tens of thousands, not millions," he said, slipping the cigarette between his lips, then inhaling deeply. He unhurriedly exhaled another smoke ring, and grinned at the result. King watched him with increasing impatience. Forsyth remained unhurried, seemingly more concerned with his creation. "A different van arrives just after the last pay-out, then collects the takings, which of course, are truly substantial." He stubbed the cigarette into the ashtray, then rubbed his chin thoughtfully. "Tomorrow, you will follow the cars to the race course, see if you can observe the events. I will follow our man Neeson. I find myself somewhat intrigued by his plans for a diversion."

"I'm more intrigued by the race course." King mused. "If it is a fact that the safe doesn't contain a vast sum of money, surely their insider would know? What the hell can they be up to?"

***

Neeson walked into the kitchen carrying a large bundle of clothes in his arms. The men were seated around the table, coffee freshly made and a plate of biscuits vanishing in front of them. Neeson pushed between Patrick and Dugan and dropped the bundle onto the table. "Here you go lads, sort yourselves out with that lot." The men reached forward and pulled the bundle apart. It consisted of navy blue overalls, the full-bodied boiler suit type, black balaclavas, black leather gloves, and black high-top trainers.

"You will be wearing them over your own clothes. Try them on now and swap if they don't fit." Neeson exaggerated a stretch as he yawned, then turned to O'Shea. "Right, I'm off now, boss. Jason will follow me in the Porsche."

"Right, stay lucky and be bloody careful. If the pigs get suspicious about that car and find out that the plates don't match, we're finished." O'Shea shook his head. "We've come way too far for things to go wrong at this stage."

"Aye, don't be worrying yourself, it'll be all right." He turned to the rest of the group, who were trying on their new garments. "Lads, I'll see you tomorrow. Don't balls it up!" He walked over to the dresser, picked a blue sports bag off the floor beside it, then walked silently to the door.

O'Shea turned to the five men and sipped his whiskey. He watched as they swapped shoes with each other, looking like an amalgamation of terrorists and plumbers, in their matching overalls and balaclavas. Finally, he replaced his glass, and leant back in his chair.

"Right, lads, get your kit off and sit yourselves back down."

***

"Where are they now?" Forsyth stubbed out his cigarette, then immediately reached for his silver cigarette case.

"In the farmhouse." King turned up the volume control, then turned towards Forsyth. "I'll need my equipment before tomorrow. If the hit is still going ahead, that is."

Forsyth extracted yet another hand-made cigarette, tapped the tip against the lid of the case, and smirked as he slipped the cigarette between his thin lips. "Oh, the hit will definitely be going ahead, old boy. I'm just not sure about when," he paused as he flicked the wheel of his gold lighter and stared at the flickering flame. "To tell you the truth, I haven't managed to pick up the executive order yet. You see, they have to be signed for, and I thought that it might prove worthwhile if we found out the full extent of what these chaps are up to." He brought the flame to the cigarette and inhaled deeply. "You see..." He exhaled the smoke and grinned, "I have rather a free hand in all of this. For the good of the operation, and all that. I'm sure HQ will understand. As long as O'Shea goes down before Friday."

King stared at him in disbelief. An executive order came from the top of the intelligence tree; and here was an MI6 liaison officer, flagrantly disregarding the order, which for all King knew, could well have come from the Prime Minister himself.

King had met only a handful of the closeted men from SIS who acted as liaison officers. Unlike its sister service, MI5, where both sexes are employed equally at all levels, the Secret Intelligence Service tended to prefer men. Privately-educated men from moneyed backgrounds. So far, all the liaison officers that King had met had been men, and *yes men* at that. Yet the more time that he spent with Forsyth, the more exceptional he appeared. Forsyth flouted the rules and was blasé not only towards authority, but also to the risk, which was building with every second that Mark O'Shea remained alive. Initially King had wanted to build some background intel on the IRA cell, but it was now Forsyth who ran the risk of taking the operation beyond its remit and beyond its vital deadline. The special operations man hated the idea of a rushed job, but with every hour the IRA quartermaster remained alive, the operation risked failure.

***

O'Shea drained the remnants from his glass, then sniffed the trace of vapour which still clung to the rim. "You know all you need to know. The time, the location, and the objective of the mission. And most importantly of all; the escape," he paused, looking at Grant. "You know your job. I know that you can do it. You also know the score if you let us down."

Grant sat in silence. It really was going ahead, and nothing that he could say or do would make any difference. All he could do now; was pray. Pray that he could pull it off. Pray that both Lisa and young David would be safe. He nodded, acknowledging O'Shea, then bowed his head. He hated Holman for getting him into this, but wished his old friend could be here nonetheless. There would at least be some comfort in familiarity.

"We shall meet here, at five-thirty tomorrow morning, for a final check. Half an hour later, you will be on the road. Be ready." He stared at each man in turn, finally fixing his cold, hard eyes on Simon Grant. "All of you."

***

"Where the hell did Danny Neeson go?" Forsyth got to his feet and paced across the room to the kitchen. He returned seconds later with a hand-wrapped packet of cigarettes and sat back down in his chair. King stared at the brown paper packet, which he did not recognise, then glanced up at Forsyth and shrugged. Forsyth opened the packet and started to replenish the silver case. "Can we track the Porsche?"

"No. I only have a tracking device on the Saab, and it doesn't work if the vehicle is more than a kilometre away."

Forsyth shook his head. "Well, that's no bloody good, is it!" He tapped the tip of the first cigarette against the case lid, then reached for his lighter.

"Don't bloody bark at me, Ian!" King growled. "I'm a specialist. I came here for an assassination, not to become PC bloody plod! I was issued with enough equipment to carry out an evaluation. There should be a whole team working on this, but as you well know, this entire operation is deniable. If the truth got out, if people knew that British intelligence assassinated key members of the IRA in the middle of the peace process, then they wouldn't blame Sinn Fein for stalling at every hurdle. As for the whole Good Friday Agreement; peace agreement, deal, talks - whatever the hell you want to call it - we all know it is doomed from the outset. Killing O'Shea won't make a shred of difference. Sinn Fein has called the shots from the start. The IRA got an agreement to get their men out of prison, and kept most of their weapons into the bargain!"

Forsyth held up a placatory hand. "Calm down, old boy. I was just thinking out loud, that's all." He lit the cigarette, then slipped the lighter back into his inside jacket pocket. "Turkey..."

"What?"

Forsyth smiled. "The cigarettes, old boy, the cigarettes," he paused, inhaled deeply, then blew out a thin plume of pungent smoke. "I noticed you looking at the packet earlier. I get them sent over from Istanbul. Spent four years over there, well, all over the Balkans actually. Found that when I returned home, I could hardly do without them."

King shook his head and found he was gripping the arm of the chair in frustration. "Ian, I don't give a damn which brand of cigarettes are giving you lung cancer." He took a deep, calming breath, then stared at him. "I am more concerned that we have let matters go too far. Tomorrow, four known IRA terrorists will be running amok with automatic weapons, while attempting to rob a racetrack. We had the chance to stop it, but we didn't."

Forsyth held the burning cigarette out in front of him and studied the smouldering tip. "It's a blend, old boy, not a brand." He smiled briefly, then rested his head back against the chair. "We can still stop it from going ahead." He slipped the cigarette back between his lips, then glanced up at him. "But then, we will never discover what the hell they were really up to. And *you* were really keen on that, if I recall correctly."

King shook his head. "I want to know as much as you do; but what if it all goes pear shaped tomorrow? What if innocent people get killed?"

Forsyth nodded. "Ah yes. The big *what if*. Come along Alex, you know how this game works, you've been undercover in Northern Ireland," he paused, looking for any trace of realisation in King's eyes. "I've been liaison officer in countless operations. I've seen your colleagues, the men you trained with in the SAS, place a car bomb under a Protestant's vehicle, just to have a Catholic shot in the head the very next night. Tit-for-tat, old boy. Don't tell me that you didn't know it went on?" King glanced down at the floor. He did know, but he had never taken part. He had been part of surveillance operations on the streets of Belfast, nothing more, but he had heard the rumours all the same. Forsyth blew a smoke ring, then stared ponderously, as it drifted with the draft towards the kitchen. "I knew of a young MI5 field agent who infiltrated a faction of the IRA. It was during the mid-eighties, back when you were probably sniffing glue behind the bike sheds…"

"I've never done drugs, Ian," King paused. "Watch your mother die from an overdose and your brothers and sisters get separated into care homes. It puts perspective onto things…"

"As I was saying," Forsyth interrupted, quite dispassionately and with no offer of an apology. "During the mid-eighties, when the IRA were receiving a great deal of weaponry and funding from the Middle East. The IRA splinter groups were becoming as bold as bloody brass; certain countries saw them as an investment. In return for weapons, ammunition and explosives, the IRA splinter groups were prepared to carry out certain tasks for their benevolence," he paused for another long drag, before blowing the pungent substance out in a long, thin plume. "This agent got in so deep, so thick with them, that his superiors were reluctant to extract him. His intelligence was superb, second to none. It was a dream come true for both intelligence services, who were receiving the best information, this side of the Russians running Kim Philby."

King frowned. "What has this got to do with our situation?"

Forsyth stubbed the half-smoked cigarette into the ever-filling ashtray and looked coldly into his eyes. "After a while the young agent was nearing detection. Several pieces of information, which had been known to only a privileged few within the IRA faction, had been picked up by the security forces a little too quickly. He was put onto several operations where he would have to be the drop man. He would have to plant a device and be responsible for many civilian fatalities. SIS weighed up the pros and cons and decided that there would always be casualties, but there would not always be such first class information." Forsyth reached for his lighter, then picked up the silver case. "The man was ordered to continue with his work, regardless of the consequences." King remained silent, thinking of the horrendous ramifications involved. An agent, sworn to defend the realm, but forced to carry out bombings so that the intelligence services could continue receiving information. Forsyth flicked the wheel of his lighter as he slipped yet another cigarette into his mouth. "You see..." He brought the flame to the tip of the cigarette, then replaced the lighter on the table. "Sometimes, you have to look at the whole picture, and not just the pretty bits. If we can achieve more than just the death of one IRA quartermaster, then we may push things closer to resolving a hideous situation. The peace deal did not achieve what it set out to do. With breakaway groups springing up like weeds, if anything the whole situation is now even more complex and volatile than before."

King looked at Forsyth and nodded in agreement. "What happened to the agent?"

Forsyth waved a hand in a dismissive gesture. "Oh, he carried out a few bombings. The IRA never suspected a thing. Then he got pulled out suddenly. Seemed that the mandarins, the powers that be, had a change of heart. An RUC officer was killed; suddenly the situation became too hot. He quit the service soon after."

King shook his head. "How could that poor man ever sleep again at night?" he mused.

"He sees the bigger picture now."

"You?" King asked sharply.

"I was offered a position in MI6 shortly afterwards," Forsyth paused. "And with the whole picture in front of me now, I sleep just fine." He looked at the specialist. "It's all a game of cowboys and Indians, Alex. But there is a bigger picture to all that we see. Nuclear weapons? Lord no, what a terrible waste of money and bad ethics. But Russia has them, will one day threaten to use them, so they suddenly seem a sound investment. This whole Northern Ireland thing is rubbish, but while we still have it and are scared to get rid of it, for whatever reason, pride more than likely, we still have to play the game."

King studied the man in front of him. He didn't know whether he respected him or loathed him. A little of both, he supposed. "Alright, what's the plan then?"

27

"What's the matter?" Lisa watched as he sank the contents of the glass in one mouthful, then slammed the vessel down onto the delicate Edwardian table. "None of your damned business, woman!" He stared at the empty glass, then raised an eyebrow. "Well? Can you not see that it's empty?" She nodded dutifully, then hurriedly stepped forward and picked up the glass. He caught hold of her by the arm, gripping the sleeve of her silk nightgown. "You're next to bloody useless." He shook his head in exaggerated despair. "Don't take the glass, just bring me the bloody bottle!"

"Sorry, Keith." She waited for him to release her from his clasp, then hurried over to the drinks cabinet. She studied the row of bottles, then turned around.

"What's the matter now?"

She glanced down at the floor, then looked up at him. "I'm sorry, I can't remember what you were drinking."

"Nor can I," Keith scoffed. He ran a hand through his greying hair, scratched at the bald patch on top. "You've taken so bloody long; it seems to have slipped my memory." He picked up his glass, then made an act of sniffing the vapour from the remnants. "Oh, brandy! That would be nice, I can hardly remember what it tastes like!"

She turned around and opened the glass-fronted cabinet. She ran her fingers along the various bottles, then stopped when she reached the bottle of D. Campeny VSOP. She took out the bottle and held it up. "Is this it?"

"Oh for God's sake, woman!" He rubbed his forehead as if it pained him, then sighed dramatically. "Yes, absolutely perfect," he paused as she walked back towards him. "For my acquaintances and your bloody mother! There's a decanter of one hundred-year-old Armagnac at the back of the cabinet. It's not labelled, so you won't have to worry about spelling it!" He laughed at his little quip, then looked at his watch as if to time her.

Lisa caught hold of the bottle, then walked back towards him. Keith looked up at her, studying her attire. She was dressed in satin French knickers and matching camisole, and was covered up with a Chinese silk nightgown. "What the hell are you dressed up like that for? You do realise that you look like a tart, don't you?" She closed her eyes, not wanting to bite. "Are you fucking ignoring me now?"

She shook her head and forced a passive smile. "No, I thought you liked me in this, that's all," she lied. She had been given no alternative. He had thrown out her comfortable pyjamas and towelling dressing gown. She had merely gone along with the outfit like a dutiful geisha. It was a game of survival.

He sneered, then shook his head. "Well?" She stared at him, confused. She knew what it would be like for the rest of the evening, when he got into one of these moods, there was just no stopping him. "The bottle, woman, the bloody bottle!" He let out a groan and picked up his glass. "Would it be too much to ask you to let go of the damn bottle?"

She glanced down, unable to conceal her surprise. Her mind had been elsewhere, trying to keep up with the man's vicious verbal onslaught. Her only thoughts were of how to keep the onslaught verbal and not let it progress to physical. She bent down and placed the decanter on the table.

Keith smiled. "Well, it's a start. Now, if we could just remember to remove the stopper and get some of it into the glass, we would be getting somewhere."

"Sorry." She hurriedly removed the ground-glass stopper, then held the decanter above the glass in his outstretched hand. She shook nervously, then clipped the neck of the decanter against the rim of the glass, spilling some of the liquid onto his trousers. "Oh my god! I'm sorry, I'm sorry!" She pulled it away in a panic, spilling yet more of the contents.

"You, stupid bitch…" he said quietly. It was the quietness that scared her the most. He stood up abruptly. "That was one-hundred-year old Armagnac!" He swung his arm out, catching her with a back-fist to the jaw. She let out a yelp as she was hurled backwards by the force of the blow, landing in a heap on the polished wooden floor. The decanter fell from her grasp, spilling the remainder of the contents on the nearby Persian rug. Keith stepped forward, bent down and tenderly picked it up. "Look what you did…" He stared down at her with contempt. He set it down on the table, then stood directly above her with his hands on his hips.

Lisa rubbed her right hand over her jaw, soothing the area, which now felt like fire upon her cheek. A trickle of blood seeped from between her fingertips and ran over the back of her hand.

Keith shook his head in despair. "You're pathetic! I've seen better than you begging at Kings

Cross. You're nothing but a cheap, common little tramp. A tramp that I pulled from the gutter." He reached down and unfastened the button to his trousers, then slowly pulled down the zip. "A whore, straight from the gutter. I took you out of it, and I can put you right back there. Don't ever forget that."

Lisa closed her eyes. She knew what he was feeling, what he had been trying for all evening. He received a perverse sexual gratification from treating her this way. He had set up the situation for maximum relish of domineering power. He had beaten her for two years now. An argument had become too heated and he had lashed out. Now it was becoming more frequent. But it had all changed three-months ago when he had come home drunk and forced himself on her. Now the arguments, the beating always led to this. It had happened a handful of times, and it shamed her more that she had stayed. That she had stopped counting and not taken David and left. But she reasoned that Keith had not yet reached his true potential. To leave him, to flee his wrath made her question what would happen to both David and herself if he ever found them. The thought made her blood run cold.

She pulled herself onto the chaise longue and looked up at him pleadingly, despairingly. "Please, Keith, don't." She pulled the silk nightgown over her shapely legs, then wiped a trickle of blood away from her full lips.

He let his trousers drop to the floor, then pulled down his boxer shorts, exposing himself to her. "I bet *he* liked you in those clothes. I bet he appreciated your prostitute outfits..."

Her pleading expression turned to a look of pure contempt. He had hurt her, violated her, and degraded her, but she was no longer scared. There was little else that he could do to her now. She just wanted to be treated like a human being again. Maybe she would get the strength to leave. Maybe she would make this the last time.

She stared into his eyes defiantly and smiled. "Yes," she said with sincere satisfaction. "Yes, *he* loved my clothes. He loved my satin, my silk, everything. And he always liked me to wear them when we made love."

"No!" Keith covered his ears momentarily in an almost childlike gesture, then screwed his face up in anger. "*He* was a nobody! A dirty, useless nobody!"

"What, like me? That's how you treat *me*! That's how you make me feel! And I hate you for it!" Lisa pulled herself up higher on the chaise longue and stared at him venomously. "He was a lot of things Keith, but at least he never laid a finger on me!" She rose to her feet and stood opposite him, less than two feet away. "And he would make love to me, like a real man, not some vile rapist!" She reached up and ripped the silk nightgown apart, revealing her small, firm breasts. "Come on then! Why don't you try to be a *real* man? See if you really are better than him!" She fell back onto the soft velvet of the chaise longue and pulled the nightgown up around her hips, exposing her long, slender legs and just a hint of her neatly trimmed pubic hair. She smiled seductively, then started to finger her nipples gently. "Come on lover, give it your best shot..." She ran her hands delicately down her flat stomach, then circled her fingertips through the small triangle of coarse pubic hair. Then, as she stared defiantly into his eyes, she spread her legs wide, her knees to her breasts, and rested her fingertips, delicately covering herself. "Take me like a real man, Keith. Make me come. There's a first time for everything…" The victory filled her with elation, and she couldn't help herself when she added, "Come fuck me, don't be quick, I want you to last as long as a *real* man does!"

He stared down at her, perplexed. Deflated, broken. He turned his gaze to his flagging manhood, limp and irrelevant. He bent down and picked up his trousers. And as he silently left the room, Lisa could swear that she saw tears in his eyes.

She *would* leave him. She knew she would. She had the strength to leave him, and she wouldn't give a damn if he found her. She covered herself up, and started to laugh and weep at the same time. It felt joyous, and she felt empowered for the first time in years.

28

Simon Grant looked at the luminous dials of the alarm clock on the bedside table. One minute to go. He groaned inwardly, having seen-in every hour, without so much as a single wink of precious sleep. He could not be bothered to wait for the alarm's monotonous tone, desperately counting off every second in between, so he reached out and switched it off, then swung his legs over the edge of the bed.

He stood up, stretched, and walked over to the sink, where he turned on the cold tap, let some water run into the stained enamel bowl, then splashed a handful over his face. It was only now that he started to feel tired; the effects of missing a full night's sleep were starting to kick in. His teeth started to chatter, and his whole body shook with the combined effects of the early morning chill and the indecent hour.

He heard footsteps approaching along the landing's timeworn floorboards, and hurriedly pulled on his trousers. A brief, but heavy knock sounded against the door, before it opened abruptly, to admit McCormick's head.

"Looks like I nearly caught yer out!" He grinned as he watched Grant fasten his belt. "Just thought I'd check that you were up and about. The boys are ready, just fixing themselves some scoff. Do yer want some?"

Grant nodded. "Yeah, just some toast, please." He slipped a grey sweatshirt over his head, then looked quizzically at McCormick. "You didn't think that I'd do a runner, did you?"

McCormick shook his head. "No. It sounds as if the boss has you too firmly by the balls for that. Nothing more you can do, except co-operate," he said, glancing briefly at the floor. "Me and the lads didn't know, we're sorry. Just do your job and we'll all get what we want."

Grant scoffed. "And what is it that you want?"

"Peace in a united Ireland," he said, holding up his hands defensively. "That's all anybody wants."

Grant sat back down on the bed and pulled on his socks. "You've got the chance of peace right now. You have the peace agreement, the supposed ceasefire. But still you kill each other, you don't want peace, you just want to rule the roost."

"Aye, whatever you think." McCormick shook his head. "You don't understand," he paused, then added, "The likes of you will never understand."

"I understand all too well," he retaliated, looking at him in earnest. "Christian, Catholic, Buddhist, Jewish, Protestant, Muslim, Hindu. Well, that was just on the housing estate where Frank Holman and I grew up. West-Indian, Pakistani, Indian, Chinese, Nigerian, Algerian... Christ knows, who else. No different from many other communities all over the country. There is the odd bit of racial violence, carried out by mindless yobs; I'm not disputing that. But do they plant car bombs? Do they blow up innocent people?" Grant shook his head in desperation. "Of course not! London is full of different cultures, yet are they machine-gunning each other?" He bent to pull on his black training shoes, then glanced back up at McCormick. "People can learn to live with their differences. Swallow your pride. Your leaders did, at the peace talks, so can you."

McCormick glared defiantly. "Nobody came into your country and separated it. Nobody decided that part of your country would become a new territory, that you would be given a new status, while your family kept theirs, just because they lived a few miles away." McCormick turned towards the door. "You just don't understand."

Grant shook his head and stood up. "Maybe I don't, maybe people like me never will. But what I do know, is that hundreds of people have died, many of them had nothing to do with the situation. They didn't even know what it was all about, but their lives were taken from them none the less. Your political leaders have recognised this; they worked hard in the peace talks, they swallowed their pride and turned towards change. They compromised. The British Government compromised. Why can't you?"

***

Forsyth peered through the thick border of rhododendron bushes that screened the house. A light shone from the upstairs window, then, moments later, a fluorescent light flickered downstairs, before brightly illuminating a window.

He pulled back a thin bushy branch, to get a clearer view of the side of the house. The black Porsche was parked next to Frank Holman's Mercedes. It squatted low, like a big cat poised ready to pounce. Its haunches were rounded, well-muscled, sleek. Compared to the new arrival, the Mercedes looked like a brick.

Behind the Mercedes, almost out of sight was Neeson's blue Saab.

Forsyth smiled. The tracking device had sounded, as he had rounded the corner and switched on the laptop. But now, he had an all-important visual.

He hopped down from the wall and strolled casually back to his Rover 620. He opened the door and slipped inside, then reached for his silver cigarette case.

On the horizon, dawn was breaking, filling the distant sky with a blaze of crimson. Forsyth flicked open the silver case and extracted one of his handmade, Turkish cigarettes. He slipped it between his thin lips and smiled. He had located Neeson in time, but only with the breaking light of dawn had he been able to confirm the presence of both vehicles. He flicked the wheel of his lighter and brought the flame to the tip of the cigarette, inhaled deeply and blew out a thin plume of smoke. He flicked the excess ash into the ever-filling ashtray, then smiled to himself. He had them now. It was just a matter of patience.

***

King brought the field glasses up to his eyes and studied the farmhouse again, remaining perfectly still, shrouded by a layer of camouflaged netting on the fringe of the thick foliage. He had been in position since four a.m. - waiting for any signs of life from within the house. He had watched the day break lazily from total blackness into the dim light of dawn. Now, at five-thirty a.m., it was almost completely light.

Lights had appeared from within the house at a little after five o'clock and both cars had been driven out from the barn and parked in front of the farmhouse approximately ten-minutes ago. The time was close; he just had to wait.

He listened intently to the chatter in his earpiece, waiting for the nervous conversation to die. It reminded him of soldier talk in the mess-room or barracks before an operation. He had accompanied soldiers in Northern Ireland, there was always nervous talk before a patrol. It struck him that the world over, whatever the side, the players were the same. The chatter died down suddenly and King new it was the much-awaited cue.

***

"Right lads! Shut yourselves up and sit the fuck down!" O'Shea perched himself on the work surface and waited for the men to do as instructed. "Time for a final check."

The men watched him intently. The atmosphere was stiff with adrenaline and anticipation. O'Shea looked at each of the men in turn. "Two hours' time, and you should be home and dry," he paused as he glanced at the courtyard outside, then turned back to his audience. "The cars are outside; Ross and Sean have loaded them up. The equipment and rifles are in the boots." He looked at McCormick. "You and Grant will ride in the Peugeot, driven by Sean. When you arrive at the racecourse, you will take the bag of equipment. Leave Grant's hands free." He picked up his cup and sipped a mouthful of coffee, then turned to the rest of the men. "You lot will ride in the Ford with Sean. Again, you will carry the equipment between you, no petty squabbling, you all carry a load." The men nodded in unison and O'Shea smiled. "Good." He then looked at Grant, who was twiddling his thumbs nervously. "Grant, you will have just under ten-minutes to get that safe open," he paused. "You can do it, can't you?" The men all turned their eyes expectantly towards Grant, watching him in earnest.

Grant looked at them, then turned to stare back to O'Shea. "Yeah, I can do it."

O'Shea smiled. "Good." He glanced at his watch, then looked at the rest of the men. "Better get going then."

Grant followed McCormick across the courtyard to where the two cars were ticking over, with Ross and Sean in the drivers' seats. Dugan and Liam got into the back of the Ford Mondeo, and Patrick, who would have been greatly restricted anywhere but in the front seat, walked around the bonnet and opened the passenger door. He turned around and held a thumb up to McCormick, who returned the gesture and opened the near side rear door of the Peugeot.

Grant walked to the front of the tiny Peugeot and looked back at O'Shea, who was leaning against the wall. O'Shea turned away, ignoring his gaze, and watched the Mondeo assume the lead and drive out of the courtyard. Grant slipped down into the passenger seat and had barely closed the door, when Sean accelerated away.

The two vehicles bounced and weaved their way down the lane, avoiding the larger potholes by occasionally mounting the grass verge. Ross swung the

Mondeo out into the road and accelerated quickly out of the blind corner. Sean pulled out, copying the manoeuvre, the little hatchback's front wheels spinning briefly as it met the damp tarmac. Then, gaining traction, it soon caught up with the larger Mondeo.

***

King waited until he heard both cars join the road and accelerate into the distance. Satisfied that they would be out of sight, he started the van's engine and drove the twenty-metres or so down the muddy lane, then pulled out onto the road.

With dawn breaking, and optimum visibility, King was in a difficult situation. He was not equipped with the tracking device and laptop, which had made his job so much easier during the past few days. Instead, he would have to rely on visual surveillance, which in the gathering light and without other traffic to act as cover, would have been difficult, with even a team of vehicles. However, he knew their destination. He was not simply following into the unknown.

King accelerated hard, taking the van's gears to maximum revs, in his anxiety to confirm his first visual. As he rounded the second corner, he caught sight of the Peugeot. He eased off the accelerator and let the distance increase to approximately three-hundred metres.

***

Forsyth stubbed his half-smoked cigarette into the overflowing ashtray and kept his eyes on Holman's property.

Several lights had flicked on and off over the past ten minutes, indicating that the people within the building were probably getting themselves ready. Now that the lights were switched off, Forsyth could swear that he heard the sound of a heavy door closing. He glanced at his wristwatch. It was six o'clock, if the plan had held, then King would already be in transit, following both vehicles towards Kempton Park racecourse.

***

Alex King had just passed the small town of Ripley and joined the A3, keeping his distance at the maximum possible for visual surveillance. The going was much easier, now that they had joined the larger and faster-moving dual carriageway. He had been able to let two vehicles overtake him and travel between the Peugeot and himself, giving him the cover that he needed to remain undetected. With any luck, the drivers of the Peugeot and the Mondeo would have no cause to become suspicious.

***

Sean glanced in his rear view mirror. There were two cars directly behind him, although he was sure that nobody had followed him from the farm.

"Problem?" McCormick asked with concern, as he leaned forward between the two front seats. "You seem a bit edgy, mate."

Sean shook his head. "The car behind," he said, squinting into the rear-view mirror. "A Ford Sierra, I think. It pulled out of a turning and has been behind us ever since."

"Should be alright." McCormick turned around casually and stared at the vehicle in question. "I checked for the first three miles and didn't see a thing." He turned back to Sean and grinned. "Most probably on his way to work."

***

King eased his speed, letting a minibus overtake him, then pull back into the inside lane further down the road. He increased his speed once more, happier now that there were three vehicles between the two targets and himself.

The traffic was increasing in both directions, which cut both ways. It would enable him to assume sufficient cover to draw attention away from his own vehicle, yet it could also develop into an infuriating barrier that could make him lose sight of the target vehicles altogether.

***

Forsyth watched Danny Neeson pull the Saab out of the entrance of Holman's property and drive carefully down the quiet road, followed closely by Jason Porter in the glistening Porsche. Both men were alone in their vehicles. Either Frank Holman was not involved in the operation at this stage, or he would be following later in a car of his own. Either way, Forsyth would have to find out later. For now, though, the most important person to keep track of was Danny Neeson. He waited for both vehicles to reach the end of the street and disappear from sight, then switched on the laptop. The specialised software came on at once, indicating Neeson's position on the road map at a distance of approximately four-hundred-metres northwest. Forsyth calmly switched on the Rover's ignition and gently pulled away.

The Saab turned on to the A24, then headed south towards Leatherhead. Forsyth could only guess that the Porsche was still following, and he would gladly have bet any amount of money that it was.

***

It was a clear day in the town of Sunbury. The traffic was reasonably light, but as they approached the racecourse, it began to grow steadily in volume. King kept his eyes strained for the Peugeot, five vehicles in front of him.

The Ford Mondeo pulled into a space on the side of the road, two-hundred metres from the main gates, and waited. The Peugeot pulled across the road and slipped into a narrow gap, twenty-metres closer to the entrance.

King cursed. With only five vehicles in front of him, he had to get off the road quickly, or drive straight past them and run the risk of being detected. For all he knew, they might have become suspicious of the periodic presence of the white Ford Escort van.

He quickly pulled into a narrow side road, which looked as if it was the entrance for a series of lockup garages. A few metres into the turning, a small pull-in space had been made to allow vehicles to pass each other in the narrow thoroughfare. King manoeuvred the van into it, switched off the engine, then quickly got out and jogged towards the entrance. He glanced at his watch: six forty-five a.m. They should still be in the cars, waiting until the last minute.

As he reached the end of the alleyway, he kept tight to the wall of the building, then cautiously peered out into the street. Both vehicles were parked with their engines switched off. From here he could clearly see the men sitting patiently, although one was staring nervously down the street out of the rear window of the Ford Mondeo.

He wanted to get closer, there were a few obstructions, and the distance was too great to identify the men individually. Across the street there was another alleyway which seemed to be offset from the road. It looked as if he would be able to observe more, yet still remain undetected. He watched the two vehicles closely, then satisfied that it was clear, he decided to make his move. He visibly jumped, startled as his mobile telephone vibrated in his jacket pocket. He hastily retreated back into the sanctuary of the alleyway, fumbled it out, and pressed the receive button. "Yes!"

"Alex, it's Forsyth here, how are you holding up, old boy?"

King cursed under his breath, only Forsyth would call just minutes from the moment that the players were due to go in. He eased his head around the corner, keeping his eyes glued to the Peugeot. "The targets are in place, seems that they're just waiting until the last moment."

"Jolly good, looks like it's a go then," he paused. *"More than I can say from this end; something very fishy going on here indeed."* King groaned inwardly, the last thing that he wanted was to have a full-blown conversation out in the field. He was used to radios, code words and the phonetic alphabet. *Are you still there, old boy?"*

"Yes, just concentrating on the players."

"Jolly good. Now, where was I? Oh yes, something very fish-like. I'm following Neeson in his Saab and that chap Jason Porter is directly behind him in the Porsche. The thing is, they are absolutely nowhere near Sunbury. They're heading in the opposite bloody direction. We're on the A24, past Dorking and still heading South."

King frowned. "I thought Neeson was going to cause a diversion for the police?"

"Exactly, bugger-all chance of that when he's over thirty-miles away."

"What about Porter?" King asked, keeping his eyes on the two vehicles. "Is he definitely following Neeson?"

"Oh, definitely. I risked a visual just a few minutes ago, the man's up his arse like Liberace."

King grinned. Forsyth certainly had a way with words. He glanced at his watch, and then double-checked the two vehicles. "Look, Ian, you will just have to stay with it, there is only a minute or two to go, and I have to get into position."

"Oh sorry old boy, lost track of time. I'll call later, bring you up to speed..."

King ended the call and slipped the mobile phone back into his jacket pocket as two hundred metres away, an unsuspecting steward opened the side gate.

***

The dot slowed dramatically, along with the sound of the incessant *bleep* that had started to plague his ears. The Saab had turned off the A24 and had taken a minor road, passing through North Holmwood. Again, the tracking receiver's tone slowed, then suddenly ceased altogether.

Forsyth eased his speed then pulled in to the side of the road and crawled along until the distance between the target vehicle and himself was down to approximately four-hundred metres. He then parked the Rover on the tree-fringed roadside, switched off its quiet engine, and retrieved a pair of compact field glasses from behind his seat. To his left a broad grass verge and a line of beech trees segregated the road from a field of young corn. He stepped out of the car, then walked through the natural barrier and hopped over the fence into the field.

***

Neeson walked towards the glistening Porsche, as Jason Porter lowered the driver's window. "Right son, are you clear on the procedure?"

"Sure, just as we did in practice."

"Okay." Neeson glanced cautiously behind him, then turned his eyes warily back to Porter. "Now, the others will be here in a while, just keep yourself calm, and whatever happens, stay in the car," he ordered. "Don't you dare bottle it on me, else I'll find you and I'll fucking kill you..."

***

Forsyth watched through the 6 x 48 magnification of the field glasses, as he rested casually against the wooden-railed fence, shrouded from either side by two hawthorn trees. He blended into the area, almost perfectly camouflaged, albeit in a country fashion, in his tweed jacket and mustard-coloured trousers. He used to wear similar attire in his youth deer-stalking on his family's Scottish Highland estate, and he could always get close enough for a shot.

***

The doors of the Ford Mondeo opened and the three men casually stepped out into the street, and walked around to the rear of the vehicle. McCormick got out of the rear door of the Peugeot and held Grant's door open. He shepherded Grant around the car, then opened the rear hatch.

Liam, Dugan and Patrick each swung a bag over their shoulders and glanced across the street at McCormick, who was holding the bag in his left hand. He nodded to the three men, then picked up his M16 assault rifle and held it as discreetly as possible down beside his right leg. The other three followed suit, holding their rifles as close to them as possible.

McCormick led the way, with Grant following, and the rest of the team closing tightly in behind them. He turned around, noticing how conspicuous they were all looking, like secret service agents minding the American president. "Keep it casual, lads." He turned back towards the entrance, then glanced across the road, all the time keeping alert, making sure that nobody had noticed them.

As the group neared the gate, a steward wearing a yellow vest stepped out onto the pavement, his hands cupped around a cigarette that he was attempting to light with a somewhat uncooperative lighter. The man looked briefly at the five men, then returned his attention to his cigarette, before suddenly realising what he had just seen. He looked back at them in sheer terror, then turned to run, but misjudged it and collided with the wall. He stumbled backwards, corrected himself, and made a frantic dash for the gates.

Patrick lunged forward, with considerable speed and agility for such a large man. He raised the butt of the rifle and brought it crashing down onto the base of the man's skull. The steward fell forward and hit the pavement hard. He was out cold.

"Right, cover your faces!" McCormick shouted, catching hold of Grant's collar and pulling him towards the gates while Patrick and Liam pulled the steward inside the grounds, and dropped him beside the wall. McCormick looked at Grant, who was staring at the steward lying motionless on the ground. "Alright, genius. Let's do this thing!"

29

McCormick kept his grip on Grant's collar, pushing him into a run and guiding him towards the main building. Grant turned his head just in time to see Patrick pounding the butt of his rifle repeatedly into the steward's face. He turned back, watching his steps, forcing himself to keep the bile from his throat. The steward would surely be lucky to survive the unnecessary beating.

Patrick caught up with the rest of the group, panting breathlessly. "He'll have a bit of a headache when he wakes up!" He laughed. "*If* the fucker wakes up, more like!"

They reached the glass-fronted door and came to a halt. Dugan, Liam and Patrick fanned out, professionally guarding their rear. Grant examined the door, then turned to McCormick. "It's locked! Bolted from the inside!"

"So?" McCormick looked at him, bewildered. "That's why you're here!"

"So, I can't unbolt a dead bolt from the outside!" He shouted, looking at the alternatives, of which there were very few. "If you can take..." He was suddenly cut off prematurely by the sound of half a dozen gunshots fired in quick succession.

Liam aimed and fired again. This time, the bullets found their mark. The unsuspecting security guard who had merely wandered into view fell to the ground as the bullets cut into his lower body. He scrambled to his hands and knees, and struggled to get away, crawling towards the relative safety of the next building. Patrick quickly stepped around Grant and released a short burst of automatic fire. This time, the security guard fell to the ground and lay still.

"Shit! Shit! Shit!" McCormick shouted. "We've lost our element of surprise!"

Patrick pushed forward and aimed his rifle at the glass door. "This won't fucking matter then!" He squeezed the trigger and fired a heavy burst at the glass. It shattered instantly, spraying glass shards and splinters of wood into the empty room. Patrick ejected the empty magazine onto the ground and quickly replaced it with a new one. "Come on then, don't waste any more time!"

McCormick dragged Grant roughly across the debris and into the building. "Right, get going! Left, then up the stairs!"

Grant ran for all he was worth. He was in a daze; his heart was pounding and his ears felt muffled and sung a high pitched whine from the gunfire. The whole moment was simply a haze of confusion.

McCormick pulled Grant back as the two men neared the top of the concrete stairwell. He held his rifle firmly between both hands, then cautiously edged his way up the last three steps. He scanned the main area through the rifle's sights, then lowered the weapon. "Right, come on, it's clear." He waited for Grant to reach the top of the stairwell. "Okay, catch your breath, we're bang on time."

Patrick pushed past Liam and Dugan, then trained his weapon at the top of the stairs. "Come on Matt, let's get the job done!"

McCormick nodded. "Just checking it was clear." He dropped the bag, then turned to Grant. "That weighs a ton! What have you got in there?" He quickly picked the bag back up, this time slinging it over his other shoulder.

Grant stared at the bag, then looked at the other men's loads. "Nothing, I only had three..." he suddenly stopped mid-sentence. "There are four bags. You each have one. I only had three bags of equipment."

"So what?" Patrick shouted at him.

"Three bags, then we dump it all and fill the bags with the money."

"So we've got more bags," McCormick said. "Big deal."

***

Sean glanced at his watch, then started the Peugeot's engine. He took out his Nokia mobile phone and kept his eyes on his watch. He silently mouthed down the second hand until it hit the twelve. He scrolled down the contacts list and pressed the dial button. He could see the signal indicator and heard the dial tone. Without looking at it anymore, he put it on the seat beside him and moved out slowly into the road.

***

Grant stared at the other men in anguish. "It's not my bag! This is bullshit! Besides, I don't need anything *that* heavy, just tools and incendiaries, thermal cutters and microphones!" He shook his head in bewilderment, then stared at the bag curiously as it emitted the muffled sound of a telephone ringtone. He pushed past Dugan, sending the small man sprawling onto his knees. Patrick tried to grab hold of him as he ran, but Grant was quicker, side-stepping, then lunging for the stairwell.

McCormick frowned in bewilderment at the sound of the ringing telephone, then glanced down at the bag in desperate recognition of what was actually happening.

The pre-ignition took them first, followed by the instant heat, which sucked the air from around them like a vacuum, then ignited it into a brilliant white flame. They were dead before the shock wave ripped their bodies apart. Dead before anyone outside would hear a sound.

Grant did not feel the heat, but heard the deafening explosion and then felt the air being sucked from all around him. He half ran, half threw himself down the second stairwell and into the foyer below. The shockwave snatched him from his feet, picking him up and throwing him to the ceiling. He felt it squeeze him, engulfing him with its pressure, then carry him across the room. He scraped against the ceiling; then felt the pressure subside, letting him fall the fifteen-feet or so to the floor, among the shards of glass and other debris.

He lay still, winded, deafened and almost paralysed with fear. Large fragments of plaster fell all around him, crashing to the floor. He saw them fall, but could hear no impact on the polished concrete floor. His eyes flickered, as he tried to lift his head, his consciousness threatening to leave him at any moment.

He gazed towards the open space that had earlier been a series of glass doors, watching the man wade through the scattered debris towards him. He looked up at him, but try as he might, was not able to focus on the man's face. He was fit and hard-looking, his dark hair cropped short and two days' stubble on his face. He held a pistol in his hand, it was pointed at the floor. The man's shirtsleeves were rolled up, and Grant could see muscles and tendons, several scars. It looked as if a tattoo had been amateurishly removed. He did not know why he noticed these details, but for some strange reason he did not focus on the man's face.

The man bent down, rested the pistol on the ground beside him and pressed both hands around his ribcage and gently squeezed. Did he feel pain? He wasn't sure, he just felt numb. Again, the man prodded and felt, this time, turning his attention to Grant's neck. Was he being asked something? He could not tell, yet he sensed vibrations; was it the man's voice? His ears were singing, whining – a shrill piercing that filled his head and left him feeling numb and drunk and left behind as time marched on.

The pain was sharp, but quickly overcome, as the man pulled him roughly to his feet. He was a dead weight and knew the man was strong. He tried to stand for him, to take some weight, but instantly felt his legs start to buckle. The man took his weight, manoeuvred him around, and then eased him over his shoulder. He squatted down to retrieve the pistol, stood back up with little effort.

Grant tried to mumble something, maybe a thank you, but even he was unsure quite what. As the man took his first steps, Grant's mind filled with emptiness, lost in a void of unconsciousness.

30

King pulled the van off of the road and into the short lay-by. He studied his rear view mirror for a few moments then, satisfied that he was free of tails, he switched off the engine. He turned around and peered over his seat at Simon Grant, who lay in the back. He was a mess, that was for sure. Although, King was aware that the injuries sustained were mainly superficial and inflicted by the splinters of glass and tiny pieces of sharp debris. The bleeding had virtually stopped, most probably conveniently plugged, for now, by the tiny slivers of glass.

Grant was unconscious, but King could clearly see the man's chest rise and fall as he breathed, and his head was tucked to one side, preventing him from swallowing his tongue. No doubt his hearing would be temporarily affected, but with luck his eardrums would not be shattered.

King had been suspicious when the Mondeo left as soon as the men had gone inside. He was curious when the Peugeot drove away a few minutes later. The explosion had come as a shock, but it had suddenly made sense in light of the two getaway vehicles leaving the scene. For a moment, King's mind had filled with the memories of destruction that he had witnessed in Northern Ireland. The residents of the street had panicked at the sound of the blast, but the specialist knew from experience that he had only minutes to investigate before the panic was replaced by unthinking curiosity and reaction. He had reacted on impulse and snatched Grant from the scene before the police made an appearance.

Grant flinched momentarily, but his eyes remained firmly closed. The man would most certainly suffer an horrendous headache, but hopefully nothing more serious.

King reached for his mobile telephone and pressed the memory button for Ian Forsyth's number.

***

Forsyth felt the vibration of his phone, which had been pre-set onto the silent ringing function to avoid unnecessary detection. He glanced once more through the compact field glasses, then fished the telephone out and pressed the receive button, before holding it closely to his ear. "Yes?" he answered quietly, not once averting his eyes from the two vehicles.

"Ian, it's Alex. Everything has gone pear-shaped at this end."

"What's the problem, old boy?"

"An explosion blew the team all to hell, but Grant's alive. He's with me. Don't ask why, I just grabbed him before the police arrived. Perhaps he'll be able to tell us something."

"An explosion? What, they blew the safe and it went wrong?"

"No."

"Well, what then?"

"An IED. A bomb. They were carrying it. Maybe they were looking to plant it and set the thing off by

mistake. I don't know though, because both getaway cars left before it detonated."

Forsyth was silent for a moment. He had eyes on Neeson, noticed the Mondeo pull into the side of the road next to him. "Hang on, old boy," he said casually. "Look, something's going on here, the Ford just turned up. Get Grant out of the way and I'll speak to you later." He broke the connection and studied Neeson and the driver of the Mondeo through the binoculars. "Now, what are you two little birdies singing about?"

***

Neeson had walked over to the driver's side of the Ford Mondeo and smiled anxiously at Ross, as the man opened his door and stepped out onto the muddy ground. "Everything go alright?"

Ross grinned. "So far, so good. I've just heard a report on the radio. They say that there was a bomb blast, or gas explosion, no news on the casualties yet, but they'll do a special update later."

"Good. Looks like they succeeded then," Neeson quipped. He glanced at his watch, then looked back at Ross. Both men looked down as a car sped past. "Did Sean get away all right?"

Ross shrugged his shoulders. "I presume so. I heard heavy gunfire not long after they went in. I thought I had better get the hell out of there. No sense in risking both of us getting caught," he paused, looked up at the sound of an approaching vehicle. Both men looked up expectantly, then turned their faces away when they saw that it wasn't Sean. The car drove past, the driver merely glanced at them.

Neeson let out a low chuckle. "That would be Patrick, I'm sure. The mad bastard always was trigger happy..." He shrugged. "Just goes to show we picked the right man for the job."

Both men looked up at the sound of a high-pitched exhaust note as another car approached, down shifting through the gears. "Aye, here he is now!" Ross exclaimed excitedly, somewhat relieved that his friend had made a safe getaway.

The Peugeot pulled erratically off the road and into the lay-by, splashing through a muddy puddle before coming to rest behind the Ford Mondeo. Sean opened his door and hastily stepped out. He slammed the door shut and held up his arms in a gesture of triumph. "You should have heard the blast! It was unbelievable; it rocked my car outside the grounds! What the hell did you have in it?"

Neeson smiled. "Four-pounds of Semtex, twenty-pounds of fertiliser packed with over six pounds of nails and screws, he said casually and watched the men's expressions. "Oh, and half a dozen cans of lighter fluid, just to help clear the remains away."

"Jesus, Mary and Joseph," Ross said quietly. "Those poor bastards..."

"No!" Neeson glared at him. "They were bastards, the fucking lot of them! Right after the peace agreement got underway, they tried to shatter it with an attack. They weren't working towards the cause like us! They had their sticky fingers in everything. Splinter groups like the INLA, IPLO, and not just at home.

Rumour is that McCormick and his team had their own little enterprise going on the side. Six months ago, a Spanish politician was shot and killed in Santander. ETA claimed responsibility, but guess where our friends had just been for a wee little holiday?" He spat on the ground in distaste. "I've no time for chequebook assassins, especially when they are using the situation at home to line their own pockets."

"What about the peace agreement?" Ross stared back at him defiantly. "What are we doing here, if we really want it to work?"

"We are protecting our future," said Neeson. "It will fail; we all know that. The British will shaft us, like they shaft everyone. But we must never be the ones who are looked on as not having tried. The likes of McCormick and his hired guns can only ruin the effect for us. We also need to keep the funds rolling in," he paused. "When the cease-fire and everything else goes by the board, we will need to fight harder and dirtier than ever before. The opposition must be overwhelmed by our superior ordinance and unlimited funds. Today has served two purposes - we get rid of a box of bad apples, while at the same time, raise enough money to buy a box of good ones." He smiled at the two men, then looked at his watch. "Right, are you ready? It's nearly time."

***

Forsyth moved further along the field, keeping tight to the fence and the row of bushes and small trees lining the roadside. Unusual for one with such a high rank within the Secret Intelligence Service, he had never seen military service. He had therefore never had formal training in camouflage and concealment techniques. On the other hand, Ian Forsyth had a quite unsurpassed talent for stalking. He had been brought up on his family's estate in the Scottish Highlands, and had been taught the art by his father's gamekeeper. From an early age, Forsyth had regularly accompanied him on deer-culling shoots. At the age of twelve, he had stalked his first stag, approaching through the long bracken and heather, from downwind and over a distance of more than four-hundred metres, and finally dropping the beast from eighty-metres with one shot from his father's Remington .30-06 rifle. Deer, hare and feathered game were far more sensitive creatures than humans. Forsyth could move through the countryside like a shadow. Grading his footsteps and controlling his breathing, he was soon level with the vehicles, his presence completely undetected.

Sean reversed the Peugeot up the road around the blind corner, then pulled in tight against the grass verge. In the meantime, Jason Porter started the Porsche's throaty engine and drove steadily down the road, halfway around the sharp right-hand bend, then pulled up tight to the hedge, keeping the powerful engine idling smoothly. He glanced nervously into his rear view mirror, tapping his fingers against the steering wheel in anticipation. He was not entirely sure of the plan, all he knew was that when he heard the sound of a car-horn, he was to pull across both lanes, switch off the engine, lift the rear engine cover and activate his hazard lights. After that, he was to stay in position and await further instructions from Neeson.

Neeson watched his mobile phone intently. The signal was strong. He glanced at his watch, then back at the screen. The ringtone chimed and he saw the number displayed on the screen. As arranged, it rang four times, then ended. The next call would tell him if they were on, or had to stand down. They had come too far, taken to big a steps to stand down now. The phone rang again, this time just twice.

They were on.

Neeson kept his eyes on the rear view mirror. In the distance, he could see a vehicle approaching. The colour seemed correct - white with a light blue trim. Then, as the vehicle got closer, he was able to make out the shape. He was positive. His contact had been as good as his word, but he was getting a great deal more out of this venture than merely money. Neeson pressed the horn, cursed when it did not sound. He fumbled for the ignition. Years of driving told him to turn the key on the steering column, but the Saab's ignition was on the centre console next to the gear lever. *Bloody Swedes,* he cursed. He switched the ignition on but the van was now far closer than he had planned it to be. He pressed the horn twice, then started the vehicle's engine and engaged first gear.

The van drove steadily past him and towards Sean, waiting in the Peugeot.

Sean waited until it was approximately twenty-metres clear, then swung out into the road, occupying both lanes. He quickly released the bonnet catch, switched on the hazard lights and hastily opened his door. As he ran around to the front of the Peugeot, he raised the bonnet, then fastened it in place, before taking the M16 out of the boot and running frantically down the road.

Upon hearing the sound of a car-horn, Jason Porter almost found himself completely overtaken with a feeling of sheer, unrelenting panic. A sense of impending doom that he could not explain. It was too late now, he would have to regain his composure and continue as planned. His old life was behind him now, too late to turn back, and without the money promised to him, he would have no existence at all. He swung the Porsche out into the road, then operated the hazard warning lights and switched off the engine. He got out, released the engine compartment catch and walked around to the rear of the vehicle and opened it up to expose the engine.

Ross waited for the security van to pass him, then pulled steadily out of the lay-by and followed, matching the vehicle's speed, at a distance of no more than twenty-metres. He looked down at the M16 in the foot-well next to him. There was no going back now.

It was all down to Neeson now, timing was everything. Between the two points where the Peugeot and the Porsche were parked, there was enough distance for them to stop the security van, while remaining completely hidden from any approaching traffic. The stretch of road had been chosen carefully. There was enough curve, that from apex to apex, there was a distance of one-hundred and eighty-metres of road that would hidden from view. The guise of a car breaking down, while occupying both lanes, would be sufficient to stop any other vehicles from passing, but would certainly not work for long.

Time was of the essence.

Neeson revved the Saab's engine as he waited, then as the security van was almost upon him; he accelerated out into the road, forcing the driver of the van to hit the brakes urgently. Neeson changed up into second, building his speed, then pulled the handbrake and turned the steering wheel to the right. The Saab skidded in the road, coming to rest broadside, in the van's path.

The driver of the van sounded the horn and quickly applied the brakes. He struggled to engage reverse gear, but before he could, Ross had pulled the Ford Mondeo across the road, just inches from the van's rear bumper.

Neeson jumped out of the Saab and aimed his silenced Glock model 19 at the windscreen, in a double-handed grip. Both the driver and the security guard in the passenger seat raised their hands, instantly conceding at the sight of the handgun. Neeson suspected that the tiny 9 mm pistol would not be a match for the toughened laminated glass of the security van, especially with the addition of the suppressor, which would lower the bullet's velocity considerably. He glanced down the side of the van and signalled for Ross to come to the front.

Ross turned to Sean, who had just reached the rear of the van and was breathing heavily from the sudden exertion. Both men took aim and fired at the vehicle's tyres. They shredded and the armoured van dropped down on one side. Both men walked around and fired on the wheels on the nearside. The van dropped lower, its underside only inches from the road. Both men stepped back and covered the front and rear doors, casually reloading their weapons.

"Take the fuckers out!" Neeson shouted. "No witnesses." He nodded to both men, then stood aside for Ross to get into the best position.

Ross calmly stepped around to the driver's door and shouldered the rifle. Both security guards signalled desperately for him not to shoot, the held their hands high, there was no mistaking the gestures. Ross fired and the glass held. He squeezed off ten rounds, and the glass spider-webbed and seemed to go loose in the door frame. He stepped closer, kept firing, and the glass finally gave out. The windscreen was covered in blood and brain matter instantaneously. He calmly reloaded a full magazine, and walked to the rear of the vehicle, where Sean was crouched low, wiring a series of small Semtex charges to the hinges and lock. There were wires hanging down to a central charge unit and he stepped backwards and around the van, feeding out the command wire. Ross and Neeson joined him and crouched down by the nearside front wheel.

Sean took out the battery-powered control unit and connected a wire to one of the terminals. "Ready?"

Neeson nodded. "Ready."

"Fire in the hold!"

"What?" Neeson frowned.

"Always wanted to say that."

"Just blow it."

"You're only supposed to blow the bloody doors off…" Sean grinned

"Worst Michael Caine ever," Ross said. "Come on man!"

Sean connected the second wire to the terminal and pressed the red button. The van rocked and the explosion was a dull thud, followed by a solid boom. The van shifted a foot forwards on its flat rubber.

Neeson stood up first, walked around to the rear of the vehicle and aimed his weapon at the smoking doorway of the security van. He advanced cautiously. He held his left hand over his nose and mouth and peered through the thick, pungent smoke. The lone security guard lay on his side, rendered unconscious by the ferocity of the blast. The IRA man aimed the pistol at the man's chest and fired two shots in rapid succession. The body threw itself into violent spasm, then lay still. Neeson stepped out from the barrage of thick smoke; breathed in some fresh air, then bellowed at the two men. "Right, come on! Get unloading!" He stood aside, allowing both men to pass. "Get everything loaded into the Saab and the Ford, quickly!" He caught hold of two heavy sacks, then walked quickly back to the Saab.

He was soon joined by Sean, who dropped both of his sacks into the boot of the vehicle and grinned excitedly. "There's a chuffing fortune here, boss! An absolute fortune!"

Neeson tried to suppress a smile. "Later! Just keep unloading!" He ran back to the rear of the security van and grabbed hold of another two sacks. He just couldn't help smiling to himself. Sean was right. If the sacks contained what they had been led to believe, then there was an absolute fortune - far more than both he and Mark O'Shea had ever anticipated.

***

Forsyth cursed the fact that he was not carrying a weapon, although he seriously doubted that he would have been able to take on three armed men and walk away unscathed. He had seen enough. He had done and seen more than most in his dozen or so years with MI6, but even he had been sickened by the way the three unarmed security guards had been so needlessly slain.

He edged his way cautiously backwards, keeping both eyes on the three men, until reached a bend in the hedgerow and was out of sight. He then retreated to the relative safety of his car. He tried to call King, but the man must have been in a blackspot. He cursed and tossed the phone onto the seat next to him. He switched on the laptop and saw the red dot indicating the Saab's position on the map. It was still stationary. His adrenalin was pumping and his breathing was erratic. He tried to breathe steadily, calm himself, but his shaking hands told him he was far from calming down.

***

With the sacks loaded evenly into the two cars, Danny Neeson turned to Ross and held out his hand. "Give me your rifle, quickly!"

Ross handed him the weapon, and Neeson snatched it out of his grasp. "And the control unit." Ross did as he was ordered, although he could not hide the confusion from his face. "Right, you two get yourselves the hell out of here and back to the farm, drive carefully and at the limit, and don't get yourselves nicked!"

Ross jumped into the driver's side of the Mondeo and opened the door for Sean. It was just short of one-hundred metres back to the Peugeot, but no doubt the man would be grateful of the short ride.

Neeson ran along the side of the security van and back to his vehicle. He opened the near side rear door and hastily pulled out two large canvas holdalls, then dragged them towards the rear of the Saab. He opened the rear hatch, then lifted out one of the heavily laden sacks. He glanced nervously over his shoulder, Sean would have reached the Peugeot by now, the road would soon be free from obstruction; the last thing that he wanted was to be seen beside the security van.

He unfastened the drawstrings and opened the two newly acquired canvas sacks. Inside, the sacks were full of waxed paper, cut into rectangular pieces. He pulled the silenced 9 mm pistol from the waistband of his trousers, then dropped it inside one of the sacks, along with the electronic control unit used to detonate the explosive charges. He refastened the drawstrings, then placed one of the stolen sacks from the armoured van into the other canvas sack, pressed it tightly in place and refastened them. With the rifle under his arm, and a heavy sack in each hand, he half carried - half dragged his load around the corner to where Jason Porter was anxiously waiting in the stolen Porsche.

Porter glanced up at Neeson as he rounded the corner, and instantly started the Porsche's throaty 3.4 litre, flat six engine. He reached over the specially adapted space, where the passenger seat had once been, and opened the door.

Neeson dragged the sacks around to the passenger side and rested them on the ground, as he placed the rifle into the foot-well. "Here, take this with you."

Porter looked at the weapon hesitantly. "What for?"

Neeson lifted one of the sacks into the specially designed space, then grinned as he picked up the second, heavier sack and heaved it into the vehicle. "Don't worry, it's not for you to use, I just don't want to chance walking back to my car with a gun on me," he paused, checking over his shoulder for any signs of approaching traffic, then looked at Porter seriously. "Right lad, get going back to the farmhouse. Don't take any chances, I don't want you getting nicked." He grinned wolfishly. "Not with over ten-million quid in cash on you!"

Porter's mouth dropped open upon hearing the amount. He swallowed, then looked nervously at Neeson. "Sure, I'll be alright." He slipped the gearbox into first gear then dipped the throttle, waking the beast. "Better get going."

"Sure, drive safely." Neeson slammed the passenger door shut and watched as the Porsche's wheels spun on the tarmac. The car accelerated erratically up the road as Porter raced through the gears. He smiled at the display. It just proved that Porter was the right person for the job. A good choice. Undisciplined and untrustworthy.

***

Jason Porter accelerated hard out of the corner and changed up to fourth. He loved the Porsche 911. He loved the sharp and precise gearbox, the closeness of the pedals. He loved the way that the bulges either side of the bonnet acted as perfect markers for both the white lines and the curb. It was as easy to thread through the country roads as a go-kart around a track. Another slick change and he was up around eighty miles per hour, and breaking for the next bend, where he would thread the car through the apex.

He had it all planned. The Irish were unlikely to kill his family if he disappeared with their money. They would be lying low after the robbery. It would be enough time to get his immediate family clear and safely away. He patted the bags beside him. *Ten million,* Neeson had said. Well, there were not many places he couldn't hide with that amount. Someplace warm, someplace where he could merge into the background. Just another young millionaire trader. He liked the idea of Monaco. And he would get to watch the Grand Prix from his own balcony. And as the cars raced past, and the champagne flowed, he wouldn't spare a thought for the family members he had left behind. Neeson could do what he wanted with them. He never sent Christmas cards anyway.

He smiled to himself. It was going to be alright. He had done his part, and what he took from them would just be a bonus for the inconvenience of having to lose his identity, to uproot his immediate family, his girlfriend's too.

The ringing halted his train of thought. He didn't have a mobile phone on him, had to surrender it to Neeson. The phone rang three times. Porter did not hear anything more before he died.

The call had activated the mercury tilt switch. Both ends of the circuit were now live. The ball of mercury, which had rolled to and fro with the vehicle's movements, was now the conductor which would complete the circuit and initiate the RDX detonator, which in turn would detonate the one-pound block of Semtex plastic explosive. All of this happened between the third and fourth ring.

As both Neeson and O'Shea had suspected, Porter was travelling away from the farm, away from Kempton Park and putting distance between the scene of the armoured vehicle robbery. The police would focus on where Porter was heading, rather than the area to the north where Neeson, Ross and Sean were now traveling to with the money.

31

King grunted as he heaved the dead weight of Grant's unconscious body onto the bed. He had walked him out of the van, up the flight of stairs and into the flat, rather than carrying him, in an effort to remain inconspicuous. At the same time, he had acted drunkenly, slurring the words of a lewd song. To any casual observer, it would look as if the two men had returned home after an all-night drinking session somewhat the worse-for-wear. It was nearly eight-thirty, but King had come home later and certainly in a worse state in the past.

He quickly undressed Grant's limp body, leaving the man's boxer shorts in place, then walked out to the kitchen to collect his compact but comprehensive first aid kit. Treatment was rapid, but thorough. The splinters of wood and shards of glass were quickly extracted with a pair of tweezers, the bleeding points dabbed, antiseptic rubbed in, and surgical plasters applied over the wounds. He felt as he went, checking for fractures, and after the swift examination, decided that Grant might have a cracked rib or two. It was evident that no pressure lay against the man's lungs, so there was little he could do; nothing more would have been attempted in hospital, save for the intravenous administration of pain killers.

King turned his attention to the egg-sized lump on top of Grant's skull. There was no bleeding, but the lump was obviously the cause of his concussion. If he did not regain consciousness within the next hour, he would drive him somewhere quiet, drop him off, and call an ambulance from a phone box. He was not overly concerned about Simon Grant's welfare; he was more interested in whatever additional information the man could possibly provide. He rolled him over onto his side, covered him with a sheet then walked out of the room, closing the door behind him.

***

Forsyth eased off the accelerator and pulled into the side of the road. He had a clear view of the farm from across the fields and could see that both the Ford Mondeo and the Peugeot were parked outside the farmhouse. Frank Holman's Mercedes was parked next to the Sierra and now there was a new addition to the fleet: a large gold BMW, parked near the entrance to the courtyard.

Neeson's Saab was travelling down the bumpy lane, on route to the farm. Forsyth watched for a minute or two, as the Saab entered the farmyard and halted outside the house. Neeson stepped out of his vehicle and performed an exaggerated stretch, then walked casually across the courtyard and up the path to the farmhouse.

Forsyth dialled King's number, spoke tersely when it was answered. "Alex, where are you?"

"At the flat."

"Are you watching?"

"No. I just got in. I had to see to Grant's injuries first."

"Injuries?"

"Blast and shrapnel. Glass and splinters mainly. He'll be okay."

"Bollocks to him, old boy. Switch the monitor on and see what's happening. It's a bloody house party down here."

King sat down heavily in the chair and switched on the monitor. Adrenalin was leaving his system. His limbs felt heavy and tired. There was no picture; the motion-activated system obviously sensed nothing to pick up. He glanced at the nearby audio receiver and could see that it was recording in the farmhouse. He turned up the volume then sat back in his seat to catch the riotous hum of high spirited voices.

***

"Congratulations, lads!" Holman patted the collection of sacks on the table, then took another long swig of whisky. "I fucking well knew you lot could pull it off!"

Ross and Sean beamed at Neeson as he entered the room. He returned a grin, entering into the party atmosphere, then glanced at the pile of sacks and thumbed towards the door. "Plenty more out there, lads, off you go!" The two men jumped up from their seats and rushed to the door, ever eager to add to the collection of money sacks, which rested on and beside the large pine table.

"So it all went to plan, then?" O'Shea asked, passing him a large tumbler of whiskey.

Neeson nodded, as he reached out and accepted the glass. "Aye, textbook perfect." He stared warily for a moment at the new arrival - a tall and thin, but hard-looking man in his mid-forties with thinning, short-cropped hair. "And this must be the infamous Mister Parker."

"Indeed." The man stepped forward, a bundle of American one hundred-dollar bills in one hand, and a large tumbler of whisky in the other. "And you're Danny Neeson," he said flatly. He dropped the bundle of money on the table and held out his hand. "Glad to meet you, after so long. Nice work."

Neeson gripped the man's hand and shook it firmly. He picked up a stack of fifty-pound notes and grinned. "Top info," he replied. He raised his glass. "To a job well done!"

Ross and Sean walked into the kitchen and dropped the rest of the sacks on the floor. Sean looked nervously at Neeson, then nodded towards the pile of sacks. "There were only five sacks in your car, Danny. There were six earlier."

Neeson grinned at O'Shea. "See how suspicious people become when there's money involved." Neeson walked over to Sean and patted him lightly upon the cheek. "Aye lad, you are right to question the money's whereabouts, but I'm afraid that it has gone forever."

O'Shea turned around and smiled. "An expensive, but necessary investment, I'm afraid." Sean nodded knowingly, although he was still none the wiser, and returned to his whiskey.

O'Shea suddenly banged his glass down on the table, then raised it triumphantly in the air. "Gentlemen!" He looked at each man sincerely. "To money, and a new and peaceful way of life!"

***

King spun around quickly, as he heard the sound of a key being placed in the front-door lock. He pulled the Browning 9 mm from his hip holster and kept it by his side, hidden from view by the arm of the chair. Forsyth appeared in the doorway, a look of anguish upon his face.

King slipped the pistol back into his holster, then looked expectantly at the MI6 officer. "What the hell's going on Ian? I've been listening in on the receiver for half an hour and they're all going haywire!" he paused as he sat back down in the chair. "Money, drinking toasts, some new guy, who's obviously well in with them. What the hell happened?"

Forsyth walked over to his chair and sat down silently. He dropped the front door key onto the coffee table, then took a small silver hip flask out of his jacket pocket. He methodically unscrewed the cap, sipped a mouthful of the contents then offered the flask to King. "Napoleon brandy, care for a jigger?"

King shook his head in frustration, exasperated near breaking point by Forsyth's casual delay. "No! Just tell me what went on!"

"Calm down, old boy. It never pays to get oneself so worked up." Forsyth took his cigarette case from his inside pocket then opened the lid gleefully. "I followed Neeson to a spot just outside North Holmwood," he paused, extracting a handmade cigarette. "The man parked his Saab in an overgrown layby and that chap Jason Porter parked the Porsche approximately two-hundred metres further up the road." Forsyth slipped the cigarette into the side of his mouth, then flicked the wheel of his gold lighter and brought the flame to the tip of the cigarette. "After I spoke to you on the mobile, the Ford Mondeo arrived, followed by the Peugeot approximately ten minutes later." He exhaled a thin plume of smoke, then smiled with satisfaction. "They positioned themselves, then waited. An armoured security van drove past a few minutes later. The man in the Peugeot sounded his horn as a signal, then pulled across the road. He popped the bonnet, then followed after the van on foot. The chap in the Porsche pulled across both lanes as well, then stayed in position. Both the driver of the Mondeo, and our friend Neeson blocked the van in the road, leaving the area of the operation out of sight, between two corners."

King frowned. "An armed robbery? An old fashioned hold-up?"

"Yes, old boy. A plain and simple, old-fashioned hold up." Forsyth flicked some excess ash into the ashtray, then slipped the cigarette back between his thin lips. "But with plastic explosive and assault rifles. It was bloody carnage, old boy. They took care of the two guards in the cab, then blew off the rear doors and shot into the back, killing whoever was inside. I'm pretty sure that there would only have been one guard in the rear of the vehicle. They off-loaded the loot into the Saab and the Ford, but unfortunately, that was when I bid my farewell. I didn't see anything after that."

"So, you don't know what happened after they unloaded?"

Forsyth blew a perfect smoke ring towards him, then smiled. "I didn't say that, old boy. I said I got out of there," he mused. "I couldn't see where the Porsche went, but I followed Danny Neeson back to the farm. Both the Ford and the Peugeot were there when he arrived."

Both men simultaneously looked towards the receiver, as the excitable banter suddenly died down, and a serious conversation began to emerge.

***

"What about the lad?" Sean asked quietly. "Where did he and his fancy car get to?"

Neeson shrugged. "He took all the evidence with him. A sack of French Francs, the electronic control unit, Ross's rifle and my pistol." He picked up his whiskey, sipped slowly, then turned back to Sean. "That and two large sacks of waxed paper cut to look like banknotes."

Sean furrowed his brow. "What do you mean?"

Neeson chuckled. "In the bottom of one of the sacks was a pound of Semtex. Jason Porter will take the credit of the armed robbery for us. Most of the interior of the vehicle will be vaporized by such a large amount of plastic explosive; leaving the forensics people with mere traces of money, electrical components, weaponry and body parts. And the chassis and VIN numbers of the Porsche, which he left the showroom with when he disappeared."

Ross stared at the floor in dismay. "But he was Okay. I thought that he was with us."

"Aye, that he was. Right from the word go." O'Shea nodded with a smile. "He has a criminal record for his part in an armed robbery and car theft. He was perfect. A few days ago, he disappeared with a brand new Porsche 911 from the classy car showroom where he worked, under a false identification and persona. When the police find his body, or what's left of it, he will have a number of burned and charred items on him, including the remains of the control unit that blew the doors off the van, two weapons, both of which were involved in killing the three guards, not to mention charred money. The waxed paper will burn amongst the real money. The whole scene will look pretty conclusive," he paused as he sipped a mouthful of whiskey, then smiled wryly. "The cops will think that he just got sloppy, blew himself to kingdom come with some explosive that he didn't use."

"So, you see, Neeson commented. "He really was with us, gave his life to the cause, so he did..."

"Nobody will ever suspect that it was the IRA who pulled off the job, there's absolutely no evidence pointing our way." O'Shea announced gleefully. "The two events will be unconnected. An ambitious but rubbish armed robber, and an IRA splinter group trying to derail the peace agreement."

Neeson turned to O'Shea. "What about the racetrack? What's been said on the television or radio?"

"The police say that it looks as if a terrorist organisation, possibly animal rights extremists, were planting a device when something went terribly wrong for them. As yet, no organisation has accepted responsibility," he said, shaking his head. "And nor will they. We are the only people who will ever know for sure. Those men were rotten to the core. They hired themselves out to the INLA and the IPLO, and used our funds in the process. They even used our intelligence and resources to set up an arms deal last autumn; PIRA never saw a penny."

"What about my interest?" Parker's voice was quiet and unassuming, yet exuded confidence. "I trust that has been taken care of?"

"Yes, of course. As agreed." O'Shea turned to both Ross and Sean. "You see, Mr Parker here, is the general manager of the security firm whose van you just hit. His company has just received a new contract with Gatwick International Airport. The money we have now was on route to the money exchanges in every terminal, just in time for the weekend. It was being taken along a devious route, that he just so happened to find out about." The Irishman beamed a smile. "The route should only have been known to the courier manager. The security team was to be told on the day," O'Shea paused. "Mr Parker saw to it that the compressed-air operated dye canisters to be placed inside the sacks as a deterrent, were recalled the day before, due to some fault or other. The company decided to ferry the money regardless, eager to fulfil their obligations so early into their contract. There was no way they could turn down such a large deal, not with the competition as it is. I seriously doubt that his company will end up keeping the contract now!"

The rest of the men all laughed, except for Parker, who remained straight-faced. "What I meant was, I kept to my side of the bargain. I supplied the relevant, but essential information. Did you keep to yours?"

Holman placed a hand on Parker's shoulder. "Weren't you listening Keith? The team was all blown to pieces. Simon Grant is dead! Lisa won't need a divorce, but what's more, a dead man can't possibly take her away from you!" Holman patted the man reassuringly on his shoulder. "And on top of that, you are now an extremely wealthy man indeed!"

***

"Bastard. The utter bastard…"

King and Forsyth both turned around, startled by the silent intrusion. Simon Grant stood in the passageway leading to the bathroom and the bedroom. He wore a pair of King's trousers and a dark grey sweater, although the outfit was far too big for him. He stepped forward and stared at the two men.

"What is going on?" he asked indignantly. "Who are you, and where am I?"

King stood up and pointed to the small sofa on the other side of the low coffee table. "Sit down over there." He turned to Forsyth and frowned, as if for guidance.

"Come now, old chap, do as he says and take a seat." Forsyth opened his cigarette case and offered it to Grant. "You are in a right old pickle; wouldn't you say?" Grant reached forward and accepted one of the handmade cigarettes, then slipped it into his mouth, his hands shaking slightly. He leaned forward as Forsyth reached out and flicked the wheel of his lighter. Grant winced, his ribs obviously causing him a great deal of discomfort. Forsyth smiled. "The least of your worries, I'd say," he smiled, blowing out a thin plume of smoke. "It would seem that you are caught slap bang in the middle. The IRA on one side, your friend Holman on the other, your wife's lover... Not good, not good at all. And now us."

Grant turned his stare to King and then back to Forsyth. "And who are you?" he asked defiantly, regaining a little composure.

"Oh, we're working for Her Majesty's Government. Don't even think of asking more, because you will not be told. Let's just say, it's a shadowy department that doesn't officially exist and we answer to very few people. Better to accept you belong to us now." Forsyth turned to King and smiled. "Please sit back down Alex, I think you're making our guest a trifle nervous."

King reluctantly sat back down, then held up his hand, as Forsyth was about to speak. "Wait." He nodded towards the receiver. "Leave the questions for later, I think we should listen..."

***

O'Shea banged his fist down on the table in an effort to regain some authority. It was time for the high-spirited banter and celebrations to come to an end. He looked seriously at Ross and Sean, then pushed a large pile of twenty-pound notes towards them and smiled. "Here, take this little lot for expenses," he paused, then pushed two large bundles of American fifty-dollar bills towards them. "And that's a little bonus for your troubles. You're both leaving tomorrow morning, at seven o'clock. Take the Ford and head for Liverpool, you know where the safe houses are. Keep your heads down for two weeks, then get yourselves back home on the ferry. Separately. And don't spend the money just yet."

Ross picked up the pile of dollars and grinned gleefully as he walked towards the door to the hallway. Sean grabbed the handful of pound sterling and beamed a smile.

"No arguing now, sort yourselves out with an equal split." O'Shea picked up the whiskey bottle, which was half-full, or half-empty, depending on your way of thinking. Today was more of a half-full day. He handed it to Sean. "Go on, get it down! A winner's breakfast! Just make yourselves scarce for a while, we've got further business to discuss." He waited for the two men to leave the room then turned to Keith Parker. "Well done. Your information was bang on the nail." He counted out the bundles of pound sterling, then slid the pile towards him. "Here, as agreed. Five-hundred-thousand pounds, or thereabouts. Keep it safe, and don't be too bloody obvious." He smiled. "You don't need to be told to hide it and wait for all of this to blow over, do you?"

"No."

"Good. I didn't realise how big a pile like that would be. Got a suitcase?"

He held up a roll of black plastic bin liners. "I work with this stuff. I knew it would be a fair old stack." Parker reached forward, trying to suppress a childlike grin. "I intend to lie low for a bit. I might well do what Holman here has done and buy myself a little holiday home in France, take it easy for a change. I've got some holiday time due. I might even look to change careers next year, once the dust has settled. Or retire altogether."

He opened up two of the bin liners and started to stack the bundles of money neatly inside. He looked across at Holman, who was still sipping from a large tumbler of whisky. "Thank you, Frank. It took a while to plan, but we finally did it."

"Fortunate that we could tie up all the factors," Holman said. "I'm pleased to have helped you with your... problem."

O'Shea rose to his feet and held his hand out across the table. Parker noted the gesture and realised that it was time for him to bid farewell. He shook O'Shea's hand firmly then gave a quick nod to Neeson. "I'd best be off. It was a pleasure doing business with you."

O'Shea waited until Keith Parker had left the house and was walking down the path before he spoke. "What about you Holman, what are your plans?"

Frank Holman set his empty glass down on the table and smiled. "I'm going to put my feet up for a change, like Parker said, take it easy."

Neeson turned to O'Shea and patted a nearby money sack. "Best be putting this lot away, we're here for a day or two more at least." He stood up and looked at Holman. "Come on, fatty," he teased. "You can help us out. Do some work for a change!"

Holman stood up reluctantly and caught hold of a sack in each hand. He grunted under the strain, obviously unaccustomed to such strenuous work, then followed Neeson out of the front door. The three men trudged across the wet and muddy yard towards the barn, avoiding the myriad of puddles as best they could. As Holman waited for Neeson to unbolt the lock, the weight proved too much for him and he released his grip on the sack in his left hand. Neeson gave the man a look of contempt, then unbolted the door and hastily stepped inside.

***

"Where do you think they've gone?" Forsyth glanced across at Grant, who simply shrugged.

"It has to be the barn," King leaned forward and switched on the monitor. There was nothing but a blank screen. He looked back at Forsyth, who seemed quite agitated at the sudden loss of communication.

Forsyth stubbed his cigarette into the ashtray and opened the silver cigarette case as he looked at Grant. "Is there anywhere else at the farm where they would perhaps store the money?" he asked, then shook his head. "Oh, hang on, all is well…"

King followed Forsyth's gaze and saw the monitor's screen flicker slightly, then reveal Neeson half-dragging, half carrying two large sacks into the cavernous space of the empty barn.

***

Neeson dropped his two sacks on the ground near a stack of musty straw bales, then turned and smiled as he watched Holman drag his sack towards him. The man was panting, his face had turned a slight tinge of scarlet, and he was sweating heavily from his deeply furrowed brow.

Neeson walked back to where Holman had dropped half of his load. He picked up the sack, slinging it casually over his shoulder, then followed O'Shea towards the pile of sacks.

"The world and their dog hates a fucking show off," Holman said sarcastically as he wiped his saturated

brow. Neeson remained silent. Holman looked around the barn, frowned, then looked at Neeson and asked, "Where are the bodies?"

Neeson shrugged. "Ross and Sean buried them someplace," he replied tersely. "Plenty of places to dig on a farm. They dumped the car too." He walked past him, then started to move the stack of straw bales. Holman watched in silence, as Neeson moved three bales aside to reveal a sheet of blue polythene covering. He dropped down onto his knees and brushed the loose scattering of straw away then carefully peeled back the section of sheet. In its place and set into the ground was a steel door, approximately one-metre wide and one and a half metres long.

"Jesus! It looks bomb proof!" Holman exclaimed. "It's sure to be safe in there."

"Aye, that's the idea." Neeson stood up and turned to O'Shea. "You get it opened, boss, and I'll go for the rest of the sacks."

O'Shea, who had been standing beside Holman, stepped forward and bent down, as Neeson jogged out of the barn. He reached down and gently twisted the combination dial, several times, in both directions, until the lock clicked open. Holman watched intently, never before had he seen such a large safe; the hinges were recessed and the rim of the door overlapped the sides. O'Shea reached under his collar and looped a length of chain over his head. Attached to the chain was a large key with a complex-looking set of wards. He slipped the key into the lock and turned it several times in both directions. Then he looked up at Holman and nodded towards the safe.

"Give us a hand, it's going to take two."

Holman bent down and eased his fingers under the rim of the door, then heaved in time with O'Shea. After much effort the door fell back against the straw-covered ground, to reveal a deep, steel-sided casing, at least two-inches thick.

O'Shea stood up and turned to the pile of sacks beside him. He opened two of them and started to count out the bundles of notes onto the ground.

Holman looked at the pile greedily; he knew that this was to be his share, and almost salivated at the sight.

"One-million pounds, as agreed." O'Shea turned his back on Holman and started to drop the sacks into the hold. "Don't spend it straight away, don't brag down the pub and don't get caught. Go and lie low. What did Parker say? A holiday home in France? Time for you to go and have a croissant and some cheese and watch the boats. In fact, I insist."

Holman dropped to his knees and grinned gleefully as he caught hold of the pile of French francs, American and Australian dollars and pound sterling. He pulled the considerable pile towards him, then took two large polythene carrier bags out of his coat pocket and proceeded to stuff them with the bundles, along with pieces of straw and debris. "Pleasure doing business with you, Mister O'Shea. An absolute pleasure!"

"Aye, just don't go getting yourself caught." O'Shea turned around and stared at him menacingly. "You know never to cross our organisation; our reach is extremely long indeed."

Holman shook his head. "I'm not stupid, you know. Tomorrow, I'm long gone."

"We will be too." O'Shea turned his back on him and continued to load the sacks into the hold.

Neeson appeared in the doorway of the barn, struggling to carry three sacks. He stared distastefully at Holman. "Are you sorted?" Holman nodded. "Aye, well get going. Myself, I wanted to put a bullet in your brain and save on your considerable fee. But, luckily for you, O'Shea is a man of his word, and said that you've done a good job and may be useful to us again in the future," he paused, glaring him. "So get your fat arse out of here before he changes his mind!" Neeson walked past him and dropped the three sacks straight into the hold.

O'Shea caught hold of the edge of the door and waited for Neeson to do the same. Between them, they lifted the door up and eased it back into position. As O'Shea twisted the combination dial and re-locked the door with the key, Neeson turned around and smiled to himself. Frank Holman had disappeared.

32

Forsyth stubbed his cigarette into the ashtray, then leaned back in his chair, making no attempt to suppress a wry smile. "Well, well, well. Whoever would have thought it?" he paused, rubbing his chin ponderously. "The IRA, so committed to the peace agreement, that they actually blow a rogue splinter group to kingdom come. A man so jealous of his girlfriend's past, so threatened by the thought of her estranged husband being released from prison and wanting to make a fresh start, that he puts together a plan where part of his payment is the husband's death!" Forsyth opened his case and took out a handmade cigarette. "Not to mention Frank Holman, the mutual friend who agrees to deliver the husband, like a lamb to the slaughter."

King nodded. "And the fact that the IRA are so dubious of the peace agreement and its duration, that they're on a fund-raising mission, the like of which we've never seen."

Grant reached forward and stubbed the butt of his cigarette into the overfilling ashtray. He winced, placing a hand over his aching ribs for comfort. "What about me, do I get arrested or something?"

King shook his head. "No. Not yet, at least. I think I may have an idea."

"Do tell." Forsyth said, incredulously. "This whole situation has gone too far. People have died, I accept responsibility for that. If we had acted sooner, those security guards, both at Kempton Park, and at the site of the armed robbery would still be alive."

"It's not all on you, Ian," said King. "I wanted more intel. I wanted to see what they were doing. If I'd just killed O'Shea, then none of this would have happened."

"You're an assassin?" Grant shook his head in despair. "What's going on?"

Forsyth looked at Grant. "I'll surmise for you. We are members of the intelligence community. We have been tasked with removing a prominent IRA member, before the peace agreement is signed in two days' time. You will never speak of us, never mention our existence to anyone. If you do, then the IRA will be the least of your worries. Understand?" Grant nodded emphatically. "Good."

"We know where the money is being kept, Ian," King paused, patted the monitor. "And we have a safecracker right here, who I am pretty certain will want to help us. Unless he would rather go to prison on terrorist related offences? Or his involvement in the armed robbery? Let's face it, coerced or not, we've got more than enough on tape to send him down."

"What are you saying, old boy?" Forsyth frowned. "That we take their money?"

"Exactly. We can't involve the police, because technically, we're operating outside of the law."

"Then what do we do with the money? Keep it?"

King laughed. "Of course not," he said. "But we don't let *them* keep it."

"So we steal their money. And then, what? Kill them?"

"We have to anyway," King said. "That was the job."

"So many loose ends," said Forsyth, tapping another cigarette on the lid of the silver case. "The police will have to be involved at some point."

"Maybe not," King paused. "As I said; I have an idea."

Grant stared at the two men warily. "I don't want to cross these people. After all, they think I'm dead. What about the safety of my family?"

Forsyth chuckled, apparently to himself. "My dear man, that was all a wonderfully played bluff. It was merely a ploy to get you to agree. Your wife's boyfriend was involved. The sole purpose from his point of view was to have you killed, but he had to come up with a plan that would suit both parties. Your wife and son could never have been safer."

Grant looked crestfallen. "No, I'm not doing it." He stood up calmly, then stared at them both. "I'm leaving."

King pointed the pistol at him. "You're not, mate."

"Now, now, Alex," Forsyth said. "It's not going to come to that. One word from an anonymous tipster to some contacts in Belfast and Simon Grant won't make it a week. Nor will his family, for certain this time." He looked at Grant. "Sit down, Simon."

Grant hesitated for a moment, then looked to reconsider. He sat down heavily in the well-worn fabric chair, that had once been a part of a suite. But not now. "What then?"

"We have a lot of loose ends. We have terrorists with ill-gotten gains, a considerable sum. We can't have that." He looked at the MI6 special operator. "Alex, you said you had an idea. I should very much like to hear it."

33

After King had laid out the bare bones of his plan, Forsyth had added some meat to them, and left to make a series of calls. He had been absent for just over five-hours. The time was now six-thirty p.m.

King had replayed all of the video recordings on the monitor, making both sketches and mental notes of the layout of the interior of the barn. After the film show had finished, he set a new tape into the receiver, to record any current conversations, then played back the audio recordings, periodically making notes on a small pad.

Grant had made them both a plate of sandwiches and was now resting in the main bedroom. He was subdued, but hopeful that he would soon be free to leave, once this last task had been completed. He had made a list of equipment he would need and King had called Forsyth on his mobile phone to set him to work acquiring it.

King heard the sound of the front door being unlocked. He stood up quickly, his hand on the butt of his pistol, which nestled tightly in the snug leather hip holster. He was aware that it was most probably Forsyth, but the months of professional training and year-long work in the field had taught him the importance of not taking chances where personal security is concerned.

Forsyth entered the flat, glanced at King's threatening posture, but proceeded to carry two large sports-bags into the room. "Only me, old boy. You really are far too edgy, try and relax a little."

King smiled. "Thanks, but *edgy* has kept me alive so far."

Forsyth walked past him, and into the lounge, and dropped the sports-bags onto the floor. King re-locked the front door, then turned to join him.

"Where's our friend?"

"He's resting in my room. I think the shock has finally caught up with him."

Forsyth sat down in his chair then took the cigarette case from the inside pocket of his jacket. "Ah, the dear of him..." he commented, somewhat condescendingly. "Be a good chap and wake him up, we have rather more pressing business to see to than making sure that Simon Grant catches up on his beauty sleep."

King made a move towards the hallway, then stopped in his tracks.

"It's alright, I've had enough rest, if that's all right with you?" Grant walked into the lounge and looked at the two sports bags on the floor. Is that my gear?"

"See for yourself, old boy." Forsyth waved an unconcerned hand, not bothering to look at Grant until he had finished lighting his cigarette. He glanced down at the notepad and pen on the coffee table, then looked up at King. "Afraid we missed something, old boy?"

King sat down in his chair and smiled. "No. Just being thorough, that's all."

Forsyth smirked, then reached into his pocket and retrieved a medium sized envelope. He passed it across to him, then leaned against the back of his chair and stared thoughtfully at the ceiling. "Grant's passport," he announced as King opened the seal of the envelope. "Under the name of Michael Roberts. Give it to him just before he needs it, then take it away again when he doesn't. There are return tickets for Le Shuttle, along with one-thousand pounds in expenses, divided equally in pounds Sterling and French francs."

King tapped the end of the envelope, letting the contents slip out into his left hand. Satisfied, he tipped them back inside and placed the envelope on the table. He looked at Forsyth for a moment, then turned to Grant. There was something amiss, something that he was unable to put his finger on. Forsyth seemed different, almost terse. The man projected an aura of arrogance at the best of times, but now he seemed somewhat indifferent. The man had made a grave error of judgement in allowing events to extend this far. The killing of the three security guards during the raid would certainly have been avoided, had Forsyth acted immediately on discovering O'Shea and Neeson's supposed plan at Kempton Park racecourse. The authorities would never have found out about the planned security van heist, but then again, the death toll would have been zero.

"Outside is a grey BMW 540i. It's a rapid yet comfortable beast, great for traveling long distances. It is two years old and registered in the name of Paul Curtis. That's you, old boy. Your counterfeit passport and driving licence are in the envelope along with Grant's."

"Same details, dates of birth and so on?" King tipped out his passport and studied the photograph. He was pleasantly surprised; the photograph was an old one, dug up from his service record, to match the passport, which was four years old. Inside were visa stamps to

Indonesia (Rep), Australia and Canada. He presumed Grant's photo had been lifted from his criminal record.

Forsyth nodded. "Everything is the same, except for the names. Both aliases are short and easy to remember. You will both pose as businessmen on a fact-finding tour. Interested in coastal holiday homes for letting on a timeshare basis," he paused, almost dreamily, then snapped back to the present. "I seriously doubt that anyone will give you so much as a second glance. We've supposedly got cross border freedom of movement now, but you get the odd check from Britain to France and vice versa."

"What about the termination order?" King asked as he flicked through his new passport.

"Goes ahead as expected. Sorry, old chum, but I didn't get you any of the weaponry that you requested," he said casually. "I didn't think that you would want to risk taking it through customs." He flicked a small length of ash into the nearby ashtray, then slipped the cigarette back into the corner of his mouth, leaving it there as he talked. "You should be able to smuggle your pistol through though. Try wiring it to the engine, under some gubbins or other, don't let the ammunition get too hot though."

King nodded, although Forsyth's suggestion was a bit too obvious for his liking. He knew many ways to get a weapon abroad. During several close protection operations, he had met civilian bodyguards who had become experts by necessity. These operatives had no help from their governments in requesting that they travel whilst armed. Although civilian bodyguards can wade through the mountains of paperwork and legislation required to carry a weapon legally in many countries, some countries remain stubbornly unsympathetic to the bodyguard's reasoning. However, paperwork and legislation are not the only ways; many a professional bodyguard had become an expert in smuggling handguns between countries. These civilian bodyguards had taught King a thing or two.

Forsyth looked at Grant, who had spread the contents of the two sports-bags out across the floor. "Everything to your satisfaction?"

"No picklocks," he said. "And I can't see the small quantity of nitro-glycerine for that matter."

"Doesn't travel too well old boy." Forsyth smirked. "It's a sure-fire way to get yourself arrested at customs as well. Sniffer dogs, for one."

King got up and rummaged into a kit bag that was near the front door. He kept anything important ready to bug out. It was an old habit, not just from his time with MI6, but from a former life on the run. A life he had left behind. He came back with a soft leather pouch. "Here, take these. They're a good selection of picklocks, should take care of most locks," he said, glancing briefly at Forsyth, who was still staring, transfixed, at the wall. "You will have to do without the explosive; we'll find another way." Again, he looked at Forsyth. The man was deep in thought. King had known officers who had lost men during his secondment training with the SAS. They had the same look as the intelligence officer. A vacant, sorry stare. He was starting to worry about the man's fitness, his ability to continue the operation.

Grant opened the case and studied the selection of keys and picks. He looked back at King and frowned. "You can use these?"

"Of course. Who do you think planted the listening devices and the pinhole camera? I'm obviously not in your league, but I can get past basic security systems and open most locks, although I have never done a safe for real, only in practice," he paused, watching Grant slip the case into one of the bags, then fasten the zip. "Besides, this will be a two-man job."

"You will head over to the farm at midnight," Forsyth announced, suddenly snapping out of his sorrowful state. "After you have retrieved the money, you will come back here, pick up the BMW and head for Folkestone where you will board Le Shuttle. Get yourselves down to Lacanau as quickly as possible and locate Frank Holman's property." He reached into his pocket and took out a small slip of folded paper, then passed it across the table to King. Here's the address. He has a French bank account, using the house just outside Lacanau as his postal address for financial correspondence, so it was relatively easy to trace."

"Where the hell is this Lacanau place? I've never heard of it," King commented.

"It's west of Bordeaux. Have you heard of that?" Forsyth asked, tersely.

"Of course," King answered defensively. "I'd just never heard of Lacanau."

"Nor had I," Grant interjected. "I can't believe Frank has a place out there. He hates French food."

"Yes, thanks for that," Forsyth chided. He looked back at King. "Well, as we've established, it's west of there. Nothing but dunes and pine forest. The odd little town, beaches and seaside towns with promenades and expensive restaurants," he paused, then added, "You break in, then get the money in a place where Holman won't come across it, but where the Irish will easily find it."

"Yes, I know," King said. Forsyth's manner was worrying him. "It was my idea. But it's not going to be easy with just the two of us. What will you be doing?"

"Oh, don't worry about me, old boy." Forsyth extracted a handmade cigarette, then passed the case to Grant, who accepted and waited for a light to be offered. "I shall be keeping an eye on Holman and informing you via mobile phone of his movements. I will also be checking that our Irish friends don't catch up with him too soon." Forsyth flicked the wheel of his lighter and reached it out in front of Grant's face. He waited for Grant's cigarette to catch. Grant hadn't smoked for ten-years and was out of practice. Today was a good day to start again. The two-inch flame flickered perilously close to Grant's eyebrows. Forsyth then brought the flame back to the tip of his own cigarette. "Alex, you know what you have to do; just get it done. When everything has been seen to, you get back here." He released out a thin plume of the pungent, scented smoke, then turned towards Grant, who was wincing at the distinctly acquired taste of Forsyth's blend of tobacco. "You will have to sign the Official Secrets Act upon your return, after that, I will see to it that you leave with sufficient funds, purely expenses. After which, you will simply disappear. Remember, if you talk you will wish the IRA had got hold of you instead. Your payment is your freedom, not to mention, revenge on your old friend Frank Holman."

"What about a rendezvous?" King asked. "In case I can't raise you on your mobile."

Forsyth shrugged benignly. "You will have to come back when the job has been completed, it will be difficult to arrange a specific time. We're not even sure that they will follow Holman immediately. I will be here to give them a push if necessary. They may well cut their losses and return to Ireland. If so, then I'm in deep you-know-what." Forsyth smiled. "The deadline will have passed. In any event, we will meet back here. I have a contact in customs at Folkestone passport control, he will let me know when your alias is back in the country, but we shall be in touch by telephone on a regular basis; so there should be no problems as far as communications are concerned."

King nodded, then glanced down at a nervous-looking Grant. "Don't worry yourself, we'll treat it like a bit of a holiday," he laughed. Grant tried to force a grin at King's attempt of humour, but it was not convincing.

Forsyth got up and looked down at King. "I will be off now, there are a few more things that I need to do." He held out his hand and stared sincerely into the specialist's eyes. "I am sorry that this whole operation went pear-shaped, but with your help, I hope we can get some sort of positive result."

King caught hold of the man's hand and shook it firmly. He knew that deep inside, Forsyth must be suffering emotional torment. Innocent people had died, their deaths could easily have been prevented, but for a gamble which had not paid off. He felt compelled to accept some proportion of the blame, after all, he had pushed for further intelligence. But then he remembered field standard operating procedure – *volunteer for nothing, admit nothing unless asked and keep your head down.* "We'll do our best," he replied.

34

Irritated, he picked up the remote control unit and pressed the button, switching to another channel. There had been no mention on BBC One's six o'clock news, but then again, he had not watched from the beginning. The Channel Four news programme would not be starting for another half an hour, so he decided to switch over to satellite channels and tried his luck with Sky News.

The correspondent was in the middle of her report, standing in the entrance to the racecourse grounds amongst the broken and scattered debris of the explosion. Fire-crews tended their appliances, while uniformed police officers were searching the exterior of the main building behind a barrier of blue and white tape. Forensic teams in white coveralls could clearly be seen on their hands and knees inside the building, carrying out their fingertip investigation.

The correspondent explained that the bomb would appear to have detonated prematurely, taking with it the group of terrorists. There was no confirmation of how many terrorists had been killed in the blast, but the police could confirm that a steward in his early-fifties and a security guard in his late-twenties had been killed prior to the explosion. No terrorist organisation had claimed responsibility, but the security forces had not ruled out the ALF, or other animal rights activists.

"Bah!" Keith Parker switched off the television and walked into the kitchen, where Lisa was giving David his tea. He looked over at the boy's plate and frowned, as Lisa dished up the food from a saucepan.

"Baked beans? They're no good for him, he wants proper food." He stared down at the boy and smiled, but already Lisa was wary.

"It's a treat for him, his favourite. Cumberland sausages, baked beans and mashed potatoes." She tried to return a smile, but her eyes held no humour.

By now he had vented his anger upon her over the last incident. Even after she had questioned his sexual performance, he had taken her - as usual - roughly and without caring. There seemed to be no way to deter the man's advances; not even humiliation had worked. She turned her back on him and went on preparing her son's meal.

Parker watched her as she spooned out a portion of creamy mashed potatoes. She was wearing a snug-fitting black cotton skirt, which came to her knees, and a red silk blouse. The outfit showed off her slim figure and proportionate curves; with each movement, the silk would hug her skin, outlining the contours of her slender, well-toned body. Parker waited until she turned around, and then he looked at her quizzically. "Are you putting on weight? I swear that each time I see you in that outfit, your hips look a little fuller," he smiled pleasantly and shrugged his shoulders. "I suppose it's to be expected at your age. What have we got for dinner?"

Lisa looked aghast at his malicious comment. She was thirty-three years old and had kept at the same nine and a half stone for the past five years, finally returning to her usual weight after a three year struggle to lose the two-stones which she had gained during her awkward pregnancy with David. It took hard work to maintain, and she felt she looked pretty good.

"Did you hear me?"

Lisa looked up suddenly. "Sorry?"

"Damn it, don't be sorry, woman, just tell me what's for dinner." He shook his head despondently. "God, woman, your head is forever in the clouds!"

She stared at him pitifully, then turned her back to him. "Sirloin steak, new potatoes and a mixed salad with basil and flat leaf parsley." She picked up her son's meal and placed it down in front of him. He smiled up at her, then started to tuck in greedily.

"Manners?" Parker stared at him expectantly.

David looked up meekly. "Thank you, mummy."

Lisa smiled at him, then turned back to the sink, where she had started to prepare their meal by washing leaves of rocket and endive lettuce. Keith Parker had always insisted that David be fed separately, and that he and Lisa should eat later in the evening, never before seven-thirty. He was not concerned that this meant twice as much work for Lisa, and never once had he offered to share in any of the domestic chores.

Parker sat down at the kitchen table and watched David, as he shovelled in large mouthfuls of sausage and baked beans. "I think that it is high time you learned some manners, young man. Manners and discipline," he said, glancing at Lisa who had just turned around from her work and was looking at him. "That is why your mother and I have decided that it would be better if you were to be sent to a boarding school." David stopped eating and looked over at his mother earnestly. "It's a nice place, in Scotland. Mountains and lakes nearby - rugby, cricket, golf, football, horse-riding, you name it.

All boys, and seriously big on academic and sporting achievement."

"No!" Lisa stared vehemently at Parker, then rushed over to David and wrapped her arms around him, hugging him close. "Don't worry darling, mummy won't make you go." She smoothed a comforting hand over his head as the boy started to sob.

"You bloody well will!" Parker fumed. "This school is going to cost me a small fortune, so don't ever say that I don't love you! Your boy will have a terrific start in life."

"You just want him out of the way!" she screamed at him.

"Of course I bloody do. The little bastard's not mine!" He looked over at the tearful boy. "Go to your room, your mother and I have matters to discuss!"

David shook his head defiantly. "No! I want to stay with mummy!" He held on to her, clutching her firmly around the waist.

Parker stood up suddenly, knocking his chair over behind him. He charged forward and grabbed the boy by his arm, pulling him violently from his mother's grasp. "I said go to your room!" He lifted the boy clean off his feet and swung him towards the door, before releasing his vice-like grip. "Now go, you little bastard!"

The boy landed in a heap on the tiled floor, then slid into the doorframe. He got to his feet quickly and ran out into the hall, screaming mournfully as he bolted up the wooden staircase. Parker turned to Lisa who was crying and screaming, near the point of hysteria. He walked calmly towards her, then smiled reassuringly as she backed away into the corner. She tried to get past him, but he pushed her back against the kitchen counter and pressed her there. "Don't cry, my darling. It will do him some good, it will give us a chance to be alone together, to sort things out. You'd like that, wouldn't you? We could try for a child of our own. I get the impression that you're not happy. Perhaps it will be better for you without having to run around after the boy? He's too much like his father," he paused and wiped away the stream of tears on her face with the back of his hand, before quickly glancing at his watch. "Now, there's something I want to watch on the television. How about having dinner earlier for a change? I think I'll have mine in the lounge." He turned and walked to the door, then glanced around as he reached the doorway. "And make sure that my steak is cooked rare, you know that it upsets me otherwise."

35

At precisely twenty-two hundred hours, King stood up and looked down at Simon Grant. "Come on mate, time to get going."

The two men had been watching the recordings of the inside of the barn, freezing the picture periodically so that they could study the safe and get a good idea of what it would be like. There was only so much that they had been able to see, but both men now knew exactly how many paces it would take to reach it in the dark, as well as the opening procedure. The combination seemed to be three turns to the left, two right, four left, one right and two left. It would help to know, but it was the exact numbers on the dial that counted. The key looked as if it had completed a whole turn to the left, half a turn to the right, then two turns to the left. Although they would have to play around with the system when they reached the safe, at least they had a good idea of what was in store for them upon their arrival.

Both men wore black denims and black leather jackets. Grant was entirely outfitted in King's clothing, and had tucked and tightened it accordingly. They would each carry a bag of equipment, although Grant's load had been considerably reduced due to his rib injury, which made heavy lifting extremely painful.

King swung his bag over his shoulder and made his way across the room. He waited for Grant to catch him up, then opened the front door. Grant stepped through the doorway and waited on the landing, as King closed and re-locked the door. He moved the drawing pin from the bannister and tucked it underneath as an indicator to Forsyth.

King led the way down the flight of steps and into the enclosed parking area reserved for the tenants of the small complex of flats. He ignored the gleaming BMW 540i and walked over to the tatty Ford Escort van, opened the passenger door then stood to the side and waited for Grant.

Grant dropped his bag into the foot-well of the vehicle and slipped into the passenger seat, while King closed the door after him then walked around the rear of the van and opened his own door. "Don't you trust me or something?" asked Grant.

King dropped down into his seat and closed the door, locking it instantly. He nodded his head towards Grant's door, signalling for him to do the same. Grant frowned at this, but locked his door even so. "Habit, basic security," he explained, then started the vehicle's engine. If I was in your position, I would probably have made a break for it long before now."

Grant shook his head. "I have a family. You don't, do you?" he stated flatly. "If you did, you certainly wouldn't risk their safety."

"No, I don't have anybody," he said, as he pulled the van out into the road, entering the light stream of traffic. He positioned the van in the correct lane, then turned to Grant. "What about your wife? Keith Parker must be extremely scared of you taking her away from him. He had the plan and the robbery coincide with your release. She must make it clear to him that she's still in love with you." King accelerated up through the gears, then steadied his speed at a legal sixty miles per hour.

Even though the road was practically empty, he did not want to risk a confrontation with the police. "Are you going to try and get back with her?"

"If you don't mind, I don't want to talk about it," Grant replied flatly. "I never wanted to lose her, but she left me because I was a criminal. A bloody crook."

King laughed mirthlessly. "And what do you think *he* is? Keith Parker is directly responsible for the deaths of three of his company's security guards, not to mention the two poor sods at the racecourse. He also tried to have you killed and got a hefty sized wedge of money on top! He's a bigger crook than you ever were, or ever will be!" Grant said nothing as he turned and gazed out of his side window, engrossed in his own thoughts. "Man, the guy must have felt threatened by you."

The two men did not speak again until they neared the farm. Grant seemed preoccupied with his thoughts. King just hoped the man would focus when the time came. He killed the engine and switched off the headlights before opening his window and looking out across the dark fields. It was a still night and the moon was full, covered periodically by the occasional scattering of dark cloud.

"What are we doing?" Grant asked, suddenly shattering the silence. "Waiting for an invite? Let's get this done."

King kept his eyes on the outside world then spoke quietly, indicating that Grant should do the same. "We are tuning in to our surroundings," he paused, then glanced briefly at him before resuming his vigil on the monochrome landscape. "Getting our night vision, distinguishing the individual sounds. There is very little wind, so sound will travel fast, both from anyone lurking out there, or from us." He turned back to Grant, as a beam of moonlight illuminated the inside of the vehicle, suddenly enabling him to make out the man's features quite clearly. "That is why I decided to leave earlier than Forsyth suggested. To give us plenty of time to adjust to our surroundings. The entrance to the farm is just over half a mile away. We will get nearer in the van, but refrain from using the headlights. I know a good place to park, well out of sight of the road. From there, we cross over the road and go in across country."

Grant studied the luminous dials on his wristwatch. "What time will we go in?"

"One hour's time. Midnight. If necessary we can wait just outside the farmyard, it will give us a rest at the same time." He glanced down at Grant's watch. "Better take that off before we go, those dials could just be enough to give us away." He reached into his jacket pocket and took out a small torch "Here, take this. It's a Mini-Maglite, with a red filter which will not destroy your night vision," he paused as Grant took the torch from him. "If you do look into a bright light, when you get back into the dark, try looking out of the corner of your eyes. The retina is made up of cells called rods and cones. Rods are sensitive to dim light and line the sides of the retina."

"Thanks." Grant slipped the torch into his pocket, then nervously tapped his fingers against the dashboard.

King smiled to himself. He knew how the man felt. Waiting was always the hardest part.

As the van crept quietly along the road, without headlights, King kept his eyes on the hedgerows that lined both sides of the strip of tarmac. He kept the van in the centre of the road using the central white lines, which were only just visible in the faint moonlight, as a guide to the vehicle's position. When he drew near to the turning, he slipped the gearbox into neutral and switched off the engine. Making doubly sure that the steering lock was off, he let the vehicle free wheel past the entrance and down the slight gradient, until they reached the entrance to the lane. He gently applied the handbrake, so as not to illuminate the vehicle with the brake-lights, then coasted into the muddy lane until the vehicle's momentum ceased altogether, bringing it to a gradual halt. He opened his door quietly, then pulled the key from the ignition and stepped onto the muddy ground. He bent down and placed the key behind the front wheel, a precaution that he had found to be most useful in such situations, then looked across at Grant. "Right, out you get; no talking, coughing or heavy breathing. I hope you're fit." He reached behind his seat and caught hold of the heavier of the two bags.

"So do I," Grant commented, as he bent forward and retrieved his bag from the foot-well of the vehicle.

The two men fastened the bags over their shoulders, linking their arms through the straps. King thoroughly checked Grant's pack for unnecessary movement or rattling, by shaking it vigorously. Grant winced as his ribs bore the brunt of the momentary assault, then breathed deeply to ease the pain. "Are you all right?"

Grant nodded. "I'll be fine, let's just get it done."

King led the way, using the faint moonlight to pick his way through the myriad of puddles that dotted the way along the muddy lane. He quickly crossed the road, then waited for Grant to catch up with him before vaulting the three-railed wooden fence.

Grant scrabbled over the obstruction. Not so adept as King, he dropped over the other side and became entangled with his bag. He struggled to free himself, until King caught hold of his shoulder and stopped him. He pushed Grant back against the fence, then gently lifted the bag free. With Grant released, King continued to lead the way along the hedge and down the gentle gradient. It was soon apparent that Simon Grant was neither fit, nor honed to this type of activity. He struggled to breathe quietly, but his intakes of breath were both erratic and noisy. His footsteps were unsure, thundering heavily, instead of being carefully, unobtrusively placed. King helped him across the small brook, catching hold of his arm and pulling him forward as he leapt over the gently running water. He helped him under the wire fence, keeping his bag from snagging, then pushed him clear. By contrast, King moved stealthily - placing his footsteps carefully and breathing steadily. As well as being far fitter than Grant, and well-practised in such activities, King had a natural affinity with this sort of exercise. His senses were instantly alert, and he was able to foresee his way silently across any obstruction, moving virtually without sound. He had operated in identical countryside in Ulster on reconnaissance operations, remaining undetected for days.

The two men climbed the gentle incline, with Grant following the MI6 operative's footsteps through the tangle of weeds and thistles. King briefly hesitated at the base of the tall hedge, and pulled Grant towards him. "We have to climb the hedge," he whispered. "I will get on top, then help you over. Watch where you put your feet."

King reached up and caught hold of an old hawthorn tree stump. He checked it for stability by giving it a sturdy tug, then eased himself up, placing his feet carefully in search of a foothold. Once on top, he held out his hand and waited for Grant to take hold. Grant pulled and scrabbled his way up, cracking a number of twigs as he reached the top. King released his grip on Grant's hand, then looked over towards the farmhouse. No lights shone from within; it would appear that the inhabitants were asleep for the night. He turned back to Grant, then leapt down from the hedge, landing quietly on the overgrown ground below. Grant eased himself down, then went to step forward, but King grabbed his arm and pulled him back into the shadows.

"No. We will wait here for a couple of minutes, I want to double check." He pulled him to his knees, then crouched beside him. "I will go first, then signal for you to follow. Watch your step, there's a lot of junk spread all over the place."

Grant nodded, then squatted down and watched the farmhouse. Only a day ago, it had been a makeshift prison for him. He had been held there by a threat to his family. Inside were the same people who had attempted to kill him, and now - he was back. He shook his head, unable to comprehend the insanity, the sheer audacity of returning. He tried to steady his erratic breathing; much of his fitness had been lost to the tedium of prison life. He was certainly not as fit as his build would suggest. He turned towards King and watched as the man silently moved out across the open ground.

King crouched low to the ground, stepping cautiously over and around the pieces of rusty scrap metal and other rubbish that was spread haphazardly across the area between the hedge and the barn. As he eased himself against the side of the barn, he looked in both directions, then signalled for Grant to follow. He watched as the man cautiously left the sanctuary of the hedgerow and stepped out into the moonlight. He successfully made it across the waste ground, avoiding the scattered debris, then stood a few feet from his right shoulder. So far, so good.

King eased the bag off his shoulder and placed it between his feet. He gently unfastened the zip and retrieved the electronic listening device. He switched it on, then placed it against the timber wall, before turning briefly to Grant. "Keep extremely quiet, do not make any sudden noises." Grant nodded as King slipped the earpiece into his ear.

King eased his way along the side of the barn, taking the device away from the wall as he walked, then placing it back against the building every three or four feet. They soon worked their way down the entire length of the building then King slipped the device back into the bag and held up his thumb. "Two people. At the far end. They must be sleeping, they're very relaxed," he whispered.

"Ross and Sean," Grant whispered. "They slept out here the whole time. I thought they'd go inside the farmhouse now that the others have…" he paused. "Gone."

"Did you see where they slept?"

"No."

King shrugged. No matter. He had his 9mm and he wasn't going to worry about using it. He made his way around the edge of the barn, Grant following closely. He stopped when he reached the smaller of the two doors, which was now fitted with a large padlock. "How do the two men get in and out?"

"I think the stone barn and the wooden barn are separate buildings. They have a door on the other side. There is a door in the internal wall, but they don't have to use it."

King contemplated this. It made sense. He had not noticed a door in the partitioning wall. He made a note to check the adjoining door. "Get the padlock off," he said.

"No problem," Grant whispered, taking the bag off his aching shoulders. He winced momentarily at the jolt of pain to his ribs, then placed the bag at his feet. He opened the bag and took out the set of picklocks, selected a thin, three-pronged pick, and set rapidly to work.

King watched Grant work, impressed at the sheer speed and expertise in which the man approached the task. Within seconds the padlock was off, and Grant had returned the picklocks to his equipment bag. King drew the 9mm pistol from his hip holster then pulled Grant to one side. He eased the door handle down then gently pushed the heavy door inwards. He held the pistol in a double-handed grip then cautiously stepped inside, moving away from the doorway and into the welcoming sanctuary of the shadows. His eyes were already accustomed to the dim light, but the inside of the barn was illuminated considerably from the moonlight that shone through the two windows near the rear of the building. He carefully sighted the pistol around the cavernous space then, satisfied that it was clear, beckoned Grant forwards.

Grant walked past him towards the bales of straw. He already knew the exact number of paces that he should take, then when he reached the small stack, he dropped his bag onto the ground and pulled the first three bales aside.

King made his way across the whole barn to the far wall. He strained his eyes in the darkness and found the door. It was an old fashioned latch type, with no lock. Two men, two trained IRA killers slept the other side of an inch and a half of wooden partition. He contemplated killing them. He had a knife on him, and knew they were sleeping. It wouldn't be difficult. And it would cover their rears as they worked on the safe. He reached for the door handle.

"Come on!" Grant whispered. That loud whisper people make that sounds more like an exhalation of air.

King hesitated. He looked around, saw a rusted milk churn and picked it up. He carried it over and placed it against the door. It wouldn't stop them from opening it, but it *would* alert him if the door swung open. After that, he'd let his friend Browning do the talking.

Grant was working at the covering of straw. King bent down, and between them the two men cleared away the loose straw, exposing the sheet of polythene. King gently peeled back the sheet, finally revealing the thick, steel door. Grant quickly opened up his bag and started to remove the various pieces of equipment that he would need. He placed them on the polythene sheet in the order in which he would use them, then picked up the medical stethoscope and carefully went to work.

King, although interested in how Grant would go about opening the safe, decided that he would be most use keeping a watch on the entrance to the building. He walked back to the open doorway, gently eased the door back until it was almost closed, then peered through the small gap, keeping his eyes firmly fixed on the farmyard with his pistol at the ready in his right hand.

Grant smoothed his hands all over the surface of the safe, then around the hinges to the side. Both O'Shea and Neeson had partially masked the camera's view, making the overall opening procedure difficult to see. Grant was aware that both locks were combination-based, and both he and King were aware of how many turns O'Shea seemed to have taken. However, what *seems*, and what *is*, are two entirely different matters. Grant decided that it would probably be wiser if he started from fresh; hopefully, this would avoid confusion, or disappointment.

He slipped the stethoscope into his ears and placed the end roughly an inch below and left of the combination dial. As he turned the dial, he smiled to himself. The configuration of tumblers and gates seemed to leap into life, rotating and sliding with one another, until he heard the first click. He eased the dial back in the opposite direction, holding his breath as he did so, desperately trying to hear the next tell-tale sound over his own rapid heartbeat.

King turned back to Grant, but the man was working with his back to him. There seemed little point in asking how it was going; the man was a professional, he would get the job done, whether or not he asked him for a progress report. He turned back to the farmhouse, then visibly flinched at the sight. Upstairs, one of the lights was on, beaming through the small gap in the curtains. King eased the door, closing the gap until it was merely a thin slit. He kept his eyes on the front door, watching for any sign of movement, then scanned the surrounding area, in case he had missed something. He cursed under his breath - he had not seen the light come on, for that crucial moment, he had been watching Simon Grant at the safe.

Grant uncoupled the stethoscope from his aching ears and let the instrument hang freely from around his neck. Having completed the combination sequence, he picked up the case containing the picklocks, then carefully opened it and selected a small diamond-tipped pick and a slightly larger titanium key. He took the Mini-Maglite from his pocket, twisted the aperture to produce a wide beam, then slipped it between his teeth. Grant rested on his stomach, wincing suddenly as his ribs bore the brunt of his weight. He bit down on the metal torch, in a bid to quell the pain, then repositioned the torch between his teeth, until the bright red beam shone against the lock. He slipped the tiny pick into the lock, then inserted the titanium key and started to probe the maze of gates inside the lock, in search of the elusive tumbler. King glanced briefly at Grant, then returned his attention to the light. There seemed even less point in worrying the man and putting him under pressure, he would not be able to work any faster without making a mistake.

After a further minute or so, which seemed like an eternity, the light in the upstairs window switched off. King kept his eyes on the farmhouse, alternating his gaze from the window to the door, then around the surrounding area. He was quite certain that the light had been due to an early morning call of nature - no doubt there had been a serious amount of alcohol consumed during their celebrations – now nature was taking its course.

Grant jiggled and probed for the final time, releasing the last of the tumblers, which could only be attempted in a specific sequence. He patiently replaced the picklocks into the case, then turned towards King. "It's done," he whispered. "Give us a hand with the door."

***

Ian Forsyth blew out a long, thin plume of pungent cigarette smoke and grinned. "Well done, chaps. Well done indeed…" He blew three perfect smoke rings, which drifted lazily across the room towards the doorway. He watched them disintegrate on the ceiling, then turned his eyes back to the monitor. King had tied the bags together, looping them over his shoulder. It was a considerable weight, possibly similar to his own, but he managed to walk reasonably freely to the door. Grant struggled with the two rucksacks of equipment. He watched as the two men left the bags in the doorway and returned to the safe. They replaced the safe lid and scattered the straw, leaving the barn as they had found it. Forsyth and King had deliberated upon how to leave the safe, deciding that if the safe were discovered too soon, then it would not allow enough time for Holman to leave for France. Of course, they were banking everything on the fact that the man would do just that. But O'Shea had insisted that the man lie low. They just hoped he would take the IRA quartermaster's advice.

Forsyth watched intently, as the two men returned to the entrance of the barn, exited with the bags and closed the door behind them. He stood up, stubbing his cigarette in the ashtray. There was nothing left to see, but he still had a great deal to do.

***

Grant re-locked the padlock using the pick-locks. He then followed King's path to the hedgerow. King was starting to feel the strain, losing his footing over the uneven ground. It was a great deal of weight, and the para-cord he had used to fasten the bags together was digging mercilessly into his shoulders. Grant felt the weight of the two rucksacks he carried, as well as the money sack. It was a heavy a load as he could manage, only adrenalin and the thought of retribution spurred him onwards. He clenched his teeth tightly together in a bid to ignore the pain that was hammering in his ribs.

King dropped his load at the base of the hedge, then turned to Grant and pointed to the shadows. "Wait here, there is something else I have to take care of."

Without further word, he bolted across the farmyard, then skidded to a halt behind the Peugeot. He kept his eyes on the farmhouse, watching intently for a few seconds; before running in a low crouch to the Ford Mondeo. Again, he checked the farmhouse, making absolutely certain that his presence had not been detected. Satisfied that all was well, he bent down, rolled onto his back, then pushed himself under the vehicle. He reached into the inside pocket of his tatty leather jacket and retrieved a tiny package. The package was approximately six inches long, by four inches wide and almost three inches thick. He reached up and rubbed the dirt away from the underside of the fuel tank, then peeled an adhesive layer from the back of the package and pressed it firmly against the roughly prepared area. He held it in place for about fifteen-seconds, then carefully removed his hand. The package remained in position, bonded securely by the quick-setting adhesive. Located to the side of the package were a ring-pin and a simple connector switch. King gently removed the pin and slipped it into his pocket. Next, he flicked the switch, then eased himself out from underneath the vehicle.

A cursory glance at the farmhouse was all that he needed, before slipping silently into the shadows and making his way back to where Grant was waiting in the undergrowth. King picked up his heavy load, then caught hold of Grant's shoulder, pulling him abruptly to his feet. "Come on. Time to move out!"

36

Back at the flat, Alex King sent Grant off to get washed and changed. Forsyth, displaying either empathy and foresight, had left a selection of clothes in what he hoped would be Grant's size and choice of style, in plain view on one of the chairs in the lounge.

With Grant out of the room, King went over to the pile of sacks and started to unfasten them one by one. He stacked the bundles into neat piles - six currencies in all. Although he did not have time to count it, he would certainly not have been surprised if the amount totalled over five-million pounds. Or even ten. He had no idea what large amounts of money looked like. Forsyth had left an extremely large, brown leather suitcase for him to use. King picked up the suitcase, carried it to the coffee table and dropped it to the floor. He opened the lid and started to stack the bundles of currency neatly into the suitcase. It was a notably tight fit, occupying almost all of the full-size suitcase, but with the money in place, he picked up the selection of clothes and arranged them on top, pressing them down tightly to avoid the money from moving around when the case would be carried. He closed the lid of the case, then applied all of his weight as he went about fastening the two large buckles to either side of the carrying handle. As he heaved the case upright onto to its tiny wheels he noticed the label attached, which read: *Frank Holman*, complete with his home address in Epsom.

King smiled wryly. As usual, Ian Forsyth had thought of everything.

"Ready to go," Grant said as he walked over to his adopted chair and sat down heavily. His hair was wet and he looked flush from his shower.

King glanced at him and nodded an approval. He looked far better in Forsyth's selection of clothes; at least the mustard-coloured slacks actually fitted him, along with the white polo shirt and tan leather jacket.

"Even the shoes are a good fit," Grant grinned, extending his right foot to show off the tan leather loafer. "Forsyth certainly has good taste, they're Lacoste."

King nodded approvingly, though not entirely sure why he had. Normally, he had no time for labels. He could never see why people went to such lengths in a vain effort to impress one another by collecting such motifs. When it came down to it, did the fact that someone paid five times the cost of an own brand really make any difference? Were people meant to jump with excitement and fall down on their backsides at the sight of an expensive logo? But then he remembered the Rolex watch he had long coveted. He would buy it one day, had resisted the soullessness of the counterfeit ones he had seen on his travels. There was no reward in shortcuts.

King hefted up the substantial weight of the suitcase then turned back to Grant. "Right, I won't be long," he said, then added, "Be sure not to go anywhere." He walked towards the hallway, then glanced back and grinned, patting the side of the suitcase. "You'll forgive me for not wanting to leave this with you, won't you?" King propped the case up against the bath and showered quickly, letting the steamy spray briefly over the muscles in his aching shoulders. He soaped himself vigorously, then rinsed the foam away before turning the dial down to its coldest setting and letting the icy spray refresh him. He wanted to awaken his senses, it was going to be a long night. He towelled himself dry, then dressed quickly in his own selection of clean clothes. He had decided to dress in smart casuals, making his and Grant's cover of businessmen interested in tourism, more credible. Adopting a style similar to Grant's, he wore a pair of new black jeans, a light blue cotton shirt and light tan desert boots. He topped it off with a smart trench coat. It looked pretty casual for most people, but for the tough specialist, it was his Sunday best.

He opened the bathroom door and dragged the heavy suitcase with him across the hallway and into his bedroom. Next, he took the Browning out of its leather holster and ejected the magazine, then pulled back the slide to eject the chambered cartridge. With the weapon cleared, he disassembled it into its five separate parts - spring, barrel, working parts, slide and magazine. He took a clean, dry cotton cloth and cleaned each part thoroughly, wiping off all traces of excess oil. With the parts relatively clean, he wrapped each piece carefully in sheets of scented tissue before placing them in individual plastic sandwich bags with self-sealing fastenings, making sure that no excess air was left in the bags before sealing them

He then took the bundles, along with five unused plastic bags, into the bathroom. He laid them down on the cabinet surface, then put the plug into the sink and ran a little hot water. Then he squeezed a whole tube of toothpaste into the sink and worked it into the hot water, creating a thick, white paste. Next, he took the packages and placed them in the sink one at a time, coating them with the toothpaste concoction. From there they went into the unused bags, which he sealed immediately. King carried the packages back to the bedroom, where he dropped them inside his sports-bag, then picked up the suitcase by its carrying handle and wheeled it towards the lounge.

Grant looked up at him expectantly as he entered the room. "Are we going now?" he asked, making a move to leave his chair.

King nodded as he pulled the heavy case through the lounge towards the front door. With Simon Grant safely seated in the BMW, he dragged the suitcase to the rear of the vehicle, then opened the boot and heaved the case inside. He dropped his sports bag beside it, then opened the zip and removed the five separate packages. King hastily removed the left-hand light panel, which houses the rear lights, brake lights and indicator bulbs, then dropped the two packages containing the weapon's slide and magazine inside. He then removed the right-hand panel and carefully placed the spring and the barrel in the compartment, before closing the panel and checking it would not come loose too easily. He closed the boot, locked it with the key, then walked around to the side of the vehicle and opened the rear offside door. He bent down and quickly pulled the bottom edge of the door panel away from its fastenings then dropped the package containing the working parts of the pistol into the door cavity. He pressed the panel back into its original position, then reapplied the studs, and fastened them securely.

King doubted that the vehicle would be subject to a thorough search either on leaving the country, or upon entering France. The more detailed searches always seemed to come on the return journey, when most travellers have by far and away exceeded their duty-free purchases, or are intent on smuggling vast amounts of cheap alcohol and tobacco to sell at a profit. King would certainly not risk bringing the weapon home, especially as it would be *tainted*, if all went to plan.

Should the vehicle be searched on the outward journey, he had taken two precautions - the scented tissues surrounding the weapon's parts had proved sufficient to outsmart trained sniffer dogs, which are unable to detect the smell of oil and nitrates over the overpowering scent. The vehicle was unlikely to be subject to search by x-ray, and a metal-detecting device could not be used for obvious reasons. However, should the vehicle be x-rayed, the high counts of glycerine, sodium magnesium silicate and sodium lauryl sulphate create a sufficient barrier of residue to deceive the x-ray's vision. The smell of the toothpaste also confused sniffer dogs further.

King opened the driver's door and got into the vehicle, glancing momentarily at Grant, who was tapping his fingers against the dashboard, obviously needing to release a great deal of pent-up nervous tension. He looked down at the two road maps, which were propped up in Grant's foot-well, leaning against the centre console. "Fancy being navigator?" he asked amiably.

Grant stopped tapping his fingers and shrugged. "Sure," he paused, picking up the road atlas of Great Britain. "What road are we looking for?"

King started the BMW's virtually silent engine and slipped the automatic gearbox into drive, then pulled out of the small parking area and onto the main road. There was a throaty rumble from the engine and exhausts as he accelerated. "We will travel down the A24, then join the M25," he said as he crawled through the roundabout and accelerated out onto the A24. "Then we want the M26. What junction is that on?"

"I thought you'd know the way."

"No." King lied smoothly. He did not want Grant in a nervous state, the task at hand was going to be difficult enough as it was. The man must regain at least a little composure. Giving Grant a role, albeit a token one, would at least take his mind off the forthcoming, and probably most difficult, part of the plan.

Grant ran his finger along the blue line that indicated the route of the M25. His finger stopped and he looked up at King. "We join the M26 at junction five."

"Great," King commented, as he overtook a slow-moving lorry, then pulled back into his original lane, resuming the speed limit. "Le Shuttle leaves from Folkestone. Can you find the exact route?"

"Sure." Grant studied the map and ran his finger along the page, struggling to keep his place against the combined effects of the movement of the car, and the dim light of breaking dawn. "We turn off onto the M20 at junction three, travel for around thirty miles, then take junction eleven, Folkestone," he said. "How long does the train take to get there? I don't fancy the idea of being underground, under the seabed for that matter, for too long."

King did his best to sound as inexperienced as Grant. Not only did he know the way without the use of road maps, he had made the journey twice before. He frowned, shaking his head. "Not long, I hope. I hate the idea of a tunnel that length. From what I gather, it takes around thirty-five minutes, with about twenty minutes or so at each end for loading and unloading the vehicles." He looked down at his black shock-proof watch, then glanced across at Grant who already seemed much more at ease. "We should board the train at seven thirty; at the very latest, we should be in France by nine o'clock."

***

Frank Holman yawned, stretched, and then swung his stubby legs over the side of the bed. He stretched again, exaggerating another loud yawn, then eased his considerable bulk off the bed. He padded across the polished wooden floorboards and into his own ensuite bathroom, and caught sight of himself in the mirror. "Morning you handsome bastard!" He let out a loud, deeply satisfying belch. "Or should I say, you handsome, *rich* bastard…" He turned on both taps and slipped the plug into the sink. The sudden rush of running water made him quickly change his plans, and he hurried over to the toilet, hopping uncomfortably from foot to foot as his desperate need grew, barely giving himself enough time to raise the seat. After the near-orgasmic pleasure of his first piss of the day, he flushed the toilet, then returned to the overfilling sink to resume his morning routine.

Danny Neeson's words had shaken him, chilled him almost to the bone. Holman had a million-pounds on him; a million reasons why O'Shea and Neeson might want to change their minds. He had decided to get out of the country today, keep out of their way for a while, then maybe help on their next job for a much smaller fee, or even for free, as a gesture of good will. A month or so beside the sea, drinking Pernod in the quiet bars, then he would return to England and contact O'Shea once more.

He had secured the money in his wall safe, setting aside sixty-thousand pounds for his French excursion. Sixty-thousand would entertain him for a month, depending on how his luck ran in the casinos of Biarritz. Even with his home near Bordeaux, he liked to stay for a few days in some of the grander hotels in Biarritz. The town had a classy, old fashioned feel to it, and the casinos were grand and luxurious. Most of his money would go on the elegant hostesses who would accompany him on such jaunts. At over five-hundred pounds a night, there was no service that they were unwilling to perform, especially for a big tipper like Frank Holman.

***

At seven a.m. Ross stepped outside the annex built onto the barn and squinted in the bright light of sunrise. It was a fine morning, the glare of the sun made worse by the dew-soaked grass in the surrounding fields.

Sean walked outside and paused at his friend's side. "Ready?"

"Yeah, I guess so. Just sniffing the air. Too much booze last night, trying to clear my head."

Sean snatched the keys out of Ross' hand. "That settles it then, you drunken bastard! I'm driving. You can't keep a car on the road at the best of times, let alone when you're half cut!" He walked swiftly down the pathway and into the courtyard.

"Slow down, you're just showing off, you bastard! You had yourself as much liquor as I did! Jesus, I need a fry-up. Let's get a good breakfast at the first services, alright?"

"Fine, but I'm still driving."

Ross bent down, picked up his small leather travel bag and followed Sean towards the Ford Mondeo. "How come you don't feel like a sack o'shit?"

"Just a tough bastard, that's all." Sean laughed as he opened the driver's door, threw his bag on the rear seat and dropped down heavily on the driver's side. "Come on lightweight! Move your drunken arse!" He slammed the door shut, then started the engine.

***

King glanced at his watch and smiled. "Any time now, you bastards," he mused.

"What?" Grant asked, turning in his seat to look at him.

"Oh, nothing," he said quietly. "Just thinking out loud."

***

Ross opened the passenger door and flopped lethargically into the seat. "Come on then, are we going or not?"

Sean engaged first gear, revved the engine then suddenly dropped the clutch. The vehicle's front wheels spun briefly on spot, and sent a mixture of mud, gravel and assorted debris over the sides of the car, before lunging violently forwards. Sean laughed out loud as Ross's head was thrown backwards into his seat. "Fast enough for you?" he smirked, watching the expression on his friend's suddenly pale face.

The tiny ball of mercury rolled backwards and impacted against the metal connector, completing the electrical circuit. The digital counter had been pre-set and instantly activated its three-minute countdown. When it reached zero, the arming switch would charge and the detonator would explode into the one-pound block of PE4 plastic explosive.

Big boy's games, big boy's rules.

***

Danny Neeson jumped up suddenly, plucked savagely from his sound and contented sleep by the familiar, unmistakable noise of the distant explosion. He leapt out of bed, quickly pulled a pair of jeans over his boxer shorts, then bolted out of the door and onto the landing.

O'Shea stood in the doorway of the master bedroom, wearing only a towel round his waist and a bewildered expression. "What the fuck was that?"

"What the fuck do you think it was?" Neeson ran past him and stared out of the landing window. "It was a fucking bomb! You've heard enough of them to know what the hell it was!" He bolted back across the landing towards his bedroom, looking at O'Shea as he went. "Get some bloody clothes on, we'll go and take a look!" Neeson knew the sound well. He had grown up with the sounds of them on the streets of Belfast. Set enough of them off in his time, and had been around to witness the ensuing carnage. He hurriedly pulled on a sweater and slipped into his tatty trainers, then ran back out onto the landing and down the narrow, wooden staircase.

O'Shea bounded after him, catching up with him in the kitchen. He was ten-years older and a stone heavier than Neeson. He struggled to catch his breath. "Ross and Sean left only minutes ago, I heard them driving down the lane. Titting about, so they were. Revving the arse off the engine and skidding in the mud. The couple of twats, they've crashed, that's what they've done…" O'Shea followed him outside.

"Bollocks! That was plastic explosive," Neeson replied as he stared out across the glistening, dew-drenched fields towards the sun. "There!" He pointed for the benefit of O'Shea, who was squinting into the direct sunlight. "Smoke. Less than a couple of miles away!"

"Let's check it out, it might not be them. Get the keys to the Saab." O'Shea walked towards the door and reached his hand out to the passenger door.

"Wait!" Neeson ran over to him and caught him by the shoulder, pulling him back forcefully. "Use your fucking head, man! If that was Ross and Sean, then there might well be a device on this!" He stepped back a few feet and cautiously started to look around the vehicle, then bent down and peered underneath. He worked his way slowly around the car, but paused suddenly at the offside, rear wheel arch. "Bastards!" He reached carefully underneath, then gently pulled out the little black box. "Fucking bastards!"

"What is it, a bomb?" O'Shea asked, peering curiously over Neeson's shoulder.

"No, looks like some kind of transmitter," he replied quietly. "We've bloody well been made!" He threw the device across the farmyard, then quickly turned back to O'Shea. "Get the keys to the barn, quickly!"

O'Shea shook his head in disbelief. "Jesus, Mary and Joseph! You don't think they...?" He turned around quickly and ran inside, not waiting for, nor wanting, an answer. He made his way frantically across the kitchen, then ripped one of the drawers out of the dresser and hurriedly snatched up a set of keys.

Neeson had already reached the barn and was waiting impatiently beside the smaller of the two doors. "Hurry up will you!" he snapped as O'Shea trudged carelessly through the muddy puddles that dotted the farmyard.

O'Shea reached the key towards the padlock with a shaking hand, only to have the key snatched from his grasp as Neeson quickly unfastened the lock. He barged through the doorway, then ran across the floor space towards the pile of straw bales. He pulled them away, throwing them frantically to the side, then ripped the polythene cover away, to reveal the large steel door.

O'Shea took the key from around his neck, then knelt down and quickly twisted the dial to offset the combination lock. He slipped the key into the lock, then frowned up at Neeson. "I locked it yesterday, it's bloody unlocked!"

Neeson caught hold of the door, and with gargantuan strength, heaved the door open, dropping it back against the remaining straw bales.

The two men stared in silence; their eyes fixed on the empty chasm in front of them. O'Shea stood up slowly, turning his back on the scene. He seemed suddenly calm, despite the discovery. "Tell me Danny, how does a killing sound to you?" he paused, looking at him briefly. "A cold, slow killing?"

Neeson turned his eyes from the empty safe and stared at him. "Frank Holman?"

"Of course! Nobody else knew the location of that safe," he said, shaking his head despondently. "Nobody else even knew we *had* a safe. Ross and Sean didn't, and Keith Parker was long gone by the time we stashed the money. I knew that it was a mistake. Letting that fat, devious bastard see the safe. He'll suffer, that's for sure."

Neeson shook his head. "There's no way that Holman would have been able to shift that lot! What about Ross and Sean?"

O'Shea glared at him. "Ross and Sean are good lads, fully committed to the cause and have been since they were in short trousers. We never showed them the safe. Never even mentioned it. Besides, I'd bet my right arm that they're spread all over the road, not two miles away. And I'll bet what's left of me, that there isn't a shred of money at the scene." He softened his expression and looked at him quizzically. "You're not seeing it, are you?" He smiled somewhat patronisingly at him. "Simon Grant took the money. Frank Holman tipped him off. I thought it was too good to be true, him setting up his old mate to take the fall, but I trusted him all the same. The bastards were in it together from the start, there is no other explanation. Grant didn't die at Kempton Park."

"Then why stop at just Ross and Sean, why not blow us to kingdom come?"

"Who knows? Perhaps they didn't have time? Perhaps they just wanted to scare us off, send us to ground? Either way, they've made a serious mistake crossing us!"

"What do we do then?" Neeson asked. "They're hardly going to hang around and wait for us to catch up with them."

O'Shea smiled wryly. "We know that Holman was planning to go to France, I doubt that he'd expect us to follow, he probably thinks we will be running back home with our tails between our legs. Stupid bastard!" He looked coldly at his fellow Irishman, his teeth clenched tightly together. "We're going to take a little trip, teach that fat bastard a lesson that he'll never forget."

"And what about Grant? I doubt he'll be hanging around for us to find him. I still don't see how Grant got away from the racetrack."

"Grant is not the immediate issue. We can catch up with him later. Right now, I want Holman's balls on a platter."

Neeson chuckled out loud. "And how do you suggest we find him?"

O'Shea grinned through clenched teeth "Oh, there are ways, my friend," he mused, somewhat cryptically. "There are ways."

***

Alex King reached for the ringing telephone as he pulled the BMW into the side of the car park at Folkestone station, loading depot for Le Shuttle. He eased the vehicle to a halt, then slipped the automatic gearbox into park before pressing the receive button. "Hello."

"Alex, this is Ian. Just thought I'd try catching up with you before you boarded the train," Forsyth paused. *"Where are you now?"*

"Folkestone," King answered. "We should be boarding the next train in around twenty-five minutes."

"Excellent," Forsyth said, then hesitated. *"I thought I'd inform you, the Irish have swallowed the bait. Hook, line and sinker. They suspect that Holman tipped Grant off about the bombing, and that he's still alive."*

King glanced across at Grant, then turned his eyes back to the array of buildings ahead of him. "Shouldn't be a problem," he said quietly. "I take it you saw their reaction to the empty safe?"

"Absolutely, old boy. Quite satisfying really."

"What about Holman? If he doesn't leave today, they could catch up with him too soon. He might be able to plead his case."

"Leave that to me, old boy. I'll see what I can do, try and keep them at bay for a while. What you have to bear in mind, is that they might not be far behind you from now on. I suggest that you get down there as quickly as possible."

"That *is* the plan." King watched a row of vehicles move slowly forward, then slipped the gearbox into drive and started to edge his way forwards. "Listen, we have to go now. You will not be able to contact me for at least another hour, so try updating me later."

"Very well, old boy. Safe journey, to both of you. Cheerio."

King slipped the telephone back into his pocket, then looked across at Grant as they slowly crawled forwards into the line of waiting traffic. "That was just an update, seems your Irish friends have fallen for it." He turned back to the line of crawling vehicles, omitting to inform Grant that they now suspected that he was alive. The last thing that he wanted to do was to put Grant under further pressure. "The only problem we could have at the moment, is if Holman doesn't leave for France today."

"Suits me, either way." Grant smiled, the thought of what the Irishmen might do to Holman obviously agreed with him.

"No. It might not." King brought the BMW to a halt as the line of vehicles came to a standstill. "If they don't find the money with Holman, he might just be able to dissuade them from harming him. He has worked with them in the past. If that's the case, they will be on an all-out search for you. And believe me, their reach is very long indeed. This time, they might just harm your family," he paused, then cut Grant off before he could protest. "Regardless of their working relationship with Keith Parker."

Grant looked away, turning his eyes towards a team of customs officers who were walking towards a stationary camper van. "You bastards," he said quietly, then turned and stared contemptuously at King. "You bastards knew that this might happen, that Holman may not leave before they catch up with him. But still you chanced it. My family's lives are at risk and there is nothing that I can do about it."

King nodded. "There was always the chance, yes. But we were giving you the chance to go free as well. You're up to your eyeballs in this, you took part in their operation. You should be doing some serious time for your involvement."

"I was threatened! My family were threatened!" Grant protested vehemently. "Their lives were at stake. I didn't have a choice."

King shook his head. "That's what you say. But you agreed to the job before they threatened you. You had already caved in to the money Holman offered you. Any threat made by them afterwards was to keep you on track."

"I was coerced!"

"I'm not sure it would look like that if it went to court," King ventured. "Where's your evidence? And now you're here to inflict some payback on Frank Holman. It's your big chance to set things right."

Grant slumped back in his seat. "We all know whose big chance this is," Grant sneered. "Your friend Forsyth's chance to sweep his mistake under the carpet. In the name of protecting sporadic peace in Northern Ireland. Your mission veered off course and people died because of your lack of direction, lack of action. Getting this money out of the hands of the IRA and letting them run amok in a personal vendetta. Perhaps they'll clear all of your loose ends up and both you and Forsyth come out with a clean pair of hands," he said. "Or maybe it will all go south and you'll get further and deeper in the shit. You can count on one thing though. None of it will stick to that man Forsyth. I hope you're aware he'll stick it all on you."

***

Neeson pulled himself out from under the vehicle, stood up slowly, then tentatively slipped the key into the lock and opened the driver's door. He released the bonnet catch, then walked around to the front of the car and cautiously lifted the bonnet.

O'Shea stared into the distance, where the steady plume of dark bluish smoke was still rising from the scene of the recent explosion. He could hear the sound of approaching sirens in the distance, and promptly turned to Neeson. "How long will it take? The police are on the scene now; they might come round here looking for witnesses."

Neeson closed the bonnet of the Saab, satisfied that there were no more devices attached to the vehicle. "I'm done now. Have you got everything?" O'Shea walked over from where he had been taking refuge behind the wall of the garden, then dropped two bags onto the ground in front of Neeson. "Here, take these, I'll go and get the rest of the gear."

Neeson picked up both bags and carried them around to the back of the Saab and opened the rear hatch. He dropped the bags into the boot space, then waited for O'Shea to reappear with two large travel bags. "Have we got travelling money?"

O'Shea placed the two bags carefully on the ground and grinned. "Aye, you leave the details to me. Have you got a weapon?"

Neeson lifted both travel bags into the boot and smiled. He unfastened the zip on one of them, reached into the bottom and retrieved a Smith & Wesson .357 Magnum snub-nose revolver. He opened the cylinder, checking that all six wad-cutter rounds were in place, then snapped it shut and slipped the weapon into the waistband of his trousers. "Why don't you leave that little detail to me?" he said coldly as he closed the rear hatch, and walked around to the driver's door. "If we don't catch up with Holman before he leaves the country, I can always stash the gun somewhere in the car before we go through customs."

O'Shea opened his door and shook his head. "No. We won't risk it. Not with our accents. Ditch it, you can always pick up something over there." He dropped down into the passenger seat and turned to Neeson as he fastened his seat belt. "Come on, I want that bastard dead. The sooner the better."

Neeson started the engine and spoke through gritted teeth. "I might just strangle the life out of the fat bastard instead."

***

Frank Holman heaved his heavy suitcase into the boot of the Mercedes and nestled it firmly against his set of Ping golf clubs, in the saloon's cavernous storage space. He was not particularly skilled at the game; nor did he profess to like it, though he liked the *idea* of it. Moreover, he had struck many a business deal in the infamous nineteenth hole, with many a tall tale to match.

He slammed the boot down then walked around to the driver's side and opened the door. Easing his considerable bulk behind the steering wheel, he closed the door and reached behind for the seat belt. He panted with the effort, stretching as far as he could, then pulled the belt triumphantly across his bloated stomach, which nestled snugly against the leather steering wheel. He started the quiet, refined engine, slipped the automatic gearbox into drive, then drove out towards the open gates, gliding smoothly over the loose gravel, before hesitating briefly to check the oncoming traffic. He pulled out and pressed down hard on the accelerator, swiftly waking the idling engine, then in the same instant, he slammed his foot down on the brake. "Bloody idiot!" he shouted, then as an afterthought, he slammed his fist against the horn and held up his middle finger in an obscene gesture. He swerved around the stationary vehicle, then stared vehemently into his rear-view mirror. "What an arsehole!" he muttered. "Stopping to use his bloody mobile phone!"

***

Forsyth kept his head down and pressed the re-dial button on his mobile telephone. He allowed Holman to reach the end of the quiet street, then pulled smoothly out into the main road. The lady on the other end of the line politely informed him, albeit through a somewhat nauseating recording, that the number he was calling was in fact unobtainable. He pressed the off button with his thumb and dropped the telephone disdainfully onto the passenger seat. Instead, Forsyth returned his concentration to Frank Holman's Mercedes, which was approximately two-hundred and fifty metres in front of him. He glanced down at the laptop, resting on the seat beside him. He had fitted the tracker soon after he arrived. A simple magnetic affair that emitted a beacon to a distance of around one-thousand metres. Once Holman was out of sight, Forsyth eased out into the road and followed the red dot on the screen.

37

Neeson swung the Saab erratically off the quiet tree-lined street and into Holman's driveway, the vehicle drifting sideways on the layer of loose gravel, then skidding to a halt.

O'Shea clenched his teeth, as he noticed the empty parking bay. "Bastard!" He turned towards Neeson, his face contorted in anger. "We can get the information we want from his slut of a wife. She'll not put up much of a fight." He reached for the door handle but was stopped in his tracks as Neeson grabbed him by the shoulder.

"No point, boss. She drives a Porsche Boxster." He pointed towards the empty space where the car had been on his previous visit. "She's obviously not here." He gripped his hands tightly around the leather steering wheel, subconsciously venting his frustration. "Most probably spent the night at her toy-boy's flat, up in Chelsea."

"She's shagging someone else?" O'Shea asked, as they walked back to the car.

"She's married to Holman. Of course she's shagging someone else!" Neeson smirked. "I gave her one, a while back."

"Did you?"

"Yeah," Neeson grinned as he got back into the driver's seat. "I came round to discuss some matters with Holman, about a month ago. He was out, but I got talking to Eileen. I'd only been in the house twenty-minutes, and I end up doing her over the kitchen table!"

"You randy bastard!" O'Shea's grin suddenly gave way to a serious pout as his thoughts turned elsewhere. He glanced down at his wristwatch, concentration ploughing deep furrows in his brow. "Supposing Holman left early this morning, he could be in France by now. Do you know where Eileen Holman's boyfriend lives in Chelsea? We haven't got the time to waste going all the way over there. Especially with the morning traffic."

"Not a clue, just a rumour that I heard whilst I was profiling Frank Holman some time ago." He slipped into first gear then drove towards the open gate at a more moderate pace. "Holman may have even departed last night, for all we know."

O'Shea nodded somewhat despondently; the morose frown still his most prominent feature. "Where are we going now?"

"Just wait and see boss. I have an idea."

***

Lisa Grant stood up from her chair and cleared the breakfast dishes away from the table. She scraped the remains of scrambled egg into the waste bin, then stacked the plates into an orderly pile, while she ran a sink full of hot water.

Keith Parker stared up from his newspaper and watched her intently as she quickly buttered two pieces of bread, then smeared them with a thick layer of strawberry jam. "Still hungry?" he asked casually, folding his newspaper neatly in half before placing it down in front of him

Lisa tensed, she had hoped that he would not have noticed. "No, I..."

"What did I say last night?" He slammed his fist down onto the table and stood up, pushing his chair back violently. "Are you so stupid as to purposely disobey me, or are you just plain forgetful?"

"Please, Keith I..." She tried to hold back her tears, but there was no mercy in his tone.

"I said no food until he apologises for his unruly behaviour!" He picked up the newspaper and started to roll it slowly into a tube, methodically creating a tight cylindrical object. "I don't care if he doesn't apologise for a week. The little bastard can starve."

"Please, Keith," she said. "He's just a little boy." She had made up her mind the moment he had pushed David to the floor. She was leaving, and she would hide from him, run from him for the rest of her days if she had to. He would never touch her son again. She wasn't scared of him anymore. Fearful for her safety and well-being, but not scared. He had crossed that line. However, she needed to be smart. Needed him to contain the beast within. And she needed to extract both David and herself when he wasn't here. When there would be enough time to pack what little they needed and disappear.

"I have spoken with both the headmaster and with the chief of governors, and they are willing to accept the boy this late in the term. He can spend the Easter holidays there with some of the boys from Asia and Africa, who don't go home except for the Christmas and summer breaks. They even suggested that he stays for their summer camp, which will give him some time to make friends with the other boys."

Lisa tensed. There was a foreboding within her. She realised where this was going, realised she had left it too late. She shook her head, tears rolling steadily down her cheeks. "Please, Keith, I'm begging you... I will do anything you want. *Anything*. I don't want David to go, I need him here with me."

He smirked condescendingly at her. "But my dear Lisa, you have *me* for company." He stepped forward and tenderly wiped the tears from her cheeks. "You'll miss the boy at first, but you'll soon forget him and we will become closer."

She tensed, her whole body rigid. She needed to ride this out. Needed him to leave the house for a few hours and she would be gone. She had it planned, they could be out of there in thirty-minutes. "Keith, let's talk about this later."

The man laughed. "We will leave today. Make a weekend of it. A nice drive up to Scotland, get David settled in on Friday, leave him an Easter egg. We can find a nice hotel, enjoy our time together and we can drive back on Monday. I've booked the time off already, I had some holiday due."

"No, don't..." she pleaded. "Keith, I'll do anything..."

"You say that you will do *anything* for me now, but the one thing that I want - you never give to me. At least, not willingly. Not anymore." She turned her eyes to the floor, unable to look at him a moment longer. He tapped the roll of newspaper against his thigh and smiled. "I think you like to be forced. You enjoy being taken," he paused. "Lord knows; you give me little alternative." She remained silent, choosing to keep her thoughts to herself. She needed to ride this out peacefully. Needed him to go to work. Or to the golf course. And then they'd be gone. "All women enjoy the thrill of saying no. Of being forced into sex. It always gives them pleasure." He placed a hand on her shoulder and squeezed, gently at first, then increasingly harder. "I watched one of those American talk shows the other day," he paused. "They referred to it as *submissive rape*. You enjoy it, don't you? The thrill of saying no, the thrill of being taken roughly?"

"Submissive? Enjoy?" she snapped. It was too late. She'd been unable to keep herself in check any longer. She pushed his hand aside and glared at him venomously. "You have absolutely no idea! You've never pleasured a woman in your life! Have you ever put yourself out, taken the time?"

Parker glared at her, his eyes ablaze. "I give you pleasure, don't I?" He watched her expression, then caught hold of her by her blouse with one hand. "Don't I?"

"Never!"

"Bitch!" He jabbed her in the stomach with the tip of the roll of newspaper, wound tightly it was like a baton. She winced, bent double and he swiped her across the face with it. "You... evil... frigid... little... bitch! How could you lie to me like that?"

Lisa rubbed her stomach, then brought both hands up to his as his grip tightened around her neck. "Please, Keith! I can't breathe!" Her voice was shallow, retarded by his vice-like grip. She dug her fingernails into the back of his hands, ripping the flesh, but suddenly let go as he released her.

Parker stared at her, breathing heavily from his physical exertion. He shook his head sympathetically then suddenly lashed out at her, catching her in the left eye with his fingertips. She gasped with the sudden shock of pain and held her hands up to her eyes. She did not see the next blow, but felt the impact, followed by another excruciating stab of pain in her lower stomach. She buckled slightly, then fell backwards against the sink unit.

Parker stood over her in a domineering posture, his hands resting firmly on his hips. She made to get to her feet but fell back against the sink unit. Then he slowly raised his right foot, held it against her shoulder, and pushed hard, sending her sprawling onto the kitchen floor. "You're pathetic, you don't even try to fight back, you just lie there, so don't say that you don't enjoy it! You want me to make love to you right now, that's why you are still lying there!" He stepped forward and started to unfasten his belt. "Well, if that's what you want... then that's exactly what you're going to get. I'll show you pleasure!" He turned suddenly, stopped in his tracks by the sound of the doorbell. "Who the bloody hell is that at this time of day?"

***

Frank Holman handed his passport to the customs officer then waited patiently for her to thumb through the pages. She returned it and smiled pleasantly, then looked expectantly towards the next waiting vehicle. Holman drove the Mercedes steadily forwards and followed the steward's instructions, manoeuvring into the appropriate lane. Twenty-minutes or so, and he would be aboard Le Shuttle, another thirty-five minutes, and he would be in France. He glanced at his watch; allowing for a couple of pit stops along the way, he should be able to reach Lacanau by evening, hopefully at a reasonable hour. He knew a lovely restaurant on the promenade at Lacanau Ocean, approximately three miles from his property. They did a good steak frites, that he would follow with a choux pastry platter, with crème patisserie and chocolate sauce.

***

Keith Parker slammed the kitchen door shut and stormed through the hallway in a rage. He smoothed his ruffled hair back into place, tested a smile at the mirror in the hallway. A little flushed, but otherwise he looked presentable. The doorbell sounded again, its shrill note agitating him even further. He twisted the key in the lock, caught hold of the brass door handle and hastily pulled the door towards him, re-engaging his business as usual smile.

Neeson moved quickly, placing a well-aimed, and powerful kick at the door as it opened. He lunged forward, advancing on Parker, who was caught entirely by surprise. He slammed his right fist into Parker's jaw, then followed through with a savage kick to the man's groin. Neeson winced, the tendons of his foot flexing too much. He managed an elbow into the side of Parker's ear as the man went down, howling like a beaten dog.

Parker fell backwards, helped by Neeson's elbow, and landed against the staircase, his head colliding with the wooden banister. He grunted, turned towards Neeson out of instinct, but was far too late for any serious attempt at defending himself. Neeson caught him by the throat with his left hand, gripping him tightly around the windpipe, then punched him in the face, twice in quick succession. Parker fell all the way down to the floor, sprawling on his stomach. He rolled over, which suited Neeson, who took the opportunity to stamp savagely into the man's groin. Neeson stepped away, limping some safe distance between them.

"You okay?" O'Shea asked.

Neeson was breathless. He turned around and looked at him. "Sure. Just hurt my foot against his nuts…"

O'Shea barged his way through the open doorway, closed the door, then quickly locked it behind him. "Right, get the bastard into that room there!" he shouted at Neeson, pointing to the doorway into the lounge. He glanced up the stairs, then looked down at Parker. "Who else is in the house?"

Parker was groaning loudly and holding his throbbing groin, but still managed to beg. "Don't hurt me, I've done nothing wrong…"

Neeson cut off his words by stamping on the man's hand, breaking a number of tiny bones, forcing him to scream involuntarily. He caught hold of Parker by his hair, then pulled him up, kicking and screaming, towards the lounge doorway.

O'Shea walked through the hallway and cautiously opened the kitchen door. He looked around, noticed Lisa, who was cowering in the corner of the room. She looked up at him, her left eye terribly swollen from Parker's vicious attack. There was blood at the corner of her mouth. "Please... please don't hurt me," she sobbed, shaking uncontrollably. "I don't want to be hurt anymore…"

O'Shea shook his head. "It's not you we want, luv. But you'll have to come with me for the moment." He stepped forward and held out his hand. "Come on, just trust me," he reassured her, a look of both pity and understanding in his eyes. "My old man used to beat up on my mother every Saturday night when he came home drunk. I saw enough to last me a lifetime."

Lisa reached up and gripped his hand, and was pulled swiftly to her feet. She winced with the pain that shot through her stomach, then wiped the tears from her eyes and walked with him as he guided her towards the lounge. She hesitated at the foot of the stairs.

"Problem?" O'Shea asked. He followed her gaze. "Is there someone else here?" He watched the hesitation in her eyes. "Don't lie to me. We mean fucking business, luv."

"My son," she said quietly, despondently. "He's in his room."

"Go and get him. Right up and back down. Call him now," he said. "I want you both right down here, no messing about calling the police. Go!"

Lisa bolted up the stairs, calling David's name as she went. The boy was ashen, shaken. He had heard Keith beating her again. She scooped him up in her arms, crying for what he was going through, what he had witnessed lately. She should have run out weeks ago, should have left when she had the chance. She had spoken to Frank Holman, asked for his help. She knew

Simon was being released and she had begged Holman to help her and David leave Keith, give them a safe place to stay. But Holman had been adamant that she should stay with Parker, just for a while longer. Just until he could make suitable arrangements.

O'Shea walked them both into the room and pointed to a leather sofa nestled in the far corner next to a large mahogany bookcase. "Sit down over there, luv. Keep quiet and don't try anything. You might want to turn the little lad around to face you." He turned to Danny Neeson and smirked. "Seems our friend here is a bit of a hard man; needs to hit his women about to keep them in line." Neeson pulled Parker to his feet and pushed him down into a hard-backed chair. He gripped him tightly around the throat, then pushed his face close to Parker's ear. "Well, now you will find out what it's like to be meet a *real* hard man…" He pushed Parker's head back against the chair, then nodded to O'Shea. "Give us a hand boss," he said. "Just keep him where he is." Neeson waited for O'Shea to grab hold of him by his shoulders, then walked around the chair and quickly unfastened Parker's shoelaces. He threaded them through the arms of the chair, then tied his hands down tightly. Next, he unbuckled the man's leather belt, wrenched it out from the belt loops and threaded it into a loop. He slipped the loop over Parker's head. The man struggled, but Neeson lashed out and jabbed him on the nose, Parker recoiled, Neeson pulled the belt tight around his neck, before handing the end of the makeshift noose to O'Shea. "Here, keep hold of this. Nice and tight, now."

Keith Parker gasped for breath as O'Shea pulled back forcefully on the belt, then slowly released it, gradually allowing him some intake of precious air. "Why are you doing this, I thought we had a deal?" he wheezed.

"A deal?" O'Shea mused. "That is exactly what I thought we had. We were to take care of Simon Grant, and cut you in on a job, while you were to supply us with all the information we would need to hold up the security van."

Lisa gasped, then held a hand over her mouth. David gasped at hearing his father's name, but Lisa hugged him close, nestled his chin into her neck.

O'Shea glanced across at her and smiled. "That's right luv, your husband is dead. Or at least, he's bloody *meant* to be." He pulled back on the belt, almost choking the man as he gasped frantically for air.

Neeson took the revolver from out of his waistband. "Holman double-crossed us. He has taken our money, and we want to know where he is. He must have tipped off Grant. And we think that you must be in this as well..." He held up the pistol, his finger resting loosely on the trigger. "Up to your spineless little neck."

"No!" Parker blurted.

"Yes!" Neeson whipped the barrel of the revolver across Parker's mouth, shattering his front teeth. He stood back and smiled as Parker spat out mouthfuls of blood, saliva and chips of enamel. "Listen to me Parker, and listen well," he paused. "Where are Holman and Grant?"

"I don't know! I'm not involved! I thought that bastard Grant was dead. *That* was our deal!" Parker lisped, then gasped suddenly as O'Shea pulled back on the belt.

"You sold us information. Three of your employees died, you agreed to that also," O'Shea said grimly. "I think you are in this up to your bloody snakelike eyeballs!" He turned to Neeson, his teeth clenched in rage. "Cap the spineless bastard!"

Neeson had knee-capped men before. He usually used a cordless drill, occasionally a length of two-by-two. A gun was too noisy back in Ulster. Not that people ever reported hearing a shot, it was never worth the risk, but in leafy suburbia the police would be round in minutes. He looked around and settled on a silk cushion from the nearby sofa. He quickly placed it against Parker's knee then pushed the muzzle of the revolver hard against it, before folding the edges of the cushion over the barrel.

"No!" Parker screamed in terror, struggling against the restraint of the leather belt around his neck. His scream was stifled to a gargle.

Neeson cocked the hammer, then squeezed the hair-trigger of the .357 magnum revolver. It kicked wildly in his hands; but although it was immensely powerful, most of the noise was suppressed by the material of the cushion. Keith Parker screamed in agony, biting his lips in a desperate bid to quell the extreme pain inflicted upon him. Lisa screamed, but held a hand to her mouth, she had turned extremely pale.

"Gag him, quickly!" O'Shea pulled a white handkerchief out from his jacket pocket and hastily threw it towards Neeson. "Hurry, before he shouts the bloody house down!"

Neeson caught the handkerchief and stuffed it forcefully Parker's mouth, letting the blood-soaked cushion fall to the floor, exposing the jagged pieces of bone and flaps of torn flesh. The .357 round had almost severed the leg. Parker was bleeding severely.

"Where... is... Frank... Holman?" Neeson asked, exaggerating each syllable. He caught hold of Parker's ear and twisted, but the man was beyond feeling more pain. "Tell us, or I'll cap yer other fucking knee!" he shouted.

"You know his address in France, don't you?" O'Shea shouted into his other ear, then pulled back on the leather belt and looked at Neeson. "Do it Danny, take his other fucking leg off and cripple the bastard for good!"

"Stop it! For Christ's sake stop this madness!" Lisa rolled David off her lap. "Stay there, my boy. Don't turn around. Everything is going to be fine..." She stood up and hurried across to a small teak writing bureau in the opposite corner of the room. She opened the lid, then rummaged quickly through a pile of papers, before holding up a palm-sized address book. "Here, it's in here. All Holman's businesses and his addresses both here and in France." She flicked through the book, found the page she was looking for and tore it out. She then held it out for O'Shea. He took the page from her and read it, before tucking it into his pocket. Lisa looked across at Parker, who rested limply in the chair. He was moaning quietly, battling unconsciousness. His knee had practically disappeared, the great power of the .357 magnum bullet had simply disintegrated the cartilage and shattered the surrounding structure of bone, which in turn, had ripped the flesh clean away. It was still bleeding heavily.

O'Shea nodded to Neeson. "Come on Danny, let's get the hell out of here."

Neeson looked at Lisa. She had returned to the sofa and was hugging David tightly to her. "Listen sweetie pie, if you know what's good for you, you won't go calling the police for a while. If you're sensible, you will give us a few minutes to get clear, and if I were you, I would forget our faces pretty damn quickly," he paused as he caught hold of the door handle. "Better get something on that knee, or he'll bleed himself dry."

Neeson closed the door behind him and moments later Lisa heard the sound of a vehicle pulling out of the drive. She started to relax a little, relieved that she had not been harmed.

"Help me." The voice was faint, as Parker spoke through the bundled handkerchief. He had managed to force most of it out of his mouth, which by now had become soaked in a sticky mass of congealed blood and saliva.

Lisa snapped to her senses. She bent down and looked at the state of his knee, not knowing what to do or how best to help him. She picked up the tattered cushion and pressed it tightly against his wound, then started to unfasten his makeshift bindings. "It will be all right, just hang on," she said quietly, attempting to put him more at ease.

"Call me a bloody ambulance, you stupid bloody bitch!" Parker clenched his teeth together, as he felt a sudden shock of pain surge through him. "Do it now or I'll bleed to death. Go on do it! Are you stupid or what?"

Lisa pulled her hands back from the knotted shoelaces and looked at David. "Honey, go upstairs and get your coat." David promptly did as he was told. Lisa looked back at Keith. "You tried to have him killed. My husband, the father of my child," she paused, shaking her head in bewilderment. "Why would you do that?"

"For Christ's sake, you stupid slut! I'm bleeding to death here, get me an ambulance!"

Unperturbed, she continued, "And those people killed in the robbery, your employees. You agreed for them to be killed as part of your heist?"

Parker grimaced in pain, then stared up at her. "Yes! I did everything that they said. For you... for us." He squinted at her, losing focus as his consciousness started to ebb away. "Now go and get me some help, you stupid cow! What the hell are you waiting for?"

She looked towards the door, then back at him, her face suddenly decisive, determined. She reached down and picked up the blood-soaked handkerchief, then stuffed it into his open mouth, so far back he started to gag. She turned round and walked to the door, wavering with her hand resting on the door handle. "Goodbye, Keith," she said quietly, almost to herself. She opened the door, then turned again and smiled at him as he moaned loudly. "There's no point in struggling. Why don't *you* just try and be submissive for change?" She closed the door gently, then turned and smiled at David as he came down stairs, carrying his coat. "Come on, sweetheart," she said, her eyes moist, but this time from tears of joy, not pain or shame. "Let's go and get you a McDonald's breakfast. You'd like that. Wouldn't you?"

"Yes please, mummy."

"And then there's that remote controlled car you wanted. How about we get that for you? We can go to the park and use it."

"Brilliant!" he smiled. "What about school?"

"I think the Easter holidays can start early," she smiled, wiping tears from her eyes. "We can go to the zoo this afternoon too."

"Yes!" His expression changed, suddenly unsure. "What about Keith?" he asked glumly.

"Keith won't be coming with us," she said. "He won't be going anywhere."

38

It was a gloriously sunny morning in north-eastern France. The sun had risen behind them, and was beaming its rays from a clear, azure blue sky. The sun was bright and Alex King was glad he would not be driving towards it. They had passed through customs trouble-free, and were now making good time as they headed towards Paris.

"How long will it take us to get there?" Grant asked, as he looked at the road signs for Paris, Le Mans and Bordeaux.

King nodded towards the road atlas in Grant's foot-well. "Check it out for yourself," he said amiably. "All I know, is that we stay on the A10 until we hit Bordeaux, after that, I'm not sure," he lied smoothly. In fact, he had planned the route thoroughly on the train journey through the tunnel, whilst Grant had slept in his seat. He was still keen to keep the man's mind active, and allow him to think of more than just the risks involved.

Grant flicked through the road atlas until he found a full map of France, indicating its motorways and major routes. "Ah, it's bloody miles!" He pointed at the page, then tapped his finger on their approximate position. "How big is France? We're here, about a quarter of the way."

King glanced at his watch. "We'd better stop off somewhere and stock up on some provisions, that way, we should be able to drive straight through. With any luck, we should be there by around six o'clock tonight." He looked at the road sign indicating the next exit. "This will do, Senlis. Looks like a small town. Besides, I'd rather make a stop before we reach Paris."

"What about Forsyth? I thought that he was going to update you, let you know if Holman was following or not. This might just be a bloody waste of time." Grant slumped back in his seat as King indicated right and entered the slip road. "And we still don't know if O'Shea and his mob are following, or whether they've already caught up with Holman."

King shook his head and grinned devilishly. "It's not a mob with O'Shea anymore, just Danny Neeson. The other two should be out of action by now, if all went well."

Grant frowned but King added nothing to enlighten him, just turned onto the road for the small town of Senlis and increased his speed.

As they entered the small town, Grant pointed across to the other side of the road. "That looks like a shop, I think it's a bakery."

King looked at the shop front and nodded. The sign simply read: *Epicer, Boulanger, Boucher.* Which simply translated as: Grocer, Baker, and Butcher.

King pulled across the road and eased the BMW to a halt outside the front entrance. He switched off the ignition and pocketed the keys. "You wait here. I'll get us some provisions. You're not a fussy eater, are you?" Grant nodded but King had not bothered to wait for a reply, he jogged towards the shop, then leapt up the four steps and into the foyer. It was three little shops in one, four if you counted the tiny dairy section to the rear of the building. King's French was not good, but most of the produce was spread out for self-service. He picked up a small wire basket and quickly helped himself to a few easy-to-eat essentials: crisps, chocolate bars, and a bottle of orange juice from the chilled cabinet. He glanced out of the window, saw Grant sitting in the car. He wondered if the career criminal could hot-wire a BMW. He suspected he could. He contemplated going out for him, but decided against it. He walked over to the cash register, dropped the basket on top of the counter, and then pointed at the savoury cabinet. With a combination of gestures and poorly spoken French, and plus an overlay of English spoken with what he imagined to be a French accent, he managed to obtain two quiches, two ham and cheese croissants and a small, cooked French bread pizza.

As he paid for the goods, and the young woman behind the counter filled two paper bags with his provisions, King wished that he had taken a course in French. At the MI6 Training Wing in Norfolk, he had been assigned Arabic. He thought it a waste of time, but it had come in handy in Iraq when he had been part of an intelligence gathering operation. Now that little lot appeared to have been sorted out, human resources had told him it would be a waste of time to continue and he was to learn Spanish to aid anti-drug enforcement in Columbia. He couldn't help thinking the middle east would be more significant in the future. That extremists would choose somewhere like Afghanistan or The Yemen to get a foothold. But he was a simple foot soldier within the intelligence world, and the brains were looking away from the middle east and watching south America and the growing drug problem. He couldn't help thinking they were looking the wrong way. He thought he'd continue with the Arabic on his own time.

He thanked the shop assistant as she handed him the bags, then walked back to the vehicle. He froze when he saw the car was empty. He dropped the bags on the ground, looked around and cursed. Grant stepped out from between the shop and another building zipping his fly.

"No bogs around here, so when in Rome..." he smiled. "What's for breakfast?"

King picked up the bags and opened his door. He handed Grant the bags as he sat in his seat. "See what you fancy," he was relieved, felt foolish for leaving him in the car in the first place. And with the money in the boot. He was used to working with team mates, not coerced criminals that would sooner jump ship if they got the chance.

Grant glanced briefly into the bag containing the quiches and turned up his nose in distaste, before looking at King. "Do you think O'Shea and Neeson will go for it? I mean, cut the bullshit. Seriously?"

King started the vehicle's quiet engine and looked at him sincerely. "If they don't catch up with Holman before he has a chance to leave, and if they are as tough and resourceful as they have previously proven themselves to be, then yes. I am positive that they will want to get hold of Holman right away." He slipped the automatic gearbox into drive and executed a three-point turn. "Now, let's get some serious miles under our belts." He glanced down at the ringing telephone, which rested on top of the centre console. He waited until he had finished the manoeuvre, then picked it up as he cruised slowly back towards the motorway. "Hello?"

"Bonjour!"

"Forsyth?" King paused. "You seem in unusually high spirits."

"Alex, it's working! Holman is on board Le Shuttle and should be on French soil any moment."

King pulled the vehicle into a lay-by on the side of the road and slipped the gearbox into neutral. "That's good news. Was it a confirmed visual?"

"Saw him with my own eyes, old chum," Forsyth said jubilantly. *"The news just gets better and better, old boy. Our Irish friends arrived not ten minutes ago, and Danny Neeson has just stepped out of the ticket office."*

King tensed. "They're on their way?"

"It would appear so, old boy. Watching them as we speak. They're heading for the boarding lanes. Looks like they'll be aboard the next train."

"Okay, if that's the case, we had better get a move on. Can you let me know if they definitely board?"

"Will try old boy, but I think you can take it for granted though; the route to France is pretty light this morning." There was a brief silence, in which King could tell that the man had paused to inhale his cigarette. The exhalation was clearly audible over the line, and King envisioned a perfect smoke ring drifting through the stale air inside Forsyth's vehicle. *"I have a few details to take care of, must dash, bye for now."*

The line went dead and King placed the mobile telephone back onto the centre console and smiled to himself. They had the lead, but only marginally. Holman had clearly been unnerved by Danny Neeson, and had decided to leave the country straight away. Planting the explosive device under Ross and Sean's vehicle had not only levelled the playing field, but prompted O'Shea and Neeson to check the money. They were now convinced that Holman had double-crossed them, and was partnered by an elusive Simon Grant. It was clear that neither Holman or Parker would have been able to empty their safe, it *had* to be Grant.

Everything was slotting neatly into place. What's more, eliminating O'Shea in France while travelling under a false name would enable King to slip back into Britain and simply disappear. The government had always denied *shoot to kill* policies, which made assassination jobs extremely difficult within the United Kingdom, even when they were officially sanctioned by the higher echelons within the intelligence services. No amount of cajoling would make the British police halt investigations, as they remain one of the most incorruptible and unanswerable police forces in the world.

King slipped the BMW's gearbox into drive and pulled out onto the quiet road. They had a mere hour's head start on Holman so there was precious little time to spare.

39

Holman pulled into the slip road, exiting the N10 from Bordeaux and taking the lesser D1 north which would take him through the town of Castelnau-de-Médoc. It was a little off route, but he had time to spare. He remembered Castelnau-de-Médoc as having a wonderful bistro on the bank of a river, where he had once ordered a Coq-au-vin so good that he had requested another portion, instead of dessert - much to the surprise of the manager, and much to the delight of the chef.

He drove along the narrow road through the thick pine forest with its wonderfully fresh, scented aroma. The sun hung bright and low in the sky, glimmering through the trees as he headed towards the town.

After a further fifteen-kilometres of quiet, near-empty road, he entered the sleepy town of Castelnau-de-Médoc with its shops and old hotels, painted fifty years ago, and never touched up since. He had not ventured into the town at this time of year before and nor, it would seem, did anyone else. The town was virtually deserted but for a few workmen who were putting the finishing touches to the shop fronts, obviously working late to get the maintenance work completed in time for the start of the summer season. He thought that the town would not have been so seasonal, but he had been mistaken.

Holman drove the Mercedes around the corner, then cursed as he realised that his favourite restaurant had closed for the winter months. Either that, or had closed down completely. The sign-written facia board that hung above the bay window was dull, with large flakes of paint peeling at the corners. The whole facade had obviously taken a violent beating from the Atlantic's unrelenting winds, even this far inland, which had encrusted the building in a thick layer of salty residue. Inside the building, the chairs were stacked haphazardly on top of the tables and the chef's specials billboards had been propped up against the empty coffee machine.

Holman kept the Mercedes moving slowly then conceded that he would find an *intermarche* for some snacks and a few groceries, and wait for the town of Lacanau Ocean, where he would eat in one of the decent seafront restaurants. He made his way back onto the D1 and headed north-west.

***

"Which way now? And this time, don't send me the wrong way down a bloody one-way street," King paused as he brought the BMW to a halt at the crossroads. "Come on Grant, we probably don't have any more time to waste!"

"Okay! Okay!" Grant studied the map in the fading light, then pointed his hand in front of King's face. "That way. I mean right."

The atmosphere inside the vehicle was tense. King was extremely tired, having driven the whole way. Then had come their second hitch. Instead of skirting the city of Bordeaux by its ring road; an error on Grant's behalf had seen them enter the city, which had proved to be a nightmare. After spending almost an hour in the rush hour traffic, and more than one erratic manoeuvre, they had finally managed to exit the rundown city, with its myriad of back streets and one way systems, but emerged onto the N10 having wasted time they did not have.

King swung the BMW erratically out of the crossroads, following Grant's directions. "Are you sure?"

"Goddamn it! I've apologised more than once! Do you want me to navigate or not?"

King ignored the outburst and looked anxiously at his watch, then returned his eyes to the winding road as it joined a bridge over a wide canal. "Just tell me where to go next." He glanced over the side of the bridge and looked down onto the banks of the river. "Seems like fishing is the national past time," he mused quietly to himself, more to ease the tension than anything else. Hordes of fishermen, young and old, were seated on the grass, fishing with long poles and talking to one another as they pulled up their lines having hooked tiny silver-coloured fish, no larger than a finger. He'd never fished before, something he'd longed to do as a child with one of his many father figures. But they were not the type to fish. Nor, do anything other than ask him to keep an eye on their car while they were with his mother. It was years later that he realised what and who they were, and why they visited his home at all hours.

Grant leaned forward, studying the road map intently, as he tried to keep his place on the page. "We want..." he looked intently at the map, "To head left, towards the beach." He looked up and saw the sign for *La Plage*. "There! Follow the sign!"

The town was rather pretty, a mixture of old and modern France. Areas of trees and neat gardens punctuated the rows of shops and houses, separating the growth of the town with small boundaries of foliage. The town seemed fresh and new, yet had a feeling of dormancy about it, as if it were waking from a deep sleep, ready for the new season to breathe precious life back into it. In many ways, it reminded King of the many coastal towns and villages of Cornwall and Devon, only coming to life upon the arrival of spring. He had once spent a spring and summer in the west country jobbing around. He aimed to buy a cottage there one day. Now his life looked to finally be on track, it was no longer merely a daydream.

King slowed the BMW, then took another left-hand turning, which took them along the seafront. The road forked in front of them, left towards the shops and restaurants along the sea wall, or right towards the beach road that led out of town in the direction of Holman's address. He pulled the vehicle into the side of the road and reached into his pocket for the directions, which Forsyth had issued him with back in England. "This is it." He rested the piece of paper carefully in his lap, then pulled back out into the road. "It's not far to go now, keep your eyes peeled. Holman's house is number one-thousand and seven, on the left and set back from the road on the dune-side, apparently."

The narrow road followed the coast behind a partial blockade of sand dunes, which parted every now and then to reveal a glimpse of the calm, shimmering ocean. The sun was setting directly to their left, turning the ocean orange on the horizon. After a few hundred metres they passed a large car park to their left, then headed into denser pine forest as they left the town of Lacanau and its outskirts behind them.

King slowed the vehicle to a relative crawl, as he passed the occasional house, set back from the quiet road. He glanced down at the instructions, then looked up with conviction. "That's it! One-thousand and seven. The properties must be numbered throughout the district. There's hardly twenty houses out here, let alone a thousand." He eased the car to a halt then looked at his watch. "Forsyth did not call to update us, so we must assume that O'Shea and Neeson are on the way. Holman could be hours away, or he could be right on our tail. It depends how he drives. That car of his could be made to hustle."

"What do we do now then?" Grant asked as he studied the property and its surroundings. "There seem to be no immediate neighbours, but the house could well be alarmed."

"It will be," King said, then pulled back out onto the road and drove on past the house. "It's with a management agency for maintenance. The company insist on their properties being alarmed. We will do it now. I don't want a premature confrontation with Holman, it will ruin everything," he paused. "I want the Irishmen."

***

O'Shea and Neeson had just bypassed the town of Carcans, having driven a different route south on the D3. The road was quiet; the traffic becoming lighter the further south they travelled. Pine forest spread out on both sides of the road, with one hundred metre firebreaks cut into it every kilometre or so.

O'Shea pointed at a group of men huddled conspiratorially around the tailgate of a four-wheel drive vehicle. "What are that lot up to?"

As they drew nearer, one of the men turned around with a double-barrelled shotgun broken over his arm. He watched the Saab dubiously as they passed, then turned back to the others. He had a bunch of dead pigeons hanging by their legs from a loop of twine.

"I guess they're game shooting," Neeson commented, then nodded towards the side of the road where a man had appeared from the forest clutching a brace of plump wood pigeons. "Another one there. Seems the French are big on hunting. I like that. Shoot your own meat, grow your own vegetables. My neighbour kept pigs when I was a lad. He shared the chops around and took payment back in chores or potatoes others grew in their back yards." He checked his empty rear-view mirror, then looked ahead at the next car, which had pulled well off the road amid a growth of bracken which fringed the edge of the dark forest.

"Aye, same here," O'Shea commented. "Simpler days. Better ones too."

Neeson slowed down, watching the man stand at the rear of his vehicle, a small Peugeot hatchback. He then eased his left foot onto the brake and tapped the accelerator with his right. The Saab jerked erratically as it slowed and he quickly switched on the hazard warning lights as he pulled into the side of the road,

"What's going on?" O'Shea sat up in his seat and stared at the hazard warning lights as they flashed intermittently on the dashboard. "Are we out of fuel?"

Neeson shook his head. "No. Just relax." He pressed down hard on the brake, but did not apply the clutch. The Saab shuddered dramatically, then stalled on the side of the road. Neeson opened his door and stepped out, scratching his head in bewilderment, before walking around to the rear of the vehicle and taking a small emergency tool kit out from the boot.

The Frenchman looked on, somewhat bemused as Neeson took a large spanner out of the tool kit and walked around to the front of the vehicle. Tourists were not among his favourite people. Indeed, from Bordeaux to Biarritz, that opinion was one shared by a great many of his countrymen. The man opened the rear hatch of his car and unfastened the cartridge belt, which hung under his ample stomach. He bent down, picked up three wood pigeons, then dropped them down into the boot before returning his gaze to the stupid foreigners who had run out of petrol.

Neeson peered through the open window at O'Shea and said, "Pop the bonnet." O'Shea frowned, but Neeson scowled at him. "Just do it!"

O'Shea quickly pulled the release catch then sat back dejectedly as Neeson walked around to the front of the vehicle, lifted the bonnet and tinkered with the engine. After a few seconds, he shut the bonnet back down then peered back inside the open window. "Pass me the map," he said tersely. He waited for O'Shea to pick the map up off the floor, then snatched it from him and walked over towards the Frenchman's vehicle. He smiled benignly as he approached, the map in one hand, a large spanner held loosely in the other. "Do you speak English?" he asked, as the man seemingly ignored his existence. *"Vous parlez Anglaise?"* Neeson smiled meekly. He shrugged an apology for his poor attempt at French, then pointed to his car. "Garage? Petrol?" He turned back to him and held out the map. "How... far... is... the... garage?" he asked loudly, just in case raising his voice would make the Frenchman understand.

The man frowned, then nodded in the direction that Neeson had been heading and held up eight fingers.

Neeson frowned. "I don't understand." He held out the map for him. "Is that kilometres?"

The Frenchman begrudgingly stepped forward and caught hold of the edge of the map. He stared at the page for a moment, then pointed at a spot approximately eight to ten kilometres from their location, and started to speak in rapid French. Neeson stepped closer and looked down at the page, then, just as the man pointed down the road, he swung the spanner up into the man's face.

The man fell backwards clutching his mouth and shattered teeth, and wailing loudly. Neeson wasted no time in following up his attack with two more vicious blows to the head. The man fell onto his stomach then rolled over onto his back and raised his hands in a desperate bid to shield himself from the rain of blows that Neeson was now delivering. Each blow struck the man in the face with a sickening crunch, and after several blows the man's hands dropped to the ground and he lay motionless. Neeson rolled him over onto his stomach, then raised the heavy spanner high above his head and directed a deadly blow to the base of the man's skull. There was a loud crack, then Neeson stood up slowly and looked cautiously around, before throwing the spanner deep into the surrounding undergrowth. Less than two paces away, a small drainage ditch cut a path neatly through the bracken. Neeson caught hold of the body by its feet and quickly dragged it towards the ditch. He heaved and rolled it, then stood back as the cadaver dropped down into the thick mud.

He wiped the sweat from his brow and returned to the small hatchback, where the .20 bore shotgun rested against the passenger door. He quickly picked it up, opened the action and looked into the breach. Both barrels were empty, although he already suspected that this would be the case, considering that the man was packing his equipment away. Neeson walked around to the rear hatch, picked up the half-filled cartridge belt, then quickly returned to the Saab.

"What the hell?" O'Shea stared at him, dumbfounded.

Neeson opened his door, placed the shotgun on the rear seat then dropped the cartridge belt into the rear foot space. "Relax," he said. "I dumped the revolver at Folkestone, couldn't chance a search. We needed a weapon, and now we have one." He calmly started the Saab's engine, selected first gear, and pulled out onto the empty road.

O'Shea looked behind him at the lonely vehicle as they pulled away and shook his head slowly, still shocked at what he had just witnessed. "Is he dead?" He turned back to Neeson and stared at him coolly. "We have no friends here. If he's dead, we could be in the shit big style."

Neeson shrugged. "It will serve the bugger right," he said calmly. "The man was bloody unhelpful."

As the Saab pulled back out onto the road and made its way into the distance, the young boy stepped out from the forest with his .410 shotgun folded over his arm, just as his father had taught him. He swung the pigeon by his side, beaming proudly. It had been his first kill and his father had not been there to witness it. He had wandered away from the clearing, out of his father's sight. He knew that his father would be angry, shooting was a strict discipline, but he also knew how proud his father would be of him. To bring home food for the table, to contribute to his modest household. Hopefully he would not be chastised when his father saw his prized trophy. He walked through the thick bracken towards the vehicle, then stood still, puzzled. He was sure that his father would have returned by now.

40

Two-hundred metres past the house, just before the next exclusive holiday home, a narrow lane branched off to the left, cutting through the dense pine forest and into the dunes.

King checked the rear-view mirror, then satisfied that there was nobody nearby to observe them, pulled into the lane and drove steadily through the muddy and sandy puddles until he estimated that he was directly behind Frank Holman's property. He steered the BMW carefully to the left, where a small passing point had been cut into the undergrowth, then switched off the engine.

"It's not dark yet, we're bound to be noticed," Grant said, shaking his head despondently. "We can't take the chance of being seen."

"I don't give a damn if we are noticed, as long as it's not Holman or our Irish friends," he paused. "Take a look around. There's nothing here, no reason for people to be here. If we can get the money in position and get the hell out before anyone calls the police, then it doesn't matter," he paused, looking at the tiny sliver of sun which stabbed savagely through the tree line. "It will be at least another hour before it's completely dark, we haven't got enough time to wait." He opened his door and stepped out over a large puddle then gently closed the door and walked around to the rear of the vehicle.

Grant followed suit, closing his door as quietly as possible. He crossed over the lane, avoiding the muddy water as best he could, then scrabbled up the small embankment and looked down the incline towards

Holman's property. There were a few islands of pine trees, growing in groups of three or four, then two-hundred metres or so of scrubby undergrowth before the final belt of pines, which bordered Holman's rambling gardens. The house nestled amongst the trees, invisible but for its terracotta roof.

"Grant!" King called out in an exaggerated whisper. "Come on, take this!" He set the bag of equipment down on a patch of pine needles, then lifted the heavy suitcase out of the boot.

Grant tentatively eased himself down the steep embankment, then picked his way through the myriad of puddles as he crossed over the lane. He bent down and picked up the heavy bag of equipment, then waited for King to close the boot of the car.

King opened the offside rear door and hastily pulled the panel away from the doorframe. He reached inside, under the electric window motor and retrieved the plastic-wrapped packages.

"What are those?" Grant asked curiously as he watched King place the tiny bundles on the roof of the car, to join the other four packages.

"Tool of the trade," he replied quietly.

Grant watched intently as King ripped the plastic off each of the packages. The toothpaste solution was crumbling like old plaster. He laid the parts out in front of him and quickly assembled the pieces, with well-practised precision: barrel into the frame, spring pressed tight against the holding lug, then the whole frame slipped inside the recess of the working parts. With the pin in place, the weapon was complete. He inserted the magazine into the pistol's butt, racked back the slide and applied the safety. He then tucked the weapon into the waistband of his trousers. Thirteen rounds. Not many for two terrorists who had both been in the game for twenty or more years. He would have preferred the odds a little more in his favour.

King slung the equipment bag over his shoulder, then picked up the heavy suitcase and pointed to a dip in the embankment. "Through there." Grant followed him through the dip, which in fact, turned out to be natural drain for excess water that had accumulated on the surface of the lane. Once clear of the makeshift passage and into the undergrowth, they cautiously picked their way towards the thick barrier of pine trees that bordered Holman's property.

King moved smoothly, placing his footsteps so as not to make any unnecessary sounds. Grant followed, somewhat less stealthily, then stood still, breathing heavily as King suddenly signalled for him to stop moving.

"What's the matter?" Grant asked quietly, his eyes darting everywhere as he cautiously crouched down beside him.

King pointed towards the far-left side of the house. "Up near the guttering, a red alarm box."

Grant craned his neck to see, then nodded. "Looks like a decoy to me," he said then looked back at King. "If you catch it right, you can see daylight through the vents. It's either a decoy to stop you looking any further and seeing the real system, or it's a poor-man's substitute; which is always a good sign."

"What do you mean?"

Grant slowly rose to his feet, keeping back behind the thick pine tree. "If someone goes to the trouble of having a fake alarm box fitted, then it generally means that they have stuff worth stealing, but are only half-hearted in their approach to protecting it."

King nodded. "That's fine, but we are not here to steal, and Holman is pretty clued-up as far as thieves are concerned." He placed the suitcase down on the soft earth and stood up, keeping close to the pine tree for cover. "I reckon it's a decoy, to stop any would-be burglar from detecting the real system. Remember, Holman doesn't live here much of the year, any system will probably go through the telephone lines to either the police, or a private security firm, or to the maintenance company."

Grant suddenly pointed to the outside light, which was fixed to the house near the left gable. "Over there, the light on the left. Near the roof. The telephone lines come in at a point just above it, but trace down the wall and into it." He looked at King excitedly. "There is no reason for the telephone line to go through a light unit, other than to alert a number if it is compromised. The light is either fake or dual purpose, it's the light that's the alarm system. They should have brought the lines in stealthily. What cowboy rigged that system up?"

King smiled. "Alright, we will go in from the right, that light may well be motion sensitive." He glanced quickly at his watch, then picked up the heavy suitcase. "We have to hurry. Follow me, and stay aware."

Grant followed him through the rambling gardens and past a large area of overgrown pampas grass, until they reached the paved patio. King looked cautiously around the area, then stepped over the timber-framed veranda and beckoned Grant forwards. Grant caught hold of the wooden rail and climbed onto the veranda and dropped his bag of equipment onto the walkway. "The window would be the best bet, but we don't want to leave any trace, so that rules out removing the pane."

King clenched his teeth together and stared at him. "I'm not here for a bloody lesson, so I am not interested in what we *can't* do. Just get us into the bloody place."

"I was just thinking out loud," Grant protested.

"Well don't, we haven't the time. Holman may be here in a matter of minutes rather than hours, after our delay. It will depend whether he stopped off somewhere. That also goes for both O'Shea and Neeson. Our little escapade in Bordeaux didn't help matters."

Grant shook his head. "Alright!" He turned back to the window and ran his hands along the underside of the frame. "There are no sensors on the exterior, but that doesn't prove that there are no sensors inside. I reckon that each room will have a PIR, or passive infrared which will detect movement," he said.

King took the bag off his shoulder and set it down on the wooden walkway, next to the suitcase. "Get everything ready, all possible tools that you should need, then pick the lock." He stepped backwards a few paces, then looked cautiously around for anybody approaching, before turning back to Grant. "Come on, hurry it up!"

Grant placed the necessary tools on the ground next to the doorstep, then reached into the bag and took out a plastic bag. He tipped the bag upside down to reveal two tightly bound bundles.

King watched as Grant unwrapped one of the bundles then slid the other across the veranda to where he was standing. "What's this?" he asked as he unwrapped it curiously.

"Just a couple of plastic carrier bags and two elastic bands." He quickly placed a plastic bag over each foot, then doubled the elastic bands around his ankles to hold them firmly in place. "Don't want mud on Holman's carpet, do we?"

King smiled to himself as he quickly pulled one of the plastic bags over his foot then bound it tightly in place. He had used the same method back at the farmhouse. Grant was obviously a true professional. The first detail that Holman would notice would be two pairs of muddy footprints in his hallway. That was what separated the professional thief from their bungling counterparts. Many victims can go days, even weeks without realising that they have been robbed. By then, the perpetrator can be safely away, free to concoct their rock-solid alibi.

Grant worked quickly and confidently. He inserted the titanium picklock into the lock, then eased a smaller, diamond-tipped key underneath and started to feel for the tumblers. After a little less than a minute, he turned to King and beamed a triumphant grin. "It's unlocked, get ready to move." He gathered up the rest of his tools and placed them into various pockets. He switched on the torch and quickly pushed the door inwards and rushed inside. There was no sign of a control panel. "Shit!" Grant was perplexed. He quickly stared around then noticed the wires from the sensor in the doorframe. He traced the wires away from the door, where they disappeared into the wall. He realised that they must have led to a coat-cupboard in the hallway.

"What's the problem?" King peered around the door and watched as Grant frantically opened the cupboard door.

Grant studied the control panel, ignoring his question. Two wires fed into the panel but only one fed out. This wire would go directly to the telephone line, but could not be cut because disconnection would halt the minor electrical current and activate the alarm via its rechargeable battery. Grant quickly reached up to the control panel and hastily typed in a four-digit code. This would now give him an extra thirty seconds, as the system would allow one mistake as a miss-type. He then took the small, rechargeable electric screwdriver out of his pocket and removed the control panel's facia. Next, he took the circuit diversion meter and held it out to King. "Quick, take this!"

He caught hold of the tiny black box and stared at the four wires that protruded from it, one from each corner. At the end of each wire was a small crocodile clip. He turned back to Grant, watching intently, as the man battled against the clock.

Grant started to cut into the wires with a small scalpel, cutting just deep enough to peel back the plastic coating and expose the bare wires. He turned around to King and held out his hand expectantly. "Quick, give it to me!" King complied, passing him the black box. Grant hastily attached a crocodile clip to both wires, then pulled the black box across the control panel and attached two more wires further along. The electrical current would now pass through the system, unaffected while Grant cut the necessary wires.

Grant turned around and smiled. "Done deal. I will have to reconnect this little lot later, but for now, we're in the clear."

***

Frank Holman had managed to pick up a few groceries and some much-needed bottles of lager at a roadside *intermarche*.

He pulled off the D6 and took the road which would skirt Lacanau's popular resort lake. It was only another ten-kilometres or so to his property, and he was trying to decide whether to freshen up, have a beer and go out for dinner, or head straight to the seafront and eat.

***

O'Shea sat up in his seat and pointed at the road sign. "Only twenty-two kilometres to Lacanau and thirty-one to Lacanau Ocean."

"So, what there's two towns called Lacanau?" Neeson asked.

"Yes. One is by a lake, the other is by the sea."

"Couldn't they come up with another name?"

"It's all in the vocabulary."

"What?"

"Three-hundred thousand known French words and one and a half million words in the English language," O'Shea said. "They must have to over-use the words they have."

"Seriously?"

O'Shea laughed. "Fucked if I know! But it's a theory."

Neeson smiled, then glanced at his watch. "I think that we should get into the town, find a quiet bar and have a drink and a steak or something, then freshen up in the toilets. After that, we can head off and find Holman's place and go in after dark, just as he's starting to relax from the long drive. Or better still, when he's asleep."

"Aye, I'll go along with that." O'Shea grinned. "Catch him while he's well and truly off guard."

***

King stood in the centre of the sparsely furnished lounge and surveyed the disheartening scene. Upon inspection, there was nowhere to hide anything. The lounge was decorated in an extremely sparse fashion. The walls were merely whitewashed, and but for a few paintings of yachts crashing through spumes of white water on full-tack, the decor had been kept to an absolute minimum. The room was furnished in the same less is more psychology, with a three-piece suite in dark cane with thick, silk-covered cushions offering the only respite from minimalism. A coffee table with a small circular lace tablecloth, and a bowl of dried flowers in the middle, was placed within easy reach of the two-seater sofa. That, in turn, was situated in front of a home cinema television complete with a video cassette recorder, a new DVD system and satellite receiver.

"Doesn't really look like Frank Holman's sort of place," King commented as Simon Grant walked into the room.

Grant shook his head. "This is Eileen's effort, believe me." He pointed at the lace tablecloth and the bowl of dried flowers. "Frank's more of your beer mat and bowl of pork scratchings man. I bet they rent this out as a seasonal holiday let. Either that, or Eileen comes here more than he does. She's cheated on him for years, most likely has a fella down here."

"Come on, let's check out the rooms upstairs." He picked up the heavy suitcase and quickly bounded up the stairs, then waited at the top for Grant to catch him up.

"How about the spare bedroom?" Grant looked at King and smiled. "Holman will take the biggest, most comfortable room. He won't give the second bedroom a glance."

"Right, let's have a look then." King pushed open the first door then closed it almost instantly. "That's the bathroom, not a hell of a lot of places to hide it in there."

Grant opened the adjacent door and glanced around. It seemed quite promising, with a dresser next to the bed and a large wardrobe against the far wall.

"This looks like the place," King called from across the landing. "Twin beds and a pine wardrobe. Pretty basic."

Grant closed the door to the master bedroom and walked across the landing to where King was standing in the doorway. He peered around the doorframe and smiled. "Just the place," he said, looking through the window at the dark sky. "If you stash it in here, I'll go down and make a start on the alarm system."

King smirked and shook his head. "Not a chance, sunshine. It's dark outside, I wouldn't want to lose you." He reached up, opened the top cupboard above the wardrobe then heaved the suitcase inside.

"You don't trust me?" Grant protested, somewhat dejectedly.

King closed the cupboard door then turned around and smiled. "Let's just say, you've been through a lot. I don't want you deciding to leg it at this late stage," he paused looking urgently at his watch. "Christ! Is that the time? Even if Holman stopped off for an hour, he'll be bloody close by now!" He made his way out of the room, followed closely by Grant who was already taking the necessary items of equipment out of his pockets.

They made their way cautiously down the stairs, making sure not slip in their new precarious footwear, which had a tendency to slide rather than grip on the highly polished wooden floorboards.

***

Holman had turned off from the ocean road and onto the track that accessed the properties in the dunes. With less than a kilometre to drive, he slowed the Mercedes suddenly at a gap in the forest and stared out across the beautifully calm, glassy ocean. The sun had gone down behind the sea, and only a trace of its burning trail could be seen, shining a dull orange glow, just a matter of inches above the distant horizon. He looked inland and marvelled at how the sky modulated from a light blue, through to a darker shade of blue with a purple hue, then finally a star-encrusted black. He eased his foot off the brake and continued on his way. The welcoming comfort of his much-loved holiday home was only a few hundred metres away.

***

Alex King waited impatiently in the front doorway as Grant set about rewiring the alarm system. He watched the road, listening intently for the sound of any approaching vehicles.

Grant worked quickly, but calmly. He reconnected the wires, then patched the plastic coating back into place with the aid of a tube of strong adhesive. He quickly placed the fascia over the control panel and screwed it back in place with the electric screwdriver, then removed the circuit diversion meter. A cursory glance to check that nothing had been left out of place, and he closed the cupboard door and walked calmly to the front door.

"Hurry up, I think I can hear a vehicle approaching!" King stood on the veranda with both bags of equipment over his shoulders, frantically beckoning Grant out of the house.

Grant gently closed the door then crouched down and slipped the titanium picklock into the lock. He turned around to King, nodding his head for him to come closer. "I can't see, it's too dark!" King dropped the bags down onto the wooden walkway and hastily rummaged through the loose equipment, desperately searching for the Mini-Maglite. "No, not that bag, the other one!"

King hastily delved into the other canvas bag, then triumphantly pulled out the tiny torch. Grant snatched the torch from his grasp, then twisted the aperture and slipped it between his teeth, playing the dull red beam onto the lock. He placed the diamond-tipped key underneath the titanium picklock and eased his way through the succession of tumblers and gates. He eased the tools out of the lock, then went to stand, when King caught hold of him roughly around the collar.

"Come on man, move your arse!" He pulled him unceremoniously to his feet and dragged him off the veranda and onto the paved patio. He released his grip, as Grant found his footing, then charged into a deep border of rhododendron bushes. Grant followed, but hesitated at the bushes, only to be pulled roughly into them. He fell to his knees, then struggled back to his feet, just in time to see the lights of a car sweep over the garden and illuminate the house.

King let out a deep sigh then smiled, baring his white teeth in the dark cover of the bushes. "That was too damn close..." He watched as Holman stepped out from his Mercedes and opened the gate to the drive, then walked stiffly back towards the bright headlights. "We'll give him time to get inside, then we'll make our way back to the car. I have a feeling that the Irishmen will not be far behind him."

"Surely Forsyth would have rung with their status by now?"

The thought was troubling King, had done for the entire day. "I'm sure he has good reason," he said.

41

"This looks alright," Danny Neeson announced as he pulled the Saab into the side of the road, then eased to a halt outside a small real-estate office. There were no road markings so he had figured that parking would be ok. "There's a bar over there."

O'Shea followed Neeson's gaze across the cobbled precinct towards the seawall. "Aye, looks okay." He unfastened his seatbelt and gave his shoulders a stretch. "Come on, I could do with a bloody drink," he paused. "And a piss."

Neeson opened his door and stepped out onto the cobbles. "I just hope that fat bastard is down here, and hasn't given us the bloody slip," he said, staring towards the sea-wall and the beach beyond, where he could hear the gentle shore break on the sand. "Parker's woman is a loose end. I'm starting to feel uneasy about letting her and that boy of hers live."

O'Shea walked around the bonnet of the Saab and fixed him with a sober gaze. "Aye well, seeing that woman on the floor brought back a lot of memories for me. My old man used to knock my mother about every Saturday night," he paused, staring distantly towards the sound of the ocean. "He used to come home after the pub, he could only drink the one night a week. My mam used to take his pay packet on a Friday and take out all the housekeeping, then go shopping on the Saturday. She gave him back what was left. That way the family got to eat. He would be full of resentment all day. Then he'd go out and get properly pissed. He'd drag himself back, there'd be an argument and he'd knock seven shades of shit out of her. Same thing every week. Week in, week out. My brother Mike, he just blew one night, he was about fifteen and built like a brick shithouse. He played a lot of rugby and boxed. He snapped and my old man ended up in hospital for about a week. He never laid a finger on her again."

"Jesus."

"I just felt sorry for her, that's all."

Neeson smiled sardonically. "Well, boss, I never knew you had a heart, until now."

"Shut up you daft bastard!" He turned towards the quiet looking bar and tapped Neeson on the shoulder. "Come on I'll buy you a Pernod."

"You can buy me a cold beer and a *Croque Monsieur*."

"What's that?"

"Basically a cheese and ham toasted sandwich."

"Well why don't they just say that? Christ, three-hundred thousand words and they have a name for a cheese and ham sandwich, but can't think of another sodding name for a town by the sea…"

***

The cordon of blue and white tape flapped in the gentle breeze, like bunting at a church fete, or village carnival. But behind this makeshift barrier of sticky plastic, lay a scene far less inviting to the general public than the prospect of tea and homemade cake. Not that the small, but growing crowd that had gathered behind the tape was in any way deterred by macabre thoughts of what lay behind the official obstruction. Far from it. The ambulance, which had pulled into the cul-de-sac with siren bellowing and lights flashing, had been stood down, and had parked unobtrusively to the side of the cordon to await further instructions. Those instructions came when the coroner's vehicle arrived. This gave the crowd something to consider, especially when the ambulance left shortly afterwards. This aspect fascinated the growing mob of onlookers, who all had their opinions as to why the services of the ambulance crew were no longer needed.

The Detective was a sergeant called Hodges, and he was here in his capacity as acting inspector. He had passed the exams, he basically needed a detective inspector to retire. He frowned at the uniformed sergeant, who had secured the scene with a handful of constables. "Parker?" he asked somewhat surprised. "Keith Parker? Are you sure?"

"Yes," the police officer reassured him. "Why, do you know him?"

"No," he replied thoughtfully. "But it seems a bit too much for coincidence."

The uniformed sergeant shook his head. "What does?"

"That robbery yesterday, out in the Hampshire countryside. The security firm that was hit had a manager called Keith Parker. I've just been pulled off it to look at this. The firm have a premises on our patch, and two of the three security guards that were killed lived here as well. As does Keith Parker."

"I see what you mean," the officer said. "That's one *big* coincidence."

"Is there a Mrs Parker?"

The uniformed sergeant nodded. "Yes, she's inside with WPC Leith. In the kitchen."

WPC Leith placed the steaming cup of sweet tea in front of Lisa Grant then pulled a chair out from under the table and sat down beside her. "Drink up, it will make you feel better." She stared benignly at the cup of tea, realising how pathetic her words must sound. As if an infusion of hot water, leaves, milk and sugar could solve the world's problems in an instant. She placed a gentle hand on the woman's shoulder and spoke softly. "Are you sure that you want to stay here tonight, Mrs Parker? I could make alternative arrangements for you."

Lisa looked up at the policewoman tearfully and shook her head positively. "If I don't stay tonight, I will *never* be able to stay. Can you understand that?" The policewoman nodded and gently squeezed her shoulder. Lisa smiled, wiping a tear from her eye. "Anyway, it's not Mrs Parker, it's Mrs Grant. Keith Parker is..." she suddenly looked aghast and corrected herself. "*Was*, my boyfriend. I'm separated from my husband, have been for some time."

The policewoman nodded amiably, not wishing to hear a full and detailed account of this woman's past. She wasn't lacking in sympathy, but she had become accustomed to her job, and the situations that it placed her in over the past six years. She was a married woman living with another man. It wasn't a Mills and Boon love story. It was a tainted and complicated affair, weaved with deception, infidelity and betrayal. For somebody, at least.

Detective Sergeant Hodges walked tentatively into the kitchen, glancing first at WPC Leith, and then turning his attention to Lisa Grant. "Mrs Parker?"

"Grant, it's Mrs Grant." The policewoman quickly interjected.

Hodges raised a hand to his mouth and coughed quietly. "I'm sorry Mrs Grant, silly mistake," he paused as he pulled out a chair and sat down opposite her at the pine table. "I know that it may be difficult at this stage, but it is essential that I ask you a few questions, is that all right?"

Lisa nodded then accepted a tissue from the woman police officer and wiped her eyes thoroughly before turning her attention back to Detective Sergeant Hodges.

"Can you think of anyone who had a grievance with your husband? Anybody who might possibly resort to this?" WPC Leith sighed, then tried to suppress a smirk as Hodges suddenly realised his mistake. "I'm sorry, Mrs Grant," he apologised, shifting uneasily in his chair. "Can you think of any reason why someone would want to kill Keith?"

She shook her head and started to sob quietly. "No, no I can't."

"Only, we have details of a robbery which took place, concerning one of the security vans, subcontracted earlier by the company that he works for."

Lisa looked up suddenly. "Works for?"

Hodges cringed. "Sorry, *worked* for." He groaned inwardly. Speaking of Parker in the present tense was the least of his worries.

Lisa shook her head. "No, I don't mean that. You said, the company that he works for. Keith was the managing director, he owned the company."

Hodges frowned and took a leather-bound note pad from his jacket pocket, opened it to the relevant page, then shook his head in negation. "No, that's not what I've got written here. I spoke to the managing director last night, a David Brown. He owns the principal share in the company. Keith Parker was in charge of accounts. He was their head clerk. He recently became their health and safety officer. According to Mr Brown, your husband..." he paused, realising that he had made the same mistake again. "Sorry, partner, had no financial decision making authority, not to speak of anyway. That is why I did not feel it necessary to interview him today. I had prioritised the main people, Keith Parker was due for a visit tomorrow or the next day, merely a routine inquiry."

Lisa Grant bowed her head to the floor, somewhat perplexed. Keith Parker had never divulged any business details to her, and once it had become obvious that they had no real future as a couple, she had not made any motion to talk to him, other than what she had deemed necessary to avoid a beating.

Keith Parker had not always treated her so poorly. For the first year, he had treated her like a princess. Keith Parker was her first love. She had bumped into him by chance, cried on his shoulder. It happens. Now she looked back on it, Keith had fuelled the fire of her anger at Simon. He had cleverly manipulated her, guided her decision to end her relationship with him. She had regretted it soon afterwards, but life is never easy and mistakes are the easiest things to make. Keith had been able to provide her with everything she could reasonably have hoped for, in the material line. A nice home, money, a loving atmosphere for her young son and above all, the stability and love that she craved.

But not for long. And she'd been trapped ever since.

Parker had changed, almost overnight. He made sure that he always got what he wanted, but soon he developed an uncontrollable jealousy of her estranged husband - and more worryingly, a deepening contempt and hatred towards young David.

She had attempted to leave him, but only once. That had been enough. Lisa had ended up in hospital from her injuries on that occasion, but for the medical staff and the police she had concocted a story about falling downstairs. She decided that it would be safer to do so. Since then, she had been a virtual prisoner, accounting for her every move, often before she had even made it, and always answerable to Parker's wrath.

"Mrs Grant?" WPC Leith soothed a hand over her shoulder, looking at her with concern. "Mrs Grant, are you alright?"

Lisa raised her head, somewhat bewildered, as she pulled herself back to the present. She looked at the young policewoman and forced a smile. "Yes. I... I just drifted off, sorry."

"Please, don't be sorry Mrs Grant." Hodges paused, satisfied that this time he had managed to address the woman correctly. "I understand that this must be a terribly traumatic time for you, but we must find out as much as we can, before the trail becomes cold."

"I understand." Lisa pulled herself straight in the chair and rested her hands around the cup of tea, taking great comfort in its warmth. "I was just shocked to hear that Keith had been deceiving me. As far as I was aware, he was the owner of the company, and was under stress because of the overall responsibility he had; trying to make deadlines, meet quotas and seek new contracts."

"I see." Hodges mused quietly. "So, today... You were out all day?"

"Yes."

"Where?"

"I took my son, David, to Hamleys. I bought him a remote controlled car he had been promised."

Hodges nodded. He was studying her face intently. "Did you go anywhere else?"

"Regent's Park," she shivered. "He used the car for hours! He's wanted it for so long..."

"And you got back, when?"

"Two-hours ago. We went to the zoo. London Zoo."

"Was it your son's birthday?

"No."

"Lucky boy." Hodges frowned. "Should he not have been at school? They break up tomorrow, don't they?"

"Yes, they do," she replied. "But he needed his mummy. Keith got it into his head that a private school in Scotland would be good for him."

"And you didn't?"

"Of course not!"

"So..."

"So we decided, or rather I decided it wasn't suitable. When I left, Keith was going to call the school and retract the application. The treat was because David had been so upset about going."

Hodges nodded. "Which school?"

"Lord knows," she said, like it wasn't even on her radar. That it was the last thing she would have done. But she knew enough about the police, and that was you never left out anything. She knew what Keith had really done for the company, but she had needed to create a smokescreen. They would not look at Keith Parker in an honest light after her little show of surprise. "It was Keith's idea, but he wound David up about it."

Hodges slipped the notebook back into his jacket pocket, then pushed the chair back from the table and rose to his feet. "Well, I can make further inquiries, but I had a thorough check done on the company today, and I can assure you that Keith Parker was not on the board of directors. I *am* sorry," he said, feeling a little awkward. "Thank you for your co-operation, Mrs Grant. WPC Leith will stay with you for a little while longer, until forensics have finished their investigations." He glanced at her swollen eye-socket and frowned. "If you don't mind me asking, how did you get that?"

"When I arrived home and found Keith, I felt light-headed," she lied easily. She was free now, only this last hurdle remained. "Before I could help myself, I wobbled and fell into the door frame." She rubbed the slight swelling gently with her fingertips, then bowed her head into her hands and started to wail. "I can't believe this is happening! Oh my God... Who would do that to him? Who?" She started to cry and pictured Keith shoving David to the ground, pictured his face as he forced himself into her. Pictured him looking down at her, dominating her, devaluing her entire being. She closed her eyes, feeling the guilt that she hadn't left sooner, hadn't taken her son out of harm's way, had left him exposed to such abuse. When she opened her eyes again she was sobbing, tears running down her face and dripping off her chin.

The policewoman wrapped her right arm around Lisa's shoulder to comfort her, but no sympathy appeared on her face. Hodges looked at the emotional woman for a moment then stepped out of the room and closed the door behind him. The lounge had become a hive of activity, with teams of forensic technicians and detectives combing the entire room for any tell-tale clue.

Keith Parker's pose was probably not as photogenic as he would have preferred but then again, he had no choice in the matter. Nor did the technician wielding the camera, who was taking photographs of the body from a variety of different angles.

Hodges peered into the lounge and watched the officers at work, then glanced briefly at the corpse. Parker's body was still seated upright in the chair, his eyes wide open, the gag still tucked generously into his gaping mouth. Hodges turned to the nearby Detective Constable who was being briefed by a forensic officer. He waited for the forensic officer to walk back into the lounge, then nodded towards the carpet. "What have you got?"

The detective looked up, then flicked a wispy tuft of blonde hair away from his eyes. "A few blood splatters. Consistent with a beating. Nothing more than fists, according to forensics." He stood up and pointed at two thick lines in the carpet's pattern, then glanced at his tatty-looking notebook. "And drag marks, running against the grain of the carpet. Proof..."

"No."

"Sorry, an *indication*, that Mr Parker was dragged from here, and into the lounge."

"Good, what else?" Hodges asked. He let his officers run, but corrected them as they went. *Proof* wasn't a word he let people use in his earshot. It was up to them to prove it after they had all the facts. He had learned this from his former Chief Inspector, and he intended to keep the practice going, especially as he was all but Detective Inspector now.

Hodges adjusted his tie, as was his habit when he needed a moment for thought, then turned to the young detective and followed the distinctive trail with his eyes. He turned back to him and frowned. "You were first on the scene, weren't you?"

The detective shook his head. "No. A mobile unit responded to the call, they were the first officers on site, put the cordon up."

"You spoke with Mrs Grant straight away?"

The detective nodded. "Yeah. Well, sort of. I gave her ten minutes or so, she was pretty hysterical when I arrived."

Hodges nodded. "What did she say?"

"She had been out with her son, I gather they went out for the day, then went to get something to eat before returning home at around seven o'clock," he said, then stared at him intently. "You don't suspect her, do you?" He pointed at the deep drag-marks in the carpet and shook his head. "She must weigh about nine or ten stone. Parker was well over six-foot tall, and must have weighed thirteen stone! There is no way that she could have beat him to a pulp, dragged him into the next room, then lifted him into the chair and tied his hands."

"I know, I know..." Hodges nodded in agreement, looked around the hallway, then peered up the staircase. "Where's the boy?"

"The woman sent him around to the neighbour's house, just before I arrived." He looked down at his notebook then turned over to the previous page. "A Mr and Mrs Palmer. At Holly Acres, number eleven." He slipped the notebook back into his pocket and perched himself on the edge of the coffee table. "Do you think this is connected? I mean, Parker worked for the security firm which had one of their vans held up yesterday, seems too much of a coincidence, doesn't it?"

"I'm positive that it's connected." Hodges nodded emphatically. "It is just a matter of how, who and why. Parker must have been involved with the heist in some way, and whoever else was involved must have seen him as a loose end."

"What about the woman, do you think she's involved?"

Hodges shook his head. "She knows nothing," he said. Lisa Grant had been an innocent. Right up until she had whisked the boy out and given him a grand day out. He knew fist marks when he saw them. Women always slipped down the stairs, or banged their face on a door or tripped over the cat. He knew desperation too. He knew the look of someone truly on the edge. And the edge was the point where it went either way. You slipped into oblivion, or you clawed your way out. He recognised Lisa Grant as someone who had clawed her way out. One slip, one false hand of hope, and she would fall to the bottom. She knew nothing of why Parker had died, but she knew everything about the moment. She had lied, he knew that. But he also knew she hadn't been involved in the man's death. Her crime? Leaving the scene and failing to get help. Her punishment? Well, Hodges had seen the bruising and newly cut lip. Maybe she had paid her punishment forward. Help wasn't always there for some. Sometimes it was more dangerous to seek help, than to stay in harm's way. He had seen it a hundred times, been to the scene when a beating had gone too far. Nobody ever meant to kill their partner, but it happened a few times a week. He had the suspicion that Lisa Grant had been close to that outcome. As close as it gets.

"You okay, boss?"

Hodges looked up. "Sorry," he said. "Lost in thought."

"Terrible world we live in," the young detective said.

Hodges nodded and left the room. It was. He had seen the world at its worst, and its best. He had seen things to keep him awake at night, things that would never leave him. He knew Lisa Grant had too. And by proximity, so would her son. He knew he was a good police officer, and that his actions made a difference. He would never take a bribe, and he would never *create* evidence. But he also knew how to play cards. He knew when to play his hand, when to fold and when to get up and walk away. He looked into the kitchen, saw Lisa Grant nursing a cup of tea between trembling hands. She wasn't play acting. She was a woman on the edge of the precipice. Fall or claw herself back? Part of that was up to Hodges.

42

Alex King kept his eyes on the house, occasionally catching a glimpse of Frank Holman in silhouette, as he walked past the lounge window.

Only minutes earlier King had brought the BMW down onto the beach road and parked it on the sandy ground behind a small copse of pine trees. Now, both he and Grant lay prone among the thick layer of sand and pine needles, within the tree line.

"What happens now?" Grant asked quietly, though somewhat impatiently. King rolled over onto his side and looked at him. "We wait."

"But what about me?"

King reached into his pocket and extracted a small piece of folded paper. He reached it across to Grant, then smiled. "Here, take this. In case anything happens to me. It's your wife's address and telephone number, at Keith Parker's house. If you try to contact her, be careful. If the Irish haven't already caught up with Parker, they soon will. Forsyth won't want him around either."

"What about my family? They're at risk!"

"You might want to get them away," he paused. "Wouldn't be a bad idea if you got the hell out of Dodge either..."

"What do you mean?" Grant asked. "Why would I have to be careful?"

King shook his head. "Let's put it this way; you have been extremely helpful, but this whole operation has gone south. Just disappear for a while. Don't become a loose end for the likes of Forsyth."

"But surely that wouldn't apply to me?" Grant protested. "I've helped turn the situation around for him."

King stared at him coldly, the whites of his eyes clearly visible in the darkness. "He messed things up. Not entirely his fault, but he had the chance to nip this in the bud. We both did. Instead, innocent people were killed. I am just advising you to stay out of sight. The fact that you were coerced will not make any difference to a man like Forsyth."

"And what about you?"

"What about me?"

"Yes. What happens when the job is done?"

King chuckled. "I'm not so sure after all this shit. I've had my taste of the shadowy world of intelligence. It's all a load of bollocks."

"And it will be that simple?"

"What do you mean?"

"Well, all this loose ends rubbish. Where does it end? Will *you* know too much?"

King thought for a moment. "You let me worry about that," he said. But it had given him something more to think about. Maybe it was time to give himself a bargaining chip, some security. He had heard of people collecting data, official orders, times and dates. It was called a security blanket and it prevented being hung out to dry. It didn't seem such a bad idea.

***

Danny Neeson downed the remnants of his beer and waited for O'Shea to emerge from the toilets. The pretty brunette behind the bar smiled at him, as she polished another glass and placed it back onto the shelf. Neeson sighed to himself, then looked up as O'Shea appeared in the narrow doorway and walked over to the table.

"Did you get the directions?"

Neeson nodded, glancing briefly at the barmaid, who smiled then placed another glass on the mirrored shelf. "Aye, and very helpful she was to. Gagging for a bit of foreigner, so she was. Must be my Gaelic charm."

"Aye well, another time, another place." O'Shea said philosophically, then placed a pile of francs on the table and made towards the door.

Neeson got up and followed, without so much as a parting glance for the pretty barmaid. They walked out of the bar, aptly named *L'Atlantique* because of its seaward location, and back towards the cobbled area where they had parked the Saab. As they reached the vehicle, Neeson glanced at O'Shea, who was staring out across the sea at the tiny lights of a group of fishing trawlers in the distance. "Where are you going with your half?"

O'Shea looked at him dubiously, then broke into a broad smile. "I like the thought of South America, they're generally good to people like us. Argentina, or Patagonia to be more precise. I'll get myself a llama farm." He laughed. "Or just sit in the hills and grow old."

"Whoever would have thought the likes of us would grow old?"

"What about yourself?"

"Australia. Beach front property and spend the days watching tits and arse."

"That's just another bloody Britain, and they're big on extradition. You'd be better off somewhere like South Africa." O'Shea stared at him grimly then grinned. "Wherever you end up, remember, you'll have more than the authorities after you. You'll have the bloody cause as well."

Neeson shook his head. "Bloody lost cause, so it is now. Agreeing to the peace agreement, handing over weapons and Lord knows what else. Christ, what will they have next? Adams and McGuinness in Westminster?"

***

King turned to Grant and pointed to the far side of Holman's property. "If you wait here, I'll go around the house. I want to watch from a point where I can see both sides of the building and check that they don't approach from the rear."

"What if this is all a waste of time, what if they don't come tonight?"

King shook his head. "Forsyth said that they were right behind Holman. He didn't telephone to let me know if there was a problem, so we can take it for granted that they'll be here soon." He pushed himself swiftly to his feet and jogged quickly across the road and parallel to Holman's property. As he drew near to the boundary of thick bushes and young pines, he could hear the sound of an approaching vehicle. He pulled back a thick branch, then charged through the bushes, just as the approaching vehicle's headlights swept around the corner, its headlights cutting a swathe of light through the darkness.

***

Neeson slowed the Saab to a crawl as they passed the house on their right. "This looks promising," he said. He drove a little further past the entrance, then glanced back towards the driveway. "That's his Mercedes! This is it!"

"Aye, right enough." O'Shea turned around in his seat and pointed to the small lay-by on the side of the road. "This will do. Pull in and kill the headlights."

Neeson eased the Saab off the road and into the sandy lay-by, approximately sixty-metres past Holman's driveway. He switched off the headlights and the ignition, then opened his door and stepped out onto the soft sandy earth, carpeted with pine needles.

As O'Shea got out of the passenger seat and quietly closed his door, Neeson reached behind the front seats and retrieved the .20 bore shotgun. He picked up the cartridge belt and took out a handful of the plastic-coated number 5 shot cartridges, then slipped them into his left-hand trouser pocket. He plucked two more from the leather belt, then opened the weapon's breach and inserted one into each barrel. He closed the breach and eased the safety catch forward with his thumb, into the off position. With the weapon loaded and at the ready, he gently closed the door and led the way towards Holman's driveway.

Neeson approached the veranda and hesitated, waiting for O'Shea, who was cautiously watching the lounge window. As O'Shea caught up, Neeson climbed the steps and stood to the side of the front door with his back to the wall, keeping the loaded shotgun pointed at the ground. "Knock," he whispered quietly.

O'Shea walked up the steps, then reached out and banged his fist hard against the solid wooden door. He heard the sound of heavy footsteps from within and tensed as he heard Holman's unmistakable south London accent.

"Who's that?" Holman bellowed. O'Shea knocked twice more. "I said, who is that?"

"Non Anglaise! Telephone?" O'Shea called out in his best attempt of a French accent.

"Fuck off!"

"Non monsieur, telephone…"

Holman unlocked the door and caught hold of the handle, pulling the door aggressively inwards. "What do you want..."

Neeson spun around and barged the door inwards, pointing the shotgun at Holman's face. "Three fucking guesses!"

Holman stumbled backwards, his hands raised above his head. "Danny! What the hell is going on?" He stared at him, perplexed.

"That's what we want to know!" O'Shea stepped into the open doorway and pointed an accusing finger at him. "Now get your fat arse into the other room!"

Neeson jabbed Holman in the back with the business end of the shotgun, catching his right kidney. Holman grunted, but managed not to cry-out out at the painful blow. Neeson jabbed him again, this time achieving the desired effect. Holman reached his right hand behind his back, trying to place his hand on the pain, but his waist was too big to contort in such a way. He winced; sucking air through tightly clenched teeth then turned around and faced the two men. "Come on, lads, what is all this? We had a bloody deal!" He straightened up, regaining a little composure.

"That's what *we* thought!" Neeson shouted.

"But I've done nothing wrong!"

Neeson nodded towards the nearby chair, motioning for him to sit down. "Sit your fat arse down!" Holman obliged, keeping his eyes on the double-barrelled shotgun. Neeson walked over to the marble fireplace. There was a base of small kindling pieces and chopped logs burning fiercely, with three larger logs on top. "I see you've lit a flame, still cold in the evenings at this time of year, isn't it?" He bent down and picked up a long-handled fire poker, keeping the shotgun steady in his right hand, the barrels aimed at Holman's midriff. Without another word, he swung the poker down onto Holman's shoulder. Holman screamed, and was off guard for the next blow to his left elbow. Neeson stepped back quickly, then grinned as he slipped the poker into the glowing base of the log fire. "Might not hurt so much, if I warm it up a bit."

"No!" Holman writhed in his chair, his whole left arm drooping, as if he'd suffered a stroke. He noticed that Neeson had lowered the barrels of the shotgun in line with his right knee. "For God's sake, Danny! Tell me what you want!"

O'Shea said, "I'll get a knife from the kitchen. Cut and cauterise! That will make the bastard talk!" He turned and ran out of the room, leaving Neeson pointing the shotgun at Holman.

"What do we want?" Neeson said quietly. "I'll tell you what we want…" He stepped forward and bent down, picking up a pair of fire tongs from the hearth. "We want our fucking money! Tell us where it is, you fat piece of shit!" He lunged forward and thrust the tongs into Holman's crotch, whilst keeping the shotgun dangerously close to him.

Holman remained motionless, staring at the tongs, which rested threateningly in his lap. He glanced up at Neeson, shaking his head slowly. "Please, Danny, don't," he begged; and then, "No!" he screamed, as Neeson clamped the jaws of the fire tongs together.

Neeson released his grip and smiled. "Come on, Holman. It's not as if you use them, is it? If it was, then your wife wouldn't have been so quick to let me take her on your kitchen table, would she?" He squeezed again, then released the pressure slightly. "Where is our money, and where is that bastard, Simon Grant?" Holman looked up at him, perplexed. He shook his head, tried to get up, but Neeson shoved him back into the chair with the muzzle of the shotgun. "Last chance, fat man!" He clamped the jaws of the fire tongs tightly together, then released them as O'Shea entered the room. He turned to O'Shea and smiled. "A bit more of this, and he'll be singing like a soprano!" Neeson dropped the tongs to the floor and stood back, wiping the perspiration from his brow with his sleeve. He handed the shotgun to O'Shea, then walked over to the fireplace. O'Shea watched, as Neeson eased the red-hot poker out of the embers and turned back to Holman.

Holman breathed erratically, panic setting in as he stared at the glowing tip of the poker. "Please Danny, in the name of God..." He slumped in the chair, unable to summon the strength to resist.

"Tell us Holman. Tell us where Grant and our money have got to." Neeson stepped forward, holding the glowing poker barely an inch from his right cheek, the heat from the metal making the man flinch. "Tell us, or I'll bend your fat arse over and stick this where the sun doesn't shine..."

"No!" Holman screamed, suddenly summoning a little strength at the terrible image. "Grant is dead, you killed him! Blew him to kingdom-fucking-come! I haven't got your bloody money!" He stared up at the Irishman, knowing that there was nothing that the man would stop at. "Please Danny, I'm begging you..." he panted. "I'm telling the truth!" He started to slump in the chair, as if he were about to lose consciousness. Neeson put the poker closer to Holman's face, then looked at him coldly before dabbing the glowing tip gently against his earlobe. Holman screamed, twisting his body to try and escape the agonising pain, and smell of burning flesh. "Argh! For Christ's sake!" He raised his hand to his ear, catching his fingers on the dry heat of the poker as he did so. Neeson stepped back a few paces and replaced the poker in the fire, rattling the embers, before setting the handle down on the hearth. He turned around to O'Shea and nodded towards the ceiling. "I'll go and take a look around the place, you keep the gun on him."

***

Simon Grant closed his eyes and swallowed, suppressing the urge to vomit. Holman had betrayed him, set him up to die. He had felt sure that exacting revenge on the man in this way, albeit by proxy, would fill him with some kind of satisfaction, but it hadn't. It just made him feel sick to the pit of his stomach. He could hear the man's screams, *felt* them run through him. He felt an overwhelming urge to help the man, a primal instinct to aid his long-term running mate, his friend. He was helpless though. He was no fighter, not against men like O'Shea and Neeson, and King had the only weapon. He knew that if he tried, he would be killed. Holman was a dead man screaming. There was no hope for him now.

Grant stood up and walked out from the treeline, then paused at the side of the road. He was not entirely sure what he intended to do. The MI6 operative was holding his passport, which, even though it was a fake, would make the return journey much easier. It would be practically impossible to cross the channel without it. But did he really want to return? There were many reasons why staying away would appear to make more sense. Lisa was with another man, a man who by all accounts would have been more of a father to his son than he had managed to be. He looked at the Saab, parked on the other side of the road, then suddenly realised that his main prerogative was to get away from this place. Away from Holman's screams.

***

Danny Neeson looked around the main bedroom, which now lay in tatters, with the bed and furniture left upturned, and the sheets ripped from the bed, after his frenzied search. He turned around and walked across the landing to the closed door that was almost directly opposite. He opened it, pushing it savagely inwards, forcing it back against the plaster wall. The room was almost bare, but for the two single beds, a large wardrobe and dressing table. He looked around, then paused, his gaze fixed on the tall, pine wardrobe.

Holman shifted awkwardly in his chair, gritting his teeth in agony, and keeping a hand pressed to his groin. He soothed his other hand over the painful burn to his ear, then glared up at O'Shea, seething. "You're a pair of sick bastards... We had a deal!"

"Aye, that's what I thought," he said. "You were warned not to cross us. It's your mistake, and you will pay."

"I should have expected this from you. You're just a fucking thick paddy. Fit for digging the roads I drive on. Well fuck you, O'Shea! A deal's a fucking deal!" Holman spat at him. He stared past O'Shea, a confused expression on his face as he watched Neeson come into the room with a large suitcase. "That's not mine!"

Neeson dropped the suitcase onto the floor, staring daggers at Holman. He popped the catches and opened it up. The money was stacked in different currencies, not a gap or space to be seen. "That's not what the label says." He bent down and held the label, turning it over between his thumb and forefinger. "Frank Holman," he said, a look of exaggerated understanding suddenly dawning on him. "Oh I see, it's *another* Frank

Holman, who just happens to live at your address. Sorry, our mistake, I think we had better be going now…"

O'Shea roared with laughter, keeping the shotgun aimed at Holman's chest. "Aye, sorry for the confusion and any inconvenience! No hard feelings!"

"I've got a petrol can in the back of the car, we can clean up this mess, good and proper," Neeson said.

O'Shea nodded. "Aye, get it done. I'll wait here, see that our friend doesn't have himself any sudden bouts of energy."

***

Grant crossed over the road and headed towards the Saab. The vehicle was parked on the opposite side of the road in a sandy lay-by, overhung by the drooping bottom branches of huge pine trees. He was not concerned with the fact that the vehicle might be locked, he could get inside in an instant, and would be able to override the ignition, and any security systems. After all, car theft had been his bread and butter when he had been younger, before he had progressed to burglary and then on to safecracking. He had two screwdrivers in his pocket that he had not returned to the bag of equipment, they were all he would need.

Neeson stepped out from the steep driveway and into the road, then suddenly stopped in his tracks, having noticed the man at the door of his car. He broke into a run, clenching both hands into tight fists, ready to take on his opponent.

Grant looked around cautiously, checking to make sure that he had not been seen. He turned his head towards Holman's house, then stared, almost frozen in horror. He attempted to run, but it was too late. Neeson was upon him, sending him heavily to the ground with a shoulder charge. The two men fell, then rolled into the road. Grant swung a wild punch, catching Neeson in the mouth. He reeled backwards, but managed to keep a hold on Grant's jacket. He regained his senses, having been caught momentarily off guard, then punched Grant in his ear. He kept hold of him, moving around for better positioning, then punched him twice more, catching him both times in the face. Grant raised both hands to his mouth, lacking all combat instinct. Neeson moved himself around further, until he was on top of Grant. He caught hold of him by the throat, pulled him upwards and executed a savage punch to his jaw. Grant fell back, cracking his head against the hard surface of the road. He lay still, unconscious, bleeding from the base of his skull. Neeson sat back in the road, breathless and perspiring after the energetic brawl. He looked down at the man, only realising that it was Simon Grant now that the man lay still.

He got to his feet, then bent down and caught hold of Grant by his ankles and pulled him out of the road, and behind the bonnet of the Saab. He looked around cautiously, then walked around to the boot of the car and opened it with the key. The red plastic petrol can was wedged dangerously between the sports bags and the rear seats. He grabbed it by the handle, then closed the boot as quietly as he could. He placed the petrol can on the sandy ground, before walking over to where Grant lay. Catching hold of him around the belt and collar, he heaved him up and over his shoulder, struggling with the dead weight, as he bent down and slowly and picked up the petrol can.

***

King groaned inwardly. He had made it across to the far side of the rambling gardens, and was now crouched amongst a clump of bushes, not twenty-feet from the path that led from the driveway to the wooden veranda. He had seen his opportunity arise, and had been ready to take appropriate action. He had planned to tackle Danny Neeson upon his return from the vehicle. With surprise on his side, King was confident that he could overcome anybody. No matter how big, strong, or experienced they were, he knew that he only needed two-seconds. Two-seconds was all the time he needed to break a man's neck.

Grant had ruined everything. King would not be able to strike an instant, deadly blow with Grant in the way, draped around the back of Neeson's neck. If a struggle ensued this close to the house, O'Shea might well hear, and with O'Shea now armed with the shotgun, that was a risk he dared not take. The shotgun required less skill and precision to use. And at night, with little visibility it would have been the better weapon.

King took a deep, calming breath. It was no good. He would have to wait a little longer. He watched, as Neeson walked steadily up the drive and onto the gravel pathway. His footsteps crunched noisily as he passed King's position, less than six paces to his right.

As Neeson stepped onto the wooden veranda, he turned, looked around cautiously, then opened the door and disappeared inside.

King moved quickly. Now was the time. Neeson would still be carrying Grant inside the house, probably into the lounge where the Irishmen could confront the two men together. He edged his way across the garden, leaping across the gravel pathway to avoid detection. He took the 9mm Browning out of the waistband of his trousers, gently eased off the safety, then held the weapon out in front of him in a double-handed grip. He carefully placed his left foot on the wooden veranda, then eased his weight slowly onto his leading foot, making sure that the wooden planks did not creak under the sudden weight. He stepped up onto the walkway then made his way silently towards the front door. The door had been left ajar. Carefully, tentatively, he eased the door inwards then stood to the side, scanning the area in front of him through the pistol's open notch sights.

Clearing buildings should never be a one-man task, he had had that drummed into him at the killing house, the live-fire training facility, on the SAS base in Hereford. But King had little choice. The activity would clearly have had to have been taking place in the lounge, he would have to risk making it the first room he tried. He edged his way along the wall, keeping the Browning out in front of him as he went. He pulled the pistol back towards himself as he neared the doorway, keeping the barrel pointed at the floor, then stepped out from the wall and crept to the side of the open door. The Browning was loaded with thirteen rounds, there were two hostile targets in the building, hopefully within this room. King knew that if he could not put an opponent down fatally with two shots, then he should not be in this line of work. But then, there was always the unexpected. And this was the first time he would have shot a man, let alone two. It had been paper targets and ketchup-filled mannequins up to this point. He took one more deep breath to steady his nerves, oxygenate his muscles, then swung into the doorway and dropped down onto one knee.

Holman lay on the floor, his body twisted at the most undignified of angles. It was clear he had been shot in the chest. Both O'Shea and Neeson lay next to him, bleeding from a fatal head-wounds. O'Shea had nothing left above the eye-line. Neeson had a neat little hole drilled in his forehead. Not as graphic as O'Shea, but ballistics were never predictable. A fee degrees' difference in angle and a lot could happen on a bullet's exit.

King stood up quickly, scanning the room for a positive target. He turned, as he saw Grant, spread-eagled on the floor behind the sofa. The man lay perfectly still, either unconscious or dead. He was not bleeding, and it looked as if he had rested where he had fallen after Neeson had been shot.

King stared at the scene in bewilderment, then snatched a breath as he suddenly realised what had transpired. He started to turn around, but was just a second too late. He tensed, flinching, as he felt the warm metal rest against the nape of his neck.

43

"Hello, old boy," Forsyth said quietly. "Fools rush in, wouldn't you say?"

King felt the barrel of the weapon push harder against his neck. "Be a good chap and drop the gun." Forsyth waited for him to discard the Browning onto the floor then pushed him forcefully across the room. King stumbled for a few paces then regained his balance and slowly turned to face the MI6 officer. It wasn't good, he was unarmed and the man had put some distance between them both.

Ian Forsyth stood in the doorway, dressed in his usual tweed outfit, complete with a yellow silk cravat and gold stock pin. He held the pistol loosely in his hands then smiled, as he slipped one of his handmade cigarettes between his thin, and now somewhat cruel-looking lips. "Sorry, old boy, just couldn't be helped," he offered by way of explanation. He reached into his trouser pocket and retrieved his gold Dunhill lighter then flicked the wheel and brought the flame to the tip of the cigarette. He blew out a thin plume of smoke then grinned devilishly. "You see, old boy, the opportunity was just too good to pass up. It *is* an awfully large amount of money. And what better way to get my hands on it than to carry out a black-ops abroad."

King stared at the pistol in Forsyth's hands, recognising it as a Heckler and Koch USP, complete with a large bulbous suppressor. *That explained the silenced shots,* he thought.

Forsyth bent down and picked up the Browning. He ejected the magazine, then threw the weapon out into the hallway, and smiled wryly. "That thing is positively archaic, you should have got yourself one of these," he said, rather proudly as he inhaled more smoke and blew it out in a thin plume. "That way, you could have taken Danny Neeson out silently outside, and not have to hold off in case O'Shea heard. Put you in a bit of a quandary, didn't it?"

"Well, some prick didn't get me my kit list."

"Sorry about that."

"How did you get here so quickly?" King stared at him hoping that Forsyth would be willing to divulge, which in turn might just buy him enough time to think of something.

"Oh, I see!" Forsyth exclaimed dramatically. "Keep me talking, get me off guard, then make your move. Sorry old boy, too bloody good for you!" he paused, moving out of the doorway, but keeping the pistol stock-still. "But now that we know that you can do nothing, I don't see any harm in playing along with your little ruse."

King glanced down at Holman, startled by the sudden movement. He looked back at Forsyth, who was already taking aim. The MI6 officer fired two shots in quick succession then smiled as Holman rolled over, exhaling his last breath. He took aim again and Holman's head disappeared in a puff of crimson.

"Sorry, old boy, slight oversight," he said casually. He turned the pistol back to King and frowned. "You really should have equipped yourself with one of these. No recoil, or very little anyway. Makes for perfect accuracy. Now, where was I? Oh yes, I flew down old boy, just hopped on a plane and flew straight into

Bordeaux Airport. Much more civilised than that God-forsaken drive. Even got here in time to set myself up and watch both you and Grant enter the house," he added, smiling superciliously. "Jolly close shave with Holman arriving like that. For a minute, I didn't think you two were going to make it."

King shook his head. "I thought that you were alright. Sure, you dressed like an old fart and acted like a pompous prick, but I thought it was an act. Your idiosyncrasy that made you stand out in a department of grey yes men. I was convinced that you were okay, in your own way."

Forsyth's face dropped. "An awfully big word in that sentence. Have you been reading a dictionary in lieu of an education?"

"I'm not stupid, Ian."

"Funny, you're stupid enough to be standing at the wrong end of a gun." He smiled. Don't tell me you hadn't given the money some thought. You could do with it more than myself. No fixed abode, other than service accommodation. No assets to speak of. What do you do with your pay check?"

There was a brother and sister from another life, who thought he was dead. There were the families of two dead marines. Money found its way by various means into their lives.

Penance.

"You wouldn't understand," King said and moved a pace and a half to where Neeson was lying on the floor. He shrugged as he eased his foot under the body's chin, then lifted the man's face off the floor and looked at the exit wound. "Thanks... you saved me the job."

"Oh, my pleasure. Nothing to it, is there?"

King nodded in agreement. "No. It's so easy, anybody can do it. It's choosing when to do it, and when *not* to do it. That's what takes a *real* man."

"Hah! Nice try! Insult my sexual prowess, and then give me the chance to redeem myself. Frankly, Alex, I don't give a hoot what people like you think about me." He nodded towards the large suitcase. "I've always been different. At boarding school, I had few friends. The same with university and the service. But who cares? I'm a rich man now, in my own right, with the know-how to remain undetected. No more dirty little jobs for me, no more pittance of a salary and a hearty slap on the back. *Oh jolly well done, Ian, good show,* I'm through, once and for all."

King stared at Forsyth, who had become extremely agitated. He was reddening in the face and starting to perspire. King knew that he had nothing to lose now, so he decided to take his chance. If he could succeed in making the man become more emotional, he might still be able to distract him. "What's your problem? I don't get any more than that. Special forces soldiers die in dirty wars all over the world and they don't get any recognition, not even in death. It's called duty."

"Don't give me that! At least if a soldier performs an act of bravery they get a bloody medal! The things I've done for Queen and country..." he trailed off, shaking his head disdainfully. You just wouldn't believe it if I told you."

"Bollocks! What did your department contract *me* to do? It wasn't all that long ago, Ian, surely you can remember? I had to kill *him*!" King kicked O'Shea's corpse, rocking the head. Part of all that was left inside seeped out onto the floor. "What did you think I would get for that? I'll tell you what I would have got for that... two things... Jack and shit! Sound familiar?"

Forsyth nodded. "Yes. But believe me, I've done *so* much more. I was only a boy when I..." he trailed off suddenly, a distant sadness in his eyes.

"We were all boys once, Ian. We grow up quickly when we serve the country. Some of us grew up quickly before all of this."

Forsyth aimed the pistol across to where Grant lay motionless, but kept his eyes on King. He lined up the sights on the man's head. "It will be quite clean and painless; I can assure you of that."

"Well it had better be a cleaner death than Danny Neeson's," King said as he bent down and felt the man's carotid artery with his fingertips. "You're pretty sloppy, Ian, he's still alive..." He reached out towards the fireplace and grabbed the handle of the fire poker and then threw it across the room at the MI6 officer.

The poker spun in the air, glowing-tip over handle, directly in line with him. Forsyth tried to evade the weapon, but there was no time. He raised both his hands, but the glowing tip caught him on the shoulder, searing the fabric of his jacket and catching the side of his neck, searing the skin. He screeched and dropped the pistol to the floor, then frantically dodged the poker as it bounced on the floor, threatening to burn his legs.

King was already up and moving, knowing full well that the only way to win a confrontation is to give it everything that you have. He powered into Forsyth, taking him to the ground and landing on top of him. Forsyth reached up and gripped King tightly around the throat, his overly-long, well-manicured nails digging deep into the flesh like claws. King countered the attack by pressing his chin down towards his neck, squashing Forsyth's thumb against his collarbone. He then grabbed hold of Forsyth's left ear and pulled. Forsyth screamed, and brought his knee up into King's groin. King fell forward and rolled over him, but managed to keep a grip on the man's ear, forcing it to part company with the rest of his head. The scream was demonic. Forsyth held the side of his head in a desperate bid to quell the savage pain, then scrabbled to his feet and bolted out of the room to the front door. King got to his feet and threw the useless piece of flesh down onto the floor. The red-hot fire poker had set fire to the corner of the sofa, and the room had already started to fill with a thick, pungent smoke. He leapt across the room, and followed the sound of Forsyth's screams out into the night.

Outside seemed darker for losing his night vision in the house. King jumped down the steps of the veranda and sprinted across the short area of over-gown lawn, then vaulted cleanly over the front gate. Forsyth was fast, he already had fifty-metres on King. As he landed, he could see Forsyth heading across the road, towards the sandy walkway that led to the beach. He quickened his pace, watching the ground carefully for obstructions. Forsyth slowed in front of him, then stopped beside a small Citroen, which had been discreetly parked under the nearby canopy of pine trees. The vehicle was obviously Forsyth's car; no doubt hired at Bordeaux Airport. Forsyth looked up as King approached, running at a frantic pace. He was obviously surprised to see him so close, there was no way that he could unlock the vehicle and get inside in time. Instead, he decided to give up all hopes of escaping by car and started to run up the steep sand dune which separated the road from the beach.

King kept up his pace, well accustomed to running from his training with the special operations wing, who trained alongside the SAS. He soon gained even more distance on Forsyth, who was struggling to reach the top of the steep dune. As King reached the top, he lost sight of Forsyth and hesitated momentarily, waiting to catch sight of him amongst the maze of dunes and waist-high sand grass.

Forsyth dived from where he crouched at the edge of the path. He caught King around the knees, tackling him to the ground. He had caught him off guard a second time and now, he was determined to make good use of the situation. He raised his hands and beat down a heavy rain of blows into King's face. Catching him in the mouth, nose and eyes with clenched fists.

King clenched his teeth together and closed his eyes until he found himself something to hold onto. He caught hold of a handful of skin on Forsyth's face, slipped his thumb inside the man's mouth to catch a good hold on the flap of cheek, then swung a savage punch. He felt it connect with something solid, felt the cheek tear and he lost his grip. He opened his eyes and started to punch the man in the face. He caught hold of

Forsyth around the neck then pulled him closer, as the two men started to slip over the dune's summit and down to the beach.

There was no such thing as a clean fight. King new this, but so did Forsyth. King had the height and weight advantage, and a decade in youth, but the man was a frenzy of motion - punching, blocking and clawing at him. He felt a heavy blow to his face, that rocked him, dulled his senses for a moment, but he kept a tight hold on Forsyth's neck and kept him close, until they had stopped moving down the sand dune. He felt another painful blow, this time to his ribs.

It's only pain! King thought. *I can take anything that you can give and more besides...* He groped at the man's face, then suddenly felt elated when he found what he had so desperately been searching for. His finger slipped in easily, but he pushed even harder despite the sickening, agonising scream. He kept pushing, slipped his other hand around Forsyth's head and gripped the nape of his neck. He pulled and pushed together, then suddenly, there was no more resistance. His finger went as deep as it could go, until the knuckle rested against the hard bone of the eye socket. He felt the warm, sticky wetness ooze over his finger and trickle across the back of his hand. Forsyth's legs kicked wildly and the man's whole body convulsed, erupting violently into a series of spine-breaking spasms. King pushed even harder, his knuckles grating against the hard texture of the bone as he twisted his finger around inside, probing and ripping the optic nerve. Forsyth went into shock. King pushed the man off him, and rolled with him until Forsyth was face down in the sand. He reached his left arm around the man's throat, cupped his fist in his right hand, and pulled backwards as hard as he could. As the neck broke, Forsyth's limbs went still. King rolled off and lay on his back, his chest heaving for breath. He looked up at the night sky, clear and starlit. Calm and silent.

He knew he had not laid there long. But he felt the adrenalin leaving him, replaced with a feeling of pure exhaustion. Almost willing him to roll over and go to sleep. It was imperative to keep moving - to keep thinking. He forced himself off, looked briefly at Forsyth's body, before wiping his bloody hand clean on the man's tweed jacket. As he stood, he brushed the sand off his clothes, checked he still had his wallet and car keys in his jeans pockets.

Smoke was in the air, a heady smell of paint and fabrics, or dry wood and roasting meat. He knew what it was without having to see it, and as King trudged up to the top of the sand dune, he noticed the great orange glow in the direction of Holman's property. He felt light-headed, the adrenalin subsiding too quickly. He could hear the voices of his instructors in his ears. They were telling him to evaluate and prioritise. From his vantage point on top the dune, he could see flashing red lights in the distance. They were heading towards him, from Lacanau. King broke into a run down the sand dune and across the stretch of rough ground which led to the road.

44

November, 1998
Stockholm, Sweden

The sun was an opaque ball, omitting as little light as was possible against the dark sky. Vast banks of rain-heavy stratus cloud hung lazily in the sky, threatening to unburden themselves and release their heavy loads upon the unsuspecting, or unprepared, below. It was cold enough for snow and the light had that golden hue to it that so often precedes snowfall. If it did, it would be the first of many flurries before the big snowfall that marked winter.

The breeze had increased dramatically to a sharp, crisp wind, and was now blowing the treetops, forcing them to sway from side to side, high above the deserted parkland. Huge drifts of fallen leaves had piled high against the series of knee-high barriers around the empty flower borders, catching the park-keepers unprepared.

Lisa Grant watched the boy kick his football into the oncoming wind, taking full advantage of watching his ball curve dramatically, as if he had just taken a goal-scoring corner kick to save the match. She smiled and wiped a lonely tear from her windblown cheek. The boy needed a man in his life - someone with whom he could kick a football and not become embarrassed, as he so often had with her. Someone to look-up to and admire, someone to aspire to. She brushed a lock of her natural brunette hair aside. The wind was picking up. The red hair was gone, it had been Parker's choice and now she made her own.

It had been seven months since Keith Parker's death. And even if she could admit it only to herself, they had been seven wonderful months. Every day seemed like a breath of fresh air, for herself, and for her son. David's new-found confidence was unbounded, and even though he was still only in his first term at his new school, in a new country, she had noted a vast improvement with his academic studies. He now had focus, contentment and confidence.

She had sold the house; Parker had actually left her provision in his will. It was as she had thought, the man *had* loved her, but he had been sick. It hadn't always been a violent relationship. But it had escalated.

The price of the house had been dropped, it seemed that people were not so keen to buy houses that had once been the scene of a brutal murder.

She looked at her watch; the evenings were becoming much darker now, summer was almost a distant memory. But it had been a wonderful summer, with forests and lakes, and a host of new experiences in a new country. Lisa loved Sweden, and so did David. It had been a wonderful few months to rediscover themselves. It was cold now, and winter in Scandinavia was an unknown, but they were looking forward to the new experiences that a frozen winter would bring as well. She looked up and watched, smiling to herself as the man jogged towards the ball and chipped it gently towards her son. She smiled. It was lovely to see.

Simon Grant turned around and walked towards her. She felt a shiver run down her spine, then looked back excitedly at him. It had been a wonderful few months, and they had fallen in love again, like teenagers. There were things they didn't talk about, would never talk about. And that was fine, because life had started for them all over again. They were a couple in love, and a family who loved each other and would never be apart again.

They hugged and kissed. The kiss lingered, became more passionate. Simon broke first, his eyes seeming to ask a question. Snowflakes started to flurry and a large one stuck on the end of his nose. She wiped it away and smiled. "Go on then," she said, and watched as he jogged back over to David and they kicked the ball to each other. The mad English, now playing football in the snow. The snow was sticking and building quickly. David had never seen snow for real, he was whooping with delight.

Lisa had grieved Simon's death. Grieved, and ached and longed for him. A man from the foreign office had visited, along with a plain-clothes police officer. The detective sergeant who had investigated Keith Parker's murder. He was a detective inspector now. They had delivered the news. Simon had been killed in a fire in south-west France. His long-time friend, Frank Holman had died too. The fire had taken hold, even starting a forest fire, and there had been little left to identify the bodies, including a third unknown male. A new process of DNA profiling, still in its infancy, had found traces of Simon Grant at the house. The men hadn't said much more, but the detective had given her a strange look when he had left. A knowing look. She had sold the house soon afterwards.

Simon had contacted her after months of trying, and when they met, it had been in Spain. The Costa-del-Sol, or the *Costa-del-Crime* as it was known for its high population of British criminals and no extradition. This was soon to change under forthcoming EU laws, and the introduction of the Euro next year. They had spent two wonderful weeks together as a family, but she knew before she had even landed in Malaga that she wanted to be with him for the rest of her life. They had decided that Sweden would be a good place to start that new life. As it turned out, it was ideal.

She watched the two play. Life was perfect.

***

Watching the man and the boy kick the ball to each other, however briefly, had suddenly struck a chord with Alex King. He had never experienced the feeling for himself. He had never known his father – in truth, nor had his mother – and he had not had that sort of relationship with the other men in his life. He was the true definition of a bastard. The bastard son of a prostitute, no less. It had given him baggage to carry his whole life. However, it was his mentor, Peter Stewart who had told him to forget what he never knew. Not to mourn something he never had. It made him a blank canvas. No baggage of having to constantly live up to another man, no benchmark for either success or failure. He had told King that he was lucky. Fathers only created imperfect expectation, nothing more. It had been enough to leave the baggage at the door of MI6.

Until now.

King was suddenly unable to explain the emotion rising from deep inside him. He'd never known his father. Never had this sort of relationship. The daily contact, the expressions of love. He tried to put it aside, he had a job to do after all, but did he want to ruin all of that for the little boy kicking the football? The kick about was only a little thing, but he knew the little things were really the biggest things of all.

It had taken six months to find Simon Grant. Six long months. Switzerland had been difficult. He had lost all trace of Grant there, but not the money. MI6 had managed to seize a vast proportion of it, but in doing so spooked Grant, and King had lost him, not picking up the trail again until three weeks later in the former East Germany. A place where it was easy to hide and stay hidden. And it was too, because King lost him again and could see no way of getting back on the trail. But then he had a revelation. Stop hunting Simon Grant, and stay close to the man's wife and son. King knew the pull they would have on him.

He nestled the field glasses against his eyes and watched as the couple strolled arm in arm. The snow was an inch deep now and falling quite heavily. The boy ran excitedly alongside, dribbling his football closely, making tracks in the snow, as he trotted to keep up with his reunited mother and father. Again, he felt empty watching.

France had been a turning point. The fire started by the red-hot poker had consumed everything. It had been burning too fiercely to attempt to put out, so King had fled the scene before the authorities turned up. He reported to his recruiter and mentor, Peter Stewart at the man's home. With Forsyth gone rogue, he went to the only man he could trust. Stewart had contacted the legal department and they had met at MI6 headquarters for a thorough debrief. King was duly assigned a researcher, two former CID missing person specialists on secondment to MI6 and a Liaison officer to report to. The team were tasked with finding Simon Grant and retrieving the missing money. The bodies had been identified by dental records. Simon Grant's was not among them. Nor was any evidence of incinerated money. Not a trace. Neeson's Saab had been taken and had been found abandoned in Marseilles, the gateway to Europe. MI6 had filed Grant as one of the dead men. This meant that Grant's fate had been sealed. MI6 wanted the money and they wanted his corpse. King had come up with the plan to steal back the money and Forsyth had padded it out accordingly. Get the Irish to go after Holman in a blood vendetta, leave all the loose ends neatly trimmed in another country and simply give MI6 the nod that both O'Shea and Neeson were terminated. King had learned that things rarely go to plan, but he had learned from it. Forsyth had intended to keep the money for himself, hence the change in attitude which King had put down to the innocent people killed during the heist. He had managed to dump the blame on Forsyth and play the hand of the dumb hired help. King was now close to bringing it all to a conclusion. Ninety percent of the money had now been accounted for and sat in an MI6 secret bank account. That had been enough to appease the mandarins. They still wanted Grant, and professional diligence was enough for King to give his all to the hunt, but he was being pressured to conclude matters and return to MI6 for further tasks.

Now he had Simon Grant in the lenses of the binoculars. It would soon be over. He watched the couple kiss again, then raised the radio to his mouth.

"Alpha Bravo Two, this is Alpha Bravo One, over," he said. He kept his eyes on the couple. They now walked hand in hand to the edge of the lake. The water was grey and cold looking. He could imagine it frozen over with ice skaters on a Sunday morning. The snow was falling on the surface of the water like gentle rain.

"Alpha Bravo One, Alpha Bravo Two, go ahead, over."

Alex King watched the boy trot over and hug his father. Grant struggled to lift him, but he did and they hugged. He spun around, and the boy looked like he was whooping with delight. The boy rubbed two handfuls of snow in Grant's face and howled with laughter when his father dropped him and scooped up some snow of his own to throw. Lisa Grant laughed and hugged them both.

"Alpha Bravo Two, this is Alpha Bravo One..." he paused. He could have been watching a snapshot of his life. A loving mother and father, walks in the park, love and protection in a family unit. But it hadn't been like that. His had another path, another start. A drug addict mother who sold sex. Little schooling and time in young offender homes. A mother so in need of a fix, she almost let a man have sex with her daughter. A fix to look the other way. King closed his eyes, shuddered at the thought. He was not a religious man, but he thanked God for the neighbour who called social services in time.

He had never seen his siblings again, but at least they had been safer than at home.

"Alpha Bravo One, go ahead, over..."

King put down the binoculars. He could see the family reach the car at the edge of the park. "Alpha Bravo Two... target confirmed as negative, over. Repeat, negative. Another false trail. Reconvene at rendezvous point, over." King put the radio back in his pocket and walked away. When he reached the exit of the park and turned around the car was gone. King felt the chill from the icy wind, and tucked up the collar of his trench coat as he climbed the snowy steps and re-entered the darkening streets of Stockholm.

Author's Note

This book took nineteen years to make it this far, but I'm glad it did. It is all the better for it now. It started out very differently, but due to the success of the Alex King novels, I thought it would make a great prequel. Those who have read the other books will appreciate the background; those who have not read the others hopefully will read them with a little insider knowledge.

So why Shadows of Good Friday? Well, it goes back to my former life training in close protection. Chatting in small groups with large beers, I came across an ex-policeman who had been involved in an investigation of an armed robbery, the manager of which, had been the insider. He disappeared, but his wife knew more than she let on. She had clearly been abused and although the policeman didn't exactly turn a blind eye, he knew she knew more, but they were unable to prove it. At the same table, another would-be bodyguard had lived a life of crime and had always wanted to get out. He always seemed to find himself pulled back in, and felt that the life he planned to have in close protection was his last chance. He would leave his associates behind, travel the world and become a new man. If he went back to crime, he may well spend more of his life inside prison than he had as a free man. After some banter, we watched him open doors throughout the pub using nothing more than a broken fork, a hairclip, a drinks straw and a selection of beermats. One of the instructors was a former SAS trooper and along with his former Royal Marine colleague, told us how they first met. The Royal Marine had been part of a surveillance operation on a high-profile member of Sinn Fein. We all knew his name and so would you. The SAS trooper was tasked with putting a device under the man's vehicle. As it was, there was some sort of compromise and the operation was aborted. Now, to this day, and put it down to the beer, but I do not know if it was meant to be an explosive device, or a tracking device. But all I knew, was that Shadows of Good Friday was already taking shape in my mind around that table. By the morning it was a working plot. While training for a new career, I had inadvertently started another.

Thank you for reading this far, I hope you enjoyed reading the story as much as I enjoyed writing it. If you wouldn't mind leaving a review, it will help keep my work visible. Here's the link to my website where you can select the book. www.apbateman.com

Thank you

A P Bateman

Made in the USA
Coppell, TX
06 December 2021